YOU'RE WEL

Also by Menna Gallie, published by Honno:

The Small Mine
Travels with a Duchess
Strike for a Kingdom

YOU'RE WELCOME TO ULSTER

by

MENNA GALLIE

*With an introduction
by
Claire Connolly & Angela V. John*

HONNO CLASSICS

Claire Connolly is a Reader in English Literature at Cardiff University. Previous editions include works by Irish novelists Maria Edgeworth and Sydney Owenson. She is editor of *Theorising Ireland* (Palgrave), co-editor of the *Cambridge Companion to Irish Culture* (Cambridge University Press) and author of *A Cultural History of the Irish Novel* (Cambridge University Press).

Angela V. John is an Honorary Professor of History at Aberystwyth University. Her most recent book is *Evelyn Sharp: Rebel Woman 1869–1955* (Manchester University Press, 2009). She is currently working on a biography of Lady Rhondda. She knew Menna Gallie well and has written the introductions for two other reprints of her novels, *Strike for a Kingdom* and *Travels with a Duchess*, also published by Honno Press.

Published by Honno
'Ailsa Craig', Heol y Cawl, Dinas Powys,
South Glamorgan, Wales, CF64 4AH.

1 2 3 4 5 6 7 8 9 10

First published in England by Victor Gollancz Ltd., in 1970
This edition © Honno, 2010

The lines on p.96, translated from the Welsh by Menna Gallie, are
from 'Profiad' originally published in *Manion*, a collection of poems
by T. Gwynn Jones (Wrexham, Wales: Hughes A'i Fab, 1932).

A catalogue record for this book is available from
the British Library.

*Published with the financial support of the
Welsh Books Council.*

ISBN 978-1-906784-19-5

Cover photograph © www.thepuravida.com
Cover design: Graham Preston
Printed by Gomer Press

Introduction

CLAIRE CONNOLLY
ANGELA V. JOHN

You're Welcome to Ulster is a bold book. It is set in 1969, the year when Northern Ireland's Troubles erupted. Published the following year, it was one of the very first novels to cover and even confront the subject.[1] Against this dramatic backdrop was an equally explosive love story that reflected the sexual liberation of the late sixties and retains its power to shock today. Moreover this heady mix came from the pen of a middle-aged Welsh woman, married to a Scot and living in England.

So who was Menna Gallie (née Humphreys) and what prompted her to undertake this audacious mixture of Irish politics, sexual adventure and self-discovery?[2] She had been born in the coalmining community of Ystradgynlais, in the Swansea Valley, on 17th March 1920 and proudly declared that her middle name Patricia was a celebration of this date. Her mother was a local woman whose father, a colliery checkweighman and small farmer, had helped to found the Labour Representation Committee in South Wales. Gallie's father, originally from North Wales, was a carpenter. She was one of three daughters in a Welsh-speaking, chapel-going, socialist household that moved to nearby Creunant when she was ten.

On completing a degree in English Literature at University College, Swansea she married W. B. Gallie, a philosophy lecturer. It was 1940 and five days later her husband left for the army. Menna Gallie meanwhile did war work in

Llandudno and London, though her son and daughter were
born in Ystradgynlais. Here she modelled for the Polish-born
artist Josef Herman who was also living in the village. He
had arrived in Ystradgynlais on a two-week visit and stayed
for eleven years.[3]

In 1950 Bryce Gallie became the first professor of philosophy at the new University College of North Staffordshire
(now Keele). Then, in 1954 he obtained a chair at Queens
University, Belfast. It was this move that launched Menna
Gallie on her writing career. Four years later *Strike for a
Kingdom*, the first of six novels, was published to great
acclamation by Victor Gollancz. She was compared to Dylan
Thomas and Gwyn Thomas (she knew them both), praised
by Eleanor Roosevelt and described as 'a born writer, indeed
almost a poet' by the *Herald Tribune*.

When asked why she began to write, she explained that the
rich use of the English language in Northern Ireland and its
symbolism influenced her. As a Welsh speaker she was fascinated by similarities between Welsh and Irish place names.[4]
Coming from a family steeped in storytelling she appreciated
the way stories unfolded in Ireland: a complicated process
that she described as more akin to mixing a fruit cake than
boiling an egg. Composing long letters to her absent husband
during the war had helped to stimulate an interest in writing
but since then she had been wife, mother and secretary
(typing her husband's lecture notes). So there had not been
'much time to be me, not much time to remember or think
about the idea that's long slipped tidily down the sink with
the dishwater, or been wrung out hard with the nappies.'
Living in Ireland freed her to become a writer, though she
was aware of the irony: 'What I owe to Ulster is of course the
peace I've found in this so-called violent country.'

Now that her children were growing up, Gallie had more
time and wanted to draw upon her rich store of family mem-

ories. A superb raconteur, she began translating her humorous, often slightly risqué stories on to the page. By combining them with her keen sense of social justice, she made her political commentary more digestible. But although inspired by Northern Ireland, her first and third novels were set in south-west Wales in the mining community she knew so well. *Strike for a Kingdom* — 'the first child of my middle age' — was written in three months and is about the effects of the General Strike on a village she calls Cilhendre. *The Small Mine* (1962) follows the same community in the aftermath of nationalisation of the mines. Reviewing the latter, the monthly magazine *Arts in Ulster* claimed that Gallie had it within her reach 'to do for the Welsh working classes something like what D.H. Lawrence did for the English working classes.'

Their historical focus is no coincidence. Living in County Down just seven miles from the depressed town of Downpatrick, Gallie felt a 'ghastly, haunting familiarity' since she was reminded 'of the men in my own country in the twenties and thirties'. Her vision of Wales was sharpened by her Northern Irish experience, while the distance freed her to write about her own land. Indeed, all but her final published novel *In These Promiscuous Parts* (1974) were written *after* she had left a locale. Her second novel *Man's Desiring* (1960) had been a retrospective nod to her recent experience of Keele though its hero was a deracinated Welsh collier's son turned academic.

When in 1967 Bryce Gallie was appointed Professor of Political Science at the University of Cambridge, Menna Gallie began reflecting back on her thirteen years in Northern Ireland in order to fashion a novel centred on its society. After a few weeks in Belfast the Gallies had moved to the Dower House on the Castle Ward Estate overlooking Strangford Lough. The home at the heart of *You're Welcome*, that of Caroline and Colum Moore, is based on this house.

Although criticising as feudal the deferential social relations
that persisted on the estate, Gallie sometimes acted as a guide
for visitors to Lady Bangor's stately home (eighteenth-
century Castle Ward was the basis for the tea party at the 'Big
House' in the novel). Gallie was a consummate cook and
hosted many dinner parties at her own house. As in the novel,
literature, politics and wine were always on the menu. Her
children attended local schools and she taught creative
writing part-time at Orangefield Boys' Secondary School in
Belfast. She also did numerous broadcasts for the Northern
Ireland Home Service and went to Yugoslavia as the PEN
(Poets, Essayists, Novelists) representative for Northern
Ireland.

So, familiarity and residence provided Gallie with creden-
tials for her writing. Indeed, as an outsider (albeit a Celt) and
as a woman it could be said that she was in an interesting
position to evaluate what *Time* magazine, in a review of the
novel, called the 'divided heart' of Northern Ireland. Place
mattered deeply to her and she always maintained that some
of her happiest years were spent there.

Conversely she found Cambridge (which she tended to
elide with the university) cold and pretentious. She told the
Birmingham Welsh Society in 1976 that 'During the long
hiraethus years' (years of longing for home) when she lived
in England and Ireland, spent a year in New York and visited
her son in Italy, she found Cambridge 'an even more foreign
place.' From a location that was definitely not home, came a
novel that attempted to explain to those outside Northern
Ireland the tragedy now unfolding there.

Yet even as Gallie was composing *You're Welcome*, the
society she missed and was depicting was being transformed.
She chose to set her narrative in the days leading up to the
Orange marches and bonfires of 12th July, thus highlighting
how the past (the defeat of James II by William of Orange at
the Battle of the Boyne in 1690 that presaged a Protestant

Ascendancy and the end of Catholic hopes) dominated and divided the present.[5] The most serious violence of 1969 (which would occur in August) had not yet taken place. But awareness of the escalation of conflict with Derry's 'Battle of the Bogside' and Belfast's serious disturbances would have affected both Gallie's writing and her readers' responses. That summer of 1969 witnessed the worst sectarian fighting since 1935: ten fatalities (eight Catholics and two Protestants) and more than 150 wounded by gunshot.

From the outset Gallie's novel conveys an undercurrent of fear. As *Time* put it, 'Her sentimental journey creates more chill than charm.' The atmosphere of foreboding derives as much from a personal predicament as a political one. At the outset of the novel, Sarah Thomas has discovered a lump on her breast and suspects that time is not on her side. In the week before her appointment for exploratory surgery, also the week leading up to the twelfth of July, 1969, she decides to leave her home in Cambridge and visit friends in Northern Ireland. Significant as this date is in Irish politics, Sarah is thinking only of her own situation. She seeks the comfort of her friends, the Moores, and wonders too if she can manage to see and sleep with James McNeil, a married Protestant journalist with whom she had a brief affair on a former visit to Belfast. A Welsh civil servant living in Cambridge who has lost her husband in the Korean War, Sarah Thomas also goes to Ireland in order to avoid Wales, where the 'blind and cannibal' affections of her family (p.10) threaten to overwhelm her fragile self-control. In connecting Wales with Ireland in this way, Gallie rewrites the more traditional plot in which an Englishman goes to Ireland or Wales, falls in love with a beautiful girl and finds a truer version of himself. Instead, she offers a more unconventional plot in which a woman finds, not so much herself, as a new understanding of her place within a set of relationships that cross national and generational boundaries.

Caroline and her academic husband Colum Moore have left the red-brick terraces of Belfast city behind. The opening pages of the novel follow Sarah's journey from Aldergrove airport to their home in County Down. Driving through the eastern edges of the city in her hired Mini, Sarah is appalled by what she sees: Union Jack bunting, Masonic symbols and murals of King Billy. The map reveals to Sarah an ancient past embedded within landscape features and monuments that predate the comparatively recent history of the Williamite wars and seem to confirm Ulster's difference. Gallie's attentiveness to local history as inscribed on the landscape is telling: the novel was written only a few years before the Royal Mail's attempt to impose a modern postcode system on the older (and still vibrant) system of '*baile*' or townlands, which was to galvanise resistance from such Northern Irish writers as Seamus Heaney and Brian Friel.

Bewildered first by the unfamiliar political landscape and then by twisting country roads, Sarah gets lost. Her anxious relationship with the Ordnance Survey map that she stops to consult every few miles echoes a familiar trope from women's writing of this period: a woman's vulnerable and uncertain place in the world mirrored in and heightened by the experience of physical dislocation. For Sarah Thomas, though, losing her way involves her in real dangers, including an uncomfortably close encounter with some local IRA men. One of them, squashed into her little hired Mini beside her, causes her to feel weak and vulnerable, both because he is armed and dangerous and because he can see the cellulite on her thighs. In this and other such moments, the novel makes Sarah's body a key register for external political conditions.

Along with its sensitivity to the layered past and an awareness of bodily realities in the present, *You're Welcome to Ulster* catalogues the main political events leading up to

August. The Civil Authorities (Special Powers) Act (Northern Ireland), 1922, which gave the Government of Northern Ireland the power to suspend many civil liberties, is central to the plot and the narrative is preceded by two pages of extracts from the legislation. Sarah's former lover James is a journalist; through him and Caroline's sister Una, a Civil Rights Activist, readers are given a vivid and immediate sense of events as they were unfolding. A host of other characters deliver pieces of reported dialogue that help to fill in this picture of Northern Ireland as it lurched towards political crisis. James and Una have both witnessed the People's Democracy March from Belfast to Derry in January 1969 (him as reporter, her as activist) and both testify to the violent loyalist response to the march and the ensuing polarisation of political opinion. Student-dominated and characterised by a high degree of non-sectarian radicalism, the march was brutally broken up at Burntollet Bridge near Derry. The violence at Burntollet Bridge, vividly described here, lost O'Neill and the Stormont government the support of middle-class Catholics, who felt that the government had allowed 'Orange rednecks to pummel the flower of their educated youth.'[6] Una is highly reminiscent of the young Bernadette Devlin, Catholic radical and founder of People's Democracy, who in April 1969 became the youngest woman elected to Westminster.

Neither, however, does Gallie sentimentalise this student generation. Una's maverick mixture of Marxism and Catholicism is held up to Sarah's stern scrutiny. Gallie's reading of Irish politics was predicated upon her Welsh socialist inheritance. (She liked to boast that the Independent Labour Party leader Keir Hardie had stayed with her grandparents.) Influenced by the Spanish Civil War and by friends in Ystradgynlais, she was briefly a member of the Communist Party in the 1930s but then spent the rest of her life as a Labour Party activist. As she explained in the 1980s:

'There was no question of one's politics. No other way of thinking – you were a socialist.'[7]

Repudiating Marxist ideology and wary of violence, Gallie's irrefragable belief in the power of the ballot box and the importance of communities pulling together for the common good was challenged by the religious and political divisions she witnessed in Northern Ireland. She had long been wary of some aspects of Welsh nonconformity and although she believed that Irish Catholics were 'provoked into every instance of violence', she could not comprehend why religion or habits of thought ran deeper than class solidarity. When living in Northern Ireland she voiced concern that there was no effective opposition at Stormont. She was especially troubled by the evident lack of waged work: 'Unemployment is the skeleton in Ulster's cupboard.'[8]

Gallie viewed politics as a process for improving living standards and admitted that it was a shock to be in a community where 'politics have nothing to do with bread and butter, where there is no community belief that something must be done politically to change social conditions.' Committed to constitutional socialism, she was active in the co-religionist Northern Ireland Labour Party.

During the 1964 election her outspoken denunciation of high unemployment and infant mortality during an open air speech provoked a Unionist into throwing chippings and a stone, just missing Gallie's eye and forcing the meeting to an abrupt end. She was also verbally assaulted after inadvertently wandering into an IRA meeting in a house in Belfast when canvassing for Labour votes. Although she saw herself as an ally of what she called 'the ill-used Catholic minority', she could not condone the use of any violence and became increasingly disillusioned about the future. She told a Welsh audience that the watchword on both sides was not change but keep, adapting lines from R.S. Thomas's poem 'Welsh Landscape': 'There is no present in Ulster and no future, there is only the past.' She added that a people cannot live on its past, however proud they might be of it.

Gallie's understanding of Northern Ireland's problems is derived not only from history, however, but also from her wide reading in Irish literature. She delights in the stagey quality of the scenes played out in the novel, and makes references to the politically-charged dramas of the Irish literary revival as well as to writers such as Brian Moore and Edna O'Brien. Meanwhile, modern cultural modes such as crime fiction and gangster films shape her vision too and arguably result in the rather clichéd depiction of the young IRA men. Yet, as she was aware, Gallie's critique of the society she observed also rested on a romanticised concept of Wales and Welshness that was itself becoming outmoded. She knew as an exile that 'this remembering with love' could be as dangerous as 'the jungle or Coney Beach, Porthcawl.' In *You're Welcome* Sarah is taken to task by Mab (a Welsh nationalist lad on the run) for still seeing the Welsh valleys as they were in the thirties. And this novel with its deliberately ambiguous title can be viewed as part of an ongoing attempt to consider meanings of national identity and, by contrast, what Welshness meant to the author.

Mab's flight from his bungled attempt to destroy a telephone kiosk in the name of Welsh nationalism links extremist Irish and Welsh nationalists. Some — but not all — readers were provided with further collusion in the form of a Prelude to the novel. These pages did not exist in the Victor Gollancz UK edition but were added to the Harper and Row American publication that appeared in the United States in April 1971 and sold over six thousand copies in the first two months. It was there that she always had her most appreciative audience.[9] The US reader's report had suggested that the relationship between Mab and Sarah and the Irish political situation and events needed to be made more explicit.[10] The

Prelude was probably therefore written to satisfy this concern, and to inform a North American readership interested in what was currently unfolding in Ireland but often ignorant of Welsh affairs, exactly why Mab was in Ulster. Set in mid-Wales, it eavesdrops on a conversation between four militant Welsh nationalists, somewhat stereotypical figures who are deliberately presented as unattractive.[11] They differ in their views but are united in their belief in a Free Wales. They await an arms cache from 'the Irish boyos' (p.1).[12]

Although the numbers active in Welsh paramilitary organisations were tiny, their existence aroused rumours and increased tension in the summer of 1969 as the Investiture of the Prince of Wales approached. John Ellis has argued that the leaders of the Free Wales Army and the Patriotic Front regarded the Investiture as 'the best chance to trigger the Welsh fight for national liberation.'[13] Nine members of the Free Wales Army were arrested and charged with public order offences. Their protracted trial in Swansea ended on the day of the Investiture.

On 1 July, the morning of the symbolically-charged Investiture at Caernarfon, exactly one week before Sarah goes to Ireland, two members of the *Mudiad Amddifyn Cymru* (the Movement for the Defence of Wales) were killed in Abergele when their bomb exploded prematurely. This organisation had been responsible for other explosions over recent years and these men became, for some, the first modern Welsh martyrs.[14] In the novel Sarah encounters Mab on the night of the Twelfth after witnessing (from a distance) Orange celebrations. She derides Mab's brand of nationalism though carefully separates these 'Baby brothers of the IRA' (p.183) from her cousin's anti-royalist, constitutionalist nationalism. She thinks of IRA atrocities in the past and 'she cringed to think of a possible repetition of similar horrors in Wales, sprouting from an unholy alliance between the implacable and the inept.' (p.197).

Writing when there was heightened sensitivity about the future of the North of Ireland and at a divisive moment in Welsh nationalist and loyalist expression, Gallie's timing is also significant for another reason. She was expressing herself at the start of a revolutionary development: the modern women's movement.

Menna Gallie did not define herself as a feminist. She was wary of labels and socialism was her priority. She explained that 'I'm not much of an -ist except that I'm a socialist.'[15] But her hatred of injustice and reaction against the way women were treated at Cambridge University (where her husband was a Fellow of Peterhouse) effectively belied any disclaimers. Written not long after the fiftieth anniversary of British women first gaining the vote, followed in 1969 by an important Divorce Act, *You're Welcome* does not so much foreshadow the priorities of the women's movement that characterised the early 1970s as reflect the sexual liberation of the late sixties. Gallie welcomed the advent of a more permissive and tolerant society in terms of gender relations. Her novel *Travels with a Duchess* (published in 1968) had taken as its protagonists two middle-aged women (one Welsh, one from Northern Ireland) and set them free on a fortnight's package holiday in Yugoslavia. It celebrated women's friendship and candidly asserted their need to affirm their (hetero)sexuality.

In *You're Welcome* Sarah's decision to contact her former lover and the consequences of this are as important as the public events that unfold during the course of the novel. Gallie's modernity is shown through her fusion of the personal and the political. The start of Chapter 8 is deliberately ambiguous. We are told that 'Sarah awoke and it was Jamesday.' (p145). It was indeed 12th July when the historic defeat of James II would dominate. But what is foremost in Sarah's thoughts is her impending assignation with James. And it is the lovers' meeting that is the subject of the chapter.

In this novel it is the women who are the dominant figures and initiators. They represent different beliefs and outlooks, ranging from the assured Catholic mother-figure Caroline to her radical sister Una and her staunchly Establishment neighbour, Lady Maxwell. Sarah has an excellent relationship with Caroline's husband, Colum, a professor of English Literature at Queens University Belfast. Their rapport is however communicated via an elaborate tissue of literary quotations, borrowed from such cultural authorities as Samuel Johnson and Edmund Burke, and does not express the lively and direct sense of shared problems and tense differences that animates conversations between the women characters.

The 'pro-Catholic, anti-government'[16] message of *You're Welcome to Ulster* was leavened by a good measure of humour: the *Birmingham Post* reviewer delighted in Gallie's wit and described the novel as a 'broth of a book.'[17] Despite Gallie's reputation for humour, however, reviewers of the early 1970s seem to have found it hard to take her irreverent mix of politics and sex. She noted that they tolerated men saying what they liked but were outraged when women wrote frankly about sexuality. In 1980 she remarked on a 'Victorian residual carry-over in literary response which would like to insist that women writers must be womanly.'

The reception of *You're Welcome* provides evidence of the persistence of these 'Victorian' attitudes. American newspaper reviews of the novel tend to praise Gallie's treatment of Irish politics but admonish her sexual morality, with one reviewer clearly disapproving of the morals of the fictional Sarah.[18] Another review contrasts the 'unconvincing, occasionally tasteless' sex scenes with the more convincing and worthwhile treatment of 'the whole problem of the North.'[19] Tom MacIntyre, on the other hand, an Irish writer from the border county of Cavan, reviewed the novel for the *Listener* and felt that Gallie had 'failed badly' in her effort to capture Northern Irish realities. Citing the reluctance of

Northern Irish poets to write about the Troubles, MacIntyre judges the novel to be lacking in 'texture', despite Gallie's knowledge of the 'ground'. The 'personal theme', however, he considers to be 'the best part of the book.'[20] The reversal of perspective from the American reviews is striking, yet what links these responses is a shared sense of disjunction between the personal and political plots that Gallie sought to connect.

A different reading of the novel's integration of its various strands is found in Nini Rodgers's 1970 review of the novel in an early issue of the radical Northern Irish magazine *Fortnight*. Gallie's novel was reviewed alongside Martin Waddell's *Meeting the British*, an altogether more conventional if also early version of the Troubles thriller that is lacking the 'pace, suspense and surprise' of the conclusion to *You're Welcome to Ulster*. Rodgers is clearly amused by the idea of Sarah going to Ulster in search of sexual pleasure, which she compares to someone who 'has chosen to go to Siberia for a holiday, or travelled to Mecca in search of alcoholic refreshment, or gone to the Falls to buy a Union Jack.'[21]

The differing perspectives expressed in the reviews, as with the different points of views realised within the novel, are part of what makes *You're Welcome* a novel of continuing relevance. As one aspect of the novel addresses the other, so our experience as readers is deepened and the nature of the fictional debate expanded. Just as the language of surgery alienates Sarah from her own body, so the dinner party discussions of Northern Irish politics threaten to estrange the Moores and their friends from fuller comprehension of the developing crisis.

Eventually, shocking events came home. In 1973, just a few years after the publication of this novel, two members of the Provisional IRA were killed in a premature bomb explosion in the grounds of the Castle Ward estate.

*

You're Welcome to Ulster avoids the tendency of Troubles novels to treat Ireland as a place of tragically insoluble problems. The likely outcomes of Sarah's visit to her surgeon and the mounting violence in Northern Ireland are gloomy, but not inevitable. Such uncertainties would have been especially powerful at the time the novel was written and continue to animate a novel characterised above all by a stimulating dialogue between differing perspectives on gender and nation.

NOTE ON THE TEXT

The 1971 edition of *You're Welcome to Ulster* is the one used here since it contains a Prelude (set in Wales) along with some other material that was not included in the original 1970 edition.

Thanks to Rhiannon Davies, the National Library of Wales, Archif Menywod Cymru/Women's Archive of Wales, Hilary Rubinstein, Kelly Sullivan, Annest Wiliam and Caroline Oakley and the Honno team.

1 See *History Ireland* July/August 2009 for assessments of the significance of 1969. For discussion of fiction about the Troubles see Patrick Magee, *Gangsters or Guerillas. The Representation of Irish Republicans in 'Troubles Fiction'*, BTP Publications, 2001 and Aaron Kelly, *The Thriller and Northern Ireland since 1969: Utterly Resigned Terror*, Ashgate, 2005.

2 For further details about her life see Angela V. John, 'Place, Politics and History: The Life and Novels of Menna Gallie', *Llafur*, Journal of the Welsh People's History Society 9/3, 2006, pp.47—57. Unless otherwise indicated, quotations come from Menna Gallie's writings in the Menna Gallie Papers L1, L4, L6 and L8, National Library of Wales, Aberystwyth.

3 The National Museum of Wales owns a 1946 Herman pastel entitled 'Attachment' depicting Menna Gallie and her baby daughter.

4 With the exception of the occasional short written feature and some talks, Gallie used English in formal communication. She did, however translate Caradog Prichard's novel *Un Nos Ola Leuad* into English (under the title *Full Moon*) in 1973 and began translating his *Afal Drwd Adda*.

5 12th July 1690 was the date of the Battle of Aughrim, between William III and the Irish armies of James II and a final decisive defeat for James. The Battle of the Boyne had taken place on 1st July but is commemorated annually on the Twelfth.

6 Paul Bew, *Ireland: the Politics of Enmity,* Oxford University Press, 2007, p. 493.

7 Interview with Menna Gallie in 1984 by Ursula Masson, SWCC AUD/544, South Wales Miners' Library, Swansea University.

8 Ulster and Northern Ireland are not coterminous: only six of Ulster's nine counties comprise Northern Ireland.

[9] The UK title was *You're Welcome to Ulster!*, the exclamation mark signifying the *double entendre*. This was not included in the US version.

[10] In the Harper and Row Papers, Rare Book and Manuscript Library, Columbia University, New York.

[11] An early draft of the US version incorporates the Prelude into the first chapter. It also places Sarah in the pub. Unknown to the plotters, she has understood their conversation in Welsh. Box 4, Notebook 1A5q, Menna Gallie Papers, Howard Gotlieb Archival Research Center at Boston University.

[12] The novel mentions international arms running as well as the claims about the IRA and Free Wales Army links. John Ellis in *Investiture, Royal Ceremony and National Identity in Wales, 1911-1969*, University of Wales Press, 2008, pp. 213—4 refers to the latter's claims of links with Irish paramilitary groups. How much this was fomented by rumour and the press is the subject of debate, as is the relative strength of the IRA in 1969 and its use of guns in response to their use by the B-Specials in August 1969. See too B.Hanley and S.Millar, *The Lost Revolution: the story of the Official IRA and the Workers' Party*, Penguin Ireland, 2009.

[13] Ellis, *Investiture, Royal Ceremony*, p.215.

[14] There is a passing reference to them in the novel on p.130.

[15] Talk given by Menna Gallie at Onllwyn Miners' Welfare Hall, May 1985, SWCC VID/132, South Wales Miners' Library, Swansea University.

[16] As described in the *Cambridge Evening News*, 12 February 1971.

[17] Review found in Box 7, folder 2, Menna Gallie Papers, Howard Gotlieb Archival Research Center at Boston University.

[18] *Denver Post*, 18 April 1971, Gallie Papers, L4.

[19] *Best Sellers*, 15 May 1971, Ibid.

[20] *Listener*, 29 October 1970.

[21] *Fortnight*, 6 November 1970.

EXCERPTS FROM
THE CIVIL AUTHORITIES (SPECIAL POWERS) ACT (NORTHERN IRELAND) 1922

1(2). For the purposes of this Act the Civil Authority shall be the Minister of Home Affairs for Northern Ireland, but the Minister a delegate, either unconditionally or subject to such conditions as he thinks fit, all or any of his powers under this Act to any officer of police, and such officer of police shall, to the extent of such delegation, be the Civil Authority as it respects any part of Northern Ireland specified in such delegation....

10. For the purpose of preserving peace and maintaining order, the Minister of Home Affairs may by order: -
    a. Prohibit the holding of inquests by coroners on dead bodies in any area of Northern Ireland specified in the order...
    b. Prohibit the holding of any particular inquest specified in the order; and
    c. Provide for the duties of a coroner and a coroner's jury (or either of them) as respects any inquest prohibited by the order being performed by such officer or court as may be determined by the order.

Under the above-mentioned Act, the authorities are also empowered to:
1. Arrest without warrant.
2. Imprison without charge or trial and deny recourse to habeas corpus or a court of law.
3. Enter and search homes without warrant, and with force, at any hour of day or night.
4. Declare a curfew and prohibit meetings, assemblies (including fairs and markets) and processions.

5.　Permit punishment by flogging.

6.　Deny claim to a trial by jury.

7.　Arrest persons it is desired to examine as witnesses, forcibly detain them and compel them to answer questions, under penalties, even if the answers may incriminate them. Such a person is guilty of an offence if he refuses to be sworn or answer a question.

8.　Do any act involving interference with the rights of private property.

9.　Prevent access of relatives or legal advisers to a person imprisoned without trial.

10.　Arrest a person who "by word of mouth" spreads false reports or makes false statements.

11.　Prohibit the circulation of any newspaper.

12.　Prohibit the possession of any film or gramophone record.

13.　Arrest a person who does anything "calculated to be prejudicial to the preservation of peace or maintainance of order in Northern Ireland and not specifically provided for in the regulations."

A PRELUDE

The scene in the pub was like a set for a television advertise-ment. An antique British hostelry, with a low, oak-beamed ceiling, a grudging light through latticed windows, a high polish on trestle tables and oak settles, a slave-driving of pewter and brass, and four young men leaning on the bar with pint mugs in their hands. At any minute now one of them would declare, with intense conviction, "It's great stuff, this—"

But instead of the commercial cliché, what he said, in Welsh, was, "Beer; aye, that was one of the things that woke me up at night inside. I went on dreaming about a foaming mug of beer long after the dreams about gorgeous girls like aching caverns had been emasculated by Her Majesty's prison diet." He drank deeply. "Christ, that's great; when did you say the Irish boyos would be here?" He was an unprepossessing youth, stoop-shouldered and thin, his black hair greasy and his skin the colour of an old chamois-leather cloth. His eyes were dark, fired with bitter-ness, and his nose had been broken and badly reset. His hands beat a continuous, compulsive drumming on the bar counter.

"They're due now, any minute. You're sure you weren't followed, Emlyn?"

"How can I be sure, mun? I did all I could. Three differ-ent cars. And I came here from Cardiff via Aberystwyth, for God's sake. And I skirted Builth to get to the pub. They couldn't ask any more, could they, fair play? Tell you the truth, you were all daft to want me here. The bloody political fuzz are on my tail; I'm a security risk to all of you. I threat-en death and damnation. I'm opting out for the time being; it's only sense."

"Yes, of course, but you are the only one who knows them and knows us. We had to have somebody we could all trust." He spoke in a cultured, clipped voice, was calm while the others fidgeted, was well dressed, in a short-back-and-sides, neat fashion, looked reliable and efficient, officer material.

Then the third youth spoke. "They're late, you know that? Not very militaristic, is it? I was expecting coordinated wrist-watches and zero hours and things." This one was a fat young man with glasses and a bird's beak of a nose probing out of a nest of fuzzy, dark whiskers; a floral shirt and a dark-brown velvet jacket, velvet trousers, sandals and no socks. His worried eyes roved the bar in frustrated expectation.

"You can't expect them on the dot, mun; got to be casual, got to take it easy. But the minute they come, I'm off, mind. I'll give you the word and then Emlyn's on his way. You've got to realise, Dafydd, that running guns isn't like selling chips and bits of fried cod."

"Can we trust them, though, Emlyn? It's a hell of a lot of money. They're asking black-market prices all right."

"Well, it is a black market, isn't it? You can't buy hard-ware on the cheap. They're taking the risks; you've got to pay for it. And where else would you get your supplies? They're the ones with contacts; been on the job for years. No, you can't trust them, but what else can you do?"

"Hold your tongue, Dafydd. We've got to have what they will offer us and there is nowhere else. Not yet, not until we've proved ourselves." The fourth spoke with a noncha-lance and an air of condescension that would have put out of countenance any blundering, heavy-footed policeman who might have looked twice at the other three. "We've still got to graduate, got to earn our degrees in violence before we can make our own contacts. Let's be academic on this one; the Irishmen we will regard as our crammers, our instructors, for the time being." He turned with a studied grace to his drink, tall, fair, self-possessed, with an academic confidence.

"Yes, well, all right, but I wish to God they'd come, all the same. Does it strike you a bit funny that they're prepared to part with ironmongery just now? You'd think they'd want to hang on to everything they've got, the way things are in the North of Ireland, wouldn't you?"

"Listen, Dafydd, these boyos are professionals. They want cash; we've got a bit and they'll use ours to invest in some more hardware. There's a lot of stuff about, in the Congo and places like that, if you've got the organisation. Selling to us is only casting their bread upon the waters." Emlyn, with twelve months hard labour behind him, for his part in attempting to blow up a reservoir in which several square miles of Wales had been drowned to water an English city, spoke with an embittered cynicism, fostered in Her Majesty's prisons. "Don't forget, it's our cash they want, whatever crap they may talk about our Celtic nationalism putting up a united front against British tyranny. No use kidding yourselves. This is business today. Bargains. If you can't meet the price, you've had it. Don't try mixing business with patriotism, good boy."

"So there's no hope of trying to beat them down with the offer of diversionary tactics over here, to keep the police busy and off their backs?"

"God, talk sense, Dafydd. What have our police to do with the North of Ireland? And we're only a handful; what could we do that would be big enough? No, no; we've got to get the explosives and pay their price. There's plenty of buyers about; guns are always in the sellers' market. Without explosives we may as well pack in here and now. Haven't you learned yet that the bang is the only trigger the Establishment responds to any longer? Those dogs only salivate at the drop of a bomb. Paving stones, petrol bombs, gelignite – they are the vocabulary of our time, those and a lovely froth of publicity. Good God, have I got to preach those lessons to you again? Will you never learn?" He kept his voice low, but it acquired a harshness, a growl, that silenced the others. They turned to their tankards, drank, and watched the door.

"Done any recruiting while I was inside?"

"Yes," Griff, the potential army officer, replied. "We got a few youngsters in. The two deaths didn't help."

"No."

"You don't think they've let us down, do you? They're late."

"Stop chewing the bloody rag, will you, Dafydd? They'll come when they can. We're not playing soldiers. What's the drill? How will you do the swap?"

"Two of them have booked rooms here for tonight and we three are staying as well; we've come to fish, the cover is perfect; and we'll be taking their suitcases instead of our own tomorrow morning. No problems there," Griff said, in his brisk, executive voice. "Once you've seen them and given them the word, Emlyn, we won't know them. Then drop into casual conversation at the bar and start a hand of cards."

"Sounds all right. Let me know how it goes; but my phone is tapped, mind, and I never did trust the post."

"Look, Emlyn, what we had in mind was to use a few of the youngsters on phone boxes for a start. Break them in. How d'you feel about that?"

"Worth a try, anyway. At least it'll get them committed. You'd better include some sanctuary arrangements in your deal tonight. Get a few safe addresses in Ireland, in case the kids have to run for it; you never know."

"Yes, thanks, we'll do that." Griff made a note in his diary.

"And don't forget to give the kids a little cash — their secret cache — to cover expenses if they do have to take a sudden holiday. Those guarded notes in their wallets will burn holes in their hearts; don't waste that urge. Mind, the guns you'll get tonight will look old-fashioned, even obsolete, but as long as they work, it doesn't matter. You get those guns. Good trade follows the flag, they used to say, but my

dictum is good violence follows the gun. We'll get nowhere
in Wales without it, even if we have to shove the gelignite up
a few arses to wake them up."

"I still can't understand why they have to ask such prices,
all the same," Dafydd nagged again. "I mean, look, there's
nothing newer than the newest gun, is there? And nothing
more out of date than a superseded gun, and yet they ask the
earth for old things that the manufacturers must be dying to
get off their hands. You'd think they'd offer us sale prices –
for discontinued stock."

"Dafydd, we are all too well aware that you come from a
good, Carmarthenshire shopkeeping family, but kindly
refrain from making bourgeois assessments of the explosives trade. We are dealing in shop-soiled goods, I grant
you, but we are hardly in a position to go in for your style of
peasant horse-dealing. Try to restrain your haggling propen-
sities, if you can, despite your grandfather's market stall.
Kindly keep the ancestral urges in check, if it isn't asking
too much of you?" This from the nonchalant, scholarly one,
who then turned to thrum the bell on the bar counter to
summon the barman.

"Oh, you bugger off, young Efan. You think you know it
all, but business is business, fair play." Dafydd's face was
pinched with anger, behind the spectacles and the birdy nose,
and he stroked his velvet paunch for comfort as he tried to
rally support for his parsimony from the hostile faces staring
him down.

"So you'd put a bargain before your ideals, then would
you, Dafydd? When you swore your oath to further the
cause of a free Wales, did you make a private reservation –
only if I can get it on the cheap? Listen, boy, there isn't anything you don't offer to get the bloody English off our backs.
Not a thing, see? Emlyn's had twelve months of it and you
dare to stand fatly there, huckstering over a few quid. You
make me sick."

"That will be all, please, both of you. I'm not in uniform, but that's an order. We will pay what they ask and concentrate our energies on the proper use of what they have to sell. That is what matters. Oh, yes, four more pints, please. Lovely night, isn't it?"

"Aye, great, mun," the barman said, "for the ducks...."

CHAPTER 1

Sarah Thomas had a little lump in her left breast. She felt about it rather like the girl who came home with a baby and no ring: "It's only a little baby, very small for its age." Sarah's lump was only a little one and very small for its age too. She'd had it there for more than two years, an old enemy now, like a mole or a corn or a crooked tooth; she'd become rather fond of it and often rolled it under her finger for company if she was alone; her little lump, not much bigger than a pea.

Her husband was dead and Sarah's succeeding, casual lovers had not cared enough or had been too polite to mention the lump; until she met the psychiatrist. Sarah, a clever girl, worked with the Ministry of Education and her psychiatrist worked with subnormal children. Things went from good to better with them until he found the lump and began a fuss. Exploratory surgery, he said, was urgent, and then went on to shatter their good thing by reassuring her that remedial corsetry was, in those days, more than adequate. He frightened the pants on Sarah. Remedial corsetry? A lump of foam rubber masquerading as a woman's breast; her left breast, the one with two beauty spots on it. Breast, font, teat, tit, secondary sexual characteristic, femininity. Exploratory surgery. They might cut it off, hack it away, a lump of malignant blubber.

She let the psychiatrist make an appointment for her with a surgeon friend of his before she said goodbye. They would explore the lump. Nobody said cancer to her. They never do. Only sometimes do they commit themselves to carcinoma. She wondered why "excreta" is a better word, or "intercourse," or "dysmenorrhea." A cancer by any other name doth stink as high.

Not that she was entirely convinced. She'd had it so long, knew it so well, her lump; so small for its age, so friendly. But when they wrote and said that she should register at the nursing home in a week and a day, the panic began to mount. It wasn't death she feared – she wasn't going to be killed by a small pea she was familiar with. It was the threatened loss of that one member that had her racked; that loss was "worse than any death could be at one"; for her was death. Never to be naked again; sportive, live and unashamed. Scarred, ugly, hidden, padded out. Christ!

Naked before her big bathroom looking glass with her full complement of teats, the handful fullness of firm flesh, she tried to put her foot upon the panic. No, no melodrama, please, it's not your line, she told her cringing self; but think, remedial corsetry, padded foam. Her terrors leered at her in the looking glass, Hieronymus Bosch and all that lot. She had seven days, at least, for what might be the last of love. Her panic screamed for passion, madness, lust. An orgiastic lunacy, a risk, a final fire in the blood, a flowering, a gag upon the scream.

But panic's like an orgasm – it has to fall and die away. All doctors are notorious pessimists. She knew her lump; they didn't. But she would have to hedge her bets, and anyway, not waste her days and nights. Eight days. A week, now. She'd go to Ireland. There she had friends, there there was comfort, and there she, once upon a holiday, had had a lover. His time had been before The Lump; he would have noticed it and been concerned, as her psychiatrist had been.

He'd been a simple, passionate, kindly man who knew about the heyday in the blood. She'd had no right to him, a husband and a father; but now she had new rights, new weaknesses, she needed him, a man. Her love for him was five years overgrown, and his for her, for all she knew, had never even truly seeded. Their relationship had been born only to finish, premised on the fact that it could only end. Their first meeting was accidental, their parting inevitable.

Sarah had been on holiday in Italy and had shared a balcony with an Irish professor of English and his wife and their first babies. She'd been attracted to them and they, good Catholics, had thought they'd seen her loneliness, too Irish to accept the notion of her chosen independence. They took her up, and took her home with them; she spent the last week of her leave in their red-brick, terraced house in Belfast, within the Catholic ghetto. There they, the Moores, introduced her to their friends, their debts, their priest; to the harsh facts of Northern Irish politics, to the realities of religious persecution, to the Orange and the Green. They gave a quick impromptu party for Sarah, inviting virtually everyone they knew who might have entertained her. And among those had been James McNeil, a Protestant journalist who wrote diatribes against the Ulster government for the more left-wing British newspapers; he was a rogue elephant among the prim-lined paddy fields of staid, conventional political commentators in the jungle of Northern Irish politics.

Sarah had immediately liked him and he had found her stimulating and rare, a woman of professional standing who succeeded in being charmingly feminine despite an almost masculine intelligence. On the evening after the party, he took her out to dinner and made love to her on the floor of his office; a silly, laughing uncommitted time they had of it. But, in the hot house of her imminent departure, a kind of frenzy sprouted feelers, like any old potato in the month of May. She fell in love with something; whether it was him or Ireland, or the Moores in him, she had never really honestly known. Ireland was a new world for her, incredible, romantic, feudal, antiquated, simple; its battles, then, like a dining-table war game. But he was Ulster's most articulate symbol and Sarah enjoyed talk. And the fact that he was not a Catholic was also a positive factor, though Sarah would have denied that most vociferously, had the notion occurred to her.

It was a temporary thing, but its context mattered to her; she had wanted it. Perhaps for the first time in her life, Sarah found that she was the one to press the kisses while the other offered the cheek. She had never conquered him; his laughter had defeated her, amusement had laid siege to every threat of passionate intensity she offered; her sexuality he found delightful, diverting, but lovemaking was a picnic, a *fête champêtre*; it was no marriage bed. Now, for her last week of love, perhaps of hope of life, he was the one; of course he was. This time perhaps she'd break him down; he owed her something, surely? She wasn't one to dissipate her love; sex, just a bit perhaps, but that was something else again. He had encouraged her commitment, hadn't he? Yes, she really ought to telephone the Moores.

But Ulster and James McNeil would demand something from her; she would have to earn her keep with them. Why not just go home and simply be her girlhood self, accepted and at rest? Did she have the courage for that? All she needed for Ulster was energy and a sense of humour. Courage was what she lacked; she hadn't the strength to carry the burden of her family's loving, caring sympathy. Much too easy, much too hard. The family, her mother, sisters, uncles, aunts, the numberless cousins rooted in their Welsh valleys, would lap her into their shawl of uncritical cosseting, their blind and cannibal affection; their love would break her up, their tears would drown her resolution. She had had it all before, when her husband had been killed, that shawling of the self in tears and love and formulated heartbreak. Home, Wales was a patterned place, a place of set responses, ready-made, ordained. Their sympathy was more than threatened flesh could take, and also more than she would dare impose on old and white-haired heads. No, she had to have a challenge to preserve her *amour propre*.

She telephoned the Moores.

"I'm due some leave and I need a holiday. Could you bear to have me?"

"Och, girl, as if you'd any need to ask. Great, I'll be at me menus and Colum at his wine lists the minute I put down this phone. It's great to hear you, you old bitch; it's been too long."

Cowardly, and remembering their devout Catholicism, she didn't mention him, the real reason for her impetuous demands on their generosity. Not yet, not yet; out of their love, their ease, their bottles would come the strength to lift a telephone, dial a number, pray and say, "It's me, I'm here in Ireland." Then it would be up to him. She knew she had been fun for him, a release, a game. So would her return, unbidden, be just a case of "Anyone for tennis?" on a wet and windy day? There's a time, a mood for games. He might not want to play. But Sarah knew that she had once disturbed his small content, had threatened his security with love. "I'll always be a bit in love with you," he'd promised when she left, bereft, for pastures new.

She'd play it light. Seven summer days to be a woman, to be a woman with a man who liked to laugh, who liked his women gay. With a brave man. That was it. It was his bravery she needed; perhaps his would spill over, buttress her. Even in Northern Ireland he had dared to speak some truths, had always dared, had risked his livelihood, perhaps his life, to tell the truth, his truth, at least. It was this bravery she courted in her panic cringe that would creep up on her when she was least prepared and, like the east winds off the Fens, would blight her little buds of confidence.

For that short week he was the one. And so was Ulster, where life, as she remembered it, was violent, lived, alive and full of colour; where fights and feuds blew up like squibs, where cynicisms and sentimentalities had the same validity; where "Och, sure" became a way of life; where dreams and shams sustained, bills were only sometimes paid, and everyone, forever, counted the cost.

One week to cancer. One week to sexual destruction. A week to know oneself alive, to be in some centre, hub. Life is most lived where life is at risk and Sarah's panics screamed for drama, for life made rich with risk, made full by laughter and fear and stress; made easy, too, by bottles, and — who knew? — by love.

She flew to Aldergrove. Then, in a hired car, a little Mini, she drove to Belfast through the small, soft, July Irish rain. She had taken this hired car because, this time, she wanted a degree of independence for her holiday; she hadn't asked herself the reason why; even to ask would have been to express a hope. But independence demanded a map, for the Moores had left Belfast to live in the country and she would have to find her way. She knew she had to drive to Belfast. She found the city *en fête*. A press of red-brick, terraced houses, set untidily about; a city without grace or shape. A run-down, down-at-heel, relegated sort of place, where nothing seemed quite to have come off. The city was *en fête* in a prim, cheese-paring, thrifty fashion. The streets criss-crossed with bunting tightly pulled, a little faded, overused; the second, fifth time around. Wet Union Jacks drooped from phallic poles above the doors of little houses, and flimsy, rickety board structures arched the streets at intervals. These bore cryptic symbols, like Masonic or Guild signs – a barred gate, an open Bible, King William III on his great white horse.

On the red gable ends of the end-of-terrace houses there were more pictures of the king, flag furled and all tri-umphant, good folk painting, brilliant in the rain, but, alas, confined to that one, exclusive, regal subject. There were graffiti too, in big white paint that shouted, "No Surrender" and "No Pope Here" and "Remember 1690" and, in slightly smaller, less confident, perhaps hurried printing, the injunc-tion to "Fuck the Pope."

But the Moores had left Belfast and the village where Sarah's welcome was lay miles away; Kilhornan, deep in the blue shadow of the Mourne Mountains, a sea village, a fishing place that only just rated a mention in small print on the Ordinance Survey map. It only earned this distinction, so the Moores claimed, because it was thigh deep in ancient monuments and National Trustings, horned cairns and sutterains and chambered graves. Sarah's competence lay in drafting minutes and inspecting schools; she was a lousy navigator and maps she found as confusing as a pattern for a Fair Isle jersey. She drove into a garage, filled the tank and asked for a map of County Down. She chatted while they hunted for it.

"Why the bunting and the arches and the jazz?"

"Woman dear, it's the Twelfth of July."

"No, not yet," she answered, positive for once. "It's only the eighth," aware of the passing days just then, one gone in the arranging, one on the journey; she knew the date. Would she ever forget her panic summer of 1969? Christ, would she get the chance to remember it?

"Sure, it's the celebrations. You'll be from across the water, I doubt, but youse'll have heard of the Battle of the Boyne, sure you will? The great Battle of the Boyne, whenever King William, God love him, beat that papish Jamie, and sent the feller packing." Exalted and bleeding from vicarious triumphs, the Orange garage hand proceeded to put her in possession of the ringing, right true Protestant facts of Ulster history. The Battle of the Boyne the only fact, and that not too well authenticated.

But, for the garage hand, it was the crucial, elemental fact, the most important battle ever fought; the battle that had ensured the preservation of the true Protestant Christian faith against the Whore of Rome, the battle that had saved Ulster and Europe from the Pope.

"Aye, the Battle of the Boyne on the twelfth day of July in 1690. 'Twas King William's self they had in them days, but we've the man today will keep his victory safe. Sure, haven't we the Reverend Dr. Ian Paisley the day? He's the boyo knows all about the Whore o' Rome, may the Protestant Lord protect him and keep him safe. And you remember this, missus; Civil Rights mean Civil War, so they do. You tell them that in England, now."

Sarah was appalled and yet delighted. Appalled that the mad religious bigotry still grew as green as grass, as orange as lilies, and yet oddly delighted that Ulster remained the same, crazy, Irish, irrational province that she'd romanticised and gone dining out on. She thought again how King William had been promoted since her history textbooks at school. For her, brought up in Wales, he'd been a notorious homosexual who had conveniently shared a throne with Mary. That reign was William and Mary, William only a second-class citizen, a hanger-on to the monarchy, rather like Albert or Edinburgh. Here, on the other hand, he was King William of Blessed Memory, emblazoned on every red-brick, Protestant gable end.

Sarah studied her map in the garage and almost despaired. All those byroads, marked in thin, wavy gray lines, those horned cairns and chambered graves. Would she have to spend the night in the welcome break of some long-standing stone? Her history tutor at the garage told her exactly how to get to Kilhornan, but she'd stopped listening. It was no use; not all that way, not twenty miles of "wee loanies" and left turns beside an infinite number of Lavery's Bars. It was too much.

Utterly discouraged, she folded her map and thanked the garageman, having registered only the general direction out of the city. At least the little blue Mini was easy enough to drive. Sarah went again past the terraces, nodded her salutations to King William and wondered about the possibilities of civil war, but mostly she concentrated on the way out.

On holiday, she left her mind to its own devices, uncorset-
ed and undisciplined. A hotchpotch of thoughts came bubbling up to the surface, bumping and shouldering each other
aside; thoughts about the Moores, and how it would be this
time; had it been too long a break? Was she perhaps an imposition? Would she see him? Now that she was there, close, it
suddenly seemed so much more difficult. Was she going to
die of cancer? She half planned her funeral and wondered
whether they would come over from Ireland for it. No,
Caroline's hands were tied with all those young, but she'd be
sure to send an expensive wreath. He, on the other hand,
would never dare, unless he sent it anonymously, from "A
Well-Wisher" – how can one be a well-wisher to the dead,
the unbelieving dead? Shut up, Sarah, she said.

She wished she could remember the last time more
clearly, but five years had been too long; what she remembered was the mood, the easy warmth, the comfort and the
welcome, almost welcome home, of the Moores' old terraced
house; and with James, the snatched-at, laughing love. With
him she'd been so possessed by sex that she remembered
properly only a few specific bits of times; his grimy office; a
bank beside the Lagan, almost a public place, where they had
risked it once, daring and scared and crazy; a wood beside a
golf course in the rain. They had never known peace and time
together; always hurried, grabbed-at, secretive, deprived, but
always gay; laughter was his thing.

The red terraces fell away, she passed the University,
Puginesque and rather nice, and then the "good end" of the
city, the best addresses, big Victorian villas, given over to
gardens and conservatories and private practices. Then a golf
course and, quite suddenly, she was out of Belfast and it was
a place of small fields and thick hawthorn hedges and, in the
rain, as green as Ireland, a strident poster green. She passed
ruined cottages without roofs, which she associated with
evictions and the Great Hunger and the Troubles; passed

large, prosperous farmhouses, opulent under their Twelfth
Day Union Jacks; through several thin, one-street villages
where every other house seemed to be a pub; but not a named
pub, no Red Lions nor Blue Boars nor Spread Eagles. No,
just a house in a row, with a discreet announcement on the
fanlight over the door, and dark paint on the downstairs
window. Sarah stopped every few miles to consult her map.
Her journey wasn't easy. There were flocks of sheep on the
road, driven by small boys on bikes and mad collie dogs,
who took the Mini for a new kind of sheep that needed
herding and who snapped and worried at her wheels.
Magpies in superstitious singles whirligigged into the hedges
and rats ran from cover, like lunatics, to dash under the
wheels of the car; she had the greatest difficulty in saving
their silly lives. Two pheasants walked elegantly across the
road, and then there was the business of the cattle. But that
was after the events of the "wee loanie."

A silly, small red light had suddenly appeared on her dashboard and kept making warning, winking faces at her. She
knew she had petrol and oil, and the garageman had checked
the water. It had to be some horrible mechanical complica-
tion, if it was anything at all. Perhaps just an idiosyncrasy of
this car, to wink at female drivers? She decided to stop at the
next garage to ask about it, stupid thing; but it would give her
a chance to make sure that she was still moving more or less
in the direction of Kilhornan.

It was another of those long thin villages and the garage,
set beside the crucified gate of a monastery, looked nastily
deserted, but Sarah Thomas, in her way, was a resolute and
determined character; she sounded her horn assertively, and
in a little while, a man appeared, liberally besprinkled with
chicken feathers and putting his fingers to his lips to entreat
for silence. There were feathers caught in his hair, they were
scattered all down his mechanic's oil-stained white coat and
one was delicately balanced in his left eyebrow.

"Oh, madam dear," he said, flapping, hen fashion, at his coat, "would you please not sound thon horn? Begging your pardon and taking the liberty, but we've just got the weans to their beds, and the smallest sound has them up again. With twelve of them, we've a hard row to furrow, so we have. How many gallons would you be wanting now? Och, it's not the petrol? A wee red light, you say? Aye, that's your fan belt, woman dear. You may just sit a wee minute for your engine to cool and I'll have youse fixed before you count the crows, so I will. Just youse wait now till I take on this new delivery of fowl that's just come in; I'll not be many minutes. Wait you there; you couldn't live on the petrol, I'm telling you. The fowl business is what keeps those weans fed."

"They can't be all your own?"

"Och, no; sure, they're all me brother's; isn't he the only one of us married?"

Sarah sat at the wheel of her Mini while the kindly man went away behind the facade of the garage, whence came the agonised calling of desperate, defeated hens. She sat and couldn't but watch more hens carried in, by their feet, in bundles, their squawking heads dangling, their legs tied, mouths agape, their crests red with affront and feathers flying. Their calling was a dirge, a keening, the saddest note she'd ever heard; but, with her fan belt gone, what could she do but wait – and promise never to eat another chicken while she lived?

After the slaughter of a few dozen hens, the gentle garage-man came back, lifted her hood and did whatever he had to do. He was testing the engine, dutifully checking his work, when another car drove in behind Sarah's, a red car driven by a young man. This driver imperiously tooted his horn and the mechanic, agonised, jerked his head out of the hood of the Mini. He waved his hands and put his fingers to his lips to beg for silence, and then a thin child of about ten appeared and was detailed to attend to the newcomers, while Sarah paid her bill and gave her thanks. "Oh, by the way, am I right for Kilhornan?"

"Aye, you are surely. But just you let thon car move on ahead and follow them. They'll be on the way near there, I reckon. I know one of those wee fellows; he lives just behind Kilhornan; and you'll not have far to go now. Safe home. That fan belt was a disgrace, so it was. And a hired car, you tell me? What is this world coming to, at all? Yes, just you get in behind that car; you'll be all right. Where else would they be going to, in the name of God, on this road with Kevin McBride in the car?"

Sarah gratefully followed the red car; it went rather faster than she cared for, but she dogged it, trustingly. Then it began to go more slowly and she was delighted, keeping sedately behind it for a few miles. Suddenly, it raced again and, thinking now that she had only a little way to go, Sarah decided to opt for safety and abandoned the chase.

After a while, however, she regretted her decision, for in the gentle, damp light that was Innisfree and Deirdre and all the sorrows, Sarah began to suspect that she was lost. Her map had acquired a strange irrelevance to the countryside since her pursuit of the red car. Now, as far as she could tell, a left turn was indicated, but could this little lane possibly be the one? Only half trusting her map, Sarah turned left off the winding, deserted country road, went left under a great overhang of untrimmed hawthorns, and so along a narrow lane with a bright green stripe of grass running down its middle, and the ditches on both sides flamboyant, like a middle-aged bride, riotous with Queen Anne's lace, maturely, serenely voluptuous. Its sweet nonsmell, the childlike smell of elderflower wine, seeped in through her open window. It was approaching the "heel of the day," in the fine rain, and the dark was gathering up.

She turned yet another bend in the lane and found her road blocked by the same red motorcar. Two young men stood beside the car. She applied her brake and turned the engine off, delighted at last to find a living soul who might be able to direct her, and feeling that the occupants of the red car were old friends by now. But she saw a momentary look of apprehension, incredulity, on their faces, and then they rushed her car. One of them wrenched open her door and, in a soft, sibilant Irish voice, he whispered, "Well, missus, what's your game? Why would you be tailing us, and where would you be off to the night?"

The whispering was utterly terrifying; a whisper in a desolate country lane, miles from anywhere. Sarah had to kill the whispering; her voice came out in a high, hoarse half shout, more obviously Welsh in accent than was her normal, cultivated diction.

"Look," she said, "I wish to get to a village known as Kilhornan, if it's any concern of yours. The garageman kindly suggested that I should follow you, but you went too fast for me and now I appear to be somewhat lost." "And where, now, would you be going to in Kilhornan?" The small raindrops dewed his dark-red hair and carefully barbered beard.

"I fail to see how it concerns you, but I happen to be visiting friends at Kilhornan; they are a family by the name of Moore."

"You know any Moores in Kilhornan?" Sarah's inquisitor asked the other, hitherto silent one.

"Only thon professor feller lives in Illnacullin House."

"Yes, that's where I'm going."

"He's the right sort. A left-footer."

"We'll have to check, all the same. O.K., missus, move over; my pal will navigate for youse for a wee while. Till we get to a phone box. And then we'll see, won't we now? We're out doing our own patrolling the day."

Clumsy, tired and feeling her years, Sarah wriggled from under the steering wheel, almost sat on the gear lever and with undignified haste scrambled into the passenger seat, too shocked to talk back. Her skirt rode up, exposing her broadening thighs, with small, purple, broken veins, to their bright young eyes. Even in those alarming circumstances she was woman enough to mind, to be shamed to humbleness. And also old enough to treat with respect these fledglings, these incomprehensible and terrifying young. For her, youth had been a time of intermittent exaltation, of infinite promise and possibilities, punctuated by black hours of humiliating incompetence and frustration. For them it seemed to mean sheer biological advantage; the rejection in advance of anything their elders had to offer by way of example or excuse; a just recognition of life's harshness flowering evilly in a positive exultation in violence.

While the silent one took over her car, the other, aggressive one, the obvious leader, loped back toward the red car, half running in long, easy strides, graceful in his tight pants and Donegal sweater, easy and controlled in his movements as a slim young cat. He opened the door of his car and poured himself in, in what seemed one graceful, tight, slim, continuous movement. Sarah's driver, despite the same kind of young physical grace, had none of that condescending slickness, that taken-for-granted superiority. To begin with he wasn't much of a driver. He crashed into reverse like a cowboy; perhaps he was a farmboy, more used to tractors and open fields than small cars in narrow lanes. Sarah didn't care for the way his confidence trembled over the wheel, nor the way he hung half out of the window to steer them backward. To the fate of the car she was by then indifferent; it wasn't her car. But it was her life.

With only a half of him in the car, conversation was difficult. Sarah let it go. She did wish he wouldn't go quite so fast; that winding lane with all the corners blind, the darkness coming on, the surface uneven, mud where it wasn't ruts and him driving in reverse, fast. Nothing for it but prayer. And

quiet speculation. She couldn't, somehow, see this one as a
crook. But the other one, the Boss Cat, he could be anything;
Sarah had seen in, or on, his eyes that film, or glint, that she
had called "the delinquent film." She didn't know how they
produced it but it was something she'd seen in, on, the eyes
of boys brought up before the headmaster, brought up before
the magistrates, in the eyes of some of the student-protest
leaders, of anarchist politicians, of psychopaths. An almost
physical barrier, barricade, a *noli me tangere*, an isolation,
rejection, a look. The bearded boy had it, that frightening "so
what?" look.

Thanks to Sarah's prayers and no oncoming traffic, they
came eventually to the end of the "loanie" and her driver
pulled the whole of himself into the car again, and let the red
car overtake him. It seemed the time for polite conversation.

"Would you care to tell me what this is all about?" Sarah
asked.

The boy didn't answer, said nothing, and Sarah watched
him struggle with his silence, his Adam's apple jerking, a
perky, nervous little register, wobbling above the would-be-
aggressive polo neck of his Donegal jersey. A black-haired
boy with high colour on his cheekbones and a look of simple,
ploughboy health. An honest, bewildered face. He might
have been film-star handsome but that he looked punch-
drunk, like a calf about to be slaughtered. A nice boy that
something had got at, hit. But he was very young and Sarah
had a healthy fear of the young, so confidently knowing
everything and nothing.

She had to respect his silence since it so obviously cost
him so much.

"All right, skip that one, but will you at least tell me
whether we are now on the road to Kilhornan?"

"Aye, we are surely."

"Do you happen to know the Moores?"

"No, but I've heard nothing against them."

"They are old friends of mine and through them I've come to love Ireland. When I needed a holiday, as I do now, I knew that this was the place to come, where I could rest and know I was welcome." Sarah laid it on for him, playing on that weakness, that bewilderment in him; at that age, with that face, he was guaranteed to be patriotic in a naïve, dreamy, romantic fashion. Given proper instruction he was, surely, a cinch for the Romantic poets and the Celtic Twilight. But before Sarah got any nearer to breaching his defences or approaching a tentative discussion of the rights of his particular kind of violence, they came to another long, thin village and saw the red car parked beside a telephone box. The first young man held the door open with his knee as he rifled through the battered blue book. The street was empty, like a cowboy film when the baddies are waiting to ambush the goodies. It rained and there was a smell of frying fish.

"You may get out and help him with the phoning," the boy said, "and, missus," he added with a sick look, laying his hand on her arm, "missus, do what he tells you, will youse? He's a boyo, so he is. Behave, now, if you're wise, but mind you, I've said nothing."

Sarah abandoned her tentative plan to make a quick dash across to one of the silent houses. What could she possibly say? They'd think she'd gone mad, was approaching a certain age, perhaps; sure the young fellows were only helping her on, telephoning to reassure her hosts that she was in good hands. No, it wasn't worth it now; Caroline would confirm her story and they'd let her go, their suspicions lulled. But why the suspicions, anyway? What were they afraid of? What were their ploys? Who could they have thought that she might be?

She left her car, shook her skirt down and walked with an assumed nonchalance and aplomb toward the telephone box. She stopped to light a cigarette on the way, a small gesture.

She passed the red car and saw a third boy, in the back seat, turn away and duck his head. The bearded one had found the number and was dialling. She heard the ringing tone and he put in the money. While he waited for the connection, he reached for her wrist and held her in an agonising grip. Sarah had rheumatism in that wrist and it was hell, but she was too damn proud to scream. For a minute the pain was all she knew and then the grip relaxed a little as he spoke and turned on the charm.

"Is that Mrs. Moore's?" A pause. She couldn't hear a thing. "Och, is that yourself, Mrs. Moore? Aye, well, tell me this. Would you be expecting a wee Welsh lady the night? Aye, seems to have lost her way, so she has. We wanted to make sure it was your house she was after. Sure, we'll set her right. No, no, think nothing to it. It's a pleasure, so it is. Aye, thanks; we'll do that sometime; never turn down the offer of a jar, but some other time then. No, no trouble at all. Good-bye, now. Good-bye."

"Satisfied?" Sarah demanded, trying to pull away, but he held her, ignoring her question. He leaned out of the booth, pushing her aside with his shoulder, and made a thumbs-up sign to the boy still sitting at the wheel of her car.

Only then did he slowly turn to Sarah. "Missus," he said, smiling with those perfect teeth glistening in the red beard, "your friend's got some childer. It was a wee boy answered the phone, and I heard some others whenever I was talking there. Just you say one word about how you came to meet us the night, and it'll be the worse for them. Got me?" He gave her wrist a vicious twist that was like toothache in every tooth. "You asked the way and we helped you on, that's all. I give your fair warning."

"No, I won't say a word about the delightful way we met. Mrs. Moore loves Ireland; I wouldn't care to upset her. She is unaware that toads like you are bred here, you beastly little – little young."

"Temper, missus, temper. Don't you be after letting your temperament get the better of your judgement. Safe home now, and God speed."

She couldn't tell him she was lost. Didn't know where to turn in this nameless, wet, deserted Irish village. The shreds of her dignity didn't allow her to ask the way; but the other boy was still standing beside her car; he understood and without asking said, "You need to drive on about three mile, take the first left-hand fork, and follow your nose to a big farmyard. Drive through the yard and you'll see the avenue to the house on your right. Have you got it now? Three mile on, take the left fork, come to the farmyard and the avenue is on your right." She could remember that much. She'd make it. "And safe home," he added. "You're welcome to Ulster, so you are."

Jesus, what a welcome. Back in the small security of her car Sarah switched on the engine and saw an arm imperiously waving her on. She needed no second bidding. She was in an odd mood by then. On one level ridiculously elated, pepped up by the melodrama, the almost comic improbability, and yet at the same time furiously angry with the participants. Her wrist was still painful and her whole body quivering rotten with fright, but she was excited and amused by the adventure. She was half smiling and yet half wild with indignation and humiliation. She felt she'd seen a wink on "the bright face of danger" and was half encouraged to wink back.

To take her mind off her thoughts there in the silence of the little car, Sarah planned the words she'd use to tell it all to the Moores; make the most of the drama; remember the shadowed narrow lane and the evil handsomeness of the one who'd telephoned and the kindness of the other, and then the third who'd ducked and hid his face. Then, with a new flush of fear, she remembered the threat: "Your friend's got some childer." Good heavens, he might have meant it; dare she say anything? Pity to waste the words she'd planned, but perhaps she ought to let it go?

It was getting perceptibly darker. The sidelights were on and Sarah thought she would put on the headlights after rounding the next bend. It was the boy who'd put on the sidelights in that lane and Sarah knew none of the switches in that car; around the corner, then, and she'd stop to investigate the dashboard. She went slowly on, in second gear, ready to stop at the next bit of straight road, and ran slap into a herd of cows or bullocks or monsters, bigger than the car. There were ten of them or a hundred, suddenly milling around her, frightened and wild, their steamy breath pouring from the black caverns of the snorting nostrils. They bumped the car and mounted each other; one of them mounted the hood of the car, and stared at her, glassy-eyed and mad, a white triangle on its black brow, and the great horns clashed against the glass. She heard something else rasp against the body of the car and felt the hurt in her flesh. Her world was black with white flashes and eyes and horns and mourning bellows of pain and despair and she was small in the middle of it in a little car, big and safe as an old salmon tin. She'd come here looking for life, but had never bargained for this: Belfast under bigoted bunting, bad boys and besotted bullocks, all in one small first hour.

The car had stalled and when she'd got over the mesmeric effect of the brute spread-eagled on her hood, she desperately felt for the light switch on the dashboard. She switched on everything she could find; heater, fog lamp, rear parking light, windshield wipers, and finally, *ex tenebris*, the headlights. The sudden, glaring new terror drove the bullock out of his fruitless coupling with the car, and he lurched to the road, to land with a heavy thump against one of his peers. Slowly, slowly, Sarah moved against the tide and added the thin shriek of her horn to the din of their anguish. Huge and heavy, they teetered away on their delicate ankles, like top-heavy swimmers in fat fur coats. They turned again as though to rend her, eyes crazed and horns lowered in threat, and then they were gone. She was through them. She put her foot down and ran for it. Then it was suddenly the first left fork and she took it and followed her nose, as the boy had said, along a road that warned: "Narrow Road, uneven surface, steep hill, one in seven." It was no idle threat, but somehow, with God's grace, she made it, and nothing came to meet her, only a woolly man riding on a bike without lights and balancing a second bike across his handlebars. And there were no lights on that second bike either. She crossed the farmyard with her heart in her mouth, her fist on the horn, one foot hovering over the brake, and the other ready to rush the accelerator. But she met no livestock in the yard.

Turn right, he'd said, out of the farmyard, for the Moores' avenue, and yes, here indeed were some gates at the bottom of a drive, old green-painted gates, hanging negligent and held everlastingly open with briars and nettles and bindweed. The ruts in the drive deep and full of rain, the inevitable bright-green grass stripe through the middle, wiping and whispering against the underside of the car. She could see the house now, big, solid, square, lights in every welcoming window and shining through a gracious Georgian fanlight over the front door.

Just as the drive ended in a wide semicircular sweep in front of the house, her offside back wheel sank into a pothole and Sarah was too damn tired to try and rev herself out. She switched off the engine and slumped over the steering wheel, stealing a few minutes to put on her sweetest smile. There were several other cars parked outside the house, so she powdered her nose and painted her mouth. She stretched a hand out and half opened the car door and came nose to nose with a great, gloomy, slobbering, canine face, grey and whiskery, with a collar on him that would have done for a horse. He was as big as a calf, and looked a man-eater. This was too much. She banged the door shut again and set her hand on the horn. She didn't care how many children were in bed, didn't care if she woke the dead. That dog was the last straw. They'd have to come and fetch her.

CHAPTER 2

They heard the feeble toot of the horn, a pathetic plea, through the boom of the party they'd laid on to welcome Sarah. The front door was opened and there was Caroline silhouetted against the light.

"It's herself," she called out, "and William Butler has her terrified." Caroline ran out towards the car, tall and with that curiously pigeon-toed lope that Sarah had forgotten about. She was followed by a drove of children.

"Come on, William Butler, come away out of that, you Irish bastard."

A tiny fair-haired innocent, no more than six years old, took the monster by his collar and heaved at him and he hung there, heraldic, his front paws dangling and his tongue pouring out, until Caroline shoved his posturing aside and Sarah was let out of her car.

"Och, Sarah, isn't it great? You've come, you're here. Away to the house now; Colum has your drink poured. You'll be needing it, I doubt." But before Sarah could totter to the house and the promised refreshment, William Butler had to welcome her. As soon as she had straightened up out of the cramping car, he came for her; he landed his floppy forepaws on her shoulders, pinning her back against the car and licking off all the newly restored make-up.

"He says you're welcome to Ireland. Pay no heed to him; come away in." Pay no heed to him and she was pinned like a dead moth to the car. William Butler was an Irish wolfhound.

"Get to hell out of it, William. He's a friendly wee soul, no mistake."

Reluctantly William gave up his prey, Caroline put her arm around Sarah, and with children tripping their feet, they

came up to the open door. The roar of the party hit them as
they crossed the threshold, but only Colum was in the hall,
with a glass in his hand.

"How are you, Sarah?" he asked with a small, formal bow.
"It is good to see you again. I have taken the liberty of
pouring you a very dry sherry, a good astringent after the
trials of a journey."

"Thank you, Colum, it's perfect. Lord, I need this." She
took one sip before she kissed him.

"Away now, Colum love, and keep that mob happy till
Sarah has a wee wash. You'll want to change, Sarah, sure you
will? But don't make a production out of it; this crowd's been
waiting to see you and we're hoping to eat in an hour, so
most of them have to be eased out by then." Caroline led the
way upstairs, followed by Sarah and all the children and
William Butler gloomily lolloping up last. The biggest boy
— Brendan, if Sarah's memory served — carried her suitcase. It was a wonderful room, large and splendid, with a vast
tester bed all hung about with white lace. There was a closet
with a washbasin and bidet, claimed by Caroline to be one of
the only three in Northern Ireland.

"You've ten minutes to paint your face and pull a dress on
you. Right, you childer, you've seen her; you may go to your
beds and I want no more sound out of you the night, mind
you."

None of the children had uttered a single word since
Sarah's arrival; they'd stared and watched and assessed; she
might as well have been in a cage or a shop window. There
were far more children than she'd remembered. There had
been five when she was last in Ireland and two since, but now
there were ten if not twelve of them underfoot, excluding the
baby, who was presumably asleep. Not even the Pope and the
Pill could have done this to Caroline in so short a time.

"I'll see you in the morning, then, shall I? Good night,
now." They turned slowly, grudgingly to go, still watching

Sarah, all the heads turned back to get a last glimpse in case she grew horns or something when they were not looking. William Butler had climbed onto the bed, however, and seemed determined to stay.

"Och, the wee treasure; he's taken a fancy to you."

"I'm sorry, Caroline. Much though I appreciate his affection, and large though this bed is, there isn't room in it for the beast and me. Kindly have him removed."

"William, you big oaf, get the hell out of it." Sadly, accusingly, he removed himself and slowly followed the children, his heart breaking in his eyes.

"Now move, girl, move. I'll just leave you in peace and see to those childer."

"They can't conceivably all be yours, Caroline? You used to have only seven, unless I've lost count."

"Save us, no; some of them are here on their holidays. But cheer up, they're away tomorrow, God be praised, and taking four of my ones with them, to give us the chance of a good crack. God, Sarah, it's good to see you."

"I know." Sarah grinned. "Ten minutes, then. I like your dress."

"Nice, isn't it? Haven't paid for it yet, mind, and it won't be fitting me long, either."

"Not again, Caroline?"

"Aye, that's the way of it. But with so many, one more makes not a hap'orth of difference."

The throb of the party reached up to Sarah through the floorboards, excited her, pleased her; her face smiled and she made a heavy pirouette toward her suitcase and the pretty, lime-green dress that was said to do things for her hazel eyes and honey-coloured hair.

Had Caroline invited him to the party? Would it have occurred to her? Perhaps the telephone call would be unnecessary after all. Why, he might actually be there, now, watching for her, pretending indifference, but waiting, his heart in those brown eyes. She felt the anticipatory clutch in her heart, the kick of hope, that gulping squeeze under her left breast, where her lump sat, temporarily forgotten.

Quickly, efficiently, she fixed her eyes, silvery green shadow and a lot of black liner. You never knew; be a boy scout, be prepared. She drank to herself in sherry before the ornate Victorian pier glass, winked and went to join the party.

He wasn't there.

Had he been asked and refused to come? Or simply not been asked? Then why not asked? Were things to be tricky? But never mind now. Don't think about it yet, don't be bleak. Duty calls. Enjoy this bit. Enjoy this foreign country.

It was good to remember; remember in this new room the same manners, the voices, the lovely antique things. Good to realise again that the myths were still at least half true. The good manners incredible, genteel, Edwardian; the voices soft and seductive, the language often Synge and the theatre, the storytelling entertaining, if somewhat professional, and the compliments soothing and warm.

Dutifully, a well-brought up girl, Sarah moved from group to group and began to notice, gradually, an excluding deference that got on her nerves. Whenever she moved in towards a group of men who seemed to be talking seriously about politics, say, or literature, they would stop at her joining to be charming to her and include her out of the discussion. She began to feel like a spy. When she said, "Look, do please go on; I want to hear about Ireland and the political situation," they would smile and ask her about Wales, or was it her first visit to the North of Ireland. They treated her like a woman in a man's world and infuriated her. The sexual segregation at the party was by then complete and she had always, anyway, avoided women's huddles. She had certainly not come all the way to Ireland to discuss the relative merits of

Lux or Fairy Snow, nor the idiosyncrasies of her cleaning woman. Indeed, whenever she happened to overhear scraps of feminine conversation during that first evening, the subject was invariably money or the Church and the price of things. It was no wonder that poor Caroline had so stridently to protest, "Sure, money's only money."

That falling over backward of politeness, that handing off, the mind-your-own-business and talk-about-what-you-understand sparked the irritation of weariness and disappointment in Sarah. She suddenly wanted to kick some arse or other. "Did you have a good journey?" was the final brush-off.

"Why, yes," she said, in her best, carrying Cambridge voice, "until I got to County Down, where I was promptly hijacked by some young thugs."

Each mannered smile remained as a rictus, the compliments wilted, aborted, the pleasantries were stilled, the room was stilled, the boom of talking whispered.

Then Colum laughed and the laugh was a neigh, a gargled giggle. "Hijacked, here? Nonsense, Sarah, you misunderstood the situation; someone a mite reckless in their do-gooding, perhaps."

"What the hell are you on about, Sarah?" Caroline, ever practical, wanted the facts. Sarah gave them; she'd rehearsed them; they came easy.

"Aye, well, that's the North of Ireland today for you," Caroline said, accepting. "Go back, my girl, go back and tell them in England. So they threatened my childer? And you told. You'll know you've put their lives at risk? You realise that? If it had been the Protestant lot you tangled with they might have had my weans' lives, have fired my house. But, thank God, I'm thinking it was the other lot, our sort. I knew by the voice on the phone there; it wasn't a Protestant voice was talking to me. Refined Falls Road, more like. Been to school with the Christian Brothers."

"Caroline, you can't be claiming to tell a bloke's religion by his voice on the telephone, for God's sake?" Sarah demanded, horrified.

"Of course I can. I don't need the face."

"But would you claim to tell by the face? Are you mad?"

"Woman, dear, there isn't one of us here the night who needs more than a voice, a face, to tell. We don't need a black skin to recognise a second-class citizen. Live here for six months and you'll get the message. We know our place, us Catholics; that's why we've got the mark on us. It's the knowing that scars you, the humility you're baptised into."

"And the criminal acceptance of it." Una, Caroline's younger sister, threw back her long, dark, straight, *avant garde* hair in challenge. "There's hardly one of you who hasn't sat back and taken it, all these years, while you wove sweet dreamy fantasies of a united Ireland, but cashed in on the crumbs partition offered you. 'Romantic Ireland's dead and gone, it's with O'Leary in the grave,' and violent protest is the only poetry of today."

"Aye, I saw you on television, Una, Maudgonning around the province in the Burntollet Bridge affair. Are you recovered at all?" a middle-aged woman, so haggard and hagged that she looked like a dirty, grey-brick derelict house, asked, in a voice that she hawked from the back of her throat, past a thousand cigarette butts. She wore a silver lamé blouse.

"Well, the pain's gone, and I have the stitches out. But recovered? Pray God I never recover. I trust I'll never be the same again."

"And was it worth it, after all?" an unidentified man asked.

"Bernadette Devlin sits in Westminster and the Unionist Party is in ruins. That's a little something, isn't it?"

"But the Special Powers Act still stands in the Statute Book and people are still denied their votes."

"What was Burntollet Bridge? Forgive my crass British ignorance."

"A student demonstration, pacific and non-partisan, demanding the basic democratic rights for all Ulster citizens. It is claimed that the police politely harassed them in the name of law and order and when extremist Protestants attacked the march the police stood by and watched. The Special Constables are said to have been active participants in the attack. For myself, I reject the story that the demonstration was communist or anarchist inspired. It was simply typical student idealism. Anyway, it was a bad wee business." He was a heavy, slumped, sag-bellied man who spoke, a slack man with a huge face gone to seed; a shovel face, vast chin disproportionate, and tiny eyes lost under eyebrows that stood out, bristling and erect like two small hand brushes. They called him Rory. "Una got clobbered by one of the thugs as she carried her pacific banner. How many stitches was it, Una? Five, I think you said?"

"Four, if we have to be precise. Four stitches, five, twenty-five – who cares? It was the blow that counted, the attack, the insane violence; the bleeding and the pain, the fright, the weariness of that ghastly, shared defeat. I didn't feel the pain at first, nor feel the trickling blood, the shock too overwhelming." Again, the hair was jerked aside, away; she seemed to use her hair instead of hands to gesture with, all cluttered as she was with cigarette and glass. The gesture with her hair reminded Sarah of the prow of some old sailing ship. "It was a legitimate march, officially permitted, and given the maximum publicity, but yet those fascist thugs were let to beat the hell out of us." She talked into a silence, into a shame, into a pride; her voice took on the beat of poetry, a Celtic, primitive beat; you might have scanned it, called it verse. "He had a chair leg, my adversary, with four big nails in it. I saw them, even counted them, as they came down; they caught what bit of sun there was. A moment of awareness, silence, fear, like when I drowned, once, long ago; he didn't get it all his own way though. I left the marks of nails on that thug face. That night I found the bits of skin in all the dirt beneath my nails. I have them still. I have them in an envelope at home. My bit of history. Some fascist skin I ripped."

But then, as they will always do, an academic broke it up, destroyed the sibyl quality, the threat of poesy. A thin, precise man with eyeglasses and a prim moustache under a questing nose, a pointing nose. "Methinks," he said, for he had felt the metre too, "methinks you bandy this word 'fascist,' Una, with too much confidence. What are you saying in our context, child?"

Her eyes relinquished all the glow of passionate recollection, common day returned, did something to her face, cancelled and reduced it. "By fascism I meant quite simply the negation of democracy, when a violent minority try to dominate the elected government, try, indeed, to cancel out the ballot box by the use of force. Not that the ballot means all that much here, but the principle remains. Isn't that what Paisleyism's all about? They attack the government, threatened the last prime minister's life, try to silence all democratic protest by violent means. I'd call that fascism, wouldn't you?"

He had the grace, at least, to shrug.

"Like Spain," said Sarah, all unmannerly, forgetting where she was, in a Roman Catholic redoubt, where religion was the *raison d'être*, the battleground.

"They're jailing priests there now," the fat man said, nicely aware of her embarrassment, "but tell me this now: what's been the typical British reaction to our bit of trouble of here?"

"Well, first, you have to appreciate the basic, abysmal British ignorance about Ireland, a complete geographic unawareness for a start; nobody too sure whether Belfast's in

the North or in the South and without the remotest idea
where the border lies. Certainly no realisation that Ulster is
still meant to be British and depends on us for its finances.
All Irishmen are Irish to the average Englishman; he makes
no distinction between North and South. And he's never
understood the fact of Ulster as a separate province; just as a
particularly noisy corner of Ireland where they carry on
about votes." They were listening to Sarah now, the party
groupings broken up, and Sarah felt secure that, for once,
she'd crossed the almost insurmountable invisible hurdle
behind which Roman Catholic Ulster barricades itself. She
well remembered how in Ulster one carries with one, like a
stench, one's British identity; how one is suspect, *agent
provocateur*, till one has somehow proved oneself by their
indefinable but stringent standards. Anglo-Saxon, on the
whole, remains *persona non*; Jewish is just as bad; black,
because rare, is fine. Scots *comme ci, comme ça*; American is
brother; but Welsh was always out, until the Welsh began a
Nationalist Front; thereafter, the Welsh became fringe benefits, officially disliked as individuals, but half acceptable as
postulants within the nationalist mystique.

Given at last a chance to speak, Sarah insisted on her say.
"In Cambridge, for example, where I work, we have the
highest figures for alcoholism in Britain – all those colleges,
you know? There, 'Irishman' has come to mean an alcoholic,
even among some of the precise academics. Your drunkard
may have a black skin or wear gold earrings, or talk Urdu,
but never mind, he's still an Irishman if he's plastered and
homeless."

"Jesus, Mary and Joseph, would you believe it? Would
you believe it, honest?"

"Another reason for the boredom with your problems is
the belief that they are merely religious, therefore, today, a bit
nonsensical; nobody cares – 'A plague on both your stupid
houses.' Though mind you, the sight, the fright of Ian Paisley

on the television has certainly kindled a lot of sympathy for your cause. And those scenes of police brutality, of course. But that's the world picture, after all; Chicago, Londonderry, Tokyo, wherever you look, there it is. That's what frightens me, this making of violence acceptable, more and more every day, more normal, more the accepted pattern."

"Christ!" Una shouted. "Don't try to divert us into a discussion of the disadvantages of television. This has been a police state since 1920 but nobody believed us till they saw it on the Box." She hammered the Adams mantelpiece and made the Chelsea figures rock. "And I'm bloody tired of saying that this is not religious struggle. It's a simple, classic example of the class war, but mention Marx or Marcuse and you all scuttle, cowering, into your holes, your warm and cosy wombs of prejudice, suspicion and discrimination. 'One man, one vote' isn't a Catholic cry, for God's sake; it's a cry from all the masses who are disenfranchised in Ulster. Jesus, you'd think we had no poor Protestants without the vote."

"Och, Una, you're too naïve by half, if not disingenuous," the prim, academic-seeming man interrupted her tirade. "You know as well as we all do that religion isn't only the opium of the poor, it is the divider of the poor, the blinker, the tool of those you call the fascists. But tell us this: what is the proportion of disenfranchised Protestants to Catholics? Perhaps ten percent at a liberal estimate? And you are perfectly well aware that the Protestant poor won't thank you for championing their cause. Your help would be like pitch; they'd feel defiled. And you well know it. The poor Protestants are the poor whites of Ulster, the real hard core of religious prejudice."

"Aye," Rory of the shovel face added. "The class war is meaningless in Ireland and always has been, may God forgive us. Take the time of the Troubles; did you ever hear tell of a Catholic or Protestant servant that warned the other sort when big house was to be fired? Not a one, though they

knew full well that the servants would be sleeping in the top
of the house and the most likely to be trapped and burned."

"I couldn't agree more, Rory," said Colum. "The notion of
working-class solidarity is a nineteenth-century myth, a myth
the Irish have never been beguiled by, having a superfluity of
others, if you'll forgive me, Una." Colum gave his sister-in-
law a little clipped bow of apology and Una turned her back
on him to mutter to Sarah, "Why will they never see the irrelevance of religion? It's politically incidental; it's too important for politics."

The party was breaking up. Sarah was once more welcomed to Ulster and wished a pleasant stay and was advised
to "think nothing to the wee lads; sure they meant no harm,
no more they did."

Six of them sat down to a superb dinner, of melon, the
local salmon poached in white wine and a strawberry
mousse. Colum served a Montrachet, dry as ice, pale gold,
exquisite. He carefully removed the table decoration of roses
before he poured the wine. Una had stayed, as well as Rory
and the prissy, academic one. Rory, it turned out, was a television director, the other a scientific farmer, though Sarah
would have been prepared to bet a hundred pounds on
University lecturer.

Sarah had heard much about "our young Una." She'd
been a Dublin University student who'd thought she had,
perhaps, a vocation but had decided in the end that she was
unworthy to be a nun. This Una, of the long hair and pre-
Raphaelite clothes and Marx, seemed hardly the girl that
Sarah'd heard about, that Caroline had prayed about. Dark,
thin, passionate; in her late twenties; with long, straight hair
worn all about her face, the flowing clothes all hung about
with beads, and the thin, nervous, almost prehensile fingers
with sore, bitten, malformed cuticles. Like Caroline, she was
tall, but while Caroline was elegant, Una was bony, stooping,
thrown together, like an old-fashioned wooden puppet, jerky,

uncoordinated. In her rare moments of repose her face was almost beautiful, her fine brown eyes were gentle and her nose was short and neat, her teeth splendid behind the wide, sensuous lips; not a nun's face, perhaps a martyr's. But her attitudes and her angers contorted her; she scowled with disapproval, fought with her face as she sought just the right pedantic thrust, and she gnawed her lower lip and her nails in irritation at the easy inanities of the conversation. An uncomfortable one, food and wine did little to mellow her; the revolution never sleeps. Yes, Sarah thought, that's why so few activists have young. No time or energy for procreation; all those barricades, that unending talk, the pamphlets, posters, angers. No perambulators.

Despite the post-party intimacy, the warmth engendered by the thought that they were chosen, special; despite the food and wine, and all the beauty of that wonderful house, paid for by Colum's now wildly successful English literature textbooks for Catholic schools, it wasn't a comfortable gathering. Roman Catholicism was the cement that bound them, but there, in Ulster, it was not so much a religious welding as a social, almost golf-club, professional linking. They were, because of their religious affiliations, members of the same social category and Sarah suspected that many of those she'd met clung to the Church not from faith but because desertion was tantamount to ratting from your own side; solidarity of the second class the real cement of Ulster Catholicism. Sarah could imagine Caroline cynically claiming that ratting got you nowhere, anyway; the bloody Protestants would always smell you out as a "wee papish from off the Falls Road." They were too different to be comfortable. Una a Marcusite; Colum, professor of English, stubbornly resisting political involvement in the holy name of Leavis and objective literary values; Rory an old-fashioned socialist, like an old, out-of-work bull, out of seed, larded with vague loyalties but, by profession, hedging all his bets. Caroline a devout Catholic, a naïve and sentimental Nationalist, a simple patriot, an anachronism. The scientific farmer, the academic *manqué*, a rejector; ready with his facts rather than his faith, his laws rather than his loyalties. A cold man; more Scots than Irish, probably a Catholic by some accident of ancient matrimony rather than positive inclination.

Sarah was the outsider, stranger, unbeliever. She sat at the table between Colum and Rory.

"I was led to believe that you were one of these Taffys, Sarah, but you say you live in Cambridge? You've been maligned, I doubt."

"No, Rory, I am a Taffy, but there aren't enough jobs for us at home. I'm an exile. It's surely a situation you're pretty familiar with over here?"

"You'll be a Nationalist, then?"

"No. Are you?"

"Och, well, now that's not a question you should be asking me."

"You asked it first."

"Aye, I did, didn't I? You know the honest truth? I don't know the answer."

"Does your job depend on the answer?"

"Aren't you the hard one? It could; aye, I'll be honest with you, it could. But tell me, what's this you do in Cambridge?"

"I work for the Ministry of Education. Does it put you off?"

"Off you, my darlin'? Talk sense now. Did you make any plans yet for your wee holiday? Would you have a minute to spare for a fat man?"

"I'm in Caroline's hands, she's the boss. But we've so much talking to do. It's been five years since I was here."

"And you came now to see the fun and games on the Twelfth Day, no doubt, the three-ring circus."

"Do you know, Rory, I'd forgotten the significance of the date when I arrived? I was tired and looking for a welcome, so I just came here, where I knew I'd find it."

"Dear Sarah." Colum put his hand over hers. "How nice to hear you say that. So good to feel 'like him with friends possessed.'" His hand was strong, workmanlike, competent, and the male warmth of it weakened Sarah, made her feel frightened, alone and small; but Rory was whispering in her ear again.

"Did you hear the one they tell about Paisley preaching down in the country? Some wee benighted place like Ballydrain or Ballynahinch, I disremember where exactly. The congregation all farmers and a handful of wives. His Reverence was thundering away against the sins of the flesh and the like, or so I'm told. 'Five minutes,' says he, 'five minutes wi' a woman, and for the likes o' that you'd imperil your immortal souls.' And more of the same; he worked the Whore of Rome in some place, I doubt, but, woman, whenever he came to the end of his peroration, 'Brothers,' says he, 'brothers, if you've any wee problems at all that's disturbing your consciences the night, would youse not come to me and ask for guidance? I'll be waiting in the vestry here to offer out a helping hand in the name of Protestant Christian charity.' Well, Sarah, I'm telling you, those farming boyos had their eyes opened. They wanted guidance all right. So what'd they do but form a deputation to ask the holy man's advice. 'Come, brother, come,' says he in the vestry, 'open up your hearts.' 'Och, well, Dr. Paisley, sir, it's not so much our hearts. But would you not be telling us, sir, how you makes it last for five whole minutes?'"

Rory had forgotten to whisper as his enthusiasm grew. Everyone was listening and appreciative, but Una held her laughter; she couldn't let it pass. "Yes, laugh at him, dismiss him, it's the easy way. You ought to be ashamed—"

"Shut up now, young Una, get on with the good food I stood cooking for you. Stop mashing that piece of salmon to death and get it down youse."

"I've had it, thanks." She pushed her plate away and lit yet another cigarette behind the curtains of her hair. She rejected strawberry mousse in favour of black coffee and thereafter addressed her remarks exclusively to the academic farmer. Sarah heard, through the meshes of other conversations, references to the cooking of official statistics, the gerrymandering of boundaries, discrimination, prejudice, civil rights, class war. Then Una's voice rose again as she proclaimed, "It will only take one death, for civil war; that's all we need."

"So get down on your knees and pray to God to save us from it," Caroline said. Her beautiful face seemed to curdle, to shrink on the bones, and the bridge of her arrogant nose sharpened, as an ugly mottled flush mounted up to her brow.

"You can't be serious?" Sarah demanded. "Surely the memories of the last one are too green?"

It was the farmer who answered her. "They are green enough to spring to life, given the right sort of encouragement. The bitterness remains, and the young are fed on old atrocities, old wrongs; here the family histories are the histories of Hungers and Troubles. But, as you say, Caroline, pray God."

A moment's thick silence. Caroline crossed herself and someone walked over Sarah's grave. Then Rory shook himself, returned to his role of fat-boy extrovert.

"Colum, boy, I know you're what's called a connoisseur, and I'm certain that's a great wee wine you're after giving us, but it might as well be lemonade for me. You wouldn't have a taste of the hard stuff hidden away, would you? Young Una has me that upset."

Sarah watched Colum wince, saw his large, blue, vulnerable eyes harden and the temper flash, but he got to his feet and thumped before Rory a bottle of Irish whiskey, a kitchen tumbler and the water jug.

"Thanks, Colum. You're a saint, so you are," oblivious to the insult of the kitchen glass. Colum collected antique Irish glass and that tumbler stood among the other glasses on the table like a bluebottle fly in a collection of butterflies.

No one offered to join Rory and Colum circulated again with the Montrachet.

"Rory, you're a pig and a vandal," Sarah said. "How can you bear to use this superb glass, Colum? Aren't you scared rotten all the time?"

"I couldn't bear to use any other." He was curt, still wounded by Rory's philistinism, and then Sarah, in her turn, put her hand over his, picked up her empty sherry glass, a flute glass, museum perfect, and peered at him down the tube of it. She saw him through the base, contorted, demoniac.

"A man who looks on glass
On that may stay his eye,
Or, if he pleaseth, through it pass
And then the heavens espy."

Colum forgot his hurt in his delight, he could always be soothed, seduced, by the apt quotation. Sarah had disliked the distorted look of him, darkly, through the bottom of her glass, fearful, as she was, of the other side of any coin. She was never one to turn over a stone nor kick away a piece of rotting wood. For her the even tenor of the days; that's why the lump—

She shook her thoughts away and kept her eyes on Colum till the face she knew was there again, his big, square head, his grey hair, like a curly fibre mat, the ugly nose, coarse and broad even between his eyes, a pubescent nose above the jut of his aggressive jaw. His skin like faded paper, virtually colourless.

"Och, well, there's nothing for me here." Roughly, ungraciously, Una got up from the table. "I'll just go home. I'll see you tomorrow, Sarah. Thanks for the meal, Caroline. No, please don't fuss. I want to walk home alone. Leave me in peace. Good night, everybody."

"Good night," they said and Caroline sighed. "Och, well, she's a lot on her mind, that same girl." And it was the end of the dinner party.

CHAPTER 3

When Sarah awoke the next morning she thought at first that she was listening to the "noises off" in a bad radio play; there were literally a raucous cockerel and squawking sea gulls and a hoarse, coughing bark that could only be William Butler. She couldn't lie in bed and count the days; she had to move, repulse the traitor thoughts. She drew back the curtains and it was like being at sea. The house clung on to, hung on the last tip of a small promontory, given over to woodland and pasture and to this one house. The tide was sweeping in, almost below the windows; she could smell seaweed and saw the brown, matted underfeathers of angry gulls who fought over bits of breakfast, and five swans were being floated in toward the house. The sea came up to the edge of the garden. A nice, messy, walled garden, with William Butler gnawing a bone in the middle of an unkempt lawn and a very small girl, in a hat, playing shop at an upended grocer's box. She talked to her imagined customers and measured out her stores of dried peas and lentils and rose petals and pushed away a ginger Agacat who had no respect for provisions and wanted his box back. The rain was all over.

In the big kitchen, Caroline, in dressing gown and curlers, was commanding the breakfast. The baby was in his high chair, covered with porridge, and the others were competently helping themselves while she cooked and served.

"Don't mind me. I'm taking a walk."

"I've no time for you now. Back in half an hour and I'll have the place civilised."

"Fine." Sarah put a box of sweets on the table for the young. "Eat these after breakfast. I'll see you all later."

"Hey, Sarah, see is young Bridget out there, would you? And send her in."

"Yes, she's in the garden. I saw her from my window. She's keeping shop."

Sarah went out through the front door and saw her car still sitting where she'd abandoned it, one rear wheel in the pothole. It didn't seem to be in anybody's way. She took the steps down to the garden and up to Bridget's shop.

"Good morning, missus; could I please have half a pound of peas?"

Bridget looked up at Sarah from under the hat. "That'll be threepence."

"O.K. Here's my threepence," and Sarah laid the pennies on her counter. "By the way, the lady in the house thought you might like some breakfast. Would you like me to mind the shop for you? I'll help myself to the peas, if you wish."

A long assessing pause.

"Yes, but don't let those others touch it. And mind thon cat; he's the cheeky one. Come on William, come for your breakfast."

She was about four, fair and fat, wearing blue jeans and a T-shirt and that hat. Obviously a very special hat, of black velour with a black ribbon and a rhinestone brooch on the front. Never one of her mother's hats. It might have been new around 1926.

She left, carrying a small fibre suitcase, and Sarah took her seat beside the box, lit her first cigarette and looked around the garden. Beyond the lawn was a rosebed and then the kitchen garden, potato flowers and broad beans and peas; a row of raspberries and then a thick hedge of gooseberries. An herbaceous border edged the kitchen garden, wild and unweeded, the lupins nearly all seeds, antirrhinums gone leggy and long, sidalceas still brilliant but falling over, unstaked. A tangle of periwinkle choked one corner and, on the other side of the path, a shrubbery, with honeysuckle and brambles climbing and clinging through the laurustinus, the berberis, the weigela, the azaleas. Sarah forgot her shopkeeping and walked towards the shrubbery. She stopped beside a rhododendron to put out her cigarette. The rhododendron leaves were glistening in the sun, like wet raincoats, and the last, lingering pink blossom fell as she watched it.

There were paths beaten through the shrubs, secret, children's paths, and, hunched, Sarah followed the ginger cat along one of them and was suddenly overwhelmed with the scent of mock orange; the tall, thin tree was struggling, stretching for the light above her head, its highest boughs all white and trembling in the breeze off the water. She cut a great armful of them and retreated to Bridget's shop to pull off the paired leaves and so expose the delicate twigs and simple, green-white flowers. A restful job, an excuse to sit in the sun. Bridal flowers, innocent. She forgot their symbolism.

Bridget came back to take over her shop and Brendan, the biggest boy, came up to Sarah and said, "My mammy says will you please come in now?" A tall, gangling, inarticulate boy with his mother's face made roughly out of putty, repressed and inhibited by puberty, gauche and clumsy, his hands and feet too big, his movements jerky as a rooster's. He walked up the garden steps with her. "And my mammy said to thank you for those sweeties," and then he stopped to stare at the buzz of a clutch of flies, starling-coloured, a settled mass on a heap of hen dung. A vicious hum. He kicked them, contemplated his shoe and turned to scrape off the mess on a stone. Sarah went in, to breakfast.

The chaos in the kitchen was now under the control of Caroline's cleaning woman, a rotund body with henna-red, tightly permed hair, a fearful squint and virtually no lips. She made up for this last deficiency by painting a pair of lips with mailbox-red lipstick over her fine moustache, and delicate beads of lipstick clung, quivering, to the little hairs.

"Good morning, madam," she said in a deep, gruff voice, like an open grave. "Isn't that the brave morning? You're welcome to Ulster, so you are. Mrs Moore is in the dining room; she wouldn't be having the likes of you in here, not with all them childer about. Now you be having a nice wee holiday and think nothing to the childer; I manage fine." As she spoke, her voice moved higher and higher out of the grave till, by the final "manage fine," she'd quite jumped out of it. Sarah hadn't been given a chance to say one word when the lady slung her tea towel onto her shoulder and leaned towards her, whispering a new note altogether, "We're expecting again, only never breathe a word I told youse." The voice went down to her black, sensible house shoes. "Myself, I digs with the right foot. I'm like yourself, the other sort." Sarah found it hard to believe that she was quite her sort — at least Sarah dealt with her moustache when it threatened — but she smiled anyway and thanked her and put down the flowers, cheerfully leaving her to the other, name-less children and the washing up.

Caroline and Sarah had breakfast alone. "Caroline, please, what is this about digging? I gather that you dig with the left foot. Strikes me as an extraordinarily inconvenient way to set about things, unless of course one happens to be left-handed."

"Yes, our sort digs with the left foot, we're left-footers. That's just a way of saying it."

"But saying what, for heaven's sake?"

"Saying we're Catholics, nit."

"Oh, and what's the other sort, then? I gather I'm one of them."

"You're a Protestant; that's the right sort here."

"Nonsense. I'm not a Protestant. I'm nothing; I'm an unbeliever."

"God, don't I know it? But here you've got to be some kind of unbeliever. You must be a Protestant unbeliever or a Catholic unbeliever. You're a Protestant unbeliever. And that's the handy thing to be; it needn't mean a fall from grace. To stop being a Protestant could be halfway to being a

Catholic. Anyway, you're harmless. Unbelievers are better than Protestants – or Catholics; depends whose side you're on."

"That's not very Christian, is it?"

"Who's talking about Christianity? Woman dear, grow up and drink your coffee."

"What are your plans for today?"

"First we get the kids sorted. Mrs. Savidge will have them up the stairs soon to make their beds and pack."

"You did say Savidge, didn't you? It is her name, not a description?"

"No, Lily Savidge. Och, I can't complain."

"Wherever do you put all the kids? What d'you do for beds to begin with?"

"Bunks, Sarah. Regimentation and bunk beds. Can't imagine what Ireland did before bunks. Featherbeds it used to be, to tell the truth; four to a bed, two up, two down, and not all the childer house-trained. That must have been a picnic. Still goes on, mind you; we're better not asking. Young Brendan is staying home with us – he wants to go fishing. And the wee ones, Bridget and Patrick, will stay, of course, but the rest are off to Donegal for a week. This friend I have, Molly Cussack, she's taken a house and caravan there, and she's taking four of mine, because I took these ones of hers. It was to let her go to London with her man. I'll bet she's back with a bun in the oven; a wee change is so damn dangerous. Look at me; Patrick arrived nine months to the day after we reached Dubrovnik on that holiday in Yugoslavia; we made this new one when a small premium bond came up and we had to celebrate. You know how we look for excuses to celebrate anything in Ireland. It's all right if you celebrate on the hard stuff; drink enough spirits and you can't raise the flag, and there's nobody saying, 'Let's risk it.' Too much spirits and you can't raise a cheer. The only contraception we poor Irish Catholics are allowed are the whiskey or the gin bottle. Och, to hell, Sarah," she said, grinding out her rare cigarette, "what a life, when we fill their glasses only to make them impotent. And there's not many can afford even that form of self-defence. What the hell is love, when you're reckoning on the almanac, and making excuses to say no? And you know me, I never know the bloody date."

There was nothing to say. Sarah helped herself to coffee.

"That's the thing about a Catholic marriage; it's always tense and hovering on the fringe of fights; you because you're scared to fall again, and him because he doesn't get it enough. Everybody biting their nails and counting mad. Did you ever hear about that wee woman who got one of those clock things, to help her keep a counting? Lived in the country, kind of trusting. She thought the clock was enough to keep her safe, like a charm, like a Saint Anthony, God help her, too. But, of course, she wanted her money back, whenever she found she was that way again."

"It never makes you feel you want to leave the Church?"

"Don't be blasphemous now, don't go thinking the Church is only sex and babies. You know me. I need it. Don't attack me, not this time in the morning, cold sober. Have a heart. Look, Colum's driving the kids to Donegal and he'll stay the night. He wants to leave within the hour, so we may move."

"Can I do anything to help?"

"Yes, clear the table and dust the furniture. You'll see we've changed it? Hope you like it, you old bitch."

"I love it. You know it's perfect, don't pretend."

"It's himself did it, of course. Not too thought out, is it?"

"No, cheer up. That battered engine and bit of chewed bone under the table supply the human touch. By the way, I cut some of your mock orange. I'll put them in the drawing room, shall I?"

"Yes, thanks; but put them high, out of reach. You might keep half an eye on the wee one for me."

Sarah made herself useful in a remote, semi-detached fashion, passing the occasional time of day with Patrick, who circumnavigated the room on his fat, napkinned bottom, with great competence. His was a sideways, crablike motion, his left leg tucked under him for leverage and the right stuck out in front, like a rudimentary grab. He elected to play with William Butler's old bone rather than the battered engine, and he had brought with him a small saucepan and a fish slice, with which he belaboured the furniture. Sarah hadn't the courage to intervene but he tired of the fish slice when the brass door handle of a corner cupboard caught his eagle eyes. Confidently assuming that such an accessible cupboard would be safely locked, Sarah risked lighting another ciga-rette and stood at the window, watching the sea. No word had been said about James McNeil; obviously Caroline wasn't going to be very cooperative. Sarah wondered whether to telephone and present Caroline with a *fait accompli*. No; the Moores were rather sticklers for good form; she mustn't be ungracious. And, God knows, she hadn't the nerve. But it was ridiculous. Hell, all she had to do was dial a number – no, to hell. Not just yet. While there's hope, there's still a holiday. She stubbed her cigarette and, idly, looked towards the quiet child in the far corner. Not only was the cupboard door open, but Patrick had surrounded himself with most of its contents — bottles and flowerpots and various interesting odds and ends, all more or less lethal — and he was busily engaged in pulling the cork out of one of the bottles with his teeth, all eight of them.

"My God, you're your mother's son, Patrick Moore." Sarah picked him up and tucked him under her arm, the bottle still dangling from his teeth. Incompetent and frightened of babies, she fled to the kitchen to look for succour.

"Put him in his pram, madam," Mrs. Savidge advised, "He'll be quiet there, thinking he's to go for a walk. And you'll not be telling him a lie, for he's to go with youse whenever the others are gone."

"What shall I give him to play with? I don't think that bottle is quite the thing, do you?"

"He likes this old soup ladle. Never was one for toys, that Patrick. Och, no, you may fasten them straps on him, madam, or the dear knows what he'll be up to."

"I'm not sure I can. Would you like to do it please, Mrs. Savidge?"

"I will, surely."

Sarah, preferring any company to her own temptations, sat at the kitchen table, dragging at another cigarette, while Patrick leaned out and hammered the sides of his pram.

"You came for the Twelfth Day, did you, madam? Did ever you see it in Ireland with the great processions and the bands and all?"

"No, I never had that pleasure. We don't have it in England."

"Do you tell me that, now? No Twelfth Day, and you a Protestant country? Mind you, I wouldn't be after talking about it to Mrs. Moore. Live and let live's my motto and what's done's done."

She came over to wipe the remnants of breakfast off the table and leaned over Sarah, speaking in that sepulchral whisper again, the globules of lipstick on her moustache pulsating with the fervour of secrecy. That close, Sarah couldn't but see that her scalp, under the thin hair, was dyed a delicate orange. Was it for the Twelfth of July, Orangemen's Day, or just the misfortunes of henna?

"In my young day, I worked for the gentry, so I did. Aye, I spent my dancing days in Ballymore Castle. They fired the place; the other sort, you know," with a jerk of her head toward the stairs. "A great shot the gentry'd had there that day and the house full of visitors and their servants. A great day, and us up since the small hours and a party for us in the servants' hall when the work was done. Them were good days, so they were; we had to work hard and the wages was small but there was plenty of sport too, and you was all right if the head servants were good ones. But, mind youse, there was some cooks would have starved us and some butlers taken advantage of us. But I mind the fire.

"We was all up in the top of the house, of course, the servants, and it was the kitchens and his lordship's library that they fired and we was cut off. The gentry woke and tried to rouse us, but we'd had a hard day of it. In the cruel end we had to jump for our lives and the gentry held blankets for us. But there was one wee girl was feared to jump and at the finish there wasn't enough of her left to give her a decent Christian burial, no more there was. But it'll do no good, thinking and remembering. There was bad on both sides and I'm for forgetting. Sure, my father, he'd have my life if he knew I was working for the other sort. Didn't he beat me once till I couldn't stand for singing one of their songs, and me too young to know the differ?"

There was no sound from Patrick during this recital. Sarah was on the edge of her chair and Mrs. Savidge's vast frame stood between her and the pram.

"You've had a hard life, Mrs. Savidge."

"Aye, sure, sunshine and shadows, sunshine and shadows, but I keep smiling. Would you care now for a wee taste of tea in your hand?"

"Well, that would certainly be very nice, if you're making it."

Mrs. Savidge turned to the Aga and Sarah saw the baby, utterly engrossed in some small thing he seemed to have found in the pram. Fingering with minute precision some little something, his fair head down between his knees and not a sound from him. Splendid; she could enjoy her tea. Then she watched him carefully pick up his new toy and bring it slowly to his mouth, experimentally. It was a large

fish hook, an evil barb, three cruel hooks dangling, swinging
from a little brass chain. Sarah rushed to the pram to snatch
the hook from him but only succeeded in frightening him and
he screamed and flung himself rigid in the pram, yelling
murder and banging his head against the back of it.

"Do something, Mrs. Savidge, for God's sake, he's got a
fish hook, he'll take his eyes out." Mrs. Savidge turned from
the stove like a competent elephant and took the hook away
from him and handed him a sweet from the depleted box. The
yells subsided but he looked at Sarah with such anger and
such hate in his swimming eyes that she retreated, fast, out of
range of that soup ladle. He was planning murder behind that
dribbling chocolate-brown face. Sarah wasn't sure that she
was overly fond of Patrick.

"He's been at the dining-room cupboard, I doubt. You
may put this hook back there, please, madam, and we'll say
no word about it, between us. Only Mrs. Moore doesn't like
him going to that cupboard."

"Why the devil does she keep fish hooks in there?"

"That'll be young James. Sure, the childer never thinks."

Poor Sarah flew to replace the hook and the bottle and to
bundle back the odds and sods as best she could. God, and in
a few more months Caroline would have another baby. How
could she survive? How could she face it? But when Sarah
was safely back in the kitchen, contemplating the tea Mrs.
Savidge had poured her, Caroline reappeared, in navy blue
ski pants and a primrose yellow blouse straight out of *Vogue*,
undefeated and beautiful.

"So you're reduced to tea, are you? Knock it back and see
the children off. Colum's just up at the door with the car."

The tea was like medicine, Indian and strong as a horse,
but Sarah took it. Had to; Mrs. Savidge had her on the end of
a fish hook. Why did she have to be so bloody competent
with her old moustache and her squint eye? Why, Sarah
thought, is a squint such an effective critical tool, permanent-

ly aghast? Mrs. Savidge gave her a conspiratorial, condescending smile as she left the kitchen, damn her.

A large grey Dormobile was parked before the front door
and a *mêlée* of children fought for precedence. Brendan was
standing, out of the struggle, picking over a box of grey-
white maggots, and Colum and Caroline were ignoring them
all and stowing luggage into the boot of the car. Bridget,
behatted, was nursing a tomato in a bath towel. After a few
minutes Caroline left Colum to the luggage and joined Sarah
at the front doorstep.

"At least indicate which of these are yours," Sarah said.
"It's like looking at fish so far."

"It's very simple. All mine are fair. There they are – Peter,
John, Kevin and Brian. Those others are Cussacks – James,
Dismus, Gavin and Philomena."

"Not Dismus and Philomena? You're joking."

"And why not? They were saints, weren't they?"

"I wouldn't know, would I? Is there any point in trying to
make contact with them now?"

"No, they're only kids, they don't register. Don't bother.
They've all seen you by daylight now, so they'll go quiet.
They had to see you because they'd heard us telling Una you
had a bit of a monkey face; there was no shifting them till
they'd seen it. They're disappointed. They were expecting
fur."

Colum eventually had the luggage disposed to his meticulous satisfaction and came up to greet Sarah with his
delightful formality.

"Good morning, Sarah. I trust you passed a restful night.
I regret having to leave so soon after your arrival. I hope to
return tomorrow to enjoy more of your stimulating company.
Alas, 'Duty, stern daughter of the voice of God' demands my
absence." He turned to the children. "Oblige me by taking
your seats," he said and the quarrelling ceased and they sat,
like private soldiers, as and when the seats came.

The tank-like car moved forward; they waved their farewells; Colum missed the Mini in its pothole by careful inches and they were left at the door in a sudden silence, four separate people momentarily caught as though in a camera lens, and then a seagull came screaming over and broke it.

"Bridget, do you want to come a walk with Sarah and me? We're taking the baby off Mrs. Savidge's hands. You may wear your hat."

"I'll think about it while youse get ready."

"We are ready."

"I'll come if Brendan doesn't touch my wee shop."

"Sure, Brendan's going fishing, aren't you, son?"

Brendan, sorting his maggots, nodded his head. "Away with you then, when she can see you go."

"Sure, I wouldn't be wanting her old shop." He said "old" as if it were "owl," but the initial *o* nearer *a*, more like "sol."

"I'm away then. I'll be back for me supper. You'll fry anything I catch, won't youse?"

"Och, you know I will, Brendan; don't I always?"

"Aye, but with her — Sarah, I mean — you might forget."

"Well, I won't; the dear knows she may fry them for you her own self."

Dragging his feet, clumsy in wellington boots, he picked up his rod, put the tin of selected maggots into a small haversack and sauntered down the drive, then broke into a run, then sauntered again. William Butler loafed along behind him.

"Would you believe me, he has those maggots in that bag with his sandwiches? That boy's himself. Right, I'll fetch the wee feller. You'll not want to be troubled with your baby on the walk, Bridget love; leave her with Mrs. Savidge in the kitchen."

I will not. I'll leave her in my shop. Mrs. Savidge might put her in the dinner; she's no sense, thon woman. But I'll take me suitcase."

"Hurry up, then. I'll just get the pram."

Sarah waited for them at the front of the house, a Georgian house of grey stone, the white door wide, a church door, with side panels of glass on either side of it and a wide, segmented fanlight stretched to embrace the door and the two panels, a flowing, sweeping pattern in the leads that was almost ethereal, like the flow of Greek garments in a bas-relief. Two windows on either side of the door and five to the first and second floors and an ancient wisteria whiskering all over it, the blossom over now, but the leaves, delicate as silk, pale brown and apple green, sneaking over the eaves and in at the open windows.

Bridget came up from the garden, carrying her suitcase, and took Sarah's hand. "We'll go on ahead, or my mammy'll be taking her time."

"Tell me about your hat," Sarah said, as she matched her stride to Bridget's. "It suits you very well."

Bridget looked up into her face, suspicious of ridicule, considered her and then, "Well, it was her ladyship gave it to me. Her ladyship likes wee girls and I'm the only one my mammy has."

"I see. Yes, you must be a great comfort to your mammy."

"I am that. You know what her ladyship says? She says your son is your son till he gets him a wife, but your daughter's your daughter for all of her life."

"Well, that's a nice little poem, isn't it?

"That's no poem; her ladyship said it."

Caroline came haring behind them down the drive, pushing the pram at breakneck, and she and Patrick laughed aloud, the same laugh. "Out of the way, we're coming. Watch out," and she let the pram go and it went racketing on, on its own, and Patrick waved the fish slice and Caroline clapped her thighs to see him go, as though she slapped the laughter out of herself, forced out the comic energy and then, suddenly, her face drained, died, and she turned into the fuchsia hedge that lined the drive and retched her soul up. There was nothing to come but slimy water; the empty retching racked her lungs and contorted the poor, beautiful face. "Oh, Sarah, Sarah, it's always like this," and her face shivered again with heartburn and the compelling push of morning sickness. She reminded Sarah of a glove you might find, lost on the road, still holding the form of the hand that shaped it, but empty, abandoned.

Bridget caught the pram and pushed it heavily forward while Sarah put her arm around Caroline's shoulders and held her head. Slowly Caroline straightened up, passed her large, competent hand over her face. "Jesus. There, I think it's over for now. Would you have such a thing as a tissue in those pants of yours? Yes, I'm all right now."

"Are you always sick in your pregnancies?"

"From the second month to the end. Always."

"But what the hell's your doctor doing about it?" "I just can't bring myself to take his bloody pills. Just can't swallow them; it's like I want to make Colum see me like this, like I want to punish him, make him suffer the bit, like me; like putting a line under all the rest of it."

"Yes, I know, but it's you doing the retching, not Colum. It's your poor body."

"What's mine's his."

"Jesus, you're mad, honest."

"I'm all right now."

"But it'll be the same tomorrow."

"Don't nag me now, don't nag. My pregnancy's mine. Just leave me in peace with it. Och, look at wee Bridget. Isn't she great, with that hat on her and all? And pushing that pram; she can't see over the top of it, God help her." Bridget, clutching the suitcase, was valiantly pushing the pram, her head ducked down to avoid the strokes Patrick was aiming at her with his fish slice. They ran to help her and she took Sarah's hand again and exchanged a look with her. All in a day's work, she seemed to say, isn't it the woman's lot? She frightened Sarah with her acceptance and then Sarah remembered how she'd nursed that tomato, and was glad, for under the black hat, for a minute, she'd seen the little face in a nun's wimple and a sense of outrage had boiled in her guts. But she had no rights, she did not count there, any more than a Hindu would have done or a Naga headhunter. She was irrelevant. Three more years and this one would be taking her first communion.

"Where are we going?"

"We'll do our usual round, up to the old castle and home by her ladyship's garden."

"Who is this ladyship, anyway? Bridget seems devoted to her."

"Lady Maxwell; she lives in the Big House yonder. She's my nearest neighbour and she has this great fancy for Bridget. Oh, she's kind enough and I'm fond of her. She's about a hundred and ten."

"She's eighty-four," Bridget corrected. "Her birthday's in August and then she'll be something else."

"Then she'll be eighty-five, won't she?"

"I'm not too sure. I'll need to ask her."

"Yes, you do that." They crossed the farmyard where, last night, Sarah had expected to run into all sorts of agrarian calamities, but the old barns and stables were abandoned, the doors unpainted and hanging askew, grass among the cobblestones and the stable clock stopped at 11.25. Ghost-grey doves still haunted the pigeon loft and muttered in their throats *tirobertigoorimewn* as they passed under their preening in the sunshine.

Bridget led them away from the road that Sarah had followed on the night before, and they pushed under an ancient archway, heavy as the Norman Conquest, and onto a track that followed the windings of the shore. An old, rutted road, still puddle brown with rainwater; there were old stone walls

on either side of the track, ruinous, collapsed; a jungle of
nettles, ivy and brambles aggressing all over them. Away to
the right, a small antique cannon sat on a stone jetty. Bridget
ran on ahead of them to search for treasures. Sarah watched
the sea birds — waders, curlews, terns and gulls — and suddenly the ridiculous face of a seal looked back at her from the
water and ducked away again and it was lovely and open and
easy and she was with Caroline.

"How very beautiful it all is. You lucky people, to be able
to live here."

"Och, well, it's Ireland. We're used to it, I suppose. I like
to be by the sea, with trees about me."

"Caroline, you remember when I was last here, you introduced me—"

"You're going to talk about James McNeil aren't you?
Does he know you've crossed the water?"

"No. Not yet. But I'd like to see him."

"It's your own business, of course," she said, suddenly
closed, cold, Catholic, "but are you thinking you ought to
disturb him again? He's settled now and seems happy enough
with that wife of his. He's been writing some half-decent
things lately, risking his neck. Following the civil liberties
lot, Una's crowd, and reporting on it to the English and
American papers. He's asking for it, thon same man, you
know that?"

"He was always brave."

"Aye, I'll give him that, and he's doing a good job now,
telling the bloody British what goes on here. It takes a
Protestant to make them listen. Were you thinking of seeing
him again?"

"I'd like to; I'd love to, really."

"Still carrying a torch for him?" The voice still harsh and
hurt.

"No. Of course not; it's been years. But he was a friend
and one seems to make fewer and fewer friends."

"Aye, that's true enough, but he's a married man, with childer and debts. You've no right—"

"Yes, Caroline, I have. I'm damned if I haven't rights to that man. He owes me a lot; I loved him far better than ever she did – you can tell by her face for God's sake; like kissing a bloody statue perched on a horse. I was kind to him, generous, comfortable. And now I need him.

"Look, I wasn't going to tell you this, but since you've got that holy look on your face, I'll have to. Thing is, I've got a lump in my breast, I may have to have it off and I want to be a woman for what may be the last time. No, no, please don't look like that, it's only a little lump. I'm not going to die of it or anything like that. I promise you, it's a little lump and I've had it for years. But the doctors say it ought to be looked at. It's probably nothing, but, just in case, I should like to see him again. I wouldn't say no to a few good prayers, either."

Caroline crossed herself. "Jesus, you're bloody calm about it. Yes, phone him, get in touch. Christ, think if I had to tell him you were dead and him all unprepared. Yes, phone him and see what he says. Better the fret than the funeral. But you'll not tell him about that, about the – sure you won't?"

"No, I don't want him for pity's sake. If he does want to see me, fine; if not, that'll be all right too, because since I've arrived and actually realised the mess over here, I feel a bit irrelevant, you know? What's a small lump, isn't it? But it would be nice to see him, if only for a drink and a bit of remembering. I know I command none of his loyalties."

"I wouldn't bank on that. He fancied you, that same wee man. If he hadn't lived here in Ulster—"

"But this is his world; this is what he lives for."

"If he's not careful it's what he'll die for too. He's sticking his neck out, you know that? What he wrote about the Burntollet march and how he bought drinks for the students after it, Jesus. I hear Billy Boy's Bully Boys have threatened to have his life. Och, no, phone him; he'd like it."

"Would he, though, Caroline? Would he? I couldn't bear to be a mere embarrassment, a politeness. That would kill me faster than the cancer that I probably haven't got. I'm five years older too."

"Cheer up; he's five years fatter. I saw him on television the other night and nearly wrote him a note to keep off the bread and potatoes, only there wasn't time; one of the weans cried or some silly thing."

As they talked Patrick slipped lower and lower into his pram, his eyelids were heavy and his grip on the fish slice relaxed. His head slowly drooped and he slept. Bridget trailed behind rattling pebbles in her pockets. They walked under tall beech trees that crowded in, between them and the water. The trees cut up the pale blue sky in lovely, airy shapes and Sarah looked down to watch the rhythms of shade and sunlight at her feet. Then a heavy, solid, deep shadow fell upon them, a cold shadow, like a fortress defying them. A tall fist of dominance, incongruous as all hell in this soft, grey, green place. A tall square lump of arrogance that sent shivers through her in the sun, and the small hairs stood erect along her arms. That giant's fist stirred the child in Sarah and something cowered from the cold cruelties, the ancient wrongs. But Bridget ran on, leaving the track and darting over the pebbles and rocks, indifferent, in her plimsolls, to the slippery, wet, purple seaweed.

"We'll have to go in; Bridget has another wee shop in there and she'll have our lives if we don't pay a visit. It's well one of the Moore kids has a notion of money. We can leave the wee fellow here; he'll come to no harm."

Slowly, heavily, they picked their way over the pebbles and slimy seaweed, slipping and squelching, saving themselves with their hands on the rough, uncomforting rocks, clinging to lumps of sea pinks, water bugle; legs astraddle, clumsy, middle-aging and corseted. They reached high-water mark and there the seaweed was crisp and dry; its crunch excited Sarah, like holidays.

The fortress was everything Norman; cold, grey, heavy, thick, functional, comfortless. A great arched entrance and an earthen floor and dusty emptiness. Bridget was already away up a narrow disastrous-looking circular stairway.

"You may as well face it. You'll have to go up. There'll be no peace till we've been. It'll do your middle-age spread a bit of good, so it will."

With considerable distaste and some trepidation, Sarah went up the staircase, more or less on all fours, bum in the air. It got darker and darker, more and more suspect, not as much as an arrow slit of light. Just before the claustrophobia reached her mouth, she reached the first floor, open, at least, if still pretty Stygian.

Caroline puffed out behind her. "I wouldn't stand too long in this part, Sarah. Too many bats. There's a special variety of big ones here, supposed to be interesting, but they can keep them for me."

Sarah flew. She floundered up the next flight of steps like a rogue rhinoceros. At the top there was light. The walls were ruinous, great untidy gaps where windows might have been and where the roof had let in the sky.

A sordid place. Pigeons' nests in the corners, untidy enough in themselves, God knows, but here made horrid: the eggs trodden on and smeared, the bits of twigs and straw scattered, robbed, and a dead chick, flattened by what might have been a heavy boot, still raw and unspeakably new. Lumps of sugar and pretty bits of broken china crunched under her feet. Pretty pebbles and pieces of given-away plastic were strewn about the floor, among cigarette butts and the empty packs. There was a great, flat, circular stone structure in the centre of the floor whose true function Sarah couldn't begin to imagine – unless it was the bottom half of that form of torture, the *poena et dure*, during which they put heavier and heavier weights on you, till you told them all, whether you knew it or not. Bridget had converted the stone into another shop and there were still some provisions on it, but she wasn't squatting behind it, waiting for customers. On the contrary, she was in a great taking, half crying and muttering to herself, running distracted from one scattered treasure to another, making uncoordinated grabs at this and then that, as a woman might run from thing to precious thing if her house were burning around her. She'd even abandoned her suitcase. In her frenzied searchings she left the chamber where Sarah stood and ran out through a narrow, ruined arching. Hoping, vaguely, to be of some remote assistance, Sarah followed her onto a narrow parapet and nearly died.

They were on a broken-down old sentry walk that seemed to hang out right over the waves; the demented child was running along it, regardless, hunting for beans and sugar. Sarah was rigid and almost seasick from the glare of sun on the water, a goodly three hundred feet below. She dared not shout in case she frightened the child, who was teetering on the edge of a shuddering gap; bits of the parapet had snapped away like rotten teeth and she was jittering about like a butterfly, on the very yawn of them. Sarah was crumpled up against the carved stone jamb of the archway, watching her, impotent with terror, when Caroline looked out at them.

"Bridget, come away out of that, you wee brat."

"Me shop's all scattered, Mammy, it's all through-other," she moaned. "It's that Brendan, he's a nasty pig. I'll kill him."

"Come out of that; I'll get you something else for the shop. Here, I tell you now."

Dragging her feet, careless of the danger and still peering to find her provisions, she came towards them and in under the arch. Caroline gave her a slap on her behind that sent her tottering forward into safety and tears, clutching the hat that had threatened to fall off with the force of the smack.

"Jesus," Caroline gasped. "Kids. And don't you be starting on your corporal-punishment balls; that wasn't punishment, that was release. Mothers must have some defences.
Shut up now, Bridget, and give us a pennyworth of sugar
lumps. You'll have to put it in the book, for me bag's in the
pram with Patrick."

"Will you not beat Brendan, Mammy? Beat him for me."
Her blue eyes were brimming and her face smeared with the
dirt off her groceries.

"Tell you something, Bridget," Sarah said, hating this talk
of beating. "I doubt if it was Brendan at all. Look, there are
cigarette stubs all around and two empty packs over there.
Someone else was probably here, unless, of course, Brendan
is a very heavy smoker?"

"No, he didn't like it, he was sick."

"Don't you think it could have been someone else then?"

"Now who the devil would come here to sit and smoke,
will you tell me that?" Caroline was suddenly alert. "I
wonder now if anybody's up to something?"

"Like what?"

"Och, nothing. Pay no heed. Somebody courting, I
doubt." Rather too casually, Caroline changed the subject.
"Look, Sarah, see over yonder, on the edge of the wood,
those walls and bits of ruins? There was a small townland
there in days gone by, but the gentry wanted the people
cleared off the estate, wanted it all tidied up and decent and
nobody being inconsiderate enough to go and die in the
Hunger. They fired the thatch of those cottages and paid the
tenants five pounds a head, to get themselves to hell out of
it and off to America. You could do it for a fiver, in the old
coffin shops. They sailed from near here, from
Ballyduggan. There's still gooseberry bushes growing
where the old gardens were. That's Ireland for you. Will
you not shut your noise, Bridget, and give us those sugar
lumps I asked for?"

Bridget gave them two grey sugar lumps apiece and tidied up the remnants of her shop, then, pigeon-toed, they went down the circular stairway, passed the bats, which Sarah preferred to take on trust, and out into God's good sunlight.

Down to the crisp seaweed again and then onto the slippery part. Sarah was more confident this time, released from that dungeon of a fortress, and the sun caressing her back. Too confident; she was rounding a rock when a heron flew up from the far side of it, flew heavy and ponderous, with a great, slow flap of his wings, and his legs, trailing like mooring ropes, almost across her face. Her legs left her, she landed hard on the old-smelling fishy seaweed, and her hands were grazed by the rock. She was too bad-tempered and outraged to move for a minute or two, not till she felt the water penetrate her seat, cold and ancient water, and there was nothing for it but to get lumpishly up and see the joke. Caroline and Bridget laughed inordinately at her wet behind, a huge dark patch, like one that Patrick might have produced, with wisps of algae caught in the creases.

"What's this you once said you were? Accident prone? We may just go home and get you changed. You're as much trouble as the childer. Are you hurted?"

"No, nothing to speak of, but it's damn cold, and such a sensitive spot. It's rather horrid actually."

Bridget was delighted; she forgot the ruin of her shop. "It's rather horrid actually," she mimicked, and ran ahead to the pram, making a little song up as she went.

"Sarah fell in the seaweed,
I wonder why she did,
Sarah fell in the seaweed,
I wonder why she did,
And now she owes me money,
I wonder will she pay,
I wonder will she pay."

Sarah walked back bowlegged, like a ploughboy, or a railway porter, cold and wet and chafed where a damp, thick seam in the crotch was rubbing her softest skin.

"Cheer up, girl; we'll be home in ten minutes and we'll have a few drinks before lunch. I've a risotto to warm and you can make the salad while I feed the childer. We didn't finish that last bottle of Montrachet and it'll just do us. There's more than half."

"Ten minutes! I shall die, I promise you."

"We'll run for it; come on."

Sarah was kept going only by the thought of a drink and dry underpants. Both, alas, were postponed. When they reached the house, Mrs. Savidge came bossing out, her breath in her fist and her voice in one of its lower registers. "Her ladyship's here," she stage-whispered. "I only passed the time of day and put her in the drawing room. Said you wouldn't be many minutes; she asked was your friend arrived and I said yes, and as nice a lady as anyone's wish to meet, so I did, begging you pardon, madam, if I'm speaking out of my place."

Bridget had darted away with a squeal of delight to greet her dear friend and Caroline said firmly. "You may forget the pants. She'll be expecting to meet you. It'll only be for a wee while. Come on; you'll do."

Mrs. Savidge had taken the pram and the sleeping child, but turned smartly at the mention of pants, the squint on the ever-ready.

"I fell in the seaweed," Sarah hastened to explain, "and I'm somewhat wet."

"Sure, her ladyship'll not mind, no more she will."

Her ladyship had no call to mind. Sarah was the one. Caroline strode to the drawing room without a backward glance and Sarah could do nothing but follow.

Lady Maxwell was listening to Bridget's song: "Sarah fell in the seaweed, I wonder why she did." She was a short, solid

old woman, like a pollarded willow, all trunk. She was
dressed in grey-green tweeds and a huge floppy straw hat,
like a Chinese peasant's, except that hers had a ruby brooch,
set in diamonds, winking on the black ribbon of it. Her thick,
old, swollen legs were covered with dense lisle stockings and
her shoes were black and sensible, like school uniform. Her
face was removed, remote in its antiquity, no longer quite a
human face, a Celtic, early Christian corbel stone. One eye
much larger than the other and both heavy lidded, the lids
white and thick as though a cushion of air lay under the skin
of them, puffing them. Her lips were lumpy and purple over
strong, stained horse teeth, and a high, mottle mauve colour
lay on her cheekbones.

"So there you are," she greeted Sarah. "This child tells me
you fell into the seaweed. Uncommon clumsy, my dear, at
your age. When you come to mine, you may have the wit to
avoid the seaweed. I've been pulling up weeds, my agapan-
thus was almost choked; it's that damned bishop, but I'll
have him out, he'll not defeat me."

"You know what the doctor said about weeding, Lady
Maxwell."

"Damn the leech; I've no need to be careful now. I've had
a good innings and I'm only playing for time. This time next
year I hope to be over there with the ancestors; I propose to
live out what's left as I see fit. Don't you agree, my dear?"
She turned to Sarah and caught her staring, standing up like
a big beanpole, unable to sit, wetly, on Caroline's best chairs.

"Would you not like a little sherry or something, Lady
Maxwell?" Caroline was a trifle nervous; best behaviour for
the gentry.

"You know I never touch it child. Still champagne was all
I cared about and we none of us can afford that any longer. It
was dear General Eisenhower who sent me the last case; his
men were stationed here, you'll remember. A nice boy. Your
husband a soldier?"

"He was killed in Korea," Sarah said.

"I'm sorry. Come to tea. Bring her up on Thursday. I'm at home."

"That's jolly decent of you; if it suits Mrs. Moore, I should like that."

"Of course it suits her. What else has she to do in this house all day? I looked at the garden as I came along. You haven't wasted much time there of late, I'll warrant you. Never mind; you cannot be expected to do everything and you will insist upon having all these wretched childer." She put her arm around Bridget's shoulder to indicate that that one, at least, was not included in the general condemnation. "Those flowers are nice. You did those. She hasn't time to strip and arrange."

"She suggested the pots," Sarah defended.

"Of course she did. I gave her that Chinese one. Got it from the last empress, the old dowager; splendid character; knew her in Peking. You be careful of that pot; Bridget's to have it."

"I'd be careful with it anyway."

"Hoity-toity, miss. Yes, you'll do. Upon my word, I must bid you good day. That cook o' mine has the temper of a fiend."

"Will you let us drive you home in the car?" Caroline asked. "I don't like to think of you walking."

"Had I wanted a motor, I would have driven my own." She glared at Caroline from under her coolie hat. "Come Bridget, you may walk with me to the farmyard and we'll let Mrs. Thomas take off her wet clothes, shall we?" She gave Sarah the most bewitching, conspiratorial smile. "Off you go, gal, and be damned to good manners. I shall look forward to seeing you tomorrow."

"Thank you, I will." They shook hands and Sarah ran for the stairs while Lady Maxwell and Bridget, both hatted like mushrooms, walked down the drive, in serious, concentrated conversation.

CHAPTER 4

The sun was stroking the back of Kilhornan that afternoon and drawing the colours out. Nineteenth-century houses in a casual row, this one washed pink, that blue, terracotta and primrose next door; shop fronts with the names above them in large, uncompromising Victorian lettering and a lot of maroon paintwork, the occasional cottage whitewashed and thatched, humping its shoulders at the neighbours. A grim old barn of a Protestant church frowned shame from its bastion of gravestones. Then the Catholic church, bald-looking and naked in its newness, with Our Lady, in the nastiest, harshest blue, eternally blessing above the porch, serenely smiling under an uncomfortable halo of light bulbs that someone had neglected to switch off.

"Would you keep your eyes on the road, woman, and take this left turn before you have us killed? Park outside that shop on the left." They had come round to the sea again and a little harbour with fishing boats and small yachts with sails and the sea spanking on the water like a picture-postcard holiday.

"Away now and look at the view while I get my business sorted here. I'll not be long." Sarah left her car and walked towards the jetty and the boats and the old men in the sun and the children. One old man bobbed at her and told her it was a brave day. It really was a brave day, bright, clean, and those little boats with their sails, like flags. She looked out and about her. There were only old men and children by the water, no other ranks, no women around their doors nor beside the shops, no men with nets, no one tending the ferry-boat. Idly, she half wondered why. Then she began to feel unfriendly standing there alone, touristy, and she joined the old man, on his wooden seat by the green, who had pointed out the bravery of the day.

"Aye, that surely is the brave day. You're welcome to Ireland. You'll be Mrs. Moore's young lady, I doubt?"

"Yes, I'm staying with her."

"Aye, well, you might be telling her me son's got what she was after," he whispered under his hand.

"Your son's got what she was after; I see," Sarah said blindly, whispering back.

"Aye, they're in the house. Begging your pardon and taking the liberty, you wouldn't put them in your wee car, now would youse? And save us all a mite of trouble?"

"Why, yes, of course, if you'd like to get them for me."

"Aye, aye, I'll do that. Just you bide there a wee minute," and he went, with small, old man's steps to a lavender-washed house and left Sarah to the serious regard of several silent children. He soon came shambling back again, bearing a wooden box before him, like an acolyte with a holy grail. It was a dirty old box, made of wooden slats, and water was fairly pouring out of it, down his ancient, baggy front.

"There you are now. Caught the day. Two rare ones. Herself will be well pleased with them." He handed her the dripping box. There were two large, live black lobsters in it, with eyes, and red antennae all over the place. Their big front claws were tied up with string, but the rest of them moved, convulsive and heavy as army tanks, rustling on the bottom of the shallow box, and the bigger one flapping his tail with ponderous malice.

"Aren't they the great ones?" he went on as he pushed the box at her. "You'll not be feared of them 'uns. He has them tied. And you the big girl too." He ignored her agonised repulsion; he was old and weak and tottery, or so he made out. Sarah was forced to take the box for shame; she carried it up to the shop like a live grenade, and heard the old rascal laugh to see her go. She half turned her head, but by then he was coughing and spitting and beating his chest. The children followed her to the open shop door. Caroline was there, giving her order.

"Caroline, for God's sake, help. Look at these monsters that evil old man has made me carry. Take them, please, I shall die."

"Och, John James got them then; bless him. Two beauties." She drooled over them.

"Take them, won't you? That big one's got his eye on me."

Caroline put the box down on the counter and ran her eyes over the shop again. "I think I've everything now. I'd like you to meet Mr. Ogle, Sarah. Mrs Thomas who's come to visit us."

"How d'you do?"

"Very well indeed, thank you madam. You're keeping well yourself? It's welcome you are and a pleasant stay to you. You've picked a brave day." The village shop had Sarah stage-struck, Abbey Theatred. "Aye, indeed, deed, it's a brave day. Except for the funeral."

"Funeral?" Caroline raised her fine, aristocratic brows. "Whose funeral, in the name of God?"

"Sure, old Mary's away. Old Mary Conville, God rest her."

"Lord, I forgot, with having Mrs. Thomas. What time's it to be?"

"Boys a boys, that's not like you, madam, sure it's not. But you'll hardly have the time to get out of this village till they're upon you from the chapel. Not now, you won't. You may wait in here and do me the honour but I'm for the procession myself. So I'll be taking off the white coat, if you'll excuse me, madams both."

"No, we'll not wait, thank you all the same."

"Now what?"

"Look, you grab those lobsters."

"I utterly refuse. Grab them yourself. What's the fuss about?"

"You heard the man. The funeral will come down the street at any minute and we can't be caught here, like sight-seers, God damn it. Take the groceries and I'll bring the lob-sters. Quick now, and turn the car. We'll hide in the pub; move now, move. Don't stall or I'll have your life."

"Right. Where's the pub?"

"That one, John Joe Magee's. In now. They're not in sight yet. We're all right."

"What about those monsters on my back seat?"

"Leave them. They'll come to no harm." Sarah had been more concerned about her back seat than the fate of the lob-sters, but they have different priorities in Ireland.

They walked into the cool dark of Magee's. The bar-room had a friendly, suspended, homely look. It was still obvious-ly the parlour and "middle room" of the Magee home, roughly knocked into one. The parlour end, by the front door, still wore its parlour wallpaper, going back to that nasty, thir-ties movement in decoration which used to be called futuris-tic – semi-squares and sharp angles and no shapes. The paper had faded into indeterminate pastel colours and was pocked with small, silver lumps. The other end, the "middle room," had been "improved" and the wallpaper colour washed; two walls were wine red and the other orange. The bar itself was very modern and plastic, a scarlet semicircle of imitation. There was no one behind the bar. This bar end of the room was furnished with old "Britannia" wrought-iron tables and there were settles along the walls. And a huge looking glass that advertised "Bushmills" in gilt.

The front end, on the other hand, still preserved its parlour elegancies; a profusion of potted plants on the mantelpiece and on the windowsill, a holy picture of the Sacred Heart over the fireplace and rigid, unyielding, chintz-covered arm-chairs, Edwardian ones with no give, made of pitch pine, a cross between a throne and a commode; not even vulgarly Victorian, merely staid, like Princess May of Teck.

As they peered their way from the sunlight, another ancient crept from an oak settle, as though from under a stone. "They're all away," he dribbled at them, "away to see poor Mary put down. You'll not get a drop till they're back, no more you will."

"Och, Mr. Wales, sure you know me? I'll help myself if you can't bring yourself to pour it."

"Is that yourself, Mrs. Moore?"

"Who else? Come on now, give me a double Irish and my friend will take a big one of the dry sherry. You'll take a wee something yourself, I'm sure. To keep out the cold, whenever the funeral's passing; God rest her."

"Aye, I will. Who's to be next, I'm asking youse. Poor Mary, poor Mary, many's the night's courting I had with that old body."

"Och, whisht now, and get us the drinks. Where's your respect, at all?"

"Mrs. Moore dear, would you not be pouring them your own self? My hands is that shaky."

"I will, surely. What's this you're having yourself?" she asked, safely separated by the bar counter from the quivering lechery of his old hands. "A double of Scotch, you said? Sure, if you say so." He stretched his dirty, battered hands for the glass and sucked up half the whiskey with a noise like a drain, in the literal blink of an eye. Then he groped in his waistcoat pocket and produced a hinged tin box. He poured snuff from it onto the back of his hand, sniffed with each nostril in turn, and came right up beside Sarah. He stank like a long-neglected dustbin. "You'll take a taste of snuff," he said, and what with the noise of catarrh and the dribbles and the dirt and the proximity of him on that warm day—

"No," Caroline said firmly, as she chalked up their drinks on a slate. "The lady doesn't indulge. You'll excuse us, Mr.

Wales; we're for the window to watch the funeral." Sarah set herself behind a flourishing red geranium and its smell was astringent and grateful after that Ancient of Days.

The funeral procession began to pass. The priest came and the fine, dark-stained coffin carried by six men, then the mourners, rigid in their best, walking stiff and solemn, like automata. There were no tears, no furled handker-chiefs; Mary had been too old. The street was quiet, desert-ed except for the little procession and a dog. But suddenly, like a clap of summer thunder, theatrical as Maria Monk, a door across the way was thrown open and a man burst out, shouting, "Daddy's dead; oh, Daddy's dead. He's killed my da, he's killed him." He threw himself upon the pavement and sobbed, beating his hands upon the paving stones. He was promptly followed by a younger man, frantic, dishevelled, his hair on end, his gestures drunken, wearing only a grubby cotton undershirt above his belted trousers. This one shouted into the horrified silence, "I've killed my daddy, I swear to God, I've killed me da." The Playboy to the life.

The staid procession shuffled, faltered, half halted; the coffin swayed. The procession seemed to consider breaking ranks, but remembered itself, died with curiosity but contin-ued to move on, slowly, respectfully, with, thereafter, hardly a sideways glance.

The two men held their postures like children in a game of statues, until the last of the mourners had passed; the Playboy stood with his face to the wall of the house, his arms out-stretched, as though on a cross, and the other lay sobbing on the paving stones in his bright brown suit, a chunk of dry dog's excreta inches from his outflung hand.

Caroline and Sarah stayed, shocked, at the window. The old man had heard nothing of the commotion.

"Jesus, Sarah, did you ever see the like of that?"

"Only in the theatre."

"I think I'd best go over. You wait here; they'll not be wanting strangers."

"I'm damned if I'll stay here with that old satyr—" Two young men came quietly, briskly, out of the house across the way. They pushed the Playboy indoors, into the wings, and then lifted the sobbing man and hustled him, also, into the decency of the house. The door was closed and the street was silent.

"Now who the devil would those be, I wonder."

Sarah knew. They were her young men; the boys of the "wee loanie," the telephoning, the threat. Those shouts of death and killing and, now, these two boys. Dare she tell Caroline? Sarah felt too bewildered to think; this final improbable coincidence after the theatricality of the hot afternoon stupefied her. But she knew she mustn't tell Caroline, not yet; Caroline would go over there, fuss, accuse the boys, anger them. And that bearded one was dangerous, a bad one; the very spit on his beard had been sadistic, spiteful. He might still harm the children, frighten them, perhaps for the fun of it, just "for badness." It was a notion that Sarah, with her dreams and ideals about progressive education, would have preferred to reject, but there, somehow, she was convinced by it. There, in Ireland, with its stage conventionality, its Hollywood diction, its terrible, living history — Mrs. Savidge and the fire, the ruined cottages and their gooseberry bushes, the ever present violence, the exhilaration of communal hate — in the context of all these, Sarah found her rationality deserting her. She couldn't think, her mind quivered, she hesitated like an old lady who hovers over a choice.

"You can't just leave me, Caroline. Look, why don't we go home and you can telephone the grocer or the priest or someone? I promise you, I couldn't possibly stay here with Casanova and not another soul in the place."

"Aye, maybe you're right. But it'll kill me till I know what it's all about, I'm telling you. John Vint's not the best, he has a heart condition. I wonder is he dead at all, girl."

"Let's just go home, shall we?"

"All right. We'll go. Una said she'd be round. Might be better if we're not out when she comes; you never know, not with her the way she is just now. Good day to you, Mr. Wales," she called.

"Good day, ladies both."

When they were safely back in the car and making for home, Sarah took her mind off her thoughts and asked, "What is it about Una? She struck me as rather prickly, shall we say?"

"Prickly? She's like a bloody hedgehog. Mind you, I've said nothing to you, but she has a few problems. You might as well know, she's left her husband. She's in a bad way, the child. He won't divorce her, thank God; he's a good Catholic, even if he was a hard one to live with."

"Poor kid."

"Aye, but she's odd, you know that? She's educated, is our Una, so she talks a lot of nonsense and suffers from ideas; you two should get on. But she ought to have more thought for her family. There's Colum's position to think of for a start; there's not many Catholics get a job like his in the North of Ireland. Una'll tell you he's the exception that proves the rule; she's maybe right. But, Sarah, he has it, he's come on; I'll not have him destroyed. The University's the one place a Catholic stands a chance here. But she has no childer; we hope to be able to swing an annulment. As long as she behaves. We couldn't take a scandal. Beats me why she never had kids. They both wanted them, and there's me, her sister, farrowing like a sow. Don't let on I said anything, now."

"What does she do? Does she have a job?"

"She's a job teaching in Belfast. She likes that and it ought to keep her, but she's forever overdrawn and hasn't a rag to put on her. Gives it all to the Cause, I reckon. She rents a little house close beside us; used to be a shooting lodge, so they say. It's pretty, like a doll's house, but I've this feeling it's haunted. It's so small and intimate, you still seem to be touching other lives there, all boxed in with you. I wonder what happened at all at the Vints'. I've half a mind to go back."

"You promised Mrs. Savidge you'd be back at four, remember? She wants to go and prepare her husband's meal, she said."

"Yes, we'd best get on. I'll phone them when we get home. They've only the two boys, the Vints. The one came running out first is a good enough feller, keeps a pub in Belfast, but's he's had his windows smashed in last week and he's closed up for a few days. But the other one, the young one, he's a bad rip, hell roast him. Never a decent job, in trouble with the peelers; he's a bad boy, that one."

Back in the house, they found Una entertaining the children. With Patrick on her lap and Bridget beside her on the sofa, she was reading *Tom Kitten* and making splendidly appropriate noises for Patrick at each picture. Sarah was relieved to see that he'd abandoned his fish slice. With the children Una was easy and relaxed, no longer the self-conscious, priggish, arrogant young woman of the previous night. Her long hair was tied back from her face with a big black bow and her laughter had brought colour into the thin cheeks. Some of the ravaged look had gone with the lifting of the curtains of her hair.

"Oh, there you are, Una. So Mrs. Savidge is away?"

"She's promised to come back to help with dinner. Did you see the village, Sarah? Impressed?"

I don't believe in it. I keep thinking it's been put on for my benefit, sheer tourism. We got *The Playboy of the Western World* this afternoon."

"God, no, it's real enough."

"I'm away to telephone. Tell Una, would you, Sarah?"

"What happened?"

"Some frantic melodrama in the village street. We were in a pub where we'd gone to hide from a funeral, old Mary Conville's, and a young man charged out of the house opposite, the Vints'. He was yelling that his daddy was murdered, and he was promptly followed by a second sort of ham actor who literally claimed to have killed his da. I'm afraid I have to confess that it struck me as naïvely comic," Sarah lied, smearing a layer of bogus sophistication over her fears. "The wretched procession hadn't a clue. It was all so ludicrous; one half expected them to break into a chorus from Gilbert and Sullivan and do a shuffle with the coffin. I had the greatest difficult in restraining Caroline from going into the house, of course, but I simply refused to be abandoned to the lecherous attentions of an old Lothario who was the only other person in the bar. And anyway, there were other people in the Vint house already, so I succeeded in dissuading Caroline."

"Yes, John Vint has a bad heart; but why should they cry murder? He's been given the last rites times without number. But you may be sure it wasn't a piece of adapted Synge. Larry Vint's never in life heard of the Playboy; I doubt whether he can write much more than his own name. But Caroline will get the facts; she keeps her hand firmly on the village pulse. I sometimes fear that this house has gone to her head and that she has delusions of grandeur."

There was a sudden scream from Bridget. Patrick had rudely torn out the picture of the Puddle-Ducks and was eating it. She snatched it back out of his mouth and despairingly tried to fit it back into its place in the book. Furious, Patrick went rigid and purple in the face and hammered his head against the arm of the sofa. Sarah retreated, fast, to help Bridget repair the book with some sticky tape, while Una gradually silenced Patrick by blowing on his face and laughing at him. Caroline returned as peace was about to be restored. She looked pale and somehow quenched.

"Get any news?"

"He's gone, God rest him. There was a fight, from what I hear. John was out in the garden, enjoying the sun, and young Larry was arguing the bit with the mother. He's been a cross to her, that same feller. John put his oar in and spoke up for Mrs. Vint and that wee one hit him, knocked him down, out there in the back yard. It's to be hoped the shock killed him, but there's to be a post-mortem."

"No need to get dramatic over that, Caroline; sudden death, the PM's automatic."

"Wait now, wait till you hear. After that shocking business we saw in the road, they brought John into the house and set him in his chair, to try and cod the doctor he'd died in his sleep. And him with the blow plain on his face and a lump on the back of his head. The doctor's still there and old Mary's procession is all packing into the Vints', so they tell me. Father O'Rourke must have got her bedded down fast. This one'll be faster than the time he took on that atheist, Una, that the Presbyterian minister wouldn't have in his churchyard."

"Poor bastard, dragged to a heaven he didn't believe existed, so that the Father could prove he was a more liberal Christian than the Presbyterian. Did you hear what the quarrel was about?"

"No." Caroline's voice was sharp and short and uncompromising. Sarah guessed the boys of the loanie were not uninvolved, but Caroline's loyalties were a mad, irrational tangle; if those boys were in the IRA, her sentimentalities would defend them against any probing.

"I'll just give these weans their tea. No word of Brendan, I suppose? You two have a crack; I'll not be long." Without the children, Una slumped again and began to gnaw viciously at an inflamed cuticle on her thumb; Sarah watched her twisting and distorting her mouth to get a purchase for the strong, clean teeth.

"Have a cigarette," Sarah suggested. "It's less painful."

Una looked up, half inclined to snap, and then, as though without the energy for anger, she gave a little, gulped, apologetic laugh and held her hand out for the packet.

"You're very solitary aren't you? Don't you think you ought perhaps to live with someone?"

"Live with in what sense? Don't for Jesus' sake suggest some nice, friendly female who'd try to save me from myself with love and forbearance. As for living with, in the other sense, this is Ireland, Sarah; we don't do things like that here."

"Then why the devil do you live in Ireland? Leave it."

"No, I couldn't. Here I have Caroline and the kids, at least. And I wouldn't abandon the fight."

"But what is your fight? You defeat me; a Roman Catholic Marxist. It makes no sense to me, I'm afraid. Shall we have a drink? I feel unhinged after Kilhornan. You remember my hijackers? Those two boys were the ones at the Vints' this afternoon. I found it not a little disconcerting."

"Were they so? It's all right then; they'll be Republicans. The Vints were always active. Yes, please, whiskey; no, no water. John's been inside more than once. But I've no patience with them; they provide a ready-made excuse for all the enemies of civil rights."

"But, as a good Marxist, aren't you glad of any disruptive force?"

"Damn you, Sarah, don't be so cold and bloody analytical. You know nothing at all about it."

"No, but I have read my Marx."

"Yes, but what do you know about being one of a suppressed minority, brought up to accept that the odds are forever against you, that you don't need a black face to be pointed at, despised, separate?" She was on her feet, all the gentleness engendered by the children dragged out of her face and the tendons standing out like thick cords in her neck. "I happen to have a job and a house and, therefore, a vote, but I'm unusual in the North of Ireland, a Catholic who's scrambled into the middle classes. No, I can't run. We've been running too long. It's got to stop."

Sarah was ashamed to realise that she was only half listening to Una. Her mind was in bits. Una's posturing bored her, despite her sympathy; the melodrama created a mood of unreality – the girl speechifying to an audience of one. And where was James? He'd been out when Caroline had telephoned his office. She'd left her number, but James hadn't called back. How soon dare she, with dignity, telephone again?

"Damn it, was there ever a country more ridiculed, more romanticised, more stereotyped, more politically used and pawned, more dismissed as a music hall joke than Ireland? We've been so staged, so theatred, that even the sewage the police pour over our demonstrations with their water cannons is dismissed like the cold tea that masquerades as strong drink in a farce."

"Och, quit the Maudgonning, Una, for God's sake." Caroline was back, with Patrick under one arm and Bridget trailing at the other hand. "Drinks? You may pour me a big one, please, Sarah." She sagged onto the sofa with a deep sigh and put Patrick on the floor. Bridget went into a far corner to sort out her suitcase. But as soon as Caroline had her glass in her hand, Patrick crawled up to her, bustling on his bottom, pointing to the drink and smacking his lips in a most peremptory fashion.

"Never a minute's peace. All right, all right; just a wee nip now." Patrick gulped a good half-inch of her whiskey and made out that he loved it. "See that? The makings of an Irishman. Sorry to break in on you, Una love, but I'm that heartsore over poor John Vint. What a holiday you're having, Sarah. But, och, I guess it's the same all over. Isn't the whole world catching up with poor old Ireland? Do you not have a phone call to make, young Sarah? Away now, and do it while you have it in mind."

"Yes. Thanks. I'll go then." God, why need it be so terrifying to phone a friend, an old friend, who would surely be
hurt to hear you'd been in Ireland without getting in touch?
Hurt, but at the same time relieved? She put her hand out to
the receiver. Withdrew it. Lit a cigarette. Look, this is why
you came to Ireland; this minute, this dialling is what it's all
about. You can't ask Caroline to do it for you again; she'd
have to tell Una, explain things. Anyway, he may still be out
of his office, out on that story; you may not have to talk to
him at all. You've got to do it now, love; don't be such a
bloody cow, get on with it.

The ringing tone. "Mr. McNeil, please."

"One moment, please. You're through, caller."

She could still ring off. But the remembered voice came.
"Hello. McNeil here."

"Oh, hello, James; this is me, Sarah. I'm in Ireland. Do
you have half an hour for a drink, I wonder?"

"Sarah. What on earth are you doing here?"

"Just visiting. I'm at the Moores'. I've been hearing wonderful things about you. I'm so glad. But I'm sure you must
be terribly busy just now, since this is the Twelfth Week and
everything." Hand him an excuse, don't force anything, play
it easy.

"Are you mad? D'you think I wouldn't make time for
you? Och, Sarah, don't think so badly of me. God, it's great
to hear you. I was about to phone Caroline; I only just got in.
Listen, just let me look in my book; yes; would Friday be any
good to you? Day after tomorrow? It'll give me a rest before
the Twelfth breaks on us. Could you manage that?"

"If you're sure you want to."

"Why wouldn't I?"

"Don't be coy, please. But you don't have to worry. Not
after five long years."

"'Five summers with the length of five long winters.'
Where shall we meet?"

"Come here, to the Moores', would you? Caroline would prefer that, I think. No overtones."

"But I'll see you alone, won't I, please?"

"Yes. I'll arrange something."

"Good girl. I'll be there at about two-thirty, then. Lovely."

"Fine. Good-bye, then."

"'Bye."

And the ping of silence.

She ran out into the garden to hide the trembling of her joy and stood staring at some stalky lupins. Her hands went up and held her small breasts, enjoyed the weight and fullness of them, her femininity, her promise. Forgetful of the reason for her journey, her mind was flooded, gulfed by unspecified, uninhibited, erotic hopes. Then she pulled her sweater firmly down and went back to join the sisters.

After dinner they walked to Una's house for coffee. It was like a doll's house, a miniature castle, with thin lancet windows, pseudo-Gothic ornamentation, an ecclesiastical front door, heavily panelled and much wrought. There were even tiny flying buttresses rising from the minute porch to the eaves. It wasn't really a house at all, a folly, a piece of nonsense, a whim, but it was utterly charming, standing on a little hill and seeming to grow out of the trees and shrubs that covered the hillside. They climbed through the trees in the last of the evening light, up mossy stone steps, with periwinkle trailing on either side and lords-and-ladies revealing their symbolic arrogant promise, darkly, under the trees. Sarah was enchanted. She thought of her promise to James. "Yes. I'll arrange something." What, more than this, could she ask?

But as they crossed the threshold, through the pretty, silly door, she felt the creep and seep of gooseflesh curdle up her arms. A lonely, half-caressive chill ran fingers down her spine. A lonely chill, partly from dank stone floors, from the faint, haunting smells of ancient drains, of mould, dry rot and secrets, and from the sudden menace of the closely guarding trees that crowded in upon them with the gathering dusk. She knew with all her folk, Celtic early conditioning what Caroline had meant by other lives "boxed in with you."

As though to ward off atavistic intuitions, Una had hung about herself some holy symbols. In the hall, blessing the telephone, there was a picture of the Virgin Mary. The background was composed of rucked sateen of a cheap and glossy blue and the Holy Mother's "pale blue gown, a little faded" clashed wickedly with its harshness. There were "pickings out" in silver paint, as garish as a fairground.

But in the little parlour, Sarah was again charmed, especially by the furniture. There were neat little Victorian waisted chairs; pretty pieces of English porcelain in a diminutive display cabinet; a fretted French love seat at the window with a Victorian sewing box beside it. A coffee table of gentle, golden walnut in the centre of the room. But on the small, cast-iron mantelpiece Una had a row of saints; the Child of Prague, the black Saint Martin, Saint Gerard, saint of mothers – all wearing an imbecile and constipated look of excessive forbearance and yearning, and behind them hung a sampler. In the first half light, this seemed to bear the simple injunction "No, No." But when Caroline had switched on a reading lamp, Sarah saw that while the commandment "No" was worked in purple stitches, and was therefore dominant, the sampler's true message was "No Cross, No Crown." Unfortunately, the "Cross" and "Crown" were done in fawn on a white background and their impact, not unnaturally, went somewhat unrecorded. The Sacred Heart of Jesus lay crowned and exposed in a "holy picture" on another wall, the heart the colour and shape of a tinned tomato. And there was, nastily, in all these holy objects a harsh insistence upon the vulgarity of Roman Catholic bric-a-brac, modern, horrid, mass-produced. A crude and cruel statement.

"What drives her to spoil this room with all this holy junk, Caroline? She knows better than this. My God, you'd think chaps like Giotto or Simone Martini had never been. What the hell's it all about?"

"Och, I know. But don't talk so loud, girl; this place is so small and she's only in the kitchen at the coffee, she'll hear youse. It may be against the things that go bump in the night here. Who the hell can tell? I know fine that I'd never live here on me own, I'm telling you."

"Lord, perhaps she feels that this is peasant art, part of her Marxism. Christ, what a paradox, the emancipated Roman Catholic's notion of Social Realism. How crazy can you get?"

"At least they're holy ones, thank God. Be quiet now; you'll not mention them whenever she comes back with the coffee, sure you won't?"

"Do you think we might take our coffee out of doors? It's a lovely evening."

"We can not. The midges would have us ate alive out there. You may put up with the saints, you heathen. At least Father O'Rourke approves of these."

Una pushed open the door with her bottom, a laden tray in her hands. "So what does he approve of, the poor old bastard, with his snuff and his bottle and the old, sour smell off him?"

"Una, I'll not have you say the like of that of the clergy. You're downright wicked, so you are." Caroline was on her feet, the blue eyes hard, her face suffused.

"Sorry, Cara, sorry. Sit down, please, you've a bad colour. You know me, I didn't think. The Church is more than the clergy, God be praised."

"You relax now, Caroline. Think of that baby."

Yes, all right, but she shouldn't, all the same."

"I've said I'm sorry, haven't I? Want me on me knees?" Bad temper on both sides now, and Una was still holding the coffee tray. Far too good a weapon in those quivering hands.

"Put the tray down, dear." Sarah spoke in a sugary, placatory voice. "That coffee smells wonderful. I'll have mine

black, please, and no sugar." Sulkily as a twelve-year-old-
girl, Una put down the tray on her walnut table and knelt to
serve them. The only light in the room came from the reading
lamp on her display cabinet, and, as she knelt there on the
floor, this light, striking the side of her face, had a startling
effect on her eyeballs. The eyes seemed to bulge and become
darkly transparent, and as she turned her head, they seemed
all staring iris and slack in their sockets. Haunted eyes. A
trick of the light, Sarah's reason said to her mind. Una's
hands were so unreliable that she filled the saucers as well as
the coffee cups. Then she thumped the pot on the floor,
covered her face with her hands; the long, dark hair swept
down to her knees and sobs tore her, racking the bony back.

Caroline recovered her temper when her sister broke; she
knelt beside her. "There now, lovie, there. It's not so bad,
sure it's not."

Una took a great shuddering breath, pushed back her hair
behind her ears and rubbed away the tears and collapsed with
one powerful, emphatic gesture, like Caroline had wiped
away the vomit in the morning. Her face was grey and
hollow, cadaverous.

"Here, drink this coffee before it's cold, after I went to the
trouble of making it for youse. Would you have a cigarette
left, Sarah, please?"

"Is there anything we can do?"

"Just leave me in peace."

"So it's peace you call it?"

"Leave it, leave it. This is my house, I have my rights.
Must have my own place."

"Tell me, Una, what do you teach at school and what sort
of children?" – and so they turned the tide and made meaningless gestures of conversation until they could politely take
their leave. One half of Sarah was dying to go, to go away
from the saints and contradictions, from the haunted atmosphere of the little house, from the embarrassments of family

quarrels; but the other half of her was afraid to leave Una; afraid of what she might do, of what the solitude might do to her.

Caroline and Sarah went down the mossy steps together, while Una held up a torch to light their way. Una had looked utterly forlorn as they'd said their lying good nights. Defenceless she'd seemed, and thin, in a short, washed-out cotton frock, and yet impregnable in her rejection of anything they might have had the effrontery to offer. The torch-light remained there at the top of the steps long after they had moved out of its small comfort. They stopped to look back and they could see it still, through the trees, when they were gone. As though Una was afraid to leave the night, to leave the friendly dark for the menace of the lighted house.

The starlit night around the two of them was full of noises; rustlings and the human-whistling call of terns; and furtiveness and scutterings in the undergrowth. And there were footsteps too, behind them, a regular heavy rustling that Sarah knew in her blood was up to no good.

"She's still standing there on her lonesome, standing in the dark. She's afraid to go in, you know that? I hate to leave her. But, Sarah, what am I to do? I've my own ones to think of." Caroline's voice was full of tears. She didn't seem to have heard the footsteps. Sarah looked back as Caroline blew her nose loudly, definitively, and thought she saw a figure that halted, merged with the trees and went. Maybe she hadn't seen it, starlight is deceptive and her eyes were not what they'd been, but Caroline's loud trumpeting startled the rooks in the trees around them. The rooks rose and swooped and thundered about their heads; they hurried, hand in hand, away to the safety, the embrace, of Caroline's warm, child-ridden house.

CHAPTER 5

When Sarah got down to the kitchen the next morning, there was no sign of Caroline. It was too early for the Noble Savage. Patrick was in his high chair, purple and screaming, Bridget was pushing toys at him, only to have them flung back at her, and Brendan was standing at the window, tall and gangling, ignoring the world.

"Good morning, everybody. Why are you just standing there, Brendan? Can't you help?"

"I'm watching thon bird out there. My mammy'll be down in a minute. She's after having one of her bouts."

"Is she sick?"

"Aye. Sure, isn't she always sick in the mornings?"

"Look, here's some porridge on the Aga. Could you feed Patrick? He doesn't exactly take to me."

"Sure, Mammy'll not be long. It's better once it's over."

"But we must shut Patrick up somehow. He's about to burst. And I'm convinced that banging his head like that can't do him any good."

"Give him a sweetie then."

"Before breakfast? Won't your mother be cross?"

"She's not here, is she? It's your only hope, so it is."

Defeated, Sarah gave Bridget a sweet to give to him. Furiously raging, he mistook the first sweet for another toy and flung it away from him. William Butler, lurking under the table, promptly ate it. The second sweet Patrick considered more soberly, slowly put it in his mouth and, perforce, stopped screaming, although his little body went on shuddering and heaving as though it were stuttering.

"What shall I do for the best now, then, Brendan?" He shrugged and turned to watch the bird. Bridget encouraged Sarah. "First my mammy sets the table and makes the toast.

And she warms the porridge; things like that. It's quite easy, I think." Sarah began to look for things to put on the table. William Butler was now pacing the kitchen, having licked the dribblings of chocolate off Patrick's face and off the tray of his high chair. She had found a tablecloth and cutlery when Caroline appeared, her hair hanging in elflock wisps, the eyes unfocused and her skin the colour of a new tombstone. She looked like a kick in the teeth.

Bridget started one of her chants:

"Patrick's had a sweetie
Before eating his porridge up.
Patrick's had a sweetie—"

"I know, I know, I heard you the first time. Who gave it? I've told you often enough, God knows."

"She gave it to Bridget to give him." Brendan said to the window.

"Sorry, Caroline, but he was yelling his head off and doing himself grievous bodily harm. I don't like this head-bumping lark; it's a sign of some fearful frustration, I'm sure."

"And wouldn't you be fearfully frustrated, if you were starving and could see your porridge there on the stove? I'll feed him first and let you get on with the table. Nobody's getting any fries this day. The very smell of the pan would set me retching again."

Brendan let out a great, exaggerated groan. "Och, I'm starving, so I am, and me a growing boy. Is there any lobster left? I could eat that."

"Yes, look in the fridge. Eat it and be damned. I hope it chokes you."

"Mammy's in a temper,
I wonder why she is.

Mammy's in a temper,
I wonder—"

"Shut up, Bridget. Brendan, take out this great brute of a dog. No, Sarah, not the best silver, that stuff in the other drawer for the kitchen. Oh, God, Patrick, will you not open your mouth like a Christian?" But Patrick was no Christian. He slammed both fat hands into his dish, splashing himself, his mother and much of the kitchen with warm, sticky cereal.

"Jesus, Sarah, d'you see what I have to put up with?" she said, wiping her face with a dish towel. "Eat, you little devil; you're getting no more sweets, so you may rest content. Make us a cup of coffee for God's sake, girl, and just flop some of the porridge in their dishes and let them get on with it. Brendan, keep an eye on that toast. I've more work with these three than all that crowd I had yesterday, I'm telling you."

"This porridge is lumpy again and the milk's off," Brendan announced, like judge and jury, and Bridget bounced on her chair to the rhythm of her chanting.

"Mammy's in a temper,
I wonder why she is.
Mammy's in a temper,
I wonder—
Och, Brendan, that's my baby you're after eating."
"It is not your baby, it's a tomato."
"Mammy, he's after eating me baby."
"Never mind, Bridget." Sarah offered another tomato. "Here's another one."
"No. It hasn't got a pretty face. I want my other one, Mammy, I want my other one."
"If he has it eaten, it's done for, isn't it? Get yourself a pretty one out of the bowl."
"No." The Moore temper was up and the porridge plate flew past Sarah's nose, as Bridget aimed at Brendan and hit

the milk jug. Brendan roared out a great male laugh, Bridget stamped and screamed, Patrick spat, Caroline administered slaps all around and Sarah lit a cigarette before mopping up what she could of the mess. William Butler had slunk in again and he licked the rest off the floor.

The Relief of Mafeking came in the form of Mrs. Savidge; and Caroline retreated with Sarah to drink breakfast off a tray in the dining room, out of sight and sound.

"Could you amuse yourself this morning? I've got to go to the village. It's my turn to decorate the altar, and it'll have to be special, with poor John Vint lying there. I'll call on Mrs. Vint to see how everything's going. And I wouldn't say no to the loan of your car, either."

"Yes, of course, take it. I think I'll look in on Una, in that case. Would I be welcome, d'you think?"

"Aye, if you've a mind to. She'd like it fine."

"She's very lonely, isn't she? I think she needs some sort of help."

"Sure, don't I know it? But what would you have me do, with seven weans of me own?"

"Are you well enough to drive yourself?"

"Aye, I've me bout over me now. I'll be all right. You remember the way to Una's?"

"Yes, I think I do; but tell me, Caroline, does she know about me and James?"

"No. You may tell her yourself, if you want. But I'll not have her thinking I'm condoning anything, remember."

"But you wouldn't object to my telling her? Perhaps even asking her to help?"

"Providing she doesn't know that I know."

"But she's bound to guess."

"Never mind; guessing's guessing, knowing's something else. But I'll have to move if I'm to get finished. Bring her back for lunch, if she wants."

*

The peaceful frenzy of life at Caroline's and the prospect of
James were soothing over Sarah's panics about her own condition; as she walked in the sunshine towards Una's house,
she was more concerned about Caroline's vomiting and the
problems of another baby than about the passing of her own
eight days. As for the threats to the children, yesterday she'd
been ridiculously frightened in the village, but it had only
been in response to the mad theatricality, and the almost
incredible coincidence. It hadn't been a rational reaction: the
Ulster countryside is sparsely populated; it was hardly surprising that she should see her young men again. But ought
she, perhaps, to be worrying about the threats against James?
No, honestly, she must try to remember to keep things in
context, the context of Ireland, where threats and quarrelling
seemed as necessary as religion and alcohol. They didn't
mean the threats and the quarrelling was only scratch deep.
Caroline had threatened, only yesterday, to take the hide off
Brendan's back for persecuting Bridget, but all she'd in fact
done was to deny him five minutes of television. She must
remember that in Ireland, words were set at a different key.

She walked under the rook-filled trees and up the Smithy
Brae, where elder trees held out their flowers, like saucers of
white lace; and all unprepared, she found herself in a corri-
dor of gorse, possessed, enchanted, overwhelmed by the
harsh yellow of the flowers, the nutty-sweet smell of them
and the sage-green spike of their leaves. "Like one that hath
been long in city pent..." The gorse, in the sun, was like a
kiss, a gasp of loveliness, like apple blossom to an adolescent
girl. Sarah saw the gorse mature, golden, the thorns sharp,
honest, a weathered green.

"James," she said aloud, into the morning, "James, be
good to me. Save me. Keep me for a little while." She tried
to cut herself a sprig of gorse, but it wasn't for the cutting.
She found its resistance reassuring, strengthening, and, com-

forted, she went on, out of the grove. She went out of the grove remembering "Fern Hill" in the pristine simplicity of the morning; remembering "Adam and Maiden," and the "farm with the cock on its shoulder," and she knew that the sun for her would grow round very soon now. The gorse had made her a promise. The climbing path to Una's house now led her up a little hill, left open and unwooded, with a clear view of the lough and the stone jetty where the antique cannon stood. The lough was still and as sheer as a piece of silk, fringed with tall trees, and a boat was coming in, heavy, deep in the water; two men at the oars and a third at the tiller. The picture was so idyllic, it so perfectly matched her mood of confidence, that Sarah simply took to her heels and ran to meet the boat, an easier way to spend her holiday morning. She bounced down the little hill toward the jetty, a tourist, if you like, agog to see, to talk, to know the working people of this strange community. These must be fishermen, she felt; perhaps she could bargain with them for some of their catch, perhaps even cadge a ride along that placid lough; at least they'd talk to her.

A holiday compulsion drove her on, a freedom, and she ran through bracken and brambles, over tussocks and tufts, to reach the shore.

The boatmen had arrived at the slip before her and the one who had been at the tiller was climbing up the steps of the jetty when, breathless, her feet almost carrying her on into the water, she burst upon them.

"Hello," she gasped, her breath in her fist. "So sorry to barge in upon you—" and the man on the steps looked up at her and he was the bearded youth of the red car again. As he ascended the steps she watched his feet, saw the beauty of the ancient stones, drying in the receding tide; she saw the everlasting colours in them, grey and purple and stone blue; she saw the seventeenth-century cannon sitting there, as meaningless, now, as a bridal cake. They gave her a sense of proportion, gave her the strength to buck this lark of somehow being half scared of a boy. "Why, hello there, we meet again," she said. "You see I've arrived safely. I never had an opportunity before to thank you for looking after me."

The young man looked up, on hearing her voice, and in his pale blue eyes there gleamed a flash of fear or hate, before that safety curtain, that shield of indifferent superiority, filmed them again. He mounted the steps and she held out her hand, instinctively, to help him to the top. His grasp was dry and powerful, a man's hand, the skin crisp and rough, vital, male. The two oarsmen waited below in the lightly bobbing boat. Sarah looked down at them, still hoping for her trip along the tranquil lough. The boat rocked and swung; they held it with their oars against the jetty.

The youth stood beside her on the silent, remote, hardly used jetty. He was dressed now in a navy blue fisherman's jersey, his grey trousers tucked into Wellington boots, his bearded chin thrust aggressively out; he looked like a Viking. The beauty of the morning still had Sarah in its thrall and she refused to be troubled by a mere boy. She looked down into the boat and spoke to the oarsmen. "D'you know, I'd love a trip along the lough in your boat. D'you think you could make room for a little one? How much would it be worth to be troubled by me?"

But before the boatmen could answer her, the boy said, "We'll not be coming back this way, missus. Sure, you might get lost again. We'll soon be pushing off; we only put in for a minute because one of our rowlocks is not too grand, and we thought we knew where we could borrow one round here. If you'll excuse us, we'll bid you good day."

"You are a friendly brute, aren't you? All right, if that's how you feel, I shall bid you a very good day too. Can't think why you have to be so beastly, I must say, nor why you have to keep dogging my holiday in Ulster."

"This is the North of Ireland, missus; Ulster was something else; and the question is who's dogging who, isn't it?"

"Well, God knows, I'd rather not dog you, if you'll
forgive my saying so. D'you know, you're not quite my idea
of fun either. Good day." Sarah turned her back on them,
feeling a little injured by such obvious rejection in a place
renowned for the elegance of its manners, but not deeply disturbed; the boy was rude, badly brought up, and probably
saw her as a symbol of British imperialist aggression. God,
he ought to meet some of her Welsh Nationalist relatives;
they'd certainly have a ball together.

Ah well, no sail on the lough then; she'd simply have to
go to Una's. Better not to mention the rebuff to Caroline,
though; it would grieve the hostess in her.

She climbed back up the hill, pulled herself up on the tus-
socky grass, stopped to take middle-aged breaths and
thought, as she paused, of another poem, a Welsh one, that
she roughly paraphrased into English, to tell James.

> Climbing, descending the withered-grass mountain,
> Hearing your voice; pausing to look into your two great
> eyes;
> If it was idle to dream of this moment,
> Was it not idle to live?

To hell with the boy and the boatmen; she could recall
James' two great brown eyes. The little hurt was passing;
nothing mattered, only think of James. She mounted the
steps to Una's house and gave a shy but Rabelaisian wink to
the lords-and-ladies, shameless under the trees. James
wanted to be alone with her. He'd asked. She would be ruthless; that resilience of the gorse had somehow matched and
bolstered her resolve. Who cared for ghosts? Or boatmen?
And as for boys…

*

Una was weeding, her back turned toward Sarah and her hair tied back in a neat ribbon. Sarah hadn't known quite what to expect; it certainly hadn't been this gentle attention to a few rock plants, this tidy sorting out of weeds.

"Hello, Una, good morning. Your sister has ditched me for good works and Mrs. Savidge isn't quite my cup of tea. I'm imposing myself on you. Can you bear it?"

"Och, it's you, Sarah. That's great. How's Caroline this morning, and the kids?"

"Sick again and the young were quite unspeakable. We've both walked out on them. Old Mrs. Savidge seems able to take them in her stride; it's that evil eye of hers."

Una ripped off a yellow gardening glove and offered Sarah her hand, but they were, somehow, clumsy over it and Sarah's first finger got excluded from Una's grasp, and it was silly and embarrassing and off-putting. Sarah thought it might be symptomatic and felt a moment's panic.

"Don't let me interrupt you. But I shan't offer to help. I'm taking my holiday seriously."

"Why don't you sit? The view's good from that stone." Sarah tried to wriggle some comfort from her haunches, but she had hardly recovered from yesterday's brush with the seaweed. The stone was hard.

"Are you weeding because you're in a good mood and want to tend flowers, or because you're in a bad mood and want to destroy your enemies? Has every wicked weed got a name on it?"

"Don't just be irritating, Sarah; I'm weeding, that's all. No need to go whimsy over it."

"No need to be so bloody bad-tempered either, is there?"

"What do you know about anything?"

"I've been a widow for a number of years. There's nothing you can tell me about sexual frustration, love; I know all the symptoms. You need a lover."

"Don't be so damned superior, so glibly right. Sex isn't everything."

"No, but it helps everything, God knows."

"I'm a Roman Catholic, Sarah, please; you're being impertinent."

"Yes. I'm sorry. But I'd still recommend a lover."

"Sarah, this is Ireland. We don't grow lovers here like blackberries. Anyway, I'm still married."

"So why don't you get a divorce?"

"Because, for the hundredth time, I'm a Roman Catholic. We hope for an annulment."

"And are you allowed lovers after the annulment? Can you marry again?"

"No to both. I wouldn't want to marry again, in any case; you haven't."

"No. There was only one man I wanted enough after David died, and he was married, firmly married. But nevertheless, I organise my sexual life. Actually, I'm seeing that other man tomorrow, for the afternoon. Might I see him here?"

Una slowly got up, slowly peeled off the other glove and stood in front of Sarah. "You mean to be alone with him? Here?"

"Yes."

"You're asking a hell of a lot."

"Yes. There are your principles, your religious scruples, your natural feminine envy, your present mood of rejection, your compulsive generosity, like Caroline's, your sympathy—"

"Shut up. How much does Caroline know?"

"Everything, except what I've just asked you. But you have to pretend to her that you don't know. There's an Irishism building up; you're allowed to know, but you mustn't allow you know. The man is a worthy bloke, actually. James McNeil. It was Caroline who first introduced us, years ago. She disapproves, of course, but she understands. It began when you were still up at the University."

"I have to think. You see that, Sarah, don't you?"

"Of course. Of course you have to think." Una turned away and walked to a rickety garden chair on her porch. There she slumped and gnawed her cuticles while Sarah remained perched on her cruel stone. A piece of stone that looked like ancient Rome, like part of the shaft of some old and elegant pillar, worked, grooved and lichened; an extension of the "folly." It was the same neo-classicism that had inspired the stone figure of a negligently draped female who leered at Sarah out of the shrubbery, wall-eyed and, apparently, "having lately suffered of the pox." There was a cherub's bust too, stuck askew and gathering green mould in the rock garden. He had a nasty, knowing smirk on his face that Sarah found not a little disconcerting. But she ignored him, armoured as she was, all girded up to fight for some small sanctuary with James.

She wouldn't speak; she wouldn't weaken, nor offer to back out. She'd asked, and she would let her asking stand. She didn't think to use her lump; too weak a weapon, anyway, in young Una's context. She sat there like a bride, selfish, ruthless, fixed, winning.

"Do you have a cigarette?" Una asked.

"Of course. No, don't get up, I'll bring it over. My God, this stone is hardly comforting."

"Thanks. Look, tomorrow I'm for Belfast. I always leave my key under that cherub; I'll be back about six. If you do come here, leave before then, and I'll know nothing about any of it."

Relief, release, joy, desire swept through Sarah like a blush, like a blow.

"Thank you Una. I know how much – oh, never mind, I'm not going to hold forth. But thanks. A lot."

"Why don't we go indoors and find you a half-decent chair? I might even manage a drink, though I warn you, in the depleted state of my overdraft, all I can offer you is Spanish burgundy."

"Anything at all would be heavenly. But why don't we have a drink here, on your terrace?" She was reluctant to leave the simple splendour of the shining morning and she hesitated, like a heavy bee, at the door of the little house.

"Och, come in, come in; it's not so bad in the clear daylight. It's only after dark that they sometimes— Go into my parlour and I'll see what I can find."

The scent of roses in the room was almost vulgarly overpowering; a great bowl of the pink ones they call The Doctor lay throwing open their strident yellow hearts, naked and unashamed, on the walnut coffee table. Sarah knelt to stare at them, into them; she stroked the golden patina of the table, like the smooth skin in the hollow of a man's back.

Una's third of a bottle of Spanish burgundy, surely two days opened, possibly three months casked, was as nasty as Sarah had feared. She drank it nobly, accommodating after her victory.

"Would you like to see the rest of the house? It might be just as well for you to know your way around." They looked into the little kitchen, the minute dining room, and mounted the steep, enclosed staircase. Sarah felt like a dinosaur. Una opened her bedroom door. There were no saints; only a crucifix above the bed and a handful of books. A white room, cold. Nothing but the crucifix relieved the white-painted walls; a narrow bed, covered with a prim white spread; a white-painted wardrobe and a thin grey carpet. A cell. She and James would be a blasphemy in there. Impossible. Hell!

But Sarah liked the bathroom. Nothing holy there. A large, rococo, gilt-framed looking glass set alongside the bath. The bath was old, stone-coloured, with cast-iron, fretted feet; the taps were brass and circular, without spouts. "Hot" and

"Cold" were done in Gothic script on circles of white china, as big as half crowns. The handle of the toilet chain was splendidly ornate, again of white china and brass, and, in the same Gothic script, it said "Pull." The walls and ceiling were papered all over with huge yellow cabbage roses and there was a warm brown carpet on the floor. The toilet was discreet; mounted on two steps of highly polished mahogany and so boxed in, so seemly, as to resemble merely a window seat. The window above it was, of course, a little casement window with leaded panes, a folly window.

From there, at the top of Una's hill, Sarah got a better notion of the geography, saw that they were on a narrow peninsula with Kilhornan at its tip, with all those little boats and sails. Caroline's house and the old fortress where Bridget had her shop stood on a subsidiary little promontory, like a thumb, away to her right. Down the slope to the left a large grey house, presumably the Big House, was just visible among trees. There was a farm or two and some scattered white cottages and the land was all cut about with hedges and lanes. Across the sea, on the mainland, farther to the left again, Sarah could see more fields and another hill, crowned with white statuary that might be anything from a war memorial to a Calvary.

She was glad of the distraction of the view. In that small bathroom Una's proximity, intensity, embarrassed her. She cringed from the confidences that seemed to be hovering between them; she simply then wanted to hold herself together, intact, as you might gently hold a blue egg, warm from the nest. James was coming, was coming here. She wanted it simple. No frayed wisps of sympathy to break the pattern of her little dream.

"What a magnificent prospect," she cliché-ed. "Your bathroom's such fun; by the way, Caroline invites you to lunch. D'you think perhaps we ought to go to Illnacullin now? She may need help, judging by this morning's form." Sarah shrugged off her guilt over Una's unspoken words. The girl defeated her, the contradictions were too much. Her devastating social aggressiveness contending with her infinite gentleness with the children; that nun's-cell bedroom coupled with the rococo looking glass over the bath; the delicate good taste of the parlour furniture given the lie by those noncarnate, sub-Pre-Raphaelite saints; her attempts to reconcile her faith with Marxist doctrine. No, it was all too much for Sarah; another time, perhaps.

A rare and blessed peace embraced Illnacullin. Patrick was asleep in his pram, Bridget deep in the arithmetics of her shop and Caroline had not yet returned. William Butler was out fishing with Brendan and Lily Savidge was on the top of the house, restoring order after the ravages of visiting children. There was no sign of lunch.

"I'll just sit and shell these peas; it's a comfortable job. Would you not get us a Tio Pepe apiece, Sarah, to take away the taste of Spanish burgundy? I still have the dregs, like iron filings, round me teeth."

Cleansed by the sherry, Sarah sat on the kitchen table, swinging her legs and painting her nails. Ashamed of her earlier rejection of Una's confidences she tried to compensate by giving her a chance to talk her politics again.

"Una, tell me something; and don't get infuriated by my ignorance, now. I was talking to someone, Caroline it must have been, about the new Divorce Act and she said you didn't have it here, and never would. She thanked God, of course. But something interrupted us and I missed my opportunity to ask why, since this province insists so vociferously that it is a part of the United Kingdom, you don't have the same laws."

"Because we have Home Rule. Nothing is automatic; this government passes the laws itself if it chooses to. You know we still have capital punishment here? That's never been abolished, and anyway, there's the Special Powers Act. They can order a flogging under it, arrest on suspicion, deny access to prisoners, search without warrants – there's hardly anything they can't do, woman." She threw a pea pod at the ginger Agacat, who was quietly doing no harm to anybody. "That cat's a Unionist spy; I can tell by his old arrogance."

"Oh, poor old pussy; did she hit him then? No, cat, no, don't come and talk to me now, my nails are wet. Remove this Unionist, Una, please. Damn him, he's knocked the bottle over, and this nice coral colour is so hard to come by – it's five years out of date. Put this bloody cat out! He's walking through it." Una shoved the cat through the back door.

"You're not going to be popular with Mrs. Savidge when she sees the mess on the table, Protestant or not."

"I'll take some remover to it in a minute. But please go on, while I dry."

"Och, to hell, what's the use? Who cares? Sometimes I just want to give up. I've taken part in almost every protest march; I've been clobbered, I've been drenched with sewage. I've sung "We Shall Overcome" till my throat gave out and my voice was a crow's croak. Were you ever on a demonstration and surrounded by enemies? The ugliness, the hate in the faces, and the fear in your guts." Her voice grew harsh and her face pinched, bleak.

"I usually contrive to carry something, a banner or a placard, to give me something to hang on to when I'm scared silly. I'm terrified of hate, and so full of it." Then she declaimed again at Sarah the brutal facts of the persecution of Catholics; the gerrymandered seats, the discrimination in jobs, in housing, the exclusion of Catholics from state appointments and state agencies, and the vitriolic savagery engendered against Catholics by the extreme right-wing Protestant fanatics, who, like the IRA, could not face the threat of progress. "Poor Colum, he's the exception to prove the rule. He has had to work at it. And a foot in neither camp."

"And now you seriously think there could be civil war?"

"Well" — she shrugged — "even you must have seen the Derry fighting on television; that wasn't so far off, was it? Our only hope is the British Army. God forgive me for saying it, but it's the unfortunate truth. I wonder what's keeping Caroline."

Their rare peace was brutally assaulted when Bridget came screaming to the house and hammered at the back door that she was too small to open. Una leaped to it, scattering peas and pods, while Sarah, with the second coat of nail polish still wet on her fingers, could do nothing but wave her hands in the air, incompetent as a man with his pants down. Bridget, hatless for once, flung herself at Una; she was still screaming and unable to get any words past the screams.

"Och, what is it, darling, are ye hurted at all? What happened you? Tell Una, tell me, sweetheart." Una was squatting on her haunches, holding the child tightly to her breast and rocking to the music of her own voice. Slowly the screaming died away and the little voice came gulping out, hiccupping, broken.

"He stole me hat, so he did. He stole me hat." She stamped her feet in furious outrage.

"Och, now, who was it, darling? Was it that wee, bold Brendan?"

"No, no, it was a man did it. Sure, I told youse, he stole me hat. He had whiskers on him."

"You're not hurted, then? It's only your hat?"

"Me hat, me hat; he came and stole me hat. Me ladyship hat."

"Who was it, then? Tell Una, tell me now." Slowly, painfully, they learned what had happened. The stranger had come in, through the gate at the bottom of the garden, had walked up to her shop, had talked to her and given her a

threepence for sugar. Then he had lifted her hat off her head
and walked away with it. She showed them the threepenny
piece that she still clutched in her grubby, sweaty little hand.

"Did you say that he had whiskers, Bridget?" Sarah asked,
and Bridget nodded her head, with the thin, fair hair parted
down the middle and worn in two optimistic plaits.

"Red whiskers they were, all on his face. Why did he want
my hat, Una?"

Una comforted Bridget with apples and the end of Sarah's
sweets, and Sarah loaned Bridget her own best hat as a temporary substitute; a large, black, droopy, Garboesque affair.
In the kitchen the two women tried to discuss the ludicrous
situation as rationally as they could.

"It's no good pretending, Una; a man with red whiskers
who does something as superficially stupid as taking that hat
must be my red-bearded one from the loanie. I saw him again
this morning, in a boat, and I'm being reminded of their
threat, but what the devil for? What can it be in aid of? I'm
frightened, Una, honest. It's so damn stupid. I find the infan-
tilism horrible, psychopathic. It's like a dirty giggle."

"Och, will you not relax, Sarah? It's not your fault. If they
were at the Vints' yesterday, the fight will have been about
them. It'll be some IRA ploy; John was active in his youth
and young Larry's involved in it yet. He's just the type.
Never able to hold a job, given to violence, fancying himself,
undereducated, frustrated."

"How refreshingly old-fashioned. That I can understand,
but all the violent young men that I know quote Marcuse or
Guevara at one, and carry Chairman Mao in their hip
pockets. They are usually over-educated and tend to be very
affluent." Sarah could hear her own voice, off-key and
clipped, would-be clever, but her belly was hysterical; she
felt macabre, like a giggling skull.

"Sure, none of the Vints would let any harm happen to
Caroline, not a one; she's been too good to them. Have

another drink." Sarah's hands shook so much that the glass was half-empty before she started on it.

"Here, stop chattering your teeth on that good glass."

"But, Una, my man isn't a Vint. He's evil, I promise you. He won't give a thought to Caroline's goodness; he'll hate her for it. I know my anarchists."

"I know the type too; they use their patriotism to justify their sadism. Here they bleat about ending Partition, uniting Ireland, as though that, by itself, would provide homes and employment. It's so stupid it has to be fake. They're a menace to the civil rights movements. They give the police an excuse to attack, by joining our demonstrations; processions being neither exclusive nor excluding. Damn it, I *wish* I knew what they are up to."

They heard Caroline at the door; Bridget heard her too and began to scream afresh.

"Mammy! A man stole my hat, Mammy. A man stole my hat, Mammy. A man with whiskers on him stole my hat."

"Well, you've got another one, haven't you? Won't that do youse?"

"This is only Sarah's old hat. It's not her ladyship's, no more it is."

"Will it not do you for now? And I'll ask her ladyship for another one for you. You can make do with Sarah's till we get you a proper one, sure you can?" Irish priorities again – it was Sarah's very best hat.

"Away now, till I get the lunch, and I promise to have a word with her ladyship." She came into the kitchen. "Drinking again? Pour me a big one; I'm dead, so I am. What's all this about Bridget's hat? I fancy yours, Sarah; if you're set on giving it away, what about me? Be a better fit, anyway."

"That, I'd have you know, Caroline, is my best hat; but Bridget was in such a state."

"I think she's lost her hat somewhere," Una came in, smooth as moisturising cream, "and made up a great tale about a man taking it; she believes it herself by now. She's got a really powerful imagination, that one."

"Lady Maxwell will give her another one. We're to go to tea today, Sarah, you remember? She's at home on Thursdays."

"Today? But I can't possibly go to tea without a hat."

"You couldn't have worn that glamour-puss affair to tea in the country, anyway. Never mind, you can go without and I'll keep the side up in my new straw. Tell you what, you can wear the black one tonight at the wake. I told Mrs. Vint you were here, and she's invited you in for a wee while this evening. Were you ever at a wake?"

"God, no. Is it frightening?"

"Don't be daft."

"I don't quite see me at a wake, somehow; hardly my kind of thing. I'd not know how to behave." Sarah buried her apprehensions in yet another glass of Tio Pepe.

"Never heard such damn nonsense; you just follow me. It'll be an experience for you. Isn't that right, Una?"

"Don't bully, Caroline; let her decide."

"She wants to see Ireland, right? So what's more Irish than a wake? Anyway, she's invited. It'll give her a chance to wear that hat of hers. What the hell's these pea pods all over the floor? Whatever were you doing here, at all? And nail varnish all over my good table; you've the place stinking, you know that? You'll need to do your nails again, Sarah; they look horrible."

"Yes, I know; I was doing them when Bridget came tearing in without her hat."

"It's odd that, not like her. She sleeps with it under her pillow, I'd have you know. Can't think what she's done with it. We'll have to hunt the crows for it. No, it's not like her, sure it's not."

"It'll turn up," Una said. "What about lunch? I am invited?"

"For all there is, you can stay. We'll need to open a tin or two. Come on then, get moving; get fell in."

They had chips with their tinned lunch and Bridget ate hers with her fingers. Sarah's hat was a big, droopy one that needed continual readjusting on Bridget's head, and every time the greasy little fingers went up to the hat, a tiny bit of Sarah's heart was chipped off. There was a neat row of greasy crescents all along the floppy front brim. Then Sarah thought about some stranger coming and lifting it off her head and inexplicably taking it away, and what was left of her heart cried for Bridget.

After lunch both children were cross and utterly disagreeable, Bridget going on and on about her hat and Patrick throwing himself about in tremendous rages.

"Let's, for God's sake, get out of this," Caroline said. Lend us your motor, Sarah. They're often good in the car. Thank God the father will be home the night."

"Yes, of course borrow the car. But I, I regret to say, am more than somewhat squiffy. I am persuaded that I ought, perhaps, not to drive. You tend to have ferocious beasts on your highways, and lunatic collies on your byways. I'll opt out, if I may. Perhaps you'll be good enough to drive us, Una? But," Sarah added, reverting to her native diction, "I'm bloody certain that I'm *not* sitting in the back seat with that monster Patrick. I know he plans to arm himself with that Anglo-Saxon fish slice."

"O.K. I'll drive, and you can sit beside me in the front."

"Tell you what we'll do," Caroline suggested. "We'll go to Ardmore. I've that embroidery to take to the nuns, and Sarah can take a wee walk up Sally's Lough; I know fine she'd like that. If you'll mind the baas, Una?"

"Let's go then."

"We're going in Sarah's motorcar,
To get sweeties in a shop.
We're going in Sarah's motorcar,
To get sweeties in a shop…"

Bridget started a new chant. Perhaps she was beginning to forget the hat.

Mrs. Savidge was left to the dishes and to bring order to the chaotic kitchen. Sarah stacked for her, while the sisters cleaned the children. Mrs. Savidge was singing cheerfully into the sink in a strong, surprisingly tuneful voice. Sarah stopped to listen to the words, and refused to believe her ears. While Caroline and Una filled her car with children and extra nappies, Sarah got Mrs. Savidge to repeat the words of her song, but Mrs. Savidge insisted that it was no song, it was a hymn, sure. Sarah put the words down quickly in her diary, writing in an excited, drunken hand.

Our Father knew thee, Rome, of old, and evil is thy fame,
Thy kind embrace — the galling chain, thy kiss — the blazing flame.
No peace with Rome, shall be our cry, while Rome abides the same,
We'll let her know that Ulster's sons will not disgrace their name.

"Och, I shouldn't be after singing thon hymn in this house, but you'll know how it is, madam; sure, you don't always be thinking what it is you're singing. Think nothing to it, madam dear, you know I meant no harm, no more I did; I wouldn't for me life hurt Mrs. Moore and you know it, madam dear, but you and me's the same sort and we know what we know, I'm thinking. Away now, and see Ireland, and safe home."

*

It was a foreign countryside. They followed a narrow coast road off the promontory and onto the mainland; passed thin, stony fields, white thatched cottages, a number of tall, glowering fortresses left by the Normans and now, occasionally, used as barns or stables; passed broken-down windmills on tiny hillocks; a poor, thin, unyielding land all cut about with dry-stone walls of massive granite lumps. They were never far from the sea. There was a beach with grey sand and rocks and not a soul on it, only sea birds with long red legs and ducks that Sarah swore were mergansers, but Caroline laughed and said, sure, they were only ducks. They passed a dolmen all tidy and National Trusted. Then, a sea town of Georgian elegance gone, Irished, to grass, gone homely; only the shop fronts and pubs robust with new paint. New paint on old facades that had a lurching, tired look, holding each other up, like exhausted soldiers after some defeat. Here there was bunting again and flags and slogans: "Rebels Beware," "Welcome, Dr, Paisley," "The Pope the Man of Sin," "No Peace with Rome." She caught the street names, English Street and Scotch Street all bedecked but Irish Street and The Shambles sullen and mute. Some brave cynic had painted "Paisley for Pope" on the paving stones. This gave Sarah a little gush of hope for the Ulster that could still laugh at its wrongs, but the sisters were silent in the town, chastened, withdrawn, under that lash of bigotry.

Beyond the town a signpost pointed to "Ballynacarrick Sutterain, Ancient Monument," and on the hill behind it was the Calvary that Sarah had seen from Una's bathroom window; stark, white, new marble.

"I wonder if it would be possible for me to see the sutterain?" Sarah asked, and Una began to slow down after the frenzy in which she'd driven to leave the town.

"No, Sarah, we can't today, not with the childer. Go you on, Una. It's not much of a place, anyway."

"It would probably interest Sarah; she hasn't grown up with it the way we have. There are three subterranean chambers, Sarah, with narrow connecting passages."

"Creeps we call them, for you've to creep on your belly to get through. Only God knows what they were for. No good that I can see, to man or beast."

"The theory is that they were built about 600 A.D., perhaps for defence or secreting treasure or even, maybe, as larders when salt was expensive and your neighbours bloody minded. This one's a spooky old place; I never cared for it, though we sometimes played there when we were young and brave. I used to hate the first bit, didn't you, Caroline, when you literally jumped out of the light and got down on your hunkers and slid into the dark?"

"You'd hate it, Sarah; probably full of spiders."

"No, nothing lives there. No toads nor frogs nor flies nor spiders. And nothing grows. Nothing but cold, dank stones; empty chambers, standing there, hidden and meaningless, for centuries. No, it's not for me. Too cold even for hauntings."

Ardmore was a fishing village with a sturdy stone jetty and boats waiting for the evening tide. They left Caroline at the wrought-iron gates of the convent, with "The Sacred Heart of Jesus" picked out in a semicircle of white paint. "Give me half an hour; we've to be in the Big House for tea."

Una drove Sarah to a field gate. "Look, if you walk through this first field, you'll come to a path that runs along Sally's Lough. It may seem a bit of a chore, but the air will clear your head for tea and the view is very lovely; utterly, utterly postcard Irish. You really ought to see it; but don't forget the time in the Celtic twilight up there, will you?"

"I'm far too scared of Caroline."

"Oh, and look out for the holy well; you'll recognise it by the bits of rag tied to the thorn tree."

Sarah crossed the field of spiky marsh grass. She came to
a stile in the stone wall that edged the field, a vast stone wall
that might have served for a revolutionary barricade but
seemed to have no function whatsoever. Once over the stile
she was on the rocky edge of a long, narrow lough, an arthrit-
ic finger of sea, probing into the low mountains, if one could
call them mountains. Rather, perhaps, the lough probed into
rocks that had acquired patchy garments of dry grass, of
moss and of heather, and ornaments of lightly rooted trees. A
little spring broke out at her feet and sogged away, down to
the lough; there was a tall, gauche-looking thorn tree beside
it, tied up with bits of rag and with bandages in bows, blood
on some of the rags and stains that might once have been pus.
Sympathetic magic; holy Ireland only a thin overlay. Sarah
crossed her fingers and followed the path above the water.
The water itself was glacier green, too deep in the cleft of the
rock to catch the sun, cold as pity, as death. On the rock face
beside her a small potato patch flourished on a bit of ground
stolen from the rocks. She saw a solitary cow on the crest.
"Two acres and a cow"; no wonder they left this beauty and
came to Birmingham.

She followed along to the summer-dry end of the lough
and saw flag irises, brilliant in a sudden burst of sun. The sea
was abandoning its claim on this last tip of its finger, and tall
water weeds grew there with purple feathery heads; she
watched the small breeze move through them and it was like
a secret animal weaving a way. The moving was no "spright-
ly dance," more like the contortions of a wounded snake.
Sarah sat on a rock. The rock mountain before her seemed
only marbled with grass and mosses, a harsh place, a poor
place, silent and empty.

She looked at the rock she sat on, looked close at it, a
tight, concentrated look, as a drunken man on a bus will
look at his small change and pick it over, with heavy,
careful deliberation. It was a pink rock. Pink, mottled with

pale grey and frilled with green lichen, if indeed this colour
was green, this colour, a pale, watery green that might be
gold, might be grey. Moss on the rock too, dark brown
moss, thick and heavy as a bear's coat. The breeze came
and blew her hair about, a small wind. She turned sentimental on her rock, the scene was so like tea cosies, like drying-
up cloths, souvenirs. She almost sang "The Mountains of
Mourne." The wind was in her hair; how nice, she thought,
it would be to abandon her hair to this little wind, take
down the elaborate combings and let it rip. She had the
front and side pieces of hair all over her face and was
feeling blindly for the crucial pins that held the back in a
tangle of back combing when a voice said, "Good evening.
Isn't that the brave day?" She peered through her hair like
a ram through the thicket and saw the heavy peasant boots
of a solitary man pass and go lumping up toward the
equally solitary cow.

She gibbered at him and felt her ardour for the lough and
windy hair retreat. She bundled her hair back into a rough,
untidy plait, all tangles and wisps, and ran down over the
lough path and passed the holy thorn tree, the thick plait
bumping on her back, as it used to when she was young and
the world was white.

They were waiting for her.

"You took your hurry," Caroline greeted her. "Was it
Indians you were playing over yonder? I see your hair, but
where's the feathers?"

"Well, how did you like the lough? Worth the effort?" Una
had the engine running and was easing off the brake as Sarah
bundled herself into the car.

"Incredible; too Irish. Like living in a tourist gift shop,
and then it hits you that it's real, all too real; but tell me, did
anyone worthwhile try to paint all this? Perhaps no Irishman
could. I'd have thought they'd never conquer the sentimentality; their brushes'd be clogged and thick with love, like

doing a death mask of your mother. Does anyone get away from the tea cosy?"

"Don't know about painters. But Brian Moore had to go to Canada to do *Answer from Limbo*," Una said, leaning over the steering wheel with a passionate concentration that reminded Sarah of Miss Judith Hearne herself.

"And Joyce in Trieste and Beckett in Paris. Yeats came and went." Sarah could turn this kind of talk on with only half a thought and anyway, someone else had said it all before.

"Yeats was Anglo-Irish." Una spat, as though Anglo-Irish was a dirty word.

"Synge?"

"Tutored by Yeats. There's Behan, but his Ireland is the literary dishcloth, made acceptable by an overlay of English obscenities. Obscenity isn't natural to the Irish." Una's voice was prim, clipped, old-fashioned.

"What about Edna O'Brien, then?" Sarah countered, fancying herself on very safe ground there.

"Lives in England, banned in Ireland. The degree of obscenity an indication of how hard she has to fight against her natural inclinations."

"Iris Murdoch?"

"Anglo-Irish, again," snapped Una. "Not obscene, anyway."

"All the incest?"

"Obscenity has to do with vocabulary, not with situations, and you know that as well as I do. Romeo gets into Juliet's bed; there's no obscenity there, just poetry and marvellous uplift."

"Sure, you used a good word there, Una. Uplift is right," Caroline giggled from the back seat.

"It's when you describe with words the mechanism of fucking that obscenity arises."

"Una said a bad word,
I wonder why she did.
Una said a bad word,
I wonder why she did."

"Yes, Bridget, I said a bad word, and I'm sorry and your mammy'll have to beat me for it and I'll tell the priest in my next confession."

"Brendan got beat for saying it, but he still says it sometimes when he forgets the beating."

"You'll not be saying it, will you?"

"No, I'm the only wee girl my mammy has; I don't say any bad words. My mammy'll beat me if I do."

"Yes, you remember that; I will beat youse, hard."

"Will you beat Una hard?"

"Yes."

"When?"

"Tomorrow."

"Will she cry?"

"Yes."

"Can I watch you beating Una?"

"You can not. Was it an ice cream you had in the sweetie shop?"

"Yes. A pink one, and Patrick had a white one."

"And what did Una have?"

"She had a cigarette and Patrick blew the match out."

"Would you put your foot down, Una, and keep off the literary discussion for the next few minutes? We'll be late for tea."

They were silent in the little car after that, Patrick sucking his thumb, half asleep on his mother's lap, and Bridget in the crook of her arm soberly watching the landscape from the shadow of Sarah's hat. Una was busy with gear lever and brake on the winding road and Sarah was left to brood.

That night she had to go to the wake thing at the house where she'd seen the bearded boy who must surely have taken Bridget's hat. She had heard that the dead body traditionally attended its own wake, that it lay there in an open coffin. But not in the twentieth century, surely? Caroline wouldn't impose that upon her? But in Catholic Ireland? Who was to know? Wake, watchnight, a vigil, a watching. Watching for what? Was it necessary to see the body in order to watch it? It sounded horribly logical. A pleasant holiday evening watching a corpse in the knowledge that her hijackers were perhaps watching her. Two vigils. And Caroline had never come clean about the fight at the Vints'.

"Caroline, what was the fight about? Did the Playboy really do for his father?"

"No, but little pigs, Sarah."

"Yes, all right."

Again they slipped into silence, that special, drowsy car silence; Sarah's other thoughts grew vaguer and vaguer and she slept.

CHAPTER 6

The Big House where they went to tea was a splendid edifice in Bath stone, of Georgian formality. The avenues were overgrown with weeds, with brambles and ivy, the box and yew hedges unclipped, the lawns like fields, unmown. Grass grew between the pebbles of the forecourt and a row of dead crows, crucified on the posts of a nearby fence, did little to make the prospect pleasing.

Her sleep seemed, superficially, to have sobered Sarah and she was driving again. Caroline was on her best behaviour under her new straw hat, a primness about her mouth and in the set of her shoulders, and a respectability in the gloved hands and the clutch on her handbag.

"Sarah, I know I don't have to ask you, but you will behave yourself here, won't you? Don't go modern and advanced and talk about art and permissiveness and that. I have to go on living here, you know that?"

"I won't let you down. I'll be the correct English civil servant and know my place. I'll even put on my English accent if you promise not to giggle."

"Giggle in the Big House? Listen, in yon place I hardly dare breathe. If they knew where I was reared—"

"Well, they don't, and the old girl obviously likes you and approves of you or she wouldn't have taken you up. But, darling, remember my formula. Think of their navels, the great common denominator. They've all got them and they all look daft, stuck there in the middle of their bellies, whether they're young, sexy, tight bellies or fat, old, flaccid ones. They're always there, and they're often dirty. Some most surprising people have dirty navels."

"That's done it now. I'll think of nothing but belly buttons all through tea. If I drop my cup, you're to blame. Oh Lord, there's a few here already. That's the judge's car and that's the Lady Molly's. Hurry now, don't make us late."

"Take it easy, Caroline; just concentrate on the navels. Is my hair terrible? I didn't have time."

"You'll do. Right then, no politics and no religion, mind; those are the two subjects we taboo here – and sex, of course."

As Caroline hauled on the rusted, antique brass bell pull Sarah wondered what the hell else was left to talk about, when you'd done the weather and the beauties of Ireland. Religion she could forswear, but sex and politics – good heavens, what else was life about? There was food, of course, and education, but that was shop.

A fat, pale girl of about fifteen opened the door to them. Protein deficiency, Sarah said to herself, while Caroline greeted her and gave their names. It turned out later that Caroline was the child's godmother, but none of these frivolities were revealed in that moment's formality. She conducted them to the front hall, which was as cold as a crypt and furnished with six of those chairs that have a circle in the seat to accommodate a chamber candlestick. Each one had the family crest on its mahogany back. There was a large sandalwood chest that reeked of the British raj and on it was a heap of country coats, tweed hats and walking sticks, silent precursors of what was in store. The pale girl knocked at a door that would have graced a baroque chapel and opened it and they went in together to the Great Hall. A splendid ornate room in the shape of an ellipse, with pillars and plasterwork and tall windows overlooking a surprisingly well-kept lawn and a dark lake. The furniture was French Empire gilt, wonderful, wonderful.

Lady Maxwell came up, shook hands and made vague introductory gestures toward the other people in the room, the men on their feet, the ladies bowing. Not one of them was under seventy and one was chocolate brown. Despite her assurances to Caroline, Sarah was feeling none too confident, her hair like a bird's nest and no hat to cover it, her good, suitable, linen suit notwithstanding. Sarah held that there are two dominant menopausal colours; navy blue if you've got a bit of sense, baby blue if you haven't. One is the colour of acceptance, make the best of a bad job and don't draw attention to your bulges; the other the colour of refusal, of "no, no, it's not true, I won't let it"; the latter tends to run to the lacy, a regression to the perambulator. Sarah was in navy blue.

A vast woman sitting on a sofa beside the handsome marble fireplace caught Sarah's eye and tapped the seat on her right. Sarah moved over and sat there, a small mouse wishing the dregs of her alcoholic storm were more securely past. She'd wakened up all awry when they'd arrived at Illnacullin and now "the skin of her bum was on her brow," as they so inelegantly say in Welsh: *"croen ei thîn hi ar ei thalcen."*

"You're the guest? Don't you love that house of theirs? A charming bijou residence is what I call it. I wish I were a guest down there. I promise you, I am eternally cold in this house. Maxwell is by way of being a sister of mine, but she never keeps a drop of liquor in the house, I'd have you know. They keep liquor down there. Very generous. Nice gel. Too many babies. Is it true? Again?"

"Yes, she is, actually."

"Damned old Pope. Always said he was an ass. You a gardener?"

"Not much, I'm afraid. I live in the city and my garden is a small, typically city garden."

"But you'll have a country Place?"

"Only a seaside cottage; little grows there but sea thistles, but I'm rather fond of them. The blue, you know, against that grey green?"

"Strange taste, I must say. Modern. Can't understand the moderns. Never did."

Another couple came into the room. A tall grey-haired man who looked like a general and probably was, and a very beautiful woman, slim and tall and dark with a flash of white hair in the black; Sarah saw the blink of diamonds from where she sat. There were the same vague, muttered introductions and while they went on, Sarah was able to look properly at the giant beside her. She had on a huge, checked tweed skirt that Sarah would have thought an insult to a problem family, a purple twin-set and a Shetland scarf of pink and green checks. The diamond bar brooch on the bolster of her bosom complemented the rings on the twisted hands. Her thick lisle stockings were badly darned with wool and she wore scuffed bedroom slippers on her swollen, tired feet. Without the diamonds, she could have been anybody at the Old People's Welfare.

"The Smiths. Rich, my dear; not multis, but rich enough. All the Smiths are rich. Meet a Smith and you smell money. All of them."

Sarah thought of some of the Cardiff Smiths she knew. They weren't multis either. God help them.

"I haven't a penny, of course, not a penny. That's why I come here for the summer. I let my London apartments to imbeciles who think it worth paying a fortune for the privilege of living in a lady's place. Impossible people who choose to spend the summer in London when nobody's there. I milk 'em, my dear, milk 'em, and why not? They pay my rent for the Season."

The fat, whey-faced girl came in and whispered to Lady Maxwell. "Thank God," Sarah's companion said, "tea at last. Give me an arm, child, help me up; my stick is there." Sarah handed her the rubber-ferruled walking stick. It was just possible that she put some of her weight on it, but most came onto Sarah's arm. Sarah very nearly buckled until she rested her hand on the frame of the sofa and, given some purchase, heaved at the giant.

Slowly, slowly, like an elephant in mush, the large woman came to her feet, and then lumbered off, like a walking oak, without a word, towards a far door and merged with the others. Sarah saw Caroline moving ahead and she followed, not knowing a soul, unconfident. Lady Maxwell took her arm.

"Come along, come along; yes, see that piece of grass at this window I have at least been able to maintain."

Sarah looked out and was startled. "Lady Maxwell, that horse the man is leading on the lawn; does it have some encumbrance on its feet?"

"Boots, child, boots."

Sarah considered that. "But why does he wear boots?"

"Hoofs, hoofs mark the grass; a horse working on a lawn always wears boots."

How ignorant one is of basic truths; to think that all the Smiths were rich, and that horses on a lawn wore boots; shoes, yes, but not boots.

"Yes, 'pon my soul, I shall continue to maintain that lawn; my dear husband used to stand here, he loved that prospect; but little else remains. Today, I'd have you know, I swept my own bedroom. I came as a bride to this house, a lady; I shall soon leave it, as a char. It is all finished."

Sarah had nothing to say to that. All right, my friends, all right, she thought, it all came off the backs of the poor, I know all that, don't be naïve. But this is utterly pathetic too, honestly; you don't have to be on supplementary benefit to deserve sympathy. It's all a matter of what you're used to, what you've learned to expect. Shut up too, you young anarchists; you have nothing to offer but your chaos, and only the chains of revolutionary government to gain; even when you preach it in the holy name of nationalism.

They were at the dining-room door, they moved in, and Sarah sat somewhere at the long mahogany table. It was just like the one in *Alice*, except that this one was without a cloth.

To her right, the chocolate-coloured Indian gentleman happened and on her left she found the tallest, thinnest, deafest lady she'd ever been privileged to meet. In her Cardiff and Cambridge bourgeois security, Sarah had always served tea in the drawing room, uncomfortably and inconveniently on laps and on small side tables. At Caroline's they hadn't much run to tea, preferring to anticipate the cocktail hour. Was this dining-room thing upper class or was it Irish? Sarah wished she knew.

Lady Maxwell poured the tea at a semicircular side table covered by the nastiest plastic cloth and there were no table napkins. Laundry bills? Idiot, the gentry didn't have laundry bills, they had laundry maids. But now, presumably, no laundry maid, hence the plastic.

Conversation wasn't easy with the thin, deaf lady. She informed Sarah about the weather and the fishing and had the sense to ask questions that could be answered with an affirmative nod, or otherwise. Like, did she fish or ride or want to borrow a horse or live in London or know old so-and-so? There wasn't much that Sarah could nod about. In despair the deaf lady talked to Sarah about hens. She farmed them. Sarah didn't quite die about hens herself, not hens *qua* hens. She rather went on, and Sarah's concentration was desultory till she came to the chick-sexer. Sarah pricked her ears at that. A long and complicated story about a chick-sexer who hadn't come when he was expected. "He didn't come and he didn't come." How utterly exhausting for you, said Sarah's filthy old mind. But then he'd turned up, unbeknownst, and had got down to it and he was sexing away happily in the barn when she came up on him. Sarah didn't dare ask any more about him; she loved him the way he was, sexing away happily in the barn.

Her Indian neighbour, together with the possible general, distributed cups of tea and then everyone sat down and offered things and accepted things and they ate toast and scones and chocolate cake, than which, in Sarah's humble opinion, there is nothing, but nothing in life nastier. She set her teeth against chocolate cake. The gentleman on her right pressed it on her, but she was firm. "I love it," she lied, "but at my age one must consider one's diet. Think of the calories."

"Fiddle-dee-dee," he said, "fiddle-dee-dee. Take a scone then and pass me the honey, would you? Set yourself up as a psychiatrist, they tell me."

"No, you've been misinformed. I work at the Ministry of Education."

"Philistines, you medicos. Insufficiently educated, understand nothing but bones. All poops, poops, poops."

"Rubbish!" Sarah wasn't taking this. "I know nothing about bones, but I would claim a modicum of culture; I am, after all, an Oxford graduate. Why," she said, thinking of colour and sympathy and all that, "my husband actually met Gandhi at Oxford. He considered that one of the greatest moments of his life."

"The Mahatma," the gentleman growled, crumbling a scone into his honey in a frenzy of barely suppressed rage. "The Mahatma, the Mahatma. I'd have you know, dear lady, that I had the pleasure of putting the Mahatma into the prison where they should have let him rot, on two celebrated occasions. Mahatma indeed."

So this must be the judge whose car they'd seen outside. An Indian judge. British raj. He mumbled on, like simmering soup.

"Man of the people, the Mahatma. But your precious Mahatma went on hunger strike on my hands; would take nothing but raisins and water. But the raisins, dear lady, the raisins had to be sent from Fortnum and Mason's; he wouldn't look at any others. Fortnum and Mason's or the death of a martyr, a holy man. Fortnum and Mason's, yes, Fortnum's." He turned to the scone that he'd crumbled into a kind of pudding in the honey he'd so copiously heaped on his plate. "Fortnum and Mason's," he growled again and then he looked at Sarah with his beautiful moss brown eyes. "The man was a poop, I tell you, a poop."

The last "poop" a half belch, half-sad sigh. By now his hands were liberally coated with honey and hundreds and thousands of crumbs were stuck to them. He looked desperately for a table napkin. His fingers dripped honey and he shook them – honestly, he shook them. The fingers got joined together; he was like Patrick with a sticky sweet. Then he leaned forward, judicial, imperious, burrowed his hands under the table and rubbed them on its underneath. Sarah felt a large, pendulant blob of honey fall onto her leg and slide thickly down her stocking, to dry, slowly, stiff and hard and sweet. "A poop, poop, poop," he said again, like Mr. Toad expiring. Why hadn't she obeyed Caroline? "No politics" were her last words. She'd gone and slid her bloody foot in it.

"Do you live in Ireland now?" she asked, ignoring the poops.

"London in the Season. Ireland for the fishing. Where's your Place?"

"She recognised the capital *P* this time. "My parents have a small Place in West Glamorganshire," she said, remembering with love and shame the half shack, half shanty that they had for holidays down in the Gower, "but duty calls me to Cambridge for most of the time, unfortunately. One must live, don't you know?"

"The tax wallahs. My dear lady, you have my profoundest sympathy. Get an accountant, get an accountant. Worth every penny, every penny."

"Oh, I do, I do, I promise you."

"Have some chocolate cake. Emma's cook makes a good one. No? Yes, yes, I will, thank you, splendid, yes, splendid."

Sarah could hear Lady Maxwell, on the judge's right, waxing furiously about some iniquity. She tapped his arm. "Ajit, Ajit, my dear, you could perhaps advise me. You know, of course, that all the servants I have left to me are Romans?"

"Poor Emma; like having rats in the house, what? Yes, like having rats. Poor Emma."

"But what is one to do? They engender these wretched undercurrents, don't you know? Today I was perhaps a little premature in the kitchen — one no longer sleeps as one did — and there at my table, in my kitchen, eating my food, I came upon a young oaf of a boy. Fortunately, my cook is too old and my kitchen maid too young to be entertaining followers to breakfast, but I wonder what the devil the fellow was about. He bolted when he saw me, ran away like a schoolboy, and I certainly have not been satisfied by their explanations. He was a hitchhiker, whatever that may mean, he was a poor starving tramp crying out for nourishment and wasn't it no more than Christian duty? You'll know their devious ways but, 'pon my soul, I don't like it. It is an established fact that I haven't a penny, but I have my things, have all this," with an encompassing wave of her hand. "I may well be put to counting the teaspoons."

"Don't be a poop, Emma, don't be a poop. Send for the police. Send for the police and have him flogged."

It was too much for Sarah. Give her a coloured face and you gave her a friend. All right, she thought, I know I'm probably the kind of white liberal that James Baldwin would spit on, but don't blame me because I don't know what they want from me. No one will tell us white liberals how to behave, what not to do. "Have him flogged," he'd said. Why in hell couldn't stereotypes stay stereotyped? She'd been so impressed to find no racial discrimination in that house; but it wasn't colour that mattered there, only background and the attitudes it produced. There colour didn't count a damn, it was still only the old class merry-go-round.

Sarah looked over at Caroline; she was pale and her face was clenched as though to hold on to her vomit. It might have been the chocolate cake, but then again it might have been

Lady Maxwell's thoughtless crack about her Roman servants. Sarah didn't like the look of her and when she saw the purplish high colour creep up to stain the taut, pale face and to clash horribly with that pale golden hair, she whispered, across the judge's fat front, "Lady Maxwell, I trust you'll forgive me, but I fear that Mrs. Moore is unwell. Would you consider it fearfully rude if I took her home? She's – well, she's—"

"Farrowing again, what? Of course, gel, of course; I shall rise and let you go without embarrassment. She has a bad colour, I grant you. Will this not be number eight? It's too much, 'pon my soul, it is. But her number six I like."

"Then we'll not prolong our leave-taking, if you'll forgive us." Sarah moved over toward Caroline. "Come on; I've told the old girl you're not well and that I'm taking you home. Bear up for the next few minutes."

They said their goodbyes and Sarah had, perforce, to shake the judge's hand, which was still a mess of honey. "Don't forget," he said, "the Mahatma was the worst thing that ever happened to India."

"Yes, I'll remember," her traitor tongue replied, "I'll remember."

In the car Caroline sat, silent, and clutched her handbag to her belly, the head in her brave new straw hat bent, desolate. Sarah lit two cigarettes and handed her one, then she removed the hat from Caroline's head and tossed it onto the back seat. She started the car. Caroline touched her arm. "No, don't go home yet, drive round a bit. Remember about yon young feller she said she found in her kitchen?"

"Yes?"

"About the police and that? I know about him. He's a feller on the run. He was hiding out in the Vints'. Mind you, I've said nothing, but that's how they came to have the fight that killed poor John, God rest him. Mrs. Vint wasn't prepared to have the feller; she's seen too much of it. She stood up to young Larry and said it wasn't to be. Larry turned nasty whenever John took her part and the wee bastard knocked the father out. But the doctor said he died of a heart attack, it wasn't the blow. With John dead on their hands they couldn't keep this feller. Even Larry saw that much, so they brought him to the Big House. Who'd have thought of her ladyship coming down to the kitchen at half-eight, and her coming at nine all these years?"

Sarah began to hope that she understood those young men of hers now; and, possibly, the other one, on the back seat of the red car, who had ducked his head. "Why is he on the run? What's he done? Wait, we'll have to stop. My hands are all over honey; this wheel's like a dirty jam jar."

"Oh, I didn't ask. Think who I am; it's best I don't know. But I couldn't turn him in, Sarah, you must see that; I couldn't grass. I've my loyalties, whoever I'm married to."

"As far as you know, he's political, is he?"

Caroline nodded, still "saying nothing." "But will her ladyship tell the peelers? It has me worried. The sergeant's a decent enough sort, our sort, but if he's pushed, he'll have to do something. Jesus, should we warn the Vints, d'you think? I don't know, I just don't know."

"But he won't be there now, surely? They can deny all knowledge. The police wouldn't go to a house with a death in it, would they?"

"No, maybe you're right; but if they thought it was IRA work they would. But where's the wee fellow now? He's nothing but a boy, a shy one and gentle, so I'm told. Mrs. Vint felt for him, but the feller that brought him was a cheeky bastard and threw his weight around. Mrs. Vint wouldn't have that. God help her, she's been loyal so long, but there comes a time. She's heartbroke with it all. What should I do, Sarah, what *should* I do, girl?"

"It's not your problem. Sit tight and breathe a few prayers."

"What else have I done all day, woman? Flog him, he said, that black bastard. Och, they're as bad as us whites, whatever you say."

"Yes, but no worse, that's all I say. Please indicate the general direction of home, love."

"You may turn right round, then left, then left again."

"That's enough for a start. I've got indigestion, have you? I saw you eat that chocolate cake."

"God, I know."

"Aluminium hydroxide in my handbag. In a white plastic thing." Caroline searched. "The mess in this bag! Nobody needs three lipsticks at the same time and four matchboxes."

"It's a phial thing."

"This it?"

"Yes. Take two; they can't harm you. And give me some, before the heartburn starts. Why do people have tea? Nothing to commend it. Not long enough to get acquainted and too long to be just a joke. Though I got my money's worth today. Honest, I'm all over honey; look at my leg."

"Yes, but put your foot back by the brake; you wouldn't know what you'd meet on these roads."

"Where now? What was the second left."

"Straight on, turn right and you're in the farmyard."

"Look at the lilies in that garden. Aren't they marvellous? Such an arrogant old colour."

"Aye. But you'll see they have the flag out too. Orange lilies, specially grown for the Twelfth. You'll not find them in my garden."

"Protestant flowers?"

"Aye; I hate this time of year, you know that? And did you hear her, on about her Roman servants? It infects us all, even the best."

"Tell you something dreadful, Caroline; we never asked her for another hat for Bridget. There'll be no peace, will there?"

"She may sleep with yours, that's all. She's fond of you; she'll be content till I get another chance with the lady."

That hat had originally cost forty dollars. The Fifth Avenue label was still in it, most carefully preserved. "Then I can't possibly go to the wake. Not without a hat."

"You can wear your head scarf. Come with me, Sarah; I'll maybe hear a wee word about that poor bastard on the run. I keep thinking of him; Mrs. Vint said he was young; just like it could be one of my own. But not a word to Colum, mind you. He'd do what he thought was his duty. He's no patience to spare for the Republicans. Says it's all madness, the nationalism."

"Me too. Though I know it's fashionable just now on the extreme left, because it's anarchistic; the first necessary step toward the final revolutionary goal. I'm not always against violence, mind, but violence needs directing; if nationalism provides the direction, for the right reasons, then one can accept nationalism. Failing all else. In Cuba violence was obviously necessary, and look at South America. But in Britain? We don't have the makings of tyrants here; our enemies are so piddling, a waste of reformist energy which ought to be better applied; Welsh nationalism, for example, seems to me to be about letting English cities use our water supplies and about having telephone instructions in Welsh. 'The tree of liberty must be refreshed from time to time with the blood of patriots and tyrants. It is its natural manure.' Patriots and tyrants, Caroline, not motorcar-licence application forms in Welsh and adolescents wanting to run the universities. No, we don't have the makings here in Britain, thank God.

"But I do wish I knew a bit more about the triggers of violence. What is it that will turn a demonstration suddenly ugly? I worry so about those kids who are at the same time both the perpetrators of violence and its victims. I *can't* think straight about it, and I keep on having this nasty right-wing suspicion that the young and idealistic are being used, you know? For God's sake, I don't mean Moscow rubles and all that balls; I'm more afraid of psychopaths and sadists cashing in on starry-eyed enthusiasms, and then sadistic judges taking it out on the honest innocents. Oh, I don't know, it's just a smell of drains somewhere. We've had a few horrible incidents in Wales; two men blown up by their own bombs, things like that."

"You sound just like Colum. But Una says you ought to encourage your enemies to violence, to win sympathy. She believes in martyrs. And don't you forget, we've plenty of tyrants in Ulster, God knows. You know how I hate the politics, but if you're a Roman Catholic over here, that makes you political, you can't help yourself; there's no politics but the religion. But whatever that wee fellow's done, even if it's not the politics, I'd have to help him. Couldn't not, Sarah."

"No, of course you couldn't."

"Och, well, it's good to be home; not a word to Colum, mind, if he's back. No, he's not, the car's not in the garage. It's a long journey he'll have of it. You realise he goes through Derry and Dungiven, where there's been trouble? It'll do him no harm in the world to see a few signs of the people's anger. He's in a cocoon, the man. None so blind. I wonder will Una stay if he's not back to let me out for the wake?"

"Let me stay."

"No, please come with me. You're asked."

Sarah slipped the car into neutral, turned the engine off and resigned herself to the wake. But she was now in far better spirits, with or without the corpse. At least she thought she knew what the bearded boy was up to; she was no longer frighteningly mystified by his attentions to her. He was surely organising the escape of the running boy and she had obviously stupidly stumbled into his devices under the overhang of hawthorns in that lane. By now her sympathies had been aroused in any case and she saw the business of Bridget's hat as a kind of oblique, romantic, Buchanesque warning and smiled at the bravado. It was almost comic, in the context of water cannons and petrol bombs, to fool around with a small girl's hat. She felt an indulgent, half-maternal fondness for his youthfulness. Yes, she'd survive the wake, and then it would be tomorrow.

CHAPTER 7

Colum telephoned to say that the car was giving trouble and that he would not be home that night. But Una volunteered to babysit so that Sarah need not miss her first wake.

"Brendan's not back. We may eat without him, though I've never known that same feller late for his meal before. He's only got two thoughts, that one, fishing and food. Where the hell is he? Will you tell me that?"

"Waiting for the sun to move off some pond or other."

"But he'll be hungry. I didn't cook them any breakfast."

"He ate the best part of a lobster and Bridget's baby tomato and porridge and enough toast for a regiment. Mrs. Savidge gave him a mountain of sandwiches and he more or less emptied your fruit basket. Perhaps he has a tapeworm."

"No, just greed."

"Probably because he's the eldest. Scared the hungry generations will tread him down."

"Doesn't give them a chance, that one. Come on, let's eat. I've done the chicken in a wine sauce, with mushrooms and green peppers. It ought to take the taste of tea out of your mouth. You wouldn't have another of those wee tablets, would you? I'd like to hang on to my chicken."

Brendan had still not returned by the end of dinner. Caroline was more angry than worried about him. If Sarah hadn't heard about the running boy at the Big House, she might have been sweating blood, but the explanation of the mystery — the boy in the back seat of the car, all that — had given her a kind of euphoria; Brendan would turn up. Children had no sense of time, especially in summer.

"Una, we'll have to go. When that wee so-and-so turns up, you'll not let him watch television, hear me? It'll be 'Danger Man' and he'll have to miss it. That'll do, till I get back. I'll

132

beat him tomorrow and he'll not go for his fishing. And you may both shut up about corporal punishment. It's all he understands; that and television. Come on, Sarah, pull on your jacket and your scarf. We'll not be long, Una; you've something to read, have you?"

"Yes, yes, of course. Go now and I'll deal with Brendan. Have a nice wake, Sarah. You'll survive."

The corpse was at the wake. Large as death, rigid as right-eousness. A brown shroud, rosary beads in the terrible hands and white satin lining the box. He was upstairs, in the bedroom, with his candles and his mourning cards and his widow. Caroline and Sarah were shown up to the room. The widow sat on a hard kitchen chair beside the open coffin and Caroline went up to her and shook hands and turned to Sarah.

"Mrs. Thomas," she said, "come to pay her respects." Sarah took the widow's hand and said, "I'm very sorry." Caroline knelt by the coffin and prayed and Sarah knelt too and had nothing to say. She looked down at the cold linoleum under her knees, shining new, vitriol green, mustard yellow and thick pink. Caroline got up and leaned over the corpse. "God rest him," she said and put down her mourning card. Sarah couldn't bring herself to look and stood there, waiting for guidance. The room was full of people, sitting on chairs, on the bed, standing around; some were praying, with beads, others quietly talking, gossiping, Sarah thought. The candle flames streamed up and the air was close, heavy. The Playboy came up to them, put his arm around Caroline's shoulder and looked with her at his father.

"Yes, sure, he's very quiet-looking, Mrs. Moore. Looks brave and harmless, sure he does?" He was half drunk, the hands on Caroline furtively lecherous, his legs unsteady and his weight drunkenly upon her. Sarah wanted to scream, to laugh, to run. Everything was so close, so intimate; near, she could see the sweat on the Playboy's brow and the coarse, unhealthy pink skin and the eyes unfocussed. There was a staleness off his clothes and the smell of old sweat off his mother's black crepe dress. She couldn't bear it. She was sorry for nobody but herself. She had to get out. She had to go, go anywhere. Those unfocussed eyes of the Playboy had got her. They might have been her own eyes looking back at her from that flushed, bravadoed face. Jesus, Jesus, let me get out of this. She turned and stumbled to the door, felt her way down the steep, ill-lighted, narrow staircase, blundering and clumsy, her feet loud on the linoleum and rattling the brass stair rods. A most unfunereal clamour she made of it, but she stood at last at the front door to breathe, and there Caroline joined her. "Come on," she said. "We have to go into the room to pass ourselves. We'll not be long. Don't be difficult now. You'll enjoy this, see if you don't."

The "room," the parlour, was thick, bunged up, with people, blue with turf smoke and the fumes of alcohol. Caroline was a changeling, gay and boisterous and calling out that they should make room for her and her guest. Wherever were their manners and wasn't there a drink in the house, at all? It was like a public bar, with a kind of professionalism about it. Cases of Guinness stood along one wall and a tin of potato crisps, bottles of Bushmills on a central table and glasses, glasses everywhere.

A fat, flushed man with spectacles and a wide gap between his front teeth was holding forth, telling a story about His Reverence the Bishop and a calf, and what John Vint had said to them both. The story was rounded, fashioned, professional, like something out of the script of a B film.

Sarah was given a tumbler of whiskey and welcomed to Ireland and Caroline sat on one of the crates and hoisted her skirt for a long stay. She had something colourless in her glass, but there was no sign of a gin bottle.

"Come on, Sarah, relax and take your hurry. Give my friend a chair there, John Joe; it's her first wake, so it is."

Sarah was grateful for the chair; her knees were still sick from the upstairs room. Someone gave her a cigarette. When the gap-toothed man had had his say, there was a kind of chorus of "Sure, there was never any harm in the man, no more he did." A pause, and then the grocer she'd met in the shop said, "Aye, you'll mind the time poor John—" and he was given the floor and the critical audience listened and polished its wits and then, like church responses, ritualistic, came the chorus, "No, never any harm in the man. A decent body, so he was."

So many people, so much laughter, so often "God rest his soul," such formal, fashioned jokes, anecdotes; such friendliness and such a lack of originality, of inventiveness, nothing impromptu, nothing unrehearsed. Caroline, on her Guinness crate, was swapping jokes and half flirting, hail-lady-well-met with the men and knocking away whatever booze she had in her glass. All the other women in the room were seated together along one wall, removed from the men. They tended to be fawn-skinned women, drawn, big-eyed, dark hair primly curled, overbabied, undersexed, in jumpers of bright harsh colours, purple and pink and strong turquoise, and battered bedroom slippers with worn imitation fur, or dead feathers. Sarah felt that she had never in life seen such a negation of sex, such a rejection, such a blasphemy. One of the women held a mongoloid child in her lap, who smoked a little pipe and looked benignly at the world.

Sarah drank her whiskey. For the first half hour she simply wanted to go, get out, but the drink and the talk and the efforts to make her welcome gradually thawed her and she forgot the corpse and rosaries and the smells up in the room above. Slowly, she began to laugh and appreciate and to feel popular. Stories and drinks and cigarettes later she looked for Caroline while it was still just possible to peer through the fumes. Caroline was in a huddle, intent, listening; perhaps she was having her wee word about the boy on the run. Sarah saw her nod and cross herself and get up to leave. She came to Sarah's chair and helped her up. "We'll be away then. Good night now, good night."

When they'd fought their way to the door and the fresh air, Caroline said, "That wasn't so bad, was it? You've had your wake. Remember what you promised me once?"

"Yes, I do; you don't want a brown shroud, it has to be white because brown never suited you. Nor do you want purple flowers. Yes, I'll remember."

"Don't you forget it, or I'll come and haunt youse, brown shroud and all. Look, there's nothing fit to drink in the house except Colum's good stuff. I'll have to call at the pub for a few things. Won't be long; I'll not keep you."

"But the pub's closed; it's after ten, I promise you."

"Did you never hear of the back door, woman? Come on; closing's nothing but a formality in Ireland."

So they went to the pub, down a narrow, pitch-black back alley, and they negotiated, to judge by the smells, what must have been the men's cloakroom and in through the back porch of the pub they'd visited on the first day. There were no lights on, only the blank television screen casting forth a dim, religious light. As far as Sarah could see, the place was packed, and there was more talk, and someone brought them a drink and old Mr. Wales, of the first funeral, pressed Sarah to snuff. She was too confused and too strangely benevolent to refuse him. He poured the fine, brown powder on the back of her hand and she sniffed it up each nostril in turn. Sneezes shook her like a rattle; she felt like a bomb; her eyes streamed, her mascara ran and in the confusion the old boy pressed her thigh with his dirty old hands. He leered and letched at her, showing his stumps of teeth and stinking to high heaven; she reared wildly out of his reach and into the glass of the man wedged behind her. He had a face like Brueghel's peasants and touched his forelock at her. He whispered in her ear, "Sure, and you'll think nothing to him, missus; he's nothing but a poor old wine victim." A wine victim; how much gentler the euphemism was. She hoped they'd call her a "poor wine victim" when the time came round.

Sarah lapsed into uncontrollable giggles when she saw one of the drinkers come close up against the television screen to count the change in his hand, his dim discovered cash. "Aye, you may well laugh," Caroline rebuked, "but money's going like snow off a ditch the night…"

And then the back door was flung open and a tall policeman stood there, big as the law, silencing as a judge's mallet.

"Come on. Out. All of you. Out. I want this place empty. You, John Joe, you've had your warning. Out now. Out of it."

The men shuffled out, in their cloth caps, dragging their feet, looking daft, like kids caught. For a moment Caroline was the imperious lady and then seemed to think better of it, but walking casually, nevertheless, taking her hurry to the door. Sarah pottered behind her, just a visitor, pretending she wasn't even there, but she was rent apart by another sneeze as she passed the law.

Caroline had neglected to collect the reinforcements she had come to buy, so they were able to run, once they were out of the alley, run from the shame of it, the humiliation. They got into the car like two fugitives.

"Jesus, I never felt so small in all my days, but I couldn't stop to pass the time with him. Not after what I was drinking."

"Why, what were you drinking?"

"The hard stuff, mountain dew."

"Caroline! Not poteen? Are you mad? How can you be such a bloody cow? Have you no regard for your baby? First you're too damn wilful to do anything about your vomiting, which can be doing the baby no good at all, and now you drink gut-rot, to poison it. If you are determined to end your pregnancy, I should have thought it more honest and moral to have taken some precautions before it began."

"Sarah Thomas, what the hell's come over you? You sound like you mean it."

"I do mean it, damn you; you're behaving like a lunatic. And here am I driving this bloody car, tight as an owl and sneezing like a pneumatic drill, thanks to being dragooned into that wake thing. If I kill us, it won't be my fault, I'm warning you. And don't expect any sympathy from me when you retch up your guts tomorrow, if, indeed, we ever see tomorrow."

There was not another word from Caroline. They sat silent in the car after Sarah's outburst. She tried to concentrate on the driving, while the road waved in her headlights and the kerb all the time seemed to come out and hit the tyres. She saw neither bullocks nor belated drinkers on the road, but they passed a big, dark semi-bus parked at the roadside with uniformed men simply gushing out of it, like squished toothpaste. They carried big, clumsy guns and wore flat uniform hats that shadowed their faces like fascism, like death.

"What the hell are those?"

"Drive like the wind, in case they halt us. They're the Special Police, the B's, out on their Protestant junketings. Special Powers, remember? Looking for that poor wee feller, I doubt." Caroline said not another word and left Sarah feeling the despised and rejected Protestant she was. Again she struggled to concentrate on the road and thought she heard a voice toll out, "Driving a car while under the influence of drink." She thought about arrest under the threat of those guns, and took a corner at about two miles an hour, with a ghastly, exaggerated caution that did nothing to help. The infernal steering wheel had a mind of its own. But the last bit was easier; plenty of room to weave in the farmyard and then, in the drive, the ruts kept her in her place. Caroline slammed out of the car as soon as it stopped. Sarah pulled at the handbrake only to find she'd had it on all the time; she remembered to turn off the lights and stalked to the house.

Mountain dew, forsooth. Caroline had it coming to her. Lord, that stupid, stage-Irish pose of hers; drinking that stuff in her condition, and simply out of some sentimental, nationalist-solidarity crap. They'd probably only made it the week before last; she might as well be on meths.

Sarah was fighting drunk as she crossed the threshold, but Caroline came running at her and threw her arms about her, almost knocking her down. "Sarah, Sarah, it's Brendan. He's never come back." Her face was ravaged, her lungs began to heave and her breath rasped and then the terrible retching started. Her eyes were red-rimmed and her face stiff with fear and drink. Una stood behind her, supporting her.

"He's drowned. I know he is, my wee boy's drowned." She vomited again, resting a hand on the doorjamb and tearing her guts out.

"Why didn't you try to get hold of us?" Sarah hectored Una as she struggled to focus and wear a brief authority, a shallow competence.

"D'you think I haven't tried to ring every number in the village? No reply, of course; everybody at the wake or swilling somewhere else. It's the doctor's day off, and not even the police barracks is answering. I couldn't leave the other kids and I've been listening to phones ringing without response for the last two hours. And you two come home plastered in a crisis like this. You know what's happened, Sarah? They have him, they've taken him. Oh Jesus, tell me why. What are they scared of you for? Or could it be Colum they're after?"

"God alone knows. Can you think of any way to get in touch with them? To try and reason? But none of it is my fault, Una, none of it. You know I didn't want to go to that damned wake thing. You know I didn't."

"You shut up," Una spat at Sarah. "You're maudlin. Get coffee going. I'll try the police again." She dialled the number. "No, they don't answer."

Sarah retreated to the kitchen. She was hysterically cursing the coffee machine and compulsively sneezing when she heard Caroline come back into the house. The sisters came to the kitchen. "What's to be done?" Una's voice was thin, disgusted.

"We'll take this coffee and then we'll drive around until we find a policeman; the village is thick with them, armed to the eyebrows. We saw them come. Caroline should go to bed and you come with me. Just give me time." Sarah's tongue was thick in her mouth and the words she looked for ran through her fingers.

"Damned if I'll risk my neck with you driving. No, I'll go myself, while you sober up. Do that and stay here with Caroline. I'll go now, though God alone knows where to start. Are the keys in the car?"

"Yes," Sarah said, in a tamed, guilty voice.

"Right; look after Caroline, if you're capable of anything."

Caroline was standing stiffly against the kitchen wall, bleak as John Vint in his coffin; she even had rosary beads between her fingers. Una tied a scarf around her head and shrugged a jacket about her gaunt shoulders, opened the back door on the night, slammed it and was gone. Caroline just stood there, silently speaking prayers while Sarah watched, blindly, the water bubbling in the percolator.

It might have been two minutes that they stood, or two years, but the coffee wasn't made when they heard the voices coming round the back. Una and someone who cried, a little crying, high voice. Sarah ran to open the door and there they stood, blinking in the sudden light, Una with her arm around Brendan, who cried and clutched his fishing rod, with William Butler glooming in the background. Caroline whispered, "Glory be to God," and then she went for him, slapped him around the head, then kissed him and then slumped onto a kitchen chair and sobbed into the tabletop.

Brendan helped himself to food, his tears and his fears temporarily forgotten, comforted by blows and kisses. They trailed after him into the drawing room, like attendant acolytes. What had happened was simple enough. He'd been walking home from his fishing and a man in a red car had stopped and offered him a lift and said William Butler could go in the back. A nice young man with a beard who'd talked to him about school and the fish and that. He'd said he'd drive Brendan round and show him a pool he knew; he wouldn't be late home, because he was saved the walk, wasn't he? When they'd gone a long way — Brendan began to cry a little again then — the man said he was afraid Brendan would have to walk the rest of the way because he'd just remembered an appointment he had in Belfast and he couldn't waste any more time on kids. He'd pitched the fishing rod out of the car and when Brendan went to retrieve it, the man opened the back door for William Butler and then he drove off and left them.

"And, Mammy, I didn't know where I was and there was not a one to ask and I walked and walked and I'm all over blisters in my Wellingtons. And I was afraid to come home; I thought you'd beat me and maybe say I made up a lie about yon man. But it is true, Mammy, it is true."

"I know, love, I know. Away to your bed now and Una will come up and look at your feet; sure, you will, Una? Had you enough to eat, son? You're sure now? Lie in, in the morning, then, and rest yourself." Brendan went limping out of the room, a tired, pale, small boy. Sarah hadn't been much drawn to him before, puberty being so mysterious and off-putting, but the sight of his drooping shoulders, the fragile young neck and the thick, bouncing fair hair, made her almost maudlin. He turned back at the door and said, "Sarah, I wonder would you put my fish in the fridge? Two roaches. I'll have them for my breakfast. Mammy, what's wrong with Sarah's face, at all? She looks awful peculiar, so she does."

"Aye; Mr. Wales gave her some snuff and she's not got the knack of it yet. God, Sarah, you ought to see yourself. You look salvaged, honest. Your mascara's run and your nostrils are like black pits, so they are. And you've a wee brown moustache on you like Ramon Novarro. If I wasn't so poorly I'd be laughing myself sick."

She didn't dare look; if she looked she'd remember it forever. Better be kind to herself and hope to forget. Easier to forget the imagined than the actually witnessed.

"I'll deal with your fish now, Brendan. I'm sorry about the face. I'll have it washed before you see me next. Sleep well, love." Back in the kitchen the coffee had boiled dry and the pot was ruined. So what? Let's have a sense of proportion about the place for a change.

"Your coffee-pot is done for, Caroline, but you'll get another. I'm sorry I blew up in the car; it was just the drink, you know?"

"Think nothing to it. Would you not help me to bed now? Una can get in with me the night. I'll not let her go home on her lonesome."

"No, you need a proper rest. She can sleep with me; God knows my bed is big enough."

"Could she? I'll go on up then. D'you think I sicked up all that bloody poteen, girl? You had me worried there in the car."

"Yes, you couldn't but have done. Don't brood about it, please, I shouldn't have gone on as I did."

"No, you were right, for once. I ought to have had more sense, but it was them including me in, giving me the special treatment, did it. You wouldn't tell Colum on me, sure you wouldn't?"

"Nit. Come on, then, let's get you to bed. Thank God that Brendan's home and you can sleep in peace."

"Thank God is right, my girl, I will."

Una and Sarah slept together in the tester bed. They lay talking, Sarah with her arm around Una, who fitted herself into the curve of Sarah's lap. She was as thin as a pair of tongs, her hipbones protruding like horseshoes and her breasts hardly lifting the bodice of Caroline's elaborate nightie. They were like the little mounds of a girl of twelve, just beginning to sprout.

Sarah and Una gnawed at the carcasses of all their problems, worried at the situation like dogs, but got no further than deciding not to tell Caroline about the continuing threat to her children. She could take no more; she probably saw nothing more sinister than sex in Brendan's abduction and a young man who had luckily put away temptation.

Relief and fear had sobered Sarah, and Una, lying curved into her lap, apologised for attacking Sarah's drunkenness. "Your head's not strong enough to take Ireland; don't kid yourself that you can take drink for drink with us. Seasoned campaigner though you may be, you haven't the head for us." Since, "intimacy" has come to mean "going to bed with," Una, in their intimacy, told Sarah a little about her marriage, her voice coming shyly through the dark. She claimed that he'd been cruel to her, but it seemed to Sarah that the cruelty she complained of was all sexual in origin. Una's husband had been interested in what struck Sarah as comparatively harmless fun-and-games, but Una hadn't felt able to ring any changes. Modesty demanded — Decency insisted — Nice people didn't do – Sarah thought of all those nuns who'd dominated Una's formative years and couldn't blame her; a strange, fastidious, passionate girl, too complex and introspective, uneasy, uncomfortable. She quietly rather sympathised with the man who'd blacked Una's eye in frustration. But what was to be done about excessive modesty? You certainly shouldn't rape against it, nor rail. Una had been formed and taught by nuns, and nuns have neither, usually, been bedded, nor have they given birth.

Sarah sighed. Had not tomorrow been the next day, Friday, Jamesday, she might have confessed to weariness of

Catholic Ulster. It was no longer the easy, holiday land of her romanticisms, her dining out. She now felt it utterly foreign to her, old-fashioned, peasant, rigid, violent, unreasonable. A place where Franco was revered as much as de Gaulle, where psychology was as suspect as communism, where politics was religion and sex wasn't permitted to be fun, even when it was permitted at all. All the lunatic violence a perversion of sexual energy?

And now, perhaps, a civil war. Whose barricades would give her shelter? Was she to be lost in their crossfire for Christ? Their special, divided, Ulster Christ, a stranger to Sarah; on the one side His Mother's milksop Son, and on the other some kind of horrific, militant changeling.

But tomorrow was tomorrow.

CHAPTER 8

Sarah awoke and it was Jamesday. She lay in the womb of bedding and felt like Molly Bloom. She daydreamed. Thought lovely dirty thoughts, planned what she might do, what they would do together. James. Darling. She caressed her lump, rolled it under her finger, but only for company, from old habit; that day she didn't believe in it. He liked girls in summer dresses; she laughed to remember him accidentally misquoting Hardy: "This is the weather the cuckoo loves and so do I. When maids go out sprig-muslin dressed, and so do I".

She'd wear a dress; hardly sprig muslin, but full of summer; light, like an advertisement for a bra. Five years older. She couldn't see the difference herself, but he was bound to, he was so damn noticing, so interested. The broken veins on her thighs; he couldn't miss those. Must on no account forget to do the hairs on her legs; he liked them smooth and silky. She'd wear stockings. But no pants? Stockings and no pants. That would amuse him. And the scent he'd liked. She rubbed her legs together in silky promise, lapped her breasts in her hands, rubbed her cheek against the silk binding of the blankets, back and forth, back and forth, sensuous as a warm cat. But God, she must get up. Caroline would be in a hell of a state after poteen, sick as a dog, and those kids demanding attention.

Only then did Sarah realise that she was alone in her great bed, that Una should have been there too. Oh well. Una was probably coping; she even seemed to like that Patrick. No, no, she must get up, this would not do. God, Una was going to Belfast, leaving her house to Sarah and James. But honestly, that nun's cell of hers; you couldn't. It would have to be the sitting-room floor. A bed would be so nice; but not that one, never. But she'd really better get up, keep Una sweet. Lord, Una'd have a bus to catch to the city. It was doubtless about to leave and Una'd miss it, feeding that worthless baby. Then her house wouldn't be empty any longer.

Dressing gown. Slippers. She'd go down as she was. Una was going to miss no buses, not today, not even if Sarah had to give Patrick his porridge herself. Hell, what a hangover. Never mind, life must go on, those kids have to be fed and Una has to catch that bus.

The morning ground itself on. Una caught her bus. Sarah and Caroline drank instant coffee and ate aspirins. Mrs. Savidge sang hymns and a song about her grandfather's orange sash. Bridget kept shop and Brendan teased her; Patrick was impossible. Caroline vomited the coffee and aspirins and Colum came home.

They had lunch.

Caroline, lying in her teeth, told Colum that James McNeil was coming down to interview Sarah about Welsh Nationalism. Una had very kindly said they could use her house for the discussion since there was no peace in Illnacullin, God knew there wasn't, with all the childer and everything and, sure, the man was a decent sort and they shouldn't waste his time, no more they should.

And Colum said, yes, he was an honest man and why didn't they have him to dinner sometime? But he didn't care for his literary style; why was there no longer any journalism like that of the early *Spectator* or *The Rambler*? There was no excuse for it. Style mattered as much as content. Didn't Sarah agree?

Sarah agreed.

Caroline reminded Colum of the letters he had to write and succeeded in shoehorning him into his workroom before it was time for James.

"Caroline, it's been too long; I'm petrified."

"I know. Here, have another gin. You'll be all right; live

up to your dress. You look like a half-warmed fish cake, honest, but the clothes are lovely. That dress is good for you and your hair looks clean and shining. Honest, you've nothing to worry about. If he gets as far as your broken veins he's there, isn't he? For God's sake, woman dear, here I am a good Catholic, aiding and abetting your adultery, lying to my husband, encouraging you and that wee man to imperil your immortal souls and you thank me by loping around like a cat that's lost her kittens to a sack. Jesus, I hate waste. I'll not have my sins wasted, hear me?"

"Yes, Caroline, I know. And so grateful; but I'm still bloody scared."

"Listen, there's the bell. Now when he comes in here you are not to look like a frightened rabbit, or you'll answer to me for it. Smile, in the name of God, smile, damn you."

Mrs Savidge showed him into the room with little grace; she recognised him, knew him for an enemy and was surly, aggressive in her servitude.

But he was there in the doorway. His arms out to embrace them both; fatter, older, more of his hair gone. The same man, but the difference more than that one new gold tooth.

Caroline was all hostess. "Och, James, it's good to see you. It's been too long. You'll take a wee drink with me, sure you will? Isn't it great to have Sarah back?" The facile Irish charm, the easy artificial bridge. Sarah's heart was in her eyes, but he went through the motions, preserved the fiction, thanked Caroline for the offered drink. He held their hands, the two of them, the same, for each a hand, a mad veneer of politeness, although he knew that Caroline knew, that she knew he knew, oh God, this Irish stuff.

Are you, damn you, are you glad to see me? Does it matter, all this balls? Why don't you kiss me, look at me, at least? Press my hand, my hand, not hers and mine, not both together. Jesus, was it for this? I'm here, I've come, give me a little kiss, you bloody blundering fool.

"You're looking very well, Sarah. How's education?"

"Christ, who cares? Did you come all this way to the country to ask me stupid questions?"

"Och, James, Sarah's herself. Take no heed to her. Himself's away in his study with letters to write, but we were wondering if you wouldn't care to have dinner with us tomorrow, on the Twelfth Night. Sure, you wouldn't want to be in the city then, when everything's all over and done with and the processions finished. It'll be Sarah's last night here and sure, we thought you'd like to come."

"Thanks. Yes, please. Unless hell breaks loose in Belfast, I'll be here."

He hadn't yet looked at her, not looked at her to meet her eyes. Why in the name of God did Caroline not just go, go away, leave them? Then Sarah saw their dilemma, saw them tied, fettered by Irish conventionality; she was damned if she'd be crucified on that worm-eaten cross. Hell, she had her rights.

"Right, then; now that the civilities are all performed, the decencies preserved, shall we go, James? That is, of course, if you still wish to talk to me alone. If you've changed your mind, of course, that's fine. We'll just stay on here with Caroline; Colum will finish his letters and Patrick will wake up and a jolly time will be had by all."

"Oh God, James, take her away; she read the riot act to me last night. I can't take it again, not twice."

He held his hand out to her, only to her. "Come along then, Sarah, if you insist. We'd better humour her, Caroline don't you think?"

"Aye, keep her sweet. It's me has to live with her."

Irritated and edgy under their heavy, affectionate teasing, Sarah walked to the door on her own and left them to founder through the politeness.

He caught up with her in the drive, short-winded, incommoded.

"James, I hate it when you do your Irish turn."

"No you don't; it's why you love me. You do love me, remember? Darling, aren't you going to kiss me?"

"Why didn't you kiss me in the house, simply and easily, when we met?"

"God knows. I was embarrassed. Have a heart. Don't sulk, Sarah, we have so little time. Don't waste it, please don't waste it. Give me your hand. Where are we going, anyway?"

"To Caroline's sister's house; she's out. We won't be disturbed."

"Let me look at you; what have the five years done to you? Nothing. No traces. You'll be thirty-nine now, isn't that right? And what have you done with yourself? Have you been happy?"

"Well, not unhappy, anyway. The job's been interesting and I've had a few things published in the education journals —" She talked of British politics and Welsh nationalism, student unrest, the obvious topics. Be gay, match your dress, Caroline had warned her, but she was too tense to let go, to venture off the safe shore of calm discussion; the measured sentences were safe. The lump of disappointment in her diaphragm was unyielding; it lay there like a piece of yesterday's chocolate cake.

Why did he have to be politely interested, why didn't he stop her, help her, shut her up? Did she sense some shame in him, was he armed, forced? His charm for her had been his ease, the sureness of his touch with people, a brisk honesty in personal relationships, an openness that demolished the thickets of shynesses, embarrassments.

They passed through the grove of gorse, but they were talking politics, discussing ministerial changes. A bleakness overwhelmed her when she remembered all she'd thought about the gorse, all that its gold had promised her. At the steps to Una's house she paused, with one foot on the bottom step. She looked down at him, a fat man, ageing, that one gold tooth a trifle vulgar; sunburn on his bald patch.

"What is it, James? Are you sorry I came?"

"Jesus, no! It isn't you. I'm sorry; I'm a bit distracted, I suppose. I have this feeling that I'm watched. You know the extremists have threatened to have my life? The peelers guard my house. God, how often have I called this a police state, and now I have to see them pass up and down behind my hedge; I keep seeing the hard hat like a bloody pendulum go up and down, up and down. My study looks that way. It's got like Chinese torture, honestly. Come on, don't just stand there looking lovely. Move, girl, move."

"I've never seen your house."

"D'you mind?"

"Yes."

"It's a semi and I mow the lawn and take a pride in my herbaceous border."

"Shut up. You'll find the key under that smirking cherub there. See it?"

"Lord, this place was made for assignations."

"Oh, I'm sure it was, though it's officially called a shooting lodge. But it's utterly feminine, isn't it? But I must tell you, there's a queer feel to the house, it's sad; old heartbreakings, discarded mistresses. I should hate to be alone in it; one would expect to hear the throaty gigglings of perverts and the cries of strangled babes, you know? It's a cold house, always cold, and a smell of damp. But please try not to mind, will you?"

They stood in the little porch. He fumbled with the key, but she pulled him toward her, hungrily found his mouth and probed it, pressing herself against him, in her pretty, silky dress. She slipped her thigh between his thighs, moved against him, and in his arms she said, "There are some holy objects, too, ghastly ones that might even make you impotent. Don't look at them, please don't look at them."

"Oh Christ; darling, Christ. Where the hell's the key? I've dropped it."

In the little parlour the roses were dead on the table and the closed doors had strengthened the ancient smells. Sarah found the bottle of Montrachet that Caroline had provided from Colum's cellar, got glasses, and left him to open the bottle while she threw away the roses, poured the water down the sink. "There," she said to the slimy water, "that's you. Now no more fooling."

He was standing before the inhibitory sampler when she came back. "Jesus, Sarah, did your friend hang this specially for you? She's got it in the wrong place; it's meant for the foot of a good Catholic bed."

"It's in the right place for today, my boy – at the foot of where our bed's to be. We couldn't possibly desecrate her bedroom. It's a cell; we'd be a blasphemy. We'll have to make do with this floor; at least there are plenty of cushions, thank God."

"Not in front of all those saints?"

"I'll turn their faces to the wall."

"You'd like a drink?"

"Of course." She dealt with the saints while he poured her drink and then he knelt to help her lay the cushions on the floor. "I'll drink it here," she said, "looking languorous."

He handed her the glass but then retreated to the love seat at the window. He looked away from her and at the view, the encompassing trees and heavy shrubs. The silence tightened, an overwound mainspring.

"Tell me about her, the girl of this house. Why does she live here on her own?"

"Perhaps to punish herself. She's a strange one, too involved for me. She wanted to be a nun, but felt unworthy; then she married and now she's left her husband. Never had the children she obviously needs. She's permanently intense, like a caged cat, but she's a good sort; after all, she did lend us her house. And she's killing herself over civil rights. She'll probably feel she has to fumigate this room after us. But she's nice, she's good. But she's also impossible. Why are we talking about her? I want to talk about us."

He turned toward her then, his face distressed, discomfited, a guilty frightened look like a mast on his warm, remembered face. "Take down your hair, my darling, loosen it and let it rip. I think I always liked your hair the most, old monkey face."

"There, my crowning glory, as they say. It's good, this Montrachet, old Caroline's blessing on our union."

"What brought you back, Sarah? Why now, after so long?"

She sat up then and hugged her knees, as though to keep the cold away. "Your politics were in the news, I wanted to see it all again. Did I go wrong? Cambridge is so inhuman, James; it's civilised itself unto death. So claustrophobic, I can't tell you. I was due some leave and I just had to get away to somewhere where there was a real, honest welcome for me, interest in me, *qua* me. There's been so much kindly indifference. I'd thought of you as part of my welcome. Sorry to have been an imposition. Drink up your wine; I won't delay you any longer."

"Oh, darling, please. Shut up, stop talking balls. Don't go cold and hurt on me. I'm in poor form, Sarah. It's like this: I—" He came then and lay down beside her on the floor; almost brutally he put his hand on her crotch, and his head on her full breasts. "Sweetheart, it's – oh God, it's just that I'm in poor form, you understand? I want you, God knows how I want you, but nothing happens. The truth is, I've nothing on me but a bloody earthworm, and I used to boast I had a two-pound trout, remember? Sarah, I'm heartsore. It isn't you; you ought to know that, God knows you ought."

"Stop then; don't rouse me any more."

"I want to. No, please let me. Take off your clothes, maybe you'll work a miracle. Let me caress you, darling, please. You've not changed a bit; your belly's still as flat, your thighs as fat. You've got this little patch of purple veins, though, haven't you? Thank God for one small sign of age. But oh, your breasts, so lovely; these two beauty spots here, how could I have forgotten these? Christ, why do I have to be like this? Help me, Sarah. Please help me, Sarah, darling, Sarah, please."

No miracle took place.

"Be still now. Talk to me. Tell me about your job, fill me in, horse's mouth stuff."

"Och, there's been so much. I'm sickened, emptied. Only God knows how it'll go on. And there's the Twelfth Day coming up tomorrow. The Orange Order is busy today, looking out the texts to preach its hatred and defiance. If only someone had the nerve to ban the Orange Order there might be some hope, but the Order has the government by the short hairs. It's the Order rules this province, Sarah, indoctrinates the innocent, the unimaginative, the lazy, keeps them blink-ered and believing. How do you discharge the poison nur-tured for fifty years among the innocently credulous? My people aren't evil; they only believe what they are taught."

"Tell me about Burntollet Bridge. Caroline said you'd written a brilliant piece about it."

"Did she so? That's kind. I wasn't on the march, of course, it was a student demonstration, but I waited for them in Derry. They were expected in the city at about one o'clock. A grey, drizzling afternoon. I was in and out of the City Hotel; it's the big one sits beside the sham-Gothic Guildhall, facing Derry's Walls. You know the symbolism of Derry's Walls?"

"Withstood the Catholic siege; apprentice boys and things. Maiden City, right?"

"They call it Maiden City now because only young girls can find work there. The crowd gathered slowly outside the Guildhall, a bit wary, remembering the other time, and yet determined, too. There was a lorry parked under the clock; a platform. We journalists were in the bar; photographers, the television people, and the civil rights officials with red-and-white armbands, nervous, biting their nails.

"People kept flurrying in and out, telling us how far the march had come, how near they were to Derry; we were a bit casual, measuring the time in drinks, you know?"

"Yes."

"Then the news of an attack came. A few miles out. A buzz of rumours. 'There's been murder done.' 'They have them thrown into the river.' 'The police is doing nothing, not a thing, just watching.' 'The Specials are on the students, half killin' them.' Meanwhile the crowd was gathering and gathering. And silent. Then the drizzled changed, a downpour, and suddenly the shouts and cheers and the clapping. It was about half-two by then."

"Where were you now?"

"At the front door of the hotel, watching them come in; singing 'We shall overcome,' of course."

"Caroline's sister was there. She had four stitches."

"You've heard it all then?"

"No, she hardly ever tells you anything. She speechifies."

"They came in two and threes; kids of eighteen and nineteen, mostly. In jeans, you know the gear. They were soaked with rain anyway, but some of them were dripping, drenched from having been thrown into the river. You never saw such weariness; days of harassment and then the ambush."

"Jesus."

"There were speeches of welcome and they stood drooping in the rain. About a dozen of the youngsters jumped into the parked lorry and stood there, soaked, their hair plastered, with their clenched fists raised. Others limped into the foyer of the hotel. St John's Ambulance men bandaged their heads and feet. They were only kids, Sarah."

"And what did you do?"

"I bought them drinks, brandies. And I talked to three of them, two fellows and a girl. One of the boys broke down, cried like a child. But the girl was just silent, silent for a long time. Shock, I suppose."

"Yes, Una talked of the shock, she didn't feel the pain of her blow for shock."

"They began to speak slowly, tired to death; they talked of a trap, engineered, they claimed, by the police; of being chased and beaten; they'd heard rumours of girls being raped, of someone drowned. But no police then. No protection. The boy who cried kept repeating 'Animals, animals, animals.'"

"And all in the name of the Protestant God."

"No, in the name of the Protestant supremacy. They slumped, with glazed eyes, in the chairs. And in the dining room the tables were all set and gay for their reception. I felt sick, Sarah, sick. I pushed through the crowd, found my car and left."

"Sure, Ireland is the saddest country ever that was seen,'" Sarah sang to him and curled his few last sad black hairs around her fingers. "Cheer up, please, James; at least you've tried to be honest, tried to mind." And together they went on singing "The Wearing of the Green," rather out of tune.

"Let's finish this bottle before we get too depressed, shall we?"

"You do have other men, don't you, darling? You're not lonely?"

"No. There have been others. Of course there have, but don't let's talk about that. Go on about the situation, just a bit. The Moores are really thinking in terms of civil war in Ulster. They must be exaggerating, surely?"

"Christ, I only wish they were. But this province is an arsenal. If I could only print one-half of what I know, my darling; I just can't tell you. The guns are everywhere. Well, first you have to realise that out in the country parts most of the men have guns; rifles for shooting rabbits and pigeons, things to eat; it's a very poor country and a shotgun is a worthwhile capital investment."

"Yes, I know about that one. Caroline has this incredible cleaning woman; bigoted as they come, I promise you, but she was telling me about the conditions of her husband's employment. It's quite, but quite feudal. He lives in a tied cottage, is not permitted to join a trade union, has a token amount deducted from his wages in return for the privilege of picking up his firewood on the estate, thereby doing a job of tidying up. And he's allowed to shoot any bird that flies along the shore, as well as any vermin; cats rate as vermin, so do badgers. Isn't it utterly wonderful? But old Mrs Savidge never sees the iniquity of it; for her, it's all privilege, kudos. Do the social scientists ever think to measure working-class kudos' values? Ever work out the more than financial value of working in, being part of, the household of a woman of title, the vicarious dignity, the small snobberies? Most important. Those stupid psephologists ought to consider it, don't you think, sweetie?"

"Darling, you can't even say psephologists. You're just a wee bit sloshed, aren't you? Our thing always was a bit like that, armoured with drink before we met, artificed with alcohol; you on holiday and me snatching at a drunken inter-lude."

"Shut up. How cruel can you get, you beast? No, tell me more about the guns; I interrupted you. Actually, I *am* a little sloshed, I must confess; I had some gin at Caroline's. I was scared of you, my friend, my very dear friend; so much for friendship. Go on about the guns."

"Och, Sarah, you can be bloody hard; all right, about the guns. Don't you dare quote me, will you, you talkative bitch? But, as you know, I've written enough against this Unionist government to have a kind of standing with the other sort, in spite of being, officially, a Protestant. I think I've earned a kind of respect from the Catholics; in their eyes I dare to think that I'm more than just a white liberal. And I love that. I really love it. I'm sorry if that shocks you, Sarah, but it builds me up; I couldn't do without it. I'm frightened and I'm weak and I'd often like to back out, but I have this lovely feeling, this precious burden of their trust. I feel they honour me. And who else does? You bitch, you'll think I'm taking the easy way out, but they make me; make me what I'd like to be. Does this make any sense? I'm so ridden with guilt and inadequacy, but their hopes make me keep hitting back like a punch-drunk boxer because they want to see me do it. And I love that; it's like having fans; it's food and drink in this aridity of Ulster. I've taken my line, my stance on the discriminated, and they depend on me to plead their cause. Can you begin to understand what I'm trying to say? I've never said any of it before, to anyone. This kind of crap needs distance, a bit of objectivity."

"Darling, darling, James, go on, you break my heart, but this is just the kind of talk I came for," Sarah mumbled as she kissed and kissed her way up his hairy forearm. "About the arsenals; go on, you never said."

"No, you distracted me, didn't you? Well, there's that initial thing about shotguns, common as lice in the countryside. You buy your licence at the ironmonger's shops; just like for a dog, you know?"

"No, but never mind. Never was a doggie person. Did you see Caroline's William Butler? Wolfhound, honestly; quite unbelievable. But very smart, madly grand, wouldn't you say? Too big for Cardiff though."

"You are sloshed, you whore; shall I go on?"

"Mmm – tell me about those lovely guns." She sat up, threw aside the long, failed richness of her heavy hair. "No, I'm not really sloshed. I'm listening; truly I'm listening."

"Well, as I said, this province is little better than an arsenal. It's said that the IRA are running guns through the South of Ireland; with government connivance, so I'm told. But I don't give too much credence to that one. What I do know is that the Southern Government refused to give the civil righters a few score gas masks to combat the CS gas, despite all sorts of arrangements to make it look like theft; the odd lorry parked and left accidentally unlocked – all that, the obvious cover. But they wouldn't play. Hell, it stands to reason, girl, the Eire government wouldn't take on Ulster, not for all the bombs in Belfast. Who would? But, and this is the frightening thing, if what I hear is true, the Protestant militants are running guns from Czechoslovakia. They come via the Congo, come by the boatloads to the small ports where smuggling's always been a way of life. Old-fashioned stuff, but nonetheless lethal. I've actually seen some of those Czech guns, Sarah."

"But, darling, you're the enemy. Why should they show *you* their guns? Are you being conned, led by the nose?"

"The Protestants didn't show me them, you nit. You really are incredibly politically naïve, you know that? No, look, some of the Protestants were rashly recruited during the last bit of fun-and-games, guns were rather wildly distributed during the panics and some of those pressed to serve were bad boyos. They've been quietly selling their guns since peace broke out, selling to the Catholics, for drinking money. God, you'll never understand Ulster; what's the good of talking? You don't have the vocabulary."

"Och, sure," Sarah said, doing a bad imitation of Caroline, "you'd not be after telling me that the good right-footers sell guns to the other sort? How's that for vocabulary, then?"

"Vocabulary's so much more than language, isn't it? Know what I mean?"

"Of course, but for God's sake, go on; talking to you is like pulling teeth. I promise you. How did you come to see the guns?"

"Well, during the first riots and the resultant panics, as I told you, recruitment went berserk. Almost anyone who didn't cross himself could become an auxiliary and was given a gun; but when the enthusiasm died down, the guns were an embarrassment to some of them. Some came to their senses and handed the guns in, but others traded them in for drink, and they've been passing them in to cover debts at the betting shops, or selling them to respectable Catholics who want to protect their wives and families; want to defend their homes, because, as even you must realise, no insurance premiums cover you from loss through riot and civil disobedience."

"God, no, that never struck me. All Colum's glass."

"You must realise that most of Ulster's pubs and the betting shops are either owned or managed by Catholics; it's the tradition. When the guns were dished out wasn't exactly a time when exact records were kept, and if the boyos are asked to account for their guns they say they've lost them, or been robbed of them, or lost them in a fight. Then there's this whisper that, after Burntollet, the B Specials may be disarmed; by definition and by function, they are all Protestants, and at Burntollet they showed their prejudiced hands rather too obviously. In their arrogant self-righteousness they forgot humble people like me and they forgot television, all that; they're no longer *persona grata* within the government – not officially, at least. But they have an armoury, Sarah, they're far better equipped than England was in 1939, and if they are made to hand in their weapons, they'd hardly be naïve enough to give them all up. If rumour is to be believed, most of them have two or three guns, not only the statutory one; and they will obviously find homes for the extra ones before they are officially disarmed. D'you know, I was offered a submachine gun and one hundred rounds last week on the black market. Offered it by a Protestant who thought I needed protection. 'Sure, Mr. McNeil,' he said, 'who'd deny youse a gun, and you threatened?'" He got up and paced the little parlour.

"Tell me it isn't true, James. I'm frightened for you."

"I only wish I could. I'll tell you something else, something I have to write about. I was in a pub the other day, in Belfast, sitting in the kitchen after hours, and a bloke came in with an old tommy gun, the kind that goes off if you sneeze. It was all taken down and sorted into bits up the front of his mackintosh. Since he saw me in the kitchen, he accepted me as the right sort and offered the gun for sale. He claimed to have bought it off an alcoholic who'd been given it during a riot by one of the B Specials. Think of it, Sarah, an alcoholic; can't you see him, drunken and mumbling and muttering and hating?" He went to stand at the window, looked out at the tangled shrubbery with blind, unhappy eyes. "God, think of the quivering hands, the unfocussed eyes, the uneasy bravado. Can't you see him? He mutters and he turns inexplicably, and he shoots; just shoots, anywhere. Wild, mad, who cares? Christ, Sarah; think, girl."

"Can't bear to. Give me a fag, fast, please. Listen, sweetie, all these guns and threats. Do you really know what you're doing? I mean, they might actually try to shoot you. I'd thought the threats were simply another Irish nonsense. Now I think I'm scared. They wouldn't really, would they? God, is that bottle quite empty?" He upended the bottle into her glass, a mere inch, and he sat again on the floor beside her.

"Tell you the truth, Sarah, most of the time I'm scared rigid, especially after an anonymous voice breathing at me down the telephone. But I go on writing from a kind of perversity; I refuse to be downed by the like of them. But I wish I could leave this place; get a job on some quiet, provincial English paper and feel safe, just safe. I'd like to drop the martyr role — I'm getting old, as you well know, my love — I'd like a chance to rest. I feel my 'struggle naught availeth'; things can only get worse here now." He picked up her left hand, with its old-fashioned coral nail polish and twisted her wedding ring round and round her finger. "Will you ever marry again, d'you think?"

She held him then, and rocked him, kissed him where his hair had gone. "Marry again? Who knows? I've had me offers, I'd have you know!"

"I should hate you to, but maybe you ought. I've never been any good to you, have I? Christ, how I wanted a child from you. I dreamed of it; I'm fond of kids."

"Did you, truly? You never gave me that bit of confidence before."

"But you knew?"

"No, but it's nice to have it to remember."

"No, don't cry. Please. It's not your line."

"No, it isn't, is it? O.K. No more tears. Come on, help me get dressed." She reached behind her for her bra, fitted her breasts into it and turning her back on him said, "Hook me, will you?"

He slid his hands under the cups of the brassiere. "Just let me hold the handfuls one more time." He knelt behind her, weighing her breasts, like pounds of sugar, bouncing them lightly on his palms, his brow pressed against her back.

She spoke before she thought. "D'you feel anything in the left one? See, there. A little lump? That's really why I came. It may be malignant. They may have to hack it off. I wanted you to remember me, to comfort me. Next week I may be nothing but remedial corsetry and scar tissue."

"No, Sarah, no. Look at me. It's true? Such a little lump?"

She nodded and her eyes swam in the waiting tears. "I'd wanted your courage to see me through. Wanted to be a woman, to be loved perhaps for the last time. I never meant to tell you, honest I didn't. I didn't want your pity. I've been so bloody good, haven't I? Why am I such a fool? Lend me your hankie, please. It may be nothing anyway. But sometimes I get scared; James, I had to say good-bye."

"Och, my sweetheart, my darling, no, lie down again. Ah, let me comfort you; no, you'll be all right, you'll see; it's such a little lump, my love, my darling. No, no, don't cry now, come on, you know I like my women gay, don't cry my sweet—" and out of sorrow, out of sympathy, out of a shared despair, somehow it came right for him and he could love her in her tears. A bursting of great dams in sorrow and in hopelessness.

When it was over and Sarah was still removed into a state of grace, of comfort, a small sense of achievement, of desire soothed, of solace, she felt James begin to heave with laughter. He left her, sat up to look down at her, his face alight, renewed.

"You did it, you old Welsh witch, you did it. God bless you, Sarah Thomas. I'll tell you something funny, Sarah. You'll grant that I'm a liberal, I hope, and never give a damn for race and all that crap? But I've always hated the Welsh; met such bastards. And yet I have to go for you; it's you performs the miracle. Mad, isn't it?"

"So I'm only a libation to your liberal conscience, then?" she said, her lips still bruised, her body languorous and long.

"Who cares? Who cares? Och, Sarah, love."

CHAPTER 9

Sarah came shyly back to Illnacullin, on her own. James had gone in his car, wisely parked at the bottom of the rutted drive, out of regard for his tyres. Colum saw her trailing up the drive and came to meet her.

"Hello, Sarah. Was it a pleasant afternoon? Lift up your face; yes, you look well. 'The lineaments of gratified desire.'"

"You knew?"

"Of course."

"And you didn't object?"

"It's a matter of conscience. It's your own, not mine. But we'll not discuss it with Caroline, shall we? She likes to preserve the fiction of my total unawareness."

"Blake was speaking of whores. I'm sorry to make you harbour a whore."

"No, no, he talked of wives, my dear. 'I would not enter in my list of friends, though graced with polished manners and fine sense, yet wanting sensibility—' No, be at ease, young Sarah; Caroline has told me something of your trouble. I understand and sympathise."

"Thank you, Colum. 'A cruel coming we had of it'. No bed of roses."

"I'm sorry. But the man has my respect. He seems a worthwhile fellow."

"And mine. He's so very nice, you know?" Then the children came, bursting in upon them, fracturing.

After their evening meal Sarah promised that they "should fold their legs and have their talk out," and Colum took her up. He poured her brandy and handed the glass to her with his little, formal bow. "She who aspires to be a heroine must drink brandy."

"Alas no heroine, but thank you for your sensibilities."

"No, Sarah, none, but I keep on trying. Shall we say 'the triumph of hope over experience'?"

Caroline ruptured their affectations like the harsh blustering of the north. "You know what they're doing out there, don't youse?" She paced the room, wrapping her arms around herself and throwing her pregnant belly forward. "It's the eve of the Twelfth; they're putting matches to their bonefires. You sit there, swilling brandy and showing off, and the fires are going up outside. They're burning us in their hearts, you know that? It'd suit them fine to have a fat priest on top of the pile. Jesus, on nights like this I hate the Protestant bastards. I'll have them to dinner, wouldn't see them starve, but tonight they'd have my life; and I theirs."

"Don't excite yourself, Caroline. You see, Sarah, as the Doctor would have said, 'The Irish are a fair people, they never speak well of one another.' No, relax, darling, this is only a folk festival, it's not significant; as meaningless today as Guy Fawkes night is in England. Don't get upset by it."

"I'm not upset myself. I wouldn't please them."

"Why do you say bonefire, Caroline? Aren't they bonfires? A good blaze?"

"No, Sarah; bonefire is the truer pronunciation. 'Bone fires' – *ignis ossium*. There is still a kind of basic honesty in our Irish vocabulary; we reject the more euphemistic 'bonfire'. Take the phrase 'to be married,' for example. We say married on, not married to; so physically exact, if you see what I mean."

"Don't change the subject, Colum. I want her to see a bonefire. She's been on about the violence and the politics; she ought to see a bit of it her own self. I've been cramped in this house all day. I'd like fine to have a wee drive."

"Mrs Savidge is doubtless at a fire, and Una seems to have abandoned us. I trust that's not significant? Did she have any plans, Caroline?"

"For tonight? Och, no, the girl's not mad enough for that, pray God. Would you not stay, and let Sarah and me out? You wouldn't mind, sure you wouldn't? Sarah ought to see it, if she's to understand Ulster. Come, Sarah, I want out."

There was no gainsaying that "I want out." There was a finality about it that neither Colum nor Sarah, nor the Reverend Doctor himself, could have withstood. Sarah would have "liked fine" to sit and swill brandy and swap quotations, but she was Caroline's friend, originally, not his; there must be no suggestion of divided loyalties.

"I'd love to see a bonefire, if you're sure you're not too tired and Colum doesn't mind."

"We'll not be long. We'll just go up the hill to watch the town. Then, maybe, we'll call on Una to see if she is all right. And don't go literary on me. There's times it gets on my nerves, though I know it's nice for Colum to find anybody who realises he's quoting at all. Get a coat on youse; there's nothing colder than a far fire."

"Caroline, you'll let it remain a far fire, won't you? You'll not go near them, sure you'll not?"

"Think I'm daft, Colum?"

Caroline took the wheel of Sarah's Mini. Whether this was a comment on her driving or an expression of the tensions that clenched Caroline, Sarah couldn't tell. They said very little to each other in the car; Caroline had gone far away, turned primitive, atavistic, masochistic. They were off, in the twentieth century, to watch the burning of Catholic martyrs; it was as simple as that. She drove to the hill that Sarah had seen, with white statuary. The little car followed the Stations of the Cross, through the grass, in bottom gear. Then they had to abandon the car and walk the steep final part. The white marble Calvary crowned the hill, the Cross and the two kneeling Marys, calm, serene. Why, Sarah asked herself, are they always serene? Jesus, if it was a son of mine up there, would I look calm? Calm? Where were the ravaged faces, the despair, where was the mother? Christianity defeated her. Acceptance is so bloody wicked, for a start. But Caroline was a devout Catholic, in her own fashion; she knelt before the meaningless, cold marble and crossed herself while Sarah looked emptily on. And having done her prescribed duty, Caroline grabbed Sarah's arm and pulled her, without a word, to the other side of the Cross. "There they are, the bastards, look at them. D'you see the fire they have?"

Now Sarah could understand why those serene faces had been so plain to her, despite the gathering night. She'd seen them in the glow of the Protestant bonfire.

The fire was built on an open square, perhaps the market place, in that solid, planter town they'd raced through yesterday. The flames tore up the darkness, floodlighting the formal regimentation of eighteenth-century streets, the tall, thin houses and their fanlights, the War Memorial, the flags, the bunting.

"Now, did youse ever see the like of that for a bonfire?"

It was certainly the biggest bonfire Sarah had ever seen in life. There seemed to be whole trees in it and there must have been gallons of petrol. The smell of burning car tyres hit them, sickening and thick. A great crowd of people, silent to the two of them on the hill. But in the flame light you could imagine the laughter and the drunkenness and see the wildly leaping boys in the piling on of more and more fuel. They saw a middle-aged woman come dancing up to the fire, fat, in a wraparound pinafore, waving the British flag. She performed a little jig, threw her head back, shouted something and laughed, and they saw the silent hands that clapped. Sarah tried to tell herself that it was only a bonfire, only Guy Fawkes, a festival, a folk holiday, they weren't even aware of the symbolism. She mustn't let Caroline infect her. Then the wind changed and the flame light was on a house wall and there it was again, huge, in white letters: "No Pope Here. Remember 1690."

Sarah shivered at the far fire, thought of Saint Joan and witches and martyrs, remembered how any little burn will throb, a cigarette burn agonising. The flames swooped up as part of the fire structure collapsed and the wild boys rushed and threw on more; an armchair, tyres, branches that could have been gorse by the spit of sparks from them. The faces were distorted, medieval and hellish; blobs of white with black open mouths and eyeballs that caught the light, pits and caverns in white shapes that might be human faces. There was a roar in the air, the roar of a fire and a mob. "Caroline, I hate this. Let's get the hell out of it. You've made your point."

"Jesus, no, we can't leave yet. Look, woman, would you look at that? Jesus, Mary, Joseph and all the saints in heaven preserve us. Look; it's the civil rights – our Una. They're marching, marching tonight, through the like of that. They're asking for it. They'll have them killed."

A thin, straggling procession of placards moved toward the fire, an anonymous, thin, wavering line of white boards that came forward and grouped itself beside the fire. There was a moment when everything was still, the flames burned steady as candles, a brave, unforgettable moment, and then the rush, the attack. Placards on the flames and bodies flung down like toys. Caroline darted forward. Sarah tried to hold her, but she pushed her in the face. "Get away out of that, this is my fight," she screamed, her face like something out of Wagner, a mythological face. Sarah caught up with her only when Caroline ran into a barbed-wire fence. With eyes for nothing but the fighting, she hadn't seen the fence; it stopped her; she lost her headlong balance and fell.

"Caroline, if you go one step further, I'll tell Colum you drank poteen, I swear I will. You promised him you'd stay away from the fire, you know you did." In the crazy lights from the fire, Sarah could see Caroline's eyes ablaze with hate for her as she sat there, frustrated, on the grass. "You've probably sat in a cow pat as well; your suit will be ruined. Only God knows how that baby of yours has survived so long. It's obviously destined to be a great Republican hero, or a parish priest, the way God preserves it. Come on now, get up; you're coming home. No heroics, love; we're both too old and you have too many responsibilities. Move, now. If you knew how daft you look, breathing fire and slaughter on your fat bottom, you wouldn't keep it up. Honest, love, there's a time for everything and we've passed it."

"Hell roast you, Sarah. Aye, we'd best go home, and maybe I'll thank you tomorrow, but don't expect a civil word from me the night."

"Just so long as I get you home. A miscarriage will be more comfortable in bed than among cow pats." Caroline lurched up from the slippery grass, the heavy thighs clumsy in a tight skirt. Sarah gave her her hands and hauled at her and got her up and onto her feet. Sarah's back was turned to the bonfire and the fighting, but Caroline was looking down upon it, over Sarah's shoulder. They were much nearer now to the marketplace and the crowds, after Caroline's charge down the slope.

"Will you look now, Sarah? Christ the night, the peelers are out. Oh Jesus, will you not look at thon one with his baton. He's hitting them; there he goes again, would you look at him. For God's sake, he's putting the boot in. Our Una's down there, she's bound to be. Hail Mary, full of Grace, there goes a petrol bomb. Holy Mary, Mother of God, deliver us, keep her safe this night...."

Blind in the flash of the bomb, Sarah clung to a post in the barbed-wire fence; a strange remoteness took hold of her, she felt removed, as though she looked merely at some picture of battles long ago in an Italian gallery; the flash and the flames merely effective chiaroscuro. The bottle bomb had fallen on the open ground, was only a challenging gesture, a thrown down gauntlet; its flames licked along the market cobbles and little, silly figures hopped out of their way. Sarah saw a figure throw something like a sack or coat, and the bright new flames went out in billows of smoke. But, momentarily, for her none of it was true, it wasn't happening; any minute now some director would cry, "Cut." But no director did. The raised arms still came down, the puppet figures fell, the flames streaked up into the shrouds of smoke and shrill screaming came, like a descant, through the deep-throated mob roar. Another petrol bomb sang from the dark, bursting into the bonfire; a surge, a gush of flame ripped into the frenzied night. The donkey bray of a fire engine added its concerto to the boom of violence. And Una was down there; there could be little real doubt, it was her fight.

Caroline was on her knees in the grass, praying aloud, a character in a Greek chorus; and Sarah stood rigidly by, numbed and shivering in the July night. She turned to Caroline and gently helped her to her feet. "Come home, Caroline, come home; this isn't for you and me. Don't kill yourself." Caroline stared at Sarah as though she'd never seen her before, as though she was bewildered by this enforced retreat from prayer; perhaps she'd been halfway through an "Our Father"; Sarah didn't know, hadn't listened to the mumbled words. Caroline looked dazed, drugged, but she silently took Sarah's offered hand and led her back towards the Calvary. Christian and Hopeful turning their backs on the Valley of the Shadow of Death. They passed the Cross and the lonely, white figures, abandoning them to the fire glare, alone. They went on in silence, brooding, tired, sickened; their eyes, in the dark beyond the fire, half blind and carrying the images of flames whenever they closed them. They walked with heads down, watching their feet, making for the car, dispirited, deflated. The grassy track was winding and narrow, symbolic of any road to Calvary; Sarah led the way, her mind full of death and despair.

She turned a corner at the Seventh Stage of the Cross and a darker shadow than the trees fell on the path; a hand grasped her arm, a quivering, nervous hand. "*Duw Mawr*," she gasped, reverting in fright to her native tongue.

"*Clywch*," a small, hoarse voice whispered. "'*Chi yw'r Gymraes sy'n aros gerllaw Kilhornan*?'"

"*Wel ie, 'n enw'r dyn. Beth sy'*?" Our minds move faster than light. In a second Sarah had gone through an atavistic terror – that young voice asking her if she was the Welsh woman staying near Kilhornan, the voice of her noncon-formist conscience; she'd remembered Caroline's condition and the need not to cause her any more alarums; she'd regis-tered rational surprise at hearing Welsh spoken, there, in Ireland and had been deluged with sympathy by that quivering hand and the thin youth of the voice. He spoke again, in Welsh.

"Is it true that you're after me? Did you come here to catch me?"

"What are you talking about, boy? I don't know who you are, never heard a word about you, *bach*."

"Is that true? Honest? I'm nearly daunted; I've had about enough."

"Oh, come now, come you."

"Sarah?" Caroline said, catching up with her. "Sarah, are you all right?" The boy slipped away among the shadows of the trees. "Why would you be talking to yourself? It's been too big a shock for you. Och, I'm sorry."

"Don't be daft. I'm not talking to myself. I've met a com-patriot. *Dewch 'nol, bach, dewch 'nol. Ffrind i fi yw hon. Gwnaeff hi ddim niwed i'chi.*"

"What the hell's going on, Sarah? Are you seeing things?"

"Caroline, I'm in my right mind, and not talking to appari-tions. There's a Welsh boy hiding in the trees and he's scared of you."

"Scared of me, for God's sake? Come out of that and let's have a look at you, boy." He moved, then, into what little light there was and, still speaking Welsh, he said, "I've got no business talking to you but, God knows, I couldn't stand it any more, see? I heard your voice, and decided to give myself up to you. I'd rather you than the local cops, and you couldn't be worse than that place where I've been hiding—"

"Wait a minute, let me translate. Listen, Caroline, he says he couldn't stand whatever it was any more and he wants to give himself up to me. He believes I've come over here to catch him. He's obviously in trouble, but I'm damned sure I won't abandon him. You're with me, aren't you?"

"You don't have to ask. Do we know who he is? Were they talking about him at her ladyship's?"

"I think so. I'll just ask; it'll be easier in Welsh."

"No need to talk to me in Welsh; I can speak English as good as you can. I know who you mean by her ladyship all right."

"So you're the boy on the run? Now, are you political or criminal?"

"Political, of course. There's a question to ask a bloke. Driven on the run I am, after attacking the English colonisation of my country."

"Save it. This is hardly the time for a Welsh Nationalist harangue. But let's get the facts clear. I'm not after you in Northern Ireland; all I did was come for a little holiday. But look, we've got a car at the bottom of the hill; let's talk in there, shall we? Mrs. Moore and I have been a bit concerned about you. My friend knows the Vints."

"Oh, Mrs. Moore, is it? It was when they heard from Mrs. Vint that Mrs. Moore's friend from Wales had decided to come for a holiday, suddenly, after five years, that they began to suspect you. And when they saw you in the village afterwards, watching the house from the pub across the way, they decided you must be looking for me. They said you were using Mrs. Moore as a front, otherwise the coincidence was too much to swallow, see? They trusted Mrs. Moore all right, but with you following us in that lane and everything; why were you there, isn't it?"

"Well, that explains a lot. What damned little lunatics. I'm nothing but an accident. We wondered where you'd gone after abandoning your breakfast in the Big House."

"You made a mistake there, boy; you should have brazened it out. The old lady might have swallowed a hitch-hiker, but when you ran, she suspicioned you. Fair enough. This your first time?"

"And never no more. Never no bloody more, I'm telling you."

"Let's go to the car. We've all had a bellyful tonight. Mrs. Moore's sister is almost certain to be in that riot down there in the town. It's frightful, incredible."

"I know; I was watching it, too. I'm sorry about your sister, Mrs. Moore. Civil rights, is she? I heard your voices while I was watching it and I was nearly going to hide again, only – well, I was afraid that's all, scared bloody rotten. Oh, there's cold I am, cold through. I've been in some place underground, where they left me. Could you put your heater on, please? Excuse me for asking."

"You weren't in the Creep, in the Lord's name?"

"Yes, that's what they called it. He said I had to stay there till it was safe for them to come back for me. And, indeed to God, I couldn't stand it any more. It was closing in on me, mun, and the dark all round and not a sound nowhere. I only had one box of matches, and I wasted those in the first hour, must have done, watching for nothing. What's fifty-two matches, isn't it? And I was expecting them back, see, any minute." The voice broke a little. "I was very frightened, no use pretending, but I'm scared of the bloke who put me down there too, listen. He had a kind of suspicion I wasn't too fond of the dark."

"That would be the one with the red beard?"

"Aye, that one. It wasn't my fault that old cow caught me, but he didn't half take it out on me. And now I don't know where to turn. They told us at home it was all organised. If you've got to run, they said, this is the route, and the boyos over there will look after you. And they went and put me down in a pit, like Joseph and his brethren, honest."

"Welsh Army, is it?"

"Never mind my affiliations. Tell you the truth, I blew up the phone box in our village. It wasn't working anyway; somebody had taken the tin opener to it. But the bobbies were coming down the road just when I'd lit the fuse and come out of the box. The sergeant said hello to me, mun. What's the sentence for a phone box? But see, what if the sergeant wanted to phone and he'd gone in there and it blew him up as well? I been worried sick, and he wouldn't bring me a paper. I don't know what's been going on."

"There's been nothing in the papers, nor on the television. It's all right, boy, he can't have been blown up, or we'd have heard. But I'll telephone a friend in Cardiff tonight and put your mind at rest. *Dewch ch'i, bach.* Not to worry."

"He told me you were in the Special Branch. Are you? But I'd rather give up than wait for that one down in the Black Hole of Calcutta. Not Queen's Evidence, mind, just bloody plain surrender."

"For the last time, I'm not out to catch you; that bloke's been leading you on."

"That was the Falls Road one that talked to me on the phone, was he, Sarah? And I thought he was a half-decent feller."

"That's what you think, missus. He's bad. I'm telling you. Look at him stealing that little girl's hat for kicks, and leaving that little boy who'd been fishing miles from home. You heard about that?"

"Of course we did; they're Mrs. Moore's children. You're getting disorientated."

"Why, Sarah, you never said a word to me, you sly wee bitch. And you knew all the time?"

"Only guessed. Where do you come from?" she asked the boy.

"From Cilhendre, in the Swansea valley."

"Small world; my granny was brought up in Cilhendre. I'm from Cardiff, but I live in Cambridge now. My name's Sarah Thomas, by the way; what's yours?"

"Mab Powell."

"Mab?" Caroline was incredulous. "Sure, that's nothing but a girl's name."

"No, Mab it is, short for Mabon. Mabon Vavasour Powell, at your service."

"His name ought to appeal to you, Caroline, Vavasour was such a great Puritan that he even quarrelled with Cromwell for being too liberal; that right, Mab? And Mabon was one of our early Welsh working-class heroes, who is said to have left eighty thousand pounds when he died. There's a socialist somewhere in your past, Mab."

"My grandfather. My mother wanted to call me Colin, but she was in bed, having me, and my father was working, so my grandfather went to register me; he was living with us. 'Colin', my mother said. 'Callin'; I never knew nobody with that name on him. Callin' who? No,' he said, 'I won't forget, Callin'.' And when he came home with the certificate, there I was, Mabon Vavasour. But he left me all the bit of money he had, fair play. I had a hundred and twenty-nine pounds when I was sixteen. Went to Israel on it. I think he'd have liked that, the old boy. Powell the Point they used to call him; always on his feet in the Labour meetings. 'Point of order, Mr. Chairman, point of order.' Fat old man he was; collier, of course."

"He wouldn't have had much patience with your politics,

good boy, but we won't start on that one. Look, we must decide on our general policy."

"Are you hungry at all?"

"Yes, I'm starving, on the quiet."

"Right; Sarah, we'll go to Una's. I couldn't go home till I know what's happened to her, in any case. We'll get him a bite there; that's the first thing."

"No, listen, though; what about him, the one who brought me here? He's been looking after me, fair play. He'll come back and he won't know what's happened. He's got a lot on his mind, and I've been enough of a nuisance to him already."

"Good. Let him steam for a bit. Let him hang around in the dark, wondering and biting his nails." Sarah switched on the headlights and began to move forward.

"He does bite his nails. How did you know?"

"You can tell by his teeth, good boy. You watch; those square, perfect teeth, sure sign. Tonight we let him stew. But you must have some way of getting in touch if things go wrong. What happens?"

"I've got no business telling you. How do I know you're not pumping me? But I've been feeling so friendless in this place, taking the blame for Mr. Vint dying and all. Bloody pariah I am, honest, with that misadventure verdict and everything."

"Misadventure nothing. The verdict was death by natural causes. We were at the wake; we know."

"Drop dead? Was it? That swine told me they were looking for me for that as well. He said they might book me for accessory. Right. I'll tell you. If anything went wrong, well, like the old cow coming when I was having my fried eggs, he'd be at that old tower place, that ruin thing about a mile and a half from the cow's place, the Big House. D'you know where I mean?"

"I know fine. So it was you was there, smoking and mucking up my wee girl's shop?"

"No, there isn't a shop there, just an old ruin it is."

"Mrs. Moore's little girl plays shop there; you probably didn't notice it. What time will he be there, if anything goes wrong?"

"Twelve o'clock in the morning. It wasn't me did it, honest, I don't smoke."

"And she's not an old cow, either; she's not half bad when you know her. It was she who gave the little girl that hat – she loved that hat. What did he do with it? Bridget would very much like to have it back."

"He's got it in the boot of his car. He was showing off about it, about the way he's keeping the Welsh bitch on her toes with it. I'm sorry, Mrs. Thomas."

"Oh, don't give me a thought. Bridget is the one; her hat was very special."

"You don't think, do you? You blow up a symbol; harmless you think, empty; and maybe a sergeant's copped it; and then, all the way over here, a little kid's special hat."

"Aye, that's the way of it. I wish to God I knew what's happening in the town."

"You don't know for sure that Una was there."

"That one? A local demo and her not in it up to the neck? No, we'll get home and find her in jail, if she's not in the hospital. She's no sense, that one; never gives a thought."

"Where are we going, then? It would be nice to know where I'm being shunted to, sometimes."

"Whisht now, we're not for the barracks. Just to my sister's place. You've missed the turn, Sarah, reverse into the corner and turn left."

"How old are you, Mab? Still at school?"

"Sixteen and a half I am; just done my O levels."

"Does your mother know where you are?"

"No."

"She'll be wondering."

"Yes, I know, mun, I know. She'll be tangling her knickers there, but what can I do? I couldn't send her a dirty postcard; 'Enjoying fine. Wish you were here. Plenty of rain.'"

"We'll have to get in touch with her."

"God, could you? I'd be, well, I'd be awful grateful, like. But the police may be watching the post. I got no business dragging you into all this. I'm very sorry. If I hadn't been so cold and hungry, I'd have managed, somehow. I feel damn small, I'm telling you."

"We'll get a word to your mother, somehow. What to do with you is the problem, isn't it? Well, here we are. Would you like me to go up to the house first, Caroline? Just in case Una is there, perhaps entertaining someone who might not sympathise with our problem?"

"Aye, please; go you on ahead, and we'll just sit here."

In the headlights of the car Sarah found her way as far as the steps up to Una's little house, but it was quickly pitch-black night around her. She had to drop on all fours and feel her way along them. She died to run, to break from the threat of the deep trees, was terrified of hurt on the narrow, steep steps. She couldn't even see the bulk of the toy house. The steps were mossy, slimy under her hands. But, gradually, her eyes were adjusting to the darkness, she could see the shapes of trees in the starlight and, at last, the ridiculous, fairy silhouette of the house. There were no lights from its windows. No Una, then. She'd better find the key. But where was the cherub in this shadowed, alarming place? Somewhere to the left, at the top of the steps. She dared to stand on her feet again, shuffled, groping with her feet, afraid to fall, afraid. Oh, to hell with it, there were matches in her car; they could all come back together now; the coast was clear. But Una? God, where was she?

Sarah gave up her dignity and the cherub together. Walking upright demanded more courage than she possessed just then. She crawled again, to where she thought the steps began, but found only the feet of the Grecian lady with the pox. Like a melodramatic beggar, she fooled about on her knees, tapping her hand on the ground to find her way. She discovered the steps only when she least expected them and lost her balance, landing hard on her wrist on the second step down; the night was as black as molasses all about her and her mind was like a jumbled jigsaw; bits of Una and the riot, Mabon Vavasour, James, her Lump, and, dominating everything, the possible ghosts leering at her from the house.

When, eventually, she had suffered her way back to the car, she found Caroline and the boy discussing nationalism with an easy rapport; Caroline had him worked up and oratorical, egging him on, with sympathy and sedition.

"If I might interrupt for a minute; the place is in darkness. I almost broke my wrist up there, I'd have you know."

"She's not there, then? You'll know where she is? In that riot."

"Try not to worry, Caroline. She's not a child, she can look after herself. She'll soon be back, you'll see." Sarah didn't believe a word she said. "But shall we try to find the key together? I gave up."

"Och, I have a spare key in my bag."

With company and matches, the steps were easier, but Sarah burned her fingers and cursed more than she ought to have done in front of the boy. Caroline opened the door and put on the lights and they saw the boy properly for the first time. Short and thin and underdeveloped, with shoulder-length, carrot-red hair. His eyes were a dark, positive brown, though, and gave him an open-eyed, naïve look of unassuming honesty. He had an eager, expectant, terrier face, as if on the perpetual *qui vive*, on the ready-steady-go. He wore a burgundy-coloured sweater, of lovingly complicated patterns, very hand-knit; Sarah saw his mother in it. Not quite the colour she would have chosen for carrots,

herself. Blue jeans, of course, below the sweater, and
scuffed suede boots. He humped a haversack. His face was
pale, and dirty; he had the look of a child at the weary end
of a long day.

CHAPTER 10

Caroline took command. She showed the boy Una's sitting room and told him to light the fire there. Sarah asked for the telephone and for permission to call Cardiff, while Caroline went to the kitchen to prepare some food. Sarah had broods of cousins in Wales; they bestrode the political spectrum, from fascist cricketers, by way of Labour councillors, to Commie chess players. One of them, Geraint Rhys, was a Welsh Nationalist and Sarah was particularly fond of him, despite the fact that she had last seen him lugging a banner in a Nationalist procession, a banner much bedragoned and reading "God keep the Prince – Away from Wales." So active was he, so close was his ear to the ground, that he loped along the valleys looking like a horseshoe, in slack, flannel bags and a leather-patched jacket, smelling out converts and possible disciples, like a bloodhound on the scent. He might never lift his head to see what was actually going on, but he would have all the Nationalist facts, he'd know what his side was up to. Sarah had his telephone number in her diary. Please God he was at home.

He was.

"Hello, Geraint, this is Sarah. Sorry to ring so late. Were you in bed?"

"Hello, Sarah, how are you, then? No, I wasn't in bed; doing a bit of marking I was, sixth form essays. But I heard you'd gone to Ireland."

"I have. That's where I am."

"Not phoning all the way from there? This is going to cost you something, good girl. Anything wrong? Not in jail are you? Watch it, *bach*, remember the family name; they haven't caught any of us yet."

"No, not jail, but don't let's waste time, right?"

"O.K., love, O.K. Only thinking of your purse I was."

"Look, this is what I want to know." She spoke in Welsh. "Has Cilhendre been in the news lately, been in your kind of news, if you see what I mean?"

"Oh, yes. No, no news."

"Are you sure? Nothing's happened there as far as you know? Phone box all right?"

"What the hell's the matter, then?"

"Are you busy just now?"

"Only in the garden and painting the kitchen."

"Right. Do something for me. Go to Cilhendre first thing tomorrow; wait, hang on a minute. I'll have to get you some details. Don't go away. I won't be long."

"Do you have to be so bloody mysterious?"

"Yes, wait now." She called to Mab. "Mab, what's your address in Cilhendre? There's no news from there, by the way; nobody's dead, at least. This is a bloke we can trust, you needn't worry. Don't stand there looking dubious; I'm sending him to see your mother. 17 Railway Terrace? Right. Geraint, you still there?"

"Yes, and the pips have gone. It's going to cost a fortune."

"Shut up about the pips; this is serious. Now, will you go to Cilhendre tomorrow and find out certainly whether there's been any trouble there, you know what I mean? And go to 17 Railway Terrace and call on Mrs. Powell. Say a friend of yours happened to meet her son, Mabon, in Ireland and gave him a lift in her car. Are you with me?"

"Yes, yes; go on."

"Find an excuse to call – you want him to organise a local youth group of your party, anything, and you wondered whether he'd come home yet. Your friend had a great time with him, and he was in good form. Stress the form, be reassuring, right? Now, will you call me back tomorrow? About sixish, say? Here's the number. And reverse the charges; I don't want you clamming up because a few pips have gone. And I'll pay all your other expenses as well, don't worry."

"You still sound bloody mysterious."

"Never mind. You do what I've asked now, good boy; it's your quarrel, not mine at all."

"I know, that's what I don't get, knowing you."

"Christian duty, that's all. The victory of crass sentimentality over my political conscience. Ireland is warping my basic standards and has utterly destroyed my better judgement."

"Right. You can leave it all to old Mr. Rhys. I won't let you down."

"I know, love. And thanks, boyo, thanks. So long, then."

"So long, Sarah, *fach*, so long now."

Mab was on his hunkers, nursing the fire in the parlour. "Well, we've begun to sort out the nonsense, my boy. My cousin will go to Cilhendre tomorrow, to see what the situation is, and he'll call on your mother. You heard my end of it, did you? It'll ease her mind a bit, at least."

"Thank you very much, Mrs. Thomas. You're very good to me. I'm very thankful, indeed to God I am. Wish I had better manners to say it right, but you know us in the valleys, scared of manners, in case somebody comes and calls us posh."

"God, yes, I know. But, Mab, don't kid yourself that I've got any sympathy for what you did. It's not the answer, boy, not the answer. I think your lot are nothing but a bunch of fascists, if you want to know. The constitutional ones, like my cousin, I can understand; they want devolution. Nothing wrong with that, it may be justified, but I happen to think that all protest voting is wrong just now. There's little enough socialism in the world; and to go and wilfully attempt to destroy one of the few Labour governments that function efficiently strikes me as utter lunacy. Look at you; you've had a good education from the state; you could have gone on to university – and what are you? A finished little fascist."

"You've been good to me, missus, but I won't let you call me a fascist, look here."

"So what else are you? Your lot, with your fancy uniforms and your piddling little bombs? Baby brothers of the IRA. And you've had enough experience of the IRA—"

"I never said it was the IRA—"

"Stealing hats and shoving you down that Creep; those are their standards. The hat off a little girl who was playing shop in the sun, in her garden. Damn it, don't talk to me."

"Don't start on him, Sarah, not till he's had a bite of food inside him. Come on Mab, get into this. Jesus, I wish to God that girl would come home, you know that?"

"Oh, thank you very much, Mrs. Moore. I'll pitch in, then. Never knew, really, what being hungry meant before this trip, not painfully hungry."

"And you stop calling him a fascist, Sarah Thomas. He's a patriot, that's what he is." Caroline's knees were dirty and stained with grass after her devotions; Sarah thought them pathetic and childlike, until she saw her own knees, equally green and dirty from crawling about on dark steps.

"Don't be so bloody old-fashioned, Caroline; nobody talks that crap any longer. Patriotism! Jesus, that's only the bait they use, to create anarchy. Out of anarchy something new will arise, they tell us. Something new. What a promise. Nazi Germany was something new, and so was Stalin. Patriotism, Caroline, 'is the last refuge of a scoundrel.'"

"Dr. Johnson," said a muffled voice, through bacon and scrambled eggs. "What did he know about the twentieth century?"

"More than you do, boyo. Telephone boxes; I ask you!"

"Well, they're a symbol, see?"

"Because the Post Office is a nationalised industry, I suppose?"

"Don't get at him, Sarah, you're hard. Sure, he's only a wee boy."

"He's old enough to have been playing about with dynamite and fuses and endangering human life. And he's almost old enough to be hanged for it in Ulster. You realise that, don't you, Mab? Capital punishment hasn't been abolished over here, under the Home Rule that you want desperately enough to blow things up for. Think of that for a bit, and I hope it gives you indigestion. I can't help thinking of your mother. You damn young, you never give the mothers a thought, do you?"

"No, fair play. I have been thinking about her."

"You should have thought long before you did it, shouldn't you?"

"Aye, you're right there, Sarah, yes, he should. I'll give you that, fair enough."

"What's your mother's age, Mabon Vavasour?"

"Mam's age? About forty, I think. Yes, forty she was last birthday. She's getting on; my daddy's forty-eight."

Caroline got up from her chair and drew a curtain, to peer out through the black window.

"And me? What's my age, Mab?"

"I wouldn't like to say, Mrs. Thomas; you got that eternal look. No, I couldn't guess, honest."

"I'm nearly as old as your mam, good boy. But I've had it easy. Would your mother look like me in trousers? Would she? That's what I mean by politics, if you can begin to see what I'm trying to say to you."

"My mother's got too much sense to wear trousers, Mrs. Thomas; she's fat and warm, like, and that's the way we want her. Well, like a bloke's mother ought to be, fair play."

"Of course you do. But what about her? Did you ever ask her if she was happy to be fat in her pinafore? The question never arose, did it? And it bloody well should have, see? It bloody well should have, damn you." Sarah lit herself a cigarette, her hands shook; she wished they'd left a little of the Montrachet that afternoon. Why was there never any decent drink in Una's house? God, she was tired. She had only come to Ireland for a bit of love, a mite of courage, a happy place to spend the suicidal time. It wasn't fair, this tangling, this involving. It was none of hers, none of it. She hadn't dreamed – She had already firmly turned her back on the simple seductions of Welsh Nationalism, regarding the movement as a temporary aberration in some of her compatriots, merely one gesture of protest among many others, a pronouncement rather than a conviction, a vague idea rather than a positive political platform. It had always bored her; provincial, she thought it, parish pump. As for the violent wing of the movement, repudiated as it was by the party itself, she had dismissed that as nothing more than the buzz of an angry mosquito, damned irritating but fundamentally harmless. Now, unwillingly, reluctantly, she was being sucked into a stupid commitment, into a quarrel as relevant to her political thinking as an African tribal dispute, and she felt bullied into taking sides with the wrong lot. But that wretchedly hungry boy was a fellow countryman, he spoke her language, was one of her own. Her sentimentality pushed her into a new awareness of the reality of factors that transcended her theoretic political attitudes. In the context of the boy's danger, there could be no questioning of general principles, of moral problems; it was no longer a matter of choice. He obviously had to be helped and be damned, for now, to the rest of it. But, God, if only she could go to bed – alone, quite alone. The price she'd had to pay for comfort was becoming pretty steep.

The boy looked up from his plate. "That was lovely, thank you, Mrs. Moore. I didn't half need that, I'm telling you."

"Och, you're welcome, sure you are. But where the hell's my sister, tell me that."

They heard the cry of voices, the sounds of footsteps, a key in the lock.

"It'll be herself." Caroline leaped towards the front door and Mab was on his feet, holding his knife and fork, all the new colour wiped off his face. "What about me? There's nowhere to hide – there's somebody with her."

"Relax, just look natural, part of the furniture. We gave you a lift, found you were Welsh and I took you up. Take it easy; she's all right herself. Leave it to us."

They crowded into the little room, dishevelled, dirty and wounded, faces stupefied by blows and pain and anger and defeat. One man limped in, his hands clutching at his crotch, and eased himself slowly, slowly, onto the couch where Sarah sat; he sat sideways and groaned. An ugly young man; thin, fair, greasy hair; crossed, crowded teeth, not overly clean, and big pale blue eyes that had a kind of loose look, as though they were slack in their sockets; there was sweat on his face and his skin had the look of slightly tarnished silver.

"What happened?" Sarah murmured to him.

"Kicked in the crotch. Oh Christ! Will they have done for me forever?"

"No, no, it'll pass," she said. "It's hell, I know, but it won't last." As if she knew anything at all about it, but a bit of hope never did a scrap of harm. Then he lapsed into himself and she began to see the others. Una's hand was burned and she was bandaging it, her face now alight with anger. She looked like a competent witch, her long hair loose and rat-tailed. Caroline was holding forth furiously, now that her anxiety was eased; like hitting Brendan when he came home late from his fishing. She shouted abuse at them for the idiot risks they'd taken in baiting the Protestants at a bonfire, asking for martyrdom.

"Och, to hell, I'm away to make youse some coffee. There's nothing else fit to drink in this place, you know that, our Una?" Caroline edged her way towards the door, shouldering and shuffling past the battered victims.

"I've a bottle in my pocket," one of them said. "It's all I

had the money for. I might have used it on those bastards at the fire, only God held my hand. At least, He let me forget I had it." He struggled the bottle out of his donkey-coat pocket, and Sarah's parching heart leaped up. But she saw the label. Sweet South African Sherry. She counted heads. No. Sweet, South African and in short supply. She'd take the coward's way out and stick to coffee, offering affront neither to her principles nor her palate. But Caroline had paused hopefully, her hand on the doorknob.

Una latched onto the bottle. "Get some glasses from the cupboard, Sarah," she threw out. "You know where they are, I think?" all *double entendre* and mean."To hell with those bloody Republicans." She hefted the bottle and swung it viciously in the air. "We ought to have known that they'd show up. Your friend was there, Sarah; red beard you said, didn't you, and devastating looks? There can't be two like that in County Down just now. The Republican lot tagged on at the end of our march and your man's placard read 'United Ireland'. So bloody original. I think his was the first petrol bomb."

"What happened in the end?"

"No deaths and no arrests. On either side. No martyrs."

"What's this you said about the Republicans, young Una? It was the Prods and peelers clobbered youse, not the Republicans." Caroline had taken a few paces back into the parlour, and her blue eyes were hard for battle.

"They gave those others their excuse; they played into their hands, and they knew it."

"Rubbish, Una," Sarah snapped. "Don't prevaricate. No one needed an excuse. You were attacked by a working-class mob; misguided, ignorant and ill informed, I grant you, but it proved the sheer nonsense of your starry-eyed myth of working-class solidarity. And be honest, wasn't it utterly provocative to invade the bonfire celebrations? You were literally asking for it, weren't you?"

"O.K., O.K. So what? We had to keep the kettle boiling. Don't you start pontificating; you don't know the local situation." Una was arrogant, and dismissing; manic, shot in the arm.

"If I might be permitted to say a word," said a short, middle-aged man with a humped back and penetrating black eyes, whose left cheek was a pulp of abrasions and dried blood. "We needed to have this march, Mrs. Thomas; it was psychologically necessary. The truth is that since the elections things have gone a wee bit flattish in the Cause." He spoke slowly, in that grudging Ulster Protestant voice that gives nothing for nothing. "You will doubtless be aware that we are all members of the People's Democracy, which is not a party in any sense, it is neither sectarian nor political; indeed, if you would care to look closely at Irish political history, you would, I am persuaded, find that the notion of political organisation is foreign to this people. We do not form parties in the British pattern; government is carried on by the elite of the opposing factions, while the rank and file are mere supporters' clubs." He took a long, slow sip at his sherry glass, put it down and looked at it severely before he continued.

"It was time we rallied our supporters. Bread and circuses, Mrs. Thomas, bread and circuses. If I might impose upon your patience for one more minute, I should like to add that the People's Democracy is fundamentally a student movement; of late the students were much involved in their examinations and by now, of course, they are, I trust, enjoying their well-earned vacations. The result has been a breakdown of what was a very informal organisation at best and we in this district were reluctant to see the enthusiasm for civil liberties flag. Therefore" — he took another, hesitant, doubting sip — "together with the local civil rights organisation, we decided, after careful consideration, to stage this protest march tonight. We asked for police permission to hold our demonstration and it was granted."

"Are you trying to cod me the peelers said you could march by the bonefires, our Una?"

"Eh, no, Mrs. Moore, I'll grant you that. They confined us to the Catholic areas, sure."

"But the open market belongs to neither Prod nor Papish," Una declared as she slopped the sherry around, "and our leader here is the Unitarian minister, for God's sake."

Then, at last, disgruntled by such arrant sophistry, Caroline banged her way to the kitchen, and the boy who'd brought the bottle said, "I wonder now would anyone have a fag to spare?" He had a nasty black eye coming up and his face was shapeless, awry, as though his centre of gravity had sifted upward toward the swollen eye and battered brow. "I hear tell there's a wee fellow on the run from the Welsh Army." He shivered. "Sooner him than me, the night." Sarah kept her eyes away from Mab, tucked away against the mantelpiece wall. No one had bothered about him; he was lost in the press, in the pains and the punishments.

They drank their sweet sherry and it put a little heart into them. Sarah forbore to comment on the source of their comfort. It was such a nasty little detail. The small thing that might finally have broken their spirits.

"Did you see thon woman who came up to me before we reached the fire?" Una asked. "She kept saying, 'Come on, come round the corner, meet me face to face without your gang, you wee bitch. I'll give youse the beating you deserve. Round the corner here without your gang, come on now, you wee coward.' Did you see her, walking beside me and shouting away, shouting away at me, and me not looking and holding up me banner and pretending she wasn't there?"

"She was mad, wasn't she?" said the hump-backed man. "She had this threadbare purple coat on her and a pink hat and her shoes were rotten, so they were. I took her in, to take my mind off; you ought to have looked at her, Una, middle-aged and shapeless, a meaningless lump. I saw her face close whenever we got to the light from the fire and she had these great blackheads and a thick coarse nose and her eyes were blank. She scared me, honest. Change of life I expect, the poor bitch."

Caroline came back with coffee and Sarah, that other poor bitch, distributed it while Caroline telephoned Colum, told him that Una had a few friends in and that Sarah was enjoying the crack; they might be late, why didn't he go to bed? Oh, yes, they were fine, fine.

She came back to the crush in the parlour and assessed them from the door. Eight punched-up men and a girl with a bandaged hand. And Mab.

"Jesus, Mary and Joseph, you ought to see yourselves, honest. We used to have a picture at home whenever I was a wean; *The Retreat from Moscow*; that's you lot. And what hell good has it done youse? Or Ireland? Drink your coffee."

"We made a gesture."

"Aye, and gave those ones out there something else for to celebrate. I watched your posters going up. Never thought to see you stoking a Protestant bonefire, our Una. You're wasting your time, you know that? No" — she held up an imperious hand — "don't start talking back at me; you're all too tired and too beat. And me, I'm the wife of a professor who knows the worth of a good job and I'm an Irish Catholic that knows the meaning of patriotism, so there's not one of youse qualified for to answer me. Whisht now, you'd best go home and lick your bruises. Una's for her bed." They recognised the voice of authority, constitutionalists that they were; they groaned to their feet and helped the kicked one up. His face still had a ghastly pallor, but Sarah thought he stood a little straighter and didn't now clutch convulsively at his genitals. She wondered whether he had ever seriously considered the priesthood; one never knew.

CHAPTER 11

When the men had gone, the women sat with Mab in the litter of cups and glasses and cigarette butts, under the forgiveness of the saints. Mab, as though to excuse his presence, began to tidy up; he put cups on a tray and recorked the empty bottle.

"Una, this is Mab Powell; he's from Wales—"

"From Wales? Not him? Not the one? Trust you two, honestly."

"Caroline and I found him wandering. I don't know how you feel toward him, after tonight's disaster, but I'll understand perfectly if you just turn him out. I appreciate that his affiliations are wrong."

"No need to be so damn formal about it, Sarah. I'll do what I can, obviously, for the wee boy. What's he done, anyway? This hand of mine hurts, you know that?"

"I blew up a phone box. But I'll go now; look, I don't want to trouble you. I'm nothing to you, and the lady can't be expected to help me now, fair play. But thank you all the same." Mab made his speech with a pathetic sincerity; he put down the tray he'd been holding, and picked up his haversack. "I'll be all right, I'll manage, honest. But you'll get in touch with my mam, won't you?"

Sarah couldn't say a word. He was perfectly right; he was nothing to the others and she had no business to speak. But as he passed her, his carroty head thrown back in a posture of bravery, Caroline got up and pulled him by the ear. "Good boy, Mab. That needed saying and I'm glad you did. But now we'll quit the heroics, and talk a bit of sense. Sit down now, and leave us peace for to think. Why you never have any drink in this house, Una, I'll never fathom. You know Sarah and me, we need lubricating. We can only think with our glasses."

"God, I'm tired. Can't we work this out tomorrow? He can sleep here tonight and we'll all see better in the clear daylight."

"No, I don't honestly think we should leave it, Una. Tomorrow we'll be inundated with young and Colum will wonder what's happening. This may be our last opportunity."

"Aye, she's right, Una, you know how she is."

"O.K., O.K. If someone would give me a fag it might help." She slipped out of her chair and sat on the floor, close to the fire. Sarah passed her a packet and Mab went down and lit a paper spill at the grate and held it for her. She smiled her thanks at him and he blushed and looked away.

"Right, then; now, young Mab, you put me in the picture. You blew the phone box and then you ran. How did you know where to run?"

"Well, our officer, see, he said, if we were in trouble, they'd see us right, over in Ireland. He gave us a few address-es to contact over here and we all had a five-pound note, in case, like. I hitched to Liverpool and caught the boat there and in the morning I found my way to this address I had in Belfast. Old-clothes shop it was, second-hand, like. Ladies' wardrobes bought and sold. Well, whatever, I went in and the smell in there was enough to drop you, honest. Shouldn't complain, I know, ought to be grateful, but I hate smells, don't you? Not so very ladylike, I said to myself; I was still sort of excited about it then, see; I could still make a little joke to myself, like. There was nobody there at the start and I was starting to wonder where to turn. Didn't like to knock the counter and shout, 'Shop,' isn't it? But after about ten minutes, mun, this old doll comes in from the back. Fat! Lord, about twenty stones of her, and her hair all bubble curls and thin. Big eyes on her and beads. I never saw so many beads. I gave her the word, quiet, and she said to come in, quick. I had to push through those old clothes she had hanging up everywhere, like curtains, and the smell, then!"

He was coming to life again, enjoying his audience, warming in their sympathy. Caroline was in tears, wiping her eyes on Sarah's headscarf; he was so small, so thin, with his red hair and that ever ready face.

"Look, I know she was risking a lot for me, jail maybe, but, tell the truth, I didn't fancy her. We went in this back room and you should have seen the clothes in there. Piles and bundles of them all over the place, all over the floor, on the gas stove, on top of the cupboards. Looked like an earthquake. She said I'd have to wait; she didn't have anybody to send on a message and her ladies would be calling. Only one proper chair was in the room, an old arm-chair, and she was sitting in that. I felt bloody daft there, standing; nowhere for me to sit, see. And I was dying to get off my feet. Couldn't sleep on the boat; Irishmen coming home for their holidays, singing and drinking and laughing, fair play. I felt a bit out of it, but I was afraid to talk too much. I got a bit of a Welsh accent, see, so I thought better not."

"Och, d'you hear him, Sarah? Got a bit of a Welsh accent, he said."

"Shut up, Caroline; I want to understand their organisa-tion. An old-clothes shop is good cover." Una's weariness was passing, her interest aroused. "What happened after that?"

"Well, I waited there, standing, for a long time and then I had to sit. I plonked myself on one of these bundles she had on the floor, fleas or not. I got used to the smell after a bit. The old bird herself was worse than the smell, in a way. She wouldn't talk, mun, not a word out of her. I tried to talk a few times, but she never answered. She sat there in this armchair, just looking at me, staring with her big old watery blue eyes. What's that word about a stare? Obelisk? No, something like that?"

"Basilisk."

"Aye, that's right, basilisk. Couldn't remember it. All I could think of was obsidian; that was right too, kind of dead and watchful at the same time."

"Go on about the shop. You sat on the bundle."

"Well, honest, I had to sit. They turned us out of the boat at half past seven and I'd been hanging about for two hours in the rain. Shops don't open till nine and nobody's rushing the gates for old clothes, on the dot. I was awful tired. And hungry! *Iesu Post*, I was bloody starving. They only had buns on the boat, second class, and the money a bit tight. Got to watch it, you never know. It was nearly dinnertime, must have been, before they came for me; that one, you know, the one with the beard, and another bloke. Awful bossy that beard was; just asked me the word and I gave it and he didn't have another word to throw at me, like I was one of the old doll's bundles, honest. They've got so much else on; I'm afraid I've been a bit of a nuisance to everybody."

"Och, cheer up, Mabon, we're enjoying the crack, sure we are."

"I don't want this to go no further, but you'll never guess where we went after. They told me to carry a big armful of the clothes to a van outside and we went on to a market, mun. They had a stall there and they were selling these clothes and bits of junk – you know, cracked jugs and odd cups and saucers and Victorian ornaments; one was a butter dish with 'A Present from Auchnacloy' done in green paint. I fancied that. And they had this lot of empty Chianti bottles, the kind with straw on them; they'd cleaned them out of some Italian restaurant and they were selling them for one and sixpence each, and people were buying them to make lamps. You wouldn't credit, would you? Anyway, they put me to sell the bottles on a corner of the stall. Open market, pouring rain and nowhere to *cwtch*."

"What's *cwtch*, Sarah, for God's sake?"

"A place to hide, a shelter. Did you sell any?"

"Well, yes, I was going great guns. They said the best place to hide was out in the open where nobody would think to look for me. I enjoyed that bit. 'Make lovely lamps, missus, only one and sixpence. We're giving them away. Come on now, where'd you get anything like this for one and six?' I sold thirty-nine for them. They gave me some tea and two meat pies for my dinner. Went down great, they did."

"Get any commission?"

"Commission? No. They were doing me a favour, seeing me right, fair play. The bloke with the beard wasn't in the market, of course, he's a bit too grand for that, but he came to fetch us with the van when the market closed and took us to the backyard of this other shop. A newsagent's it was. They gave me another cup of tea there and I sat in the back place by myself. That bloke, the beard, I won't tell you his name, he spoke to the chap behind the counter and gave the instructions. But he didn't tell me nothing, not a word, mun, only, 'Wait there till you're told to move.' Not the type I take to, myself. Deadpan type; bit old-fashioned in his line, I thought, to tell the truth. I think he got stuck in a groove, in one of those 1940s films. But anyway, mun, about six o'clock, the man from the shop comes out to me, 'Get away out of it now,' he said, 'and stand by that bus stop across the road. When you see a red Mini-Cooper coming up, in about five minutes — they've just been on the phone to say they're on the way — you thumb a lift, and when they stop, get in there fast. Hurry up, lad, don't keep thon feller waiting. He's the hard one. Good luck to youse, now, and safe home.' Decent bloke he was; those were the kindest words I'd had since I came. Can't blame them, mind, I'm a nuisance to them. It's a busy time for them in Ireland. Oh, I'm sorry; I've put my foot in it again, haven't I?"

"Never mind. It's not your fault that everything is all through-other over here. God knows."

"There was another chap in the car with us. He was all right. I liked him; he tried to talk to me a bit, but he was scared rotten of the boss cat, the beard. Who'd blame him? That one had me cringing in there in the back seat; he's got this gun he carries. Big Luger it is. I told you he was stuck in a groove, didn't I? The decent bloke didn't want to interfere with you, Mrs. Thomas, he said it would draw attention to us, but the other one said, no, he had to know who you were, coming up the lane like that. He said he was the professional, he knew. The good bloke was only some sort of guide, a contact. He knew those people, the Vints, where the man died. It was my fault in the end, no denying. If they hadn't brought me there, see?"

"The man had a bad heart, he was bound to go." Una dismissed Mab's sentimentality.

"Och, no, it's true enough what he says. If we get you out of this mess, lad, don't you be forgetting John Vint, God rest him."

"What were you doing in the lane then, Mab, where I ran into you?"

"Waiting for the word from Larry Vint that we could come, that his mother would have me. We were expecting him on his bike, quietly, and then we heard this car coming and thought that he'd got a lift from somebody; nobody uses that lane but the farmer who lives there and he's one of them. We knew he'd gone home already. The bloke got mad when he heard the car, thought Larry was breaking his orders. All he wants is 'Aye, aye, sir,' and 'Permission to speak, sir?' and 'Kiss your arse.'"

"Mab!"

"Oh, sorry. After he'd phoned and checked your story, he decided you were clean, but with you tailing our car like that and then turning out to have a Welsh accent when they had me in the car, well, you can understand his worry, can't you? Later on he heard you'd come over here a bit suddenly.

mpetuously, and he began to suspect you again. Or he said he did, anyway, but I'm not really convinced that he did suspect you at all. But he enjoyed it, see, the possibilities of danger, the lovely threat you might be. Cops and robbers. He wanted to believe the Special Branch was after him, it made him feel great, big; he hasn't been in the Organisation very long, and he likes drama, that one. He had me believing him, of course, and I think he kind of enjoyed frightening me."

"But, Mab, this is a crazy time to run to Ulster, with all the trouble we have here; didn't you think of that?"

"Well, our officer said, see, 'If you have to run, run to Ireland, the Organisation will help; the North is safer than the South,' and so I did. I had to run."

Sarah's flesh crept at the thought of the IRA atrocities in the past, the risks, the loss of life, the hangings in British jails, the beatings-up in Ulster. She cringed to think of a possible repetition of similar horrors in Wales, sprouting from an unholy alliance between the implacable and the inept.

"There's been this old investiture of the Prince of Wales, see, and there's been a security scare on. They'll arrest you for holding a firework. Mrs. Vint said she'd have me that first night, but no longer, and then, next day, they had the fight and there was nothing for it but to run again. I felt terrible then, you won't believe. Mrs. Vint was very nice to me."

Mab looked down at his dirty hands to hide the weakening of his face, hide the threat of tears; then he clenched his hands, a positive, mature gesture, and looked up again. "Mrs. Thomas, you've got to realise that everybody's scared daft just now; they see double meanings in every word and spies behind every bush. Nobody's quite sure of anybody. See, Mrs. Thomas, this isn't a film script, it's real, terrifying. You seem to be trying to be so objective about it, weighing things logically, like. But you can't. We were all ready to believe him when he said you'd come after me, especially when you saw him again in the boat; we were — what's the word? — yes, we were conditioned to suspect everybody, frightened of shadows. You try going on the run for a bit and see how your sense of proportion lasts. I know now that nobody in their right minds would take you for a cop, but who's in their right minds here? And he was wild with you about that boat thing. It was after that he took the hat."

"In the name of God, what's all this about a boat? You have me foundered, so you do." Caroline's voice was beginning to lose patience.

"I saw a boat on the lough and asked for a sail and the bearded boy was on it, that's all. What the hell was wrong with that?"

"No, but, see, he was on his way to meet some high-ups in the Organisation and then he couldn't risk it, after seeing you; he still wasn't sure, because you seemed to turn up so pat all the time. So there was a breakdown in their arrangements. They got discipline in that organisation; you don't keep high-ups waiting at a rendezvous; it's too dangerous for a start. They tore slow strips off him when he was able to make his contact, later on. You gummed up the works and he likes to run things like on a quarterdeck." Mab, whose spirit seemed to rise and fall like the bounce of a rubber ball, drew himself up, squared his thin, pathetic shoulders and gave a smashing, heel-clicking salute, grinning confidently now at his fascinated audience of three. "Tell you the truth, I'm not always quite sure that he's right in his head, all cunning and no common, if you know what I mean. It's like his mind is turned inside out, anything simple has got to be complicated, I'm telling you; life, the way he looks at it, is like a tangle of wool the kittens have had a go at. Mrs. Thomas was like an answer to a prayer for him, honest."

"Lord, Sarah," Caroline said, a trifle pettishly, "I'd be half suspecting you myself, if I didn't know the likes of you. You might think of the childer."

"But in a place this size, with only about two and a half inhabitants, how could I help running into him? It's not my fault that you choose to live in the heart of the Republican recruiting ground, Caroline." Sarah was hurt, brisk and somewhat cold, in her weariness. "We more or less know the rest, I think. They put you in the Big House and her ladyship caught you there and after that you were in the Creep until we found you, right?"

"More or less, yes."

"In the Creep? Lord, sooner you than me, lad."

"And the beard will be at the old fort tomorrow at twelve? That's the arrangement if anything goes wrong and you've lost touch?"

"Yes. But – I don't like to say this, but I'm not looking forward to seeing him, honest."

"No. I shall see him."

"You, Sarah? Is it mad you are, woman dear? You can't be drunk, that's for sure."

"That chap has kicked me around enough. I'm not myself for nothing. Make up a bed for Mab, Una, and get to bed yourself. I'm not too worried about Mab; that cousin of mine would have heard if anything was seriously wrong. I told you he was deformed from keeping his ear to the ground, didn't I? You can't keep secrets in Wales, can you, Mab? Any trouble would have leaked. You haven't blown up the sergeant. He must have known the phone was out of order, surely?"

"Of course, come to think, he'd been round looking to see whose tin opener was busted the day before."

"There you are, then. Relax. We'll sort it out, somehow." Sarah was so emotionally exhausted that she hardly knew what she said, where she got the energy to articulate, but, in that little room where she had been with James, she knew she had some debt to pay, some thanks to give.

"Let's go then, Caroline. You drive; I'm far beyond it." And in her pretty, sacred summer dress, she lumped her way to the door, singing "The Men of Harlech," out of tune.

"Jesus, you *can't* be drunk, Sarah. What's with you, a all?"

"Let's go home. I'm tired, tired, tired. There's been to much. I'm not equipped. Let's go."

CHAPTER 12

It was the glorious Twelfth of July and there would be no
Protestant help for those who were left-footers. Caroline had
hinted to Mrs. Savidge on the previous day that she would
appreciate some help with dinner on the Twelfth; the processions and the excitement would be over by that time, sure
they would? But she had foolishly gone on to say that Mr.
McNeil was expected, he was an old friend of Mrs. Thomas',
and it would be nice to have him for her last evening.

"Madam, I've worked for you and the Professor, both, and
as God's me witness, I've not a thing against youse. And
Mrs. Thomas, as kind a lady as ever stopped; makes her own
bed and folds her own bath towel her own self. But I'd have
you know, madam, there's limits. Work for the other sort,
yes, when the money's short and everything two prices in the
shops, but serve that one, who's a traitor to our side, I will
not, no more I will. No, not if it means my place. Mind you,
there's some of us would have his— You may give me the
road, madam, but you'll excuse me thon night. I'll not
wrench a cloth, no, nor dry a dish, for the likes of thon wee
man. Sure, me own man would have my life for it. It's more
than Protestant human flesh will bear, so it is, begging your
pardon, and sorry to be speaking out of me turn. No, this is
where I hangs up me dishcloth."

On the morning of the Twelfth, Sarah went to Una's house
to see what the night had brought. She hated what Mab had
tried to do and what, politically, he stood for, and yet she
loved him; for the name he bore, for his unbroken voice and
valley accent, because he had a mam, because she knew him
in her blood. She was prepared to swear he'd had no need to
run, but perhaps the running was part of what he'd dreamed
about. His first time out, and the threat of the law, sauntering

down the village street, just as he left the phone box. Who wouldn't then have run? But something had gone wrong with his attempt. It must have. Old Geraint would have heard; he knew it all.

Mab was asleep and Una drinking coffee on the terrace when Sarah broke upon her broodings. Her face reminded Sarah of the mummified head of the Blessed Oliver Plunkett she'd seen in Drogheda Cathedral. Una complained of her burned hand. Sarah rebandaged it.

"No developments overnight, then? No IRA boys trying to snatch back our shorn lamb?"

"No. Not a one. He's exhausted, the boy. D'you think there'll be trouble for him yet?"

"No, honestly, I've got faith in that mad cousin of mine. I think Mab panicked. But I'll beard the beard, God save the mark, at twelve in the old fort. I hate that place. The thought of all those bats. But I'll frighten that young thug. I hate his type. I fear them, Una. They so deny my work, all that I've done, my faith, you know? One turns out bad, like that one, one who'll do things 'just for badness.' Defeating. Makes one despair. Have you ever been alone in bed, in a foreign city, say, and heard the church bells say, 'In vain, in vain' to you? Sometimes they say, 'Too late, too late.' That's the end, that one."

"How was it yesterday? I'm sorry I forgot the roses. But you forgot to wash the glasses."

"It wasn't a bit easy, love. And without this place to come to, it would have been a compete rout, an utter fiasco."

"I suspected you were a bit too damn sure. You're too old to learn now."

"I never presuppose misery because I hardly ever seem to think in terms of anybody but myself; just dream my own dreams on my own terms. Before I came to Ulster this time, all I saw was my own need for simple, physical comfort. I could easily have found it somewhere else, and probably a far more competent one. But I went sentimental, faked a bit. Good God, I hadn't really missed him in five years, let's face it; but when my crisis hit me suddenly I had to run, run far, and he was my farthest comforter. Maudlin I was, to tell the truth. Maudlin. Wanted pampering, that's all; I had to run to Daddy; kiss it better, please, kiss, kiss. This crap of love, this lying, lying love. I never really mean a bloody word of it. But it is so easy, and they seem to like it, even when they run away."

"What crisis?"

"What? Oh, my crisis? I thought you knew. I may have cancer in my breast. That's why I fled."

"God, I'm sorry. You wouldn't like to live with it cut off, not you."

"No. Though I would, even if it won't be fun. But today I'm doing my brave turn, with that boy and his sexy teeth. And don't you dare imagine that I'm doing it for anything but selfish reasons. I want to slap him down; he's pushed me around and I simply won't have it. I also want to slap down the threat he offers to the stuff that I believe in; education is my thing, after all, and he spits in my professional eye. I want to clear the air too, my air. I came here all agog for passion, renunciation, fond farewells, and he's had the nerve to put me out. D'you believe this catalyst stuff? Did I engender things? But I'm damn sure I'm going to bring the light of common day into the nonsense of that old fortress, that nursery world of stupid violence, this cops-and-robbers balls of yours. I've had it. It gets on my nerves, too bloody phoney."

"God knows I wish you luck, but, Sarah, nobody fools with the IRA. And that one's armed."

"*Third Man* stuff. Why, even Mab said he was in a groove. He won't harm me; I'm too sophisticated. And if he were to hasten my departure, think what an obituary James would write." She smiled. "You know he's coming to dinner tonight? Hope you approve."

"Sarah, shut up. You're telling lies – all that about hastening things. I know you are."

"You want to feel my lump?"

"No."

"Who would? Here, have a fag. Look, you must see that I can't just go home tomorrow, with Mab perhaps under my arm; go to my nursing home to wallow in self-pity and just forget that horrid boy. He'll go on, that one, persecute with petty things, take his mean little revenges. He hates, you know, that's his function. He hates you for your civil rights thing, Colum he'll regard as a Poujadist and Caroline's archaic loyalties won't matter a damn. His handsome young-manhood is dedicated to destruction. Such a waste, as well. So" — Sarah shrugged — "I've got to tidy this thing up, see?"

"I won't let you—"

"You can't stop me, love, I'm off. I'll be back here at sixish to hear what my cousin has to tell me. Forgive the melodrama of my lump. Bad theatre, wasn't it?" She ran, bravadoed down the mossy steps, aware of what she'd said to Una, what for the first time she'd actually put into words; that he might only hasten things. But not believing it, still not believing it; demanding connivance from them all by means of a threat that she was only using as an excuse, a justification. Not true. No. Only a new behaviour pattern, an embellishment, a blackmail.

But they had accepted it. Believed it. Four people now believed that she might have cancer, might even die of it. They took her word for it. But she was lying. Wasn't she? She'd only used her lump as and when the need arose. A superstitious flush engulfed her: you get what you give, my girl, watch out. Four people heartsore, sick for her. What Providence had she not tempted, flaunted?

Blindly, she walked back to Illnacullin, afraid of death, afraid of life, solitary and tired. But bullied, driven, by the job she'd so braggardly sworn to do. And in that ghastly place. Did she really have to go? The boy would surely go away when Mab was gone? But how would he know that Mab had gone? Perhaps he honestly believed that she was there to trace old Mab and might even mount a rescue operation, waving his Luger and everything. God, now she was at the melodrama once again; one must really try not to let them infect one. Yes, she had to go. But first a drink. She had walked from Una's with her head bent, her hands clasped behind her back; occasionally she'd kicked a stone out of the ruts in the scruffy track, as a slow, unhappy child will do. A drink, yes, and then she'd cope. It was only this Irish atmosphere, so bad for her. She must get back, get back to Cambridge. No melodrama in the Fens, in academic cloisters. Cambridge was sane and safe; no waste of emotion there in sympathy and friendliness; no emotion, to tell the truth. Sometimes it made life easier, if less lived. Of course she'd cope. A brandy would be best, a drop of the hard stuff to help her past the bats.

She raised her head as she approached the promise of the house and saw the motorbike.

A motorcycle in the drive. A big, efficient bike, labelled "Police". She hovered over it like a heavy, blundering moth, aimless, defeated. They knew then? Mab was for it; old Geraint had been badly out of touch; she might have known. But why were the police at Illnacullin? Mab wasn't here. But she and Caroline were, the aiders and abetters. That Special Powers thing; suspicion was enough. Good God, she'd miss the nursing home. Could she plead her breast the way women used to plead their bellies in the bad old days? Should she go into the house to be with Caroline or run back to Una, help her bundle Mab out again? But where? Hell, what was the meaning of escape, anyway? What was the good of running, except to wear you out? She might as well go in and know the worst.

The drawing-room door was open. She went in. Caroline and Colum were with the sergeant; Sarah remembered him from the humiliation of the pub on the night of the wake. He sat, on the edge of his chair, turning his cap in his hands, between his frightening, uniformed knees. He looked embarrassed; like anyone in uniform, he seemed naked and almost pathetic without his hat. But he wore his gun in its bright, black leather holster. Whom was he going to arrest? Policeman. Enemy. The tension in the room was almost tangible. The men stood up as she came in and greeted her a little overheartily, she thought. Caroline had a bad colour, but was covering up, as ever, with offers of strong drink.

The sergeant held a glass; it wouldn't be Caroline, then. With a noisy gust of forced laughter, Caroline introduced the sergeant to Sarah.

"How d'you do? We met before. You turned me out of the pub, remember?" Never strike your colours till you know what your enemy holds. "What have I done this time? I wasn't there, I promise you. I have an alibi, whatever it was." Sarah laid on the fake nonchalance, the ease; a visitor, amused, patronising the locals, the accent now entirely Cambridge, the Protestant ascendancy to the life.

"Aye, I know it, ma'am. And I'm truly sorry, so I am. That's partly why I came round the day, to be perfectly honest with youse, Mrs. Moore. I'd never have done that to the likes of you, and well you knows it. But it's this new inspector we have; he's a hard one on the closing time, the man. I'd been tipped the wink, so I had. And, I'll tell you no lie, I was afraid I'd blotted my copybook in this house. I couldn't bring myself to mention it, not till the lady there brought it up her own self."

"Trust her. She's herself, so she is."

"Aye, well, no hard feelings, Mrs. Moore? Sure there's not?"

"Not a bit of it, Michael; you had your duty to perform. 'We must dare to do our duty as we understand it.'"

Sarah knew from the heightened tone of Colum's voice that he was quoting something, but in that state of the game, who cared? Was that only why he had come round? Only because he'd blotted his copybook? Dare they hope?

"I'm glad we've got that out of the way, because there was something else I had to mention, begging your pardon and taking the liberty."

He turned his cap and couldn't look them in the eyes. A decent peeler with his duty to perform. Caroline's lips were moving in prayer: "Hail Mary, full of Grace...." Sarah had a bland smile pasted on her lips as she got up to offer him a cigarette; her thoughts were stuck like the dumb end of a gramophone record.

Guiltless, ignorant, Column asked, "What was that other matter, Michael? 'Conscience doth make cowards of us all.' You have us alerted."

"Och, sure, it's only the Police Ball. You were always good about buying the tickets, though I've yet to see you come. But with me making a fool of Mrs. Moore, there, and her with her friend and all, I was hesitating to ask youse. I've been feeling awful bad about it, so I have."

The Police Ball. Would they wear their guns to it? Only the Police Ball.

"Of course, Michael, of course. We'll not promise to attend, but here's something towards the expenses. You'll know I'm a busy man."

"Thank you, sir. It's very good of you. God knows it is."

Sarah was so weakened by relief, so stupefied by the return of hope, that she heard herself saying, "Wait, I'll give you something too." Sarah, who hated the police, hated their guts, hated, wrote him a cheque; libation, thank you, God.

But time was passing, and now time had become relevant

again. She had a date at twelve. She caught Caroline's eye and looked hopefully toward the brandy bottle.

"Sarah," Caroline said, "wasn't there something you said about wanting to take pictures of the old fort when the light was right? Not that I know the first thing, mind you, but you said something about midday, did you not? But here's a wee sherry," she lied, pouring out a brandy big enough to drown in. "You'll want to take a drink with the sergeant to show him that all is forgiven, I'm sure."

"Yes, of course. *Iechyd da*, sergeant. That was a bit of Welsh for you. I did rather want to catch the light."

"Aye, well, go you on ahead and I'll follow with the childer while the lunch is cooking."

"But don't delay, Sarah. You expressed an interest in seeing the Twelfth Day procession. You'll not wish to miss too much of the television presentation."

"No, indeed, Colum. Thank you for reminding me. Just give me about fifteen minutes Caroline. And don't give another thought to the pub, my dear sergeant. At least you didn't arrest me. Hope to see you on my next trip and have a lovely ball."

"Thank you Mrs. Thomas, and good-bye. You're welcome to Ulster, so you are. And safe home."

"'Bye now." Sarah had never owned a camera in her entire life, but her handbag was a big one; it might, just, have taken a camera, she hoped. She went out through the garden gate; Bridget was, as usual, keeping shop, but breaking the no-customer monotony by trying to teach William Butler to beg. It wasn't a successful exercise. Brendan, greatly daring, was tinkering, doubtless disastrously, with the motorbike and Patrick was looking on from his pram. Sarah saw them through set teeth and ran. She didn't pause to pass the time of day; given time, she'd think; given half a chance, she'd back out. The sergeant had done something to her knees and the brandy was taking its time.

Deaf to temptation, she ran on, under the trees and onto the shore; careful on the damp seaweed and half enjoying the bounce of the crisp bit. Up, then, and into the old ruin, whizzing past the bats, on all fours up the circular stairs and at last into the light of Bridget's second shop. Armoured and brave, or fairly brave, to cope with the bearded youth.

But there was no one there. The place was empty.

The boy had let her down.

Sarah had never even considered this. Her plans, her bravery, had presupposed the boy's being in that place at that time; his *Third Man* stuff, his groove; he, more than anyone, was meant to play his part. This was ridiculous. Sarah felt affronted, like a girl in all her makeup whose boyfriend hasn't come. She was insulted. She walked to the window slits; but the fields and the sea were empty. Nothing but some black-and-white cows on a distant pasture. She sat beside the shop and lit a cigarette. Give him ten minutes. Damn him. Damn him. Where the hell was he? She paced the floor a bit and saw the crushed baby pigeon, dry now, if vaguely feathered, and, because removed by dryness, less obscene, as a skeleton is less than a hanged man. But there were two new eggs in the untidy pigeon's nest, though no fat bird sat on them. What had driven her away, that sluttish mother pigeon? You, lumbering up those stairs, she told herself, don't go getting fanciful and seeing clues. But even while she dismissed her thought, something residual reminded her of that awesome parapet, that sentry walk where Bridget had gone to look for bits of shop. Would he have dared to hide out there, for all this time? Might he have seen her, heard her climbing up, and ducked? Would he have been brave enough to stand there waiting, till she gave him up? Good God, God, she had no right; not to leave him there, perhaps terrified, with the lough at full tide those hundreds of feet below him. She'd have to look, at least.

She ventured to the edge of the crumbling stone lintel, gripped with both hands at the deep carved stonework of what had once been the solid doorframe to de Courcey's sentry walk. Scared to the quivering of her toenails, she stood on the edge of the old doorstop and, hesitating, peered out.

And there he was. Rigid and silent, looking out over the water, and standing only a few feet to her left on that crumbling insecurity with the tide hammering in. She could have touched his right hand and there was something maternal in her that wanted to. His arm was held stiffly down along his side, the hand turned inward, towards the wall, as though to clutch a purchase on its unrelenting face. The hand quivered, strained, the tendons taut, and the sun shone on the fine golden hairs on it and on the ugly, coarsened fingers and the hideous bitten nails.

"For Christ's sake come in from there, you fool. I want to talk to you and I haven't all day. Oh, please come in; you scare me, honest. I'm suitably impressed, I promise you, but, please, come on in here where I can talk to you. Jesus, damn you, you'll do no good to man or beast if you fall into that tide. I want to talk to you about an old-clothes shop and about Chianti bottles. Stop the heroics now, there's a good boy, and don't bother waving your Luger at me when you come, either." By then the brandy had arrived.

"Come, we've passed that stage," she added, impatient, schoolteacher fashion. And then he came, slipping through the archway with that same easy grace, that cat saunter of his. She had to grant him that, the braggart, the little bastard.

"Here, sit down; have a cigarette, it'll soothe you. Now look, don't worry any more about the Welsh boy, Mab Powell. I ran into him last night. And it was all your own fault. He couldn't stand the damp and the dark of that Creep place another minute; he's hardly more than a child, after all. Mrs. Moore and I had gone up to the hill where the Calvary stands to watch the bonfire in the town. He'd come out of the Creep and was attracted to the fire — he was very cold, you understand — then he heard us talk, recognised my Welsh voice, which is fairly rare in Ulster, and simply gave himself up. His guilt and homesickness overwhelmed him. You'd aggravated it all, of course, by lying to him about the verdict on John Vint and by claiming that I had come here to look for him. I'm simply here on holiday, my Welshness quite coincidental, but coincidence doesn't fit the groove, does it?"

The boy made no response to Sarah. He smoked her cigarette and looked away from her.

"I'm taking him back to Wales with me tomorrow, to face anything he has to face. He wants to thank you and the others for everything you did for him. He's aware that he came at a difficult time for you. He's not going to say anything that will incriminate you; he will be honourable, I think. He thought that it was all going to be splendid and romantic, but it turned out to be painful and sordid. You know that yourself, don't you?"

He didn't answer, still wouldn't look at her as she sat there on the same cold stone seat. He picked up a spent match and carefully prised out the dirt from a cavity on the face of Bridget's counter, concentrating, meticulous. The grubby lumps of sugar and split peas and pretty, broken bits of pottery were scattered around the ugly hand.

"But the Mab thing isn't all I have to talk to you about. There's your persecution of me through Mrs. Moore's children. You don't deny that?"

Still no word, no glance in her direction.

"That has got to stop. Hear me? I leave here tomorrow. Your job is finished and I don't want to hear that you've been continuing your unpleasant little tricks for sheer spite. I believe you capable of it, on the side."

A quick flick of the eyes toward her, but no reply, no defence, no anger.

"I warn you, we know all about Powell's adventures. We refused to do anything to help him till he told us the whole tale, and, of course, your lies about the verdict on Mr. Vint didn't exactly strengthen his loyalties to you. When he gets home, if he's arrested, he's going to tell the British police that he failed to make any contacts in Belfast and that he had to give up. But Mrs. Moore and I know the truth, we know about the old clothes, the doll with the beads, the market, the newsagent, the lot. Any more of your petty sadism and Mrs. Moore will blow the whole gaff to the police. Maybe that's not much of a threat to you, personally; you could be a long way off by then, but she can put your Belfast friends on the spot, yes, even Larry Vint here in Kilhornan. You know as well as I do that here in Ulster they don't bother too much about evidence; they'll arrest on suspicion and then they'll make them sing. You won't be popular with your superior officers when they learn that their network was destroyed because you wanted to play games with kids, will you? Mrs. Moore is a Nationalist and wouldn't want to inform, but she'll do it; you struck at her children, that was a stupid mistake. So it's up to you, boy. Damn you, have you been listening to anything I've said? If we are to believe half we're told, I gather that your organisation's arm is even longer than that of the police. I wouldn't envy your fortune."

He played with his matchstick and Sarah had to move from her seat beside him and walk to the arrow slits. She had to move about, in case he smelled the fear that burned like an ulcer in her stomach; fear has a heavy, rotten breath. Silence was a weapon that she'd never had to fight, never had paused to evaluate. She knew that she held all the cards, but there was a deadness in the boy's face, a complete refusal, rejection, that reduced her to a mere articulate lump. It was then she realised in all her cringing flesh that the boy had it in him to kill her; kill her because she held all the cards, kill her because he'd been proved wrong about her, kill her for pride, kill her for "badness," for bloody hate, a symbolic act, a shriving. She was alone with him in that old, ruined, heraldic fortress. It was the Twelfth of July and she was a British Protestant; all the ingredients of a Republican gesture were there. Nor was there a soul in sight.

He needn't use the Luger; only a push over the parapet into the wild tide, a careless visiting photographer, taking stupid risks.

"I sympathise with Mab's activities, of course," she lied into the tight silence. "I mean, I sympathise with his ideals, if not his means. Wales needs Home Rule, it's our only hope of economic recovery." She looked out and down to where Caroline had left Patrick in his pram that first time, all those violences ago. But there was no one there.

"I'd be the last to wish to break the valuable contact Free Wales has with you more experienced people over here, but if you force me to, I shall, I swear it." She turned to look at him again, and lit a cigarette, a screen. And then he looked up at her. Assessed. Perhaps he'd heard the wilting of resolve. Something sparked in the blankness of his eyes. She couldn't stare him down. She felt her age, his age. Back once again to the arrow slits of those remoter wrongs; she felt her weariness as she paced the earthen floor, felt her boredom with fanaticism and, like a pistol in her back, she felt the push of all his youthful dedication, the youngness of the boy, that lovely thing that here had gone awry and sour, corrupted by a foul community. She slipped her hands around the worked stone of the arrow holes and found a strange new strength from these symbols of simpler aggressions. Hopeless of succour, stripped, reduced, alone with questions that she couldn't even form, she looked out again, as one looks up from arguments, turns one's eyes away to see one's own perspectives. She didn't glance to where Caroline might have been; she saw the sea, the seaweed and the heron on his rock and they were all as meaningless as she. She had no answers to the questions that she couldn't ask. Like him, she only had her prejudice to see her through. She felt bewildered, helpless, middle-aged and set in the concrete of her time, her thoughts, responses preordained, conditioned. What right had she? The boy was young, at least, and had some freedom left, some hope. She was threatened, stuck, cemented in her facile, leftist attitudes. Was his the better way? The archaic setting, antique sacrifice, the brandy and the literary hotchpotch of her mind drove her to turn to him again, to offer, to renounce.... But, when she looked, she saw him biting his bitten nails with that same ghastly, careful nicety.

No. God! No, not this one, not worth, unworthy. The Sarah that she knew came back again; Jesus, fair play, she thought, sacrifice needs a half-decent audience, one must be allowed to choose one's moment for the taking off. Hers wasn't for the likes of him, his beauty notwithstanding. And, down below, like little minicars in children's games, she saw Caroline with the pram and Bridget. The sergeant was with her, settling his bike up on the stand and leaning over it to listen as Caroline held forth; he seemed to be paying attention, nodding the uniformed head.

Sarah felt purged. "Come," she said to the boy. "Come quickly. D'you see Mrs. Moore down there; d'you see who that is with her? She's ready to tell him everything, unless I go to join her. We'll give Mab to the police and he'll sing to this lot here; he's only a boy, he couldn't help himself." He came up behind her to peer over her head through the arrow slit; he had to rest his hand on her shoulder, lean against her.

She turned her head to speak to him; their faces were so close she could have kissed him, almost wanted to kiss him, soothe him, apologise for having all the cards, but all she said was, "There's only one exit from this place and he's wearing his gun." Her hand went up and she stroked his cheek. "Good-bye, now. Don't forget. My friend is much wiser and stronger than I am. Remember that." And then she ducked out of their strange embrace and ran to the daunting circular stairway. No hands and knees this time; there was something that demanded dignity, something that had nothing to do with people looking on. There were only the bats to watch her and they were blind, but still no hands and knees, no bloody groping in the dark.

The sergeant stayed with Caroline until Sarah joined them, then said good-bye again and repeated that she was welcome to Ulster. But he was wrong. He was welcome to it. Sarah had almost had it.

"How did you manage the sergeant, genius?" she asked Caroline as he left them.

"It was just a thought. Isn't everybody feared of the uniform? I got him to take a look at the lock of our boat-house. It was myself had been at the lock; there was a recipe in the boat I was wanting and I'd misremembered where I'd put the key. Didn't manage to break in, mind you, but you could see the marks of me. I showed them to Michael and kept him chewing the rag till I saw you. Hope I did right. God help him, too; it's not easy being a peeler, and him a left-footer."

"I think I've managed to persuade the boy to leave us all alone. Thank you for being so good to that old Mab. He's Wales, you know?"

"Och, it's no more than I'd do for any poor bastard. And what's more, I like the fellow, he's got a bit of sense. Colum may go on about his old constitution and Una about her civil rights, but it's me's in the right of it; we need a free, united Ireland. There's Colum saying time will heal all the breaches. What's this he says? Aye, 'the logic of history,' he says, 'the inevitability of progress.' Our Una's all for accepting the border too; *fait accompli* she calls it. What about my French accent, then? She has it that nationalism clouds the issues like votes and houses and jobs. She says they're worse off in the South of Ireland; all right, but they need the North to make them prosperous, don't they now? Mind, I hate the politics, but I'll help any poor devil who fights for Ireland. Sure, I'm the simple one, but it makes life easier."

"So who were you fighting for today? That boy back in the fort is a champion of Irish Nationalism and it was you who really circumvented him, turning up like that with the cop."

"You'll not say a word to Colum, sure you won't? He'll be sitting there now, watching the Twelfth Day on the television and kidding himself there's no harm to it. Keep him innocent, Sarah, it's the only way. He's too many principles, thon same man; he's too good to live."

They walked on, with the children, out of the dark shadow of the ruined fort and into the broken sunshine under the beech trees. Sarah felt the sweet prickle of the sun on her back and then paused to look back again. It was only an old ruin where Bridget kept a shop. Sarah rubbed her hand along the seat of her pants because her fingertips still carried a memory of the boy's warm skin. She wished she could dismiss the memory as a temporary moment of misdirected sex.

"I never asked, was young Mab all right when you went over to our Una's?" Caroline asked, dredging Sarah back to commonplace, safe reality.

"Fast asleep, exhausted," she answered.

"What's to happen to him, at all?" Caroline sighed and crossed herself.

"God knows. We'll wait and see what my cousin has to say tonight."

They watched the Twelfth on television. It was not a day when wise Catholics walked abroad. There was yet another layer of bunting on the Belfast streets. The official buildings and the little terraced houses all beflagged, boastful, proclaiming their eternal loyalty to the British Crown if not exactly to the British way of life.

The Loyal Orangemen were marching to the clamour of drums and flutes and tambourines and bagpipes. Their invasion of the city had begun early in the morning but still they came, as Colum indeed said, "in never-ending line." They carried their banners high, like a medieval army; King William danced upon his charger; the cameras closed on Queen Victoria bestowing a Bible on a noble savage; General Gordon, up to some mystery in Egypt; the Walls of Derry, Maiden City; Mount Pottinger's Imperial Orange lodge; the Apprentice Boys of Derry; the Sandy Row Imperialists. Sarah was surprised to see so many temperance lodges. She hadn't associated the British monarchy, nor indeed Northern Ireland, with excessive temperance, but we live and learn.

A small boy with the angelic face of a mental defective came past the cameras, carrying an open Bible on his outstretched palms; a bevy of girl pipers with fat knees uplifted; and again the cameras panned, this time on a drummer, on one man who walked a bit apart, with a drum much larger than himself, one who beat and beat with a dogged, wooden persistence and wore a bowler hat.

"That's one of the Lambegs, Sarah, that big drum. That fellow will be after beating thon in his protest and his triumph the day, till the blood streams from his beating hands. Sure, isn't it a point of honour with them? The blood has to stain the parchment, hell roast them."

It was the incongruity that defeated Sarah. The sashes they wore across their chests and the banners they carried were said to be predominantly brilliant-orange-coloured, flamboyant, triumphant. But they marched with a rigid, militant bleakness. Bigoted, stiff, uncompromising, unsmiling, in bowler hats, best suits, stiff white collars and the white gloves which seemed to be *de rigeur*. Children held obligatory sad sixpenny flags that drooped. Sarah found it all utterly dreary, merely dull. Colum had described it as a festival, but there seemed to be no fun, no magic, no sense of carnival. It was a show of force, a dour threat, a misery and, to Sarah, infinitely boring. The dead hand, the dead hand of dogma, the Red hand of Ulster a taste of death in the mouth.

"Cold hearts," Colum said, "cold hearts and very muddy understandings."

Sarah saw two young miniskirted girls in the crowd that flooded the pavements. They were eating candyfloss and one of them yawned widely, embarrassing the camera, which hastily left them. They said it all for Sarah. A bore. What's on the other channel? Lord, the same thing. Why don't we just eat?

"Aye, it looks harmless enough there. But I'm telling you, it'll only take one shot, one death. Our patience is going like snow off a ditch; there'll be trouble somewhere the night, pray God."

CHAPTER 13

They took their lunch and Colum talked about his journey back from Donegal. He was incensed against the newspapers and the broadcasters; claimed that they exaggerated every small event, and were, indeed, the breeders of the present violence. "We idiot Irish have a pathological dislike of disappointing. We behave like stage Irishmen because they want us to. God knows, I even do it myself, in England. Just now the television cameras come, so someone throws a brick or petrol bomb, or clouts a head because 'Sure, you wouldn't see the wee sods come for nothing?' Take the covering of the Dungiven violence. My dears, I drove through the town and saw nothing untoward. No burned and looted shops, no bandaged heads, no state of siege, just an ordinary country place going about its normal business. Ulster needs just one year without television cameras or radio reporters. Every Irishman is an actor *manqué*. Just deny us an audience, and that would end the violence, I promise you. First it's the cameras, then it's the fights."

"No cameras and no civil rights?"

"Sarah, the civil rights will come. It's in the logic of history. Democracy will slowly evolve in Ulster, given time and given peace. Why, they are still disputing Darwin in the churches here. The time span is different, and you must realise, Sarah, that Ireland is Ireland, something quite special; it was never an offshore European island. You must remember that the Romans never came this far; we've never known their discipline, their order. That is a fundamental truth, I'd have you know."

"And were there cameras at Burntollet Bridge the day my Una got that blow?"

"No, Caroline, I grant you that. But surely you'd agree that that was a sport, a freak affair?"

"Why, Colum?"

"Because it had no religious overtones. That was an intellectual, academic exercise which, in turn, provoked a purely political, fascist response. Those young people were students, behaving in the accepted, student-protest fashion; they were irrelevant, out of the Ulster context. Unlike Una, I see the conflicts in this province as purely religious in origin. The conventional hatreds, the traditional feuds, the patterns of Ulster, the religious fights, these are the ones encouraged by publicity, because they can be stage-managed; we've been rehearsed for them, we know our lines and our cues. Do I make myself clear?"

"Clear as mud. Would you not pass the rice?"

"Tell me, Colum, how did you get your Chair, if it's not an impertinent question? It's not that I doubt your obvious qualifications, but you're a Roman Catholic?"

"Aye, you may well ask," Caroline said.

"No, it's a fair question. To begin with, my name. Moore is not an Irish name, certainly not an exclusively Catholic name. I was sent to school in England and read English in Oxford, as you know. I must confess that I suspect I was awarded my original lectureship without the suspicion that I was a Roman Catholic. Without wishing to sound immodest, my academic success thereafter, my publications, what have you, precluded the appointment of anyone else to the Chair when it fell vacant. I was patently the obvious choice. Don't let Caroline and Una influence you unduly, Sarah; the University, at least, has no built-in anti-Catholic prejudice. Of course, English literature is relatively harmless, like geography, let's say, and unlike history, or philosophy. But remember, we take in students of both persuasions and the local authorities give them equal grants."

"Aye, Sarah, but it's when they come to look for jobs. If

they went to Saint Malachi's or the Christian Brothers' School, then who cares what the University may have done for them? They can always tell by the school, Sarah. We'll excuse you now, Colum love. I know you've work to do and Sarah understands. You'll not forget we've asked McNeil to dinner. It's to be fillet steak. You'll get the wine?"

"Is it indeed? Does he know his wines, young Sarah? Would he deserve a good one?"

"At least he won't ask you for the hard stuff, like Rory."

"Rory! He's out of the history. I warn you, Caroline, he's had his last meal in this house. I will not suffer Vandals; you'll not forget?"

"No, Colum, I won't. Away now and leave Sarah and me to the dishes."

"When do you propose to eat?"

"About eight?"

"You'll remind me in time to open the bottles? There ought to be one Montrachet left for the pudding."

"No, there's not. I know because I thought I'd use it to poach the trout last night and there wasn't one."

"Montrachet for cooking? Caroline, are you quite mad?"

He left them then, shaking his head, abstracted and haloed by the professorial mystique, his eyes heavy; he would sleep, but only in the holy sanctuary of his study.

"God forgive me for lying to him, but it was you and James had the last of that Montrachet. Was it worth it, girl? You never said."

"Then it was. Yesterday it was worth it, I suppose. But nothing's easy any more." Sarah got up and piled the dirty plates, needing a job to cover up the temptings of a giggling disloyalty. "Oh, well, he's getting on, you know?"

"Thank God."

"He said he loved me, though. He's glad I came, I know he is. He said he'd like a child by me."

"Sarah, don't tell me you didn't—"

"If it's happened, it's happened. But at my age? No, all I've ever produced is my lump. What can I do to help you with dinner?"

"Plenty. We'll have a crab soup first, then the steaks, and I thought meringues with the first raspberries for the pudding. That ought to please you. You may deal with the crabs; I have them cooked."

Sarah dealt with the crabs and then she entertained Bridget and Patrick with the pincers. Slowly, suspiciously, Patrick began to accept her; the kitchen floor was littered with bits of shell and she spent most of the afternoon under the kitchen table, playing with the children and lying fallow.

And then it was time to change her clothes, time to give up the easy afternoon, and walk to Una's house for her cousin's telephone call, time to take on the burden of her adult responsibilities. It was her green, sophisticated cocktail dress she wore that early evening; no Hardy summer dress for James this time; that time was passed...

In the kitchen, when Sarah came back, Bridget was firmly rejecting the notion of bed, and it was feared that Patrick had swallowed some crab shell; Bridget insisted that the sun was shining, that it was afternoon, it wasn't fair. "Bridget," Sarah said:

"In winter I get up at night
And dress by yellow candlelight,
In summer, quite the other way,
I have to go to bed by day.

"Don't you know that yet? Come along, let me take you up, and I'll tell you some more poems."

"What poems?"

"Well, come to bed and hear them. Shall we say them on the stairs?" Sarah dredged the hated *Garden of Verses* up and resigned herself to helping Bridget fold her best Fifth Avenue hat up small, to fit under her pillow.

Caroline, having decided to leave Patrick and the crab shells to the mercy of Providence, was drinking sherry and had a glass ready for Sarah.

"Now, you'll drink that and take your hurry. Before you move one step from this house you'll write out that wee poem about going to bed by day. God, why did I not have it years ago? You'd think himself would have thought of it, wouldn't you, and him with all his old poems and his quotings? Here, I've the pen and paper ready, put it down. Worked like a charm, so it did. I'll not forget you for this."

It was only two minutes past six when Sarah got to Una's and the telephone was ringing as she climbed up the steps. The door was open and Una was saying, "Yes, I'll pay for the call. It's your man, Sarah, ringing from Cardiff."

"Right, thanks. Hello? Geraint? Yes, this is me. You went, then?"

"Yes; panic's over. What the hell are you cooking, good girl?" He spoke in Welsh.

"Just tell me what happened."

"Can I spread myself, or are we counting the pips?"

"It's on me. None of your cheese-paring."

"Well, I went up the valley, like you said. The phone box looked all right when I passed it in the bus so I thought I'd go round to the pub first to hear the news. They told me somebody's taken a tin opener to the phone box and the GPO is tired of mending it, waste of time. Can I charge the pint as well? In a good cause?"

"Yes, yes; for God's sake get on with it, love."

"The old kiosk was still there; out of order, yes, that's nothing new. But I thought I'd better take a proper look, just to see for myself how these Vandals carry on, if you see what I mean, destroying government property and everything. I knew what to look for, mind, I wasn't born yesterday; and you needn't laugh, my girl, I've saved your bacon, all right. There were two sticks of you-know-what stuck down behind the box thing that you put your money in. Only Jesus knows why they hadn't gone off. Damp fuse or some damn thing; there's no class in explosives these days. Now, when I was young—

"I risked my life for your boyo, Sarah. I actually picked those things out and shoved them in my two pockets. Me! I can't believe it myself yet, honest. Don't bother asking me how I did it; it must be the beer they sell up there. I'm still incredulous. Me, mind, old Rhys."

"Thank you, oh, thanks, boy. I'll never forget this."

"But I'm glad you sent me there, girl; I've never seen such magnificent desolation. Can I go on?"

"You can talk all night. I love you."

"Did you see his mother?"

"Yes, I'm coming to that. What a girl, eh? Bloody marvellous."

"Was she tangling her knickers?"

"Sarah, where do you pick up your language? No, she wasn't; she was fine. We had a lovely chat. She told me Mabon was probably on one of these things called hitch-hikes; he was always on the go; nothing new."

He was a notorious mimic, Sarah's cousin, quite unable to forego the chance to do a turn. He did Mab's mother. "'You know what they are these days, can't say a word to them. Student power they call it; they've even got it in the grammar schools now. Any minute, they'll be starting in the infants'. It's the food they get, see? Bread and butter we were brought up on, mostly, and the top of my father's boiled egg, in turns. But they get school dinners now and I got a few spare shillings in my purse, so you needn't start your old Welsh Nationalism with me, boyo; no, I've had enough from our Mabon. No, come you, the Labour Party have saved my old kids from a diet of bread and butter, with chips for a special treat, whatever, even if the kids have got a bit cheeky with it.

It shows a bit of spirit, mun. No, they're all right, the young ones. Come to their senses in time; crooning it was in my day, see, drove my mother mad. But this old world tames us all in the end, you watch.'"

"She put you in your place, then. What else?"

"It's those pips again, but I must finish this bit. She told me her Mabon was a good boy." His voice reverted again. "'Worried he is, see, waiting for his results, the old O levels on his little mind. Mean so much, isn't it? But it'll be lovely having him on the mantelpiece, framed, in his capangown. It won't take him away from us, not our old Mab; but there's some, mind, in this very village that hardly know their parents no more, not since they got the letters after their names. Leave alone those that lent their mothers a few shillings when things was tight.'"

"You're not making this up, are you? Make it true; she's been on my mind."

"She's great. I'm telling you. She said it was a pity for everybody, because the parents didn't know their kids either. 'They're in a different world, our kids, but, look, I'll be in a different world if I don't get on with Jim's dinner.' I asked her if he was still working. Had to, Sarah; if you'd seen that desolation I was on about. All the pits in that valley are closed; nothing there, nothing, only desolation and demolition and a few dirty sheep. It'd break your heart, Sarah. That valley, by itself, is a total and utterly convincing argument for nationalism. It's all you need to see, girl."

"His father is working, is he?"

"Not for long. He's got a few weeks left, but he's been declared redundant. Redundant. A man in his prime. It's a bloody shame."

"Yes, he's younger than you."

"The old lady waxed very eloquent about redundancy."

"Take it easy, Ger, with your 'old lady'; she can only give me a year."

"Sorry, love. She threatened me with her dishcloth and said, 'Not even your old Nationalists can make heaven on earth. Give the Labour a change, I say, and fair play; a gang of new civil servants who can talk Welsh isn't going to bring this valley back to life, good boy, say what you like. We got to move with the times, and coal is finished. Oil it is now, and schools and hospitals for all those Arabs; you think of that too. Time they had something. God help.'"

"Oh, love her heart. She's got a bit of sense. Pity she didn't go to work on Mab."

"Good boy, is he? Keen?"

"Yes. He's not for you."

"Watch it, Sarah. You may be in Ireland, but don't get confused; you're not the Virgin Mary. I've been counting the pips. That last was the fourth lot. You must remember to tell me how much this call costs. I feel like Rockefeller. I'm wearing my heavy glasses and smoking a fat cigar."

"Who cares what it costs? If you knew what it was worth, my boy. Jesus, the relief. Thanks, Ger; I can't tell you—"

"Don't give it a thought. Any time, old girl, any time. I buried that stuff in my garden, by the way. Must have been old, or something, thank God."

"I'll never thank you enough. I'll be in touch as soon as I'm back in Cambridge. We'll have a drink in Cardiff and I'll spill my beans then, right?"

"So long, then. Be good. Home Rule for Wales."

"Right. So long, pal."

She put the receiver down slowly, tired now, middle age catching up with her. She stole a precious minute to sit on the hall chair and a great flush of weakness engulfed her.

Mab was pacing the floor in the sitting room, weak to know what she'd heard. He was pale again, that white, cancerous look that only redheads take. She came into the room, sat down and carefully crossed her legs, lit a cigarette and let him stew. Caroline had worked on her; she was beginning to

James took Sarah's hand under the cover of the dining table, squeezed it, hard. It was all that, publicly, he could do, a casual friend of Sarah's, a married man, "with childer and debts." He had no right to speak and reassure her, she had no right to turn to him and say, "Comfort me, just comfort me." A mistress with no right to command, a lover with no right to say he loved. The pressure of his hand was strong on hers, almost cruel, twisting the small bones. She took up her glass. "I'm sorry, chaps, but here's to Ulster." Drank, tasted, appreciated, dredged up the strength to indicate her pleasure to Colum, and then said, like a challenge, "Yes, right then, this is the Twelfth of July. Shall we all promise to meet on the next Twelfth Day, providing none of you are jailed?"

They drank to that and Caroline crossed herself. "Pray God," she whispered, into the laughter. Sarah gave herself a mental dressing-down, always the well-brought-up girl, and then she found that she could listen to the talk again, be with the company, at ease. As long as James could hold her hand.

Mab and Una had set up their barricades and were sniping at each other with statistics and sentimentalities. He was stating the formal position of the Welsh Nationalist Party, his young face eager, ever ready, and the Welsh accent and newly broken voice singing his enthusiasms, the words tripping each other up like the sound of fast water racing over pebbles in a Welsh mountain stream. Sarah loved his every sound and feared his every word. Gradually everyone was listening. "See, what you lot don't understand is capitalist rationalisation. That hasn't got anything to do with countries, nor with human beings going redundant; it's only concerned with profits. Look, do you honestly think you've got high unemployment over here because you've got so many Catholics? You can't believe that the big capitalists care whether you cross yourselves and think the Pope's infallible. My Aunt Fanny! In Wales we've got twice the unemployment they've got in England, and if half of us didn't leave to find jobs somewhere else, we'd be nearly as badly off as you are. Look at my old man; redundant he is, and he's not much older than you Mrs. Thomas. Now if we had our own government for Wales, we'd have a proper planned economy for Wales as a unit, not as a useful but forgotten piece of England." He buried his fears of Sarah in his glass of Château Haut Smith Lafitte 1959. "And the bloody English couldn't steal our water power then, without asking, and kiss your arse for the money. We got to have decentralisation, see?"

Caroline laughed and tousled his long hair as she got up to remove a dish. "Och, Mab, aren't you the great one? We'll see you in Parliament yet," and Mab blushed ferociously, partly from pride and partly from the realisation that, again, he'd talked too much, forgotten his manners and his place.

"All right, Mab," Una said, biting, rather than sharpening her claws. "We've got this magic decentralisation here in Ulster already, and look at us."

"Aye, fair enough, but we haven't got your history, have we now? We haven't got a civil war to forget, nor the same seeds of violence ready to sprout." He spoke down into his plate, shy, but sticking to his guns.

"Careful, Mab," Sarah said. "We've got a few kindergarten IRA types in Wales too, don't forget." Mab looked across at Sarah from under his brows; indebted to her, but dying to have his fling, his adolescent fling against her as a symbol of the so-called progressives of the Education Establishment. It was James who saved him from the answer that he might have given. "Oh, nonsense, Sarah, a handful of silly boys. But Wales is hardly economically viable. You're too small."

Thinking of the wild way in which Mab had chosen to pronounce "decentralisation" in his last outburst, Sarah stammered in with, "Actually, James, the Nationalists would argue that New Zealand, Israel, Iceland, Albania, what have you, all have smaller populations than Wales and yet are self-governing and have a seat at the U.N."

"Yes, and we don't live on the backs of the English tax-payers, neither, look here. You, in Ulster, get a grant of about one hundred million pounds a year from Westminster, but we, in Wales, by ourselves, paid more tax on fags and tobacco than they spent on the whole of the Health Service last year; not only our bit of it, mind, the whole of it – visiting Americans, the lot." Mab made an expansive gesture which nearly knocked his depleted wine glass over; Una saved it. "We got to have decentralisation, I'm telling you."

It was as obvious to Una as to the others that Mab was "under the weather," unaccustomed as he was to Caroline's standards of liquid hospitality, but that socially destructive urge in her, that itch to be ungracious, to destroy the simple easiness of conversation, drove her to argue with him.

"I repeat. I insist. Look at Ulster. And look at the standard of life in the Irish Free State – dependent on German and Japanese capital investments, those bloody tainted sources."

"Una," Colum interposed, "full employment and good social services are benefits you must be able to afford. They neither come from heaven nor by decree."

Bitchy, Una snapped at Colum, "Oh, we know that in your position you can't talk politics, and that the police are your buddy boys, so you may just shut up, brother-in-law."

"I was under the impression that you prescribed to the notion of civil rights, Una. Freedom is only for those who think like you, I take it? 'The only liberty is liberty connected with order, that not only exists along with order and virtue, but cannot exist at all without them.'"

"Why the hell you think, Colum, that you have only to quote something for it to become, automatically, a true and irrefutable statement, I'll never fathom. But I know my Burke too; I shall cap you for once. 'There is, however, a limit at which forbearance ceases to be a virtue.' But to return

from Colum's retreat into eighteenth-century polemic, why
the Welsh don't look at Ulster beats me."

"Och, our Una, hold your tongue and show respect. Are
you telling us you'd have Ireland back under the yoke of the
English? Is it betraying the Easter Rebellion you are, and
siding with the Black and Tans?"

"Jesus, Caroline, don't be more naïve than you can help.
Let's confine this discussion to the North, today, and forget
the sentimental trimmings. Here we have the decentralisation
from Westminster and the Home Rule the Welsh claim they
want. And what do we have? A fascist police state."

Mab was nodding his head, "winding the clock of his
wit," when James' voice coldly cut across the threat of family
coils and of adolescent girding. "Una," he said, "I suspect
you are much more naïve than you accuse Caroline of being.
Unless you are deliberately disingenuous. It is simply crap,
my girl, to think in terms of a Marxist solution to Ulster's
problems. Indeed, I feel there never will be a solution in
Ulster. It's like a bunion on the sole of Europe that neither
surgery nor manipulation will cure. Just something that one
has to grin and bear. Look, let's be realistic, for a change.
Small improvements like a more equitable distribution of
houses, a reform of the electoral system, these would obviously be something; in the short term, they might do a little
to create a new atmosphere, in the sense of the government's
acceptance of the need for them. But both extremist factions
would reject them and they would deliberately see to it that
they'd cost, in civil strife, far more than they'd be worth. The
right-wing Protestants and the active Republicans would see
in any democratisation of Ulster a positive threat to their
respective campaigns of hate. The right wing only exists to
keep the Ulster Catholics down, where they belong, and the
Republican militants want revolution – want to see the
Catholics suffer enough to rebel. As a Marxist, Una, you'll
appreciate that. You might, possibly, by your civil rights

movement, do some good, in the very short term; but in the long term, Ulster is bound to go from bad to worse."

"Oh, James, don't be so damn depressing," Caroline begged. "This is a dinner party, not a wake. But, you know, you are right in a way, for even if you give us votes and houses, there isn't much you can do about the unemployment and the poverty, sure there's not."

"So Una's right, James?" Sarah asked. "The only answer is revolution of some kind – whatever your definition of revolution?"

"Look," he answered, "in my book — not being a nihilist — revolution only makes sense in terms of the solutions that it offers. What would be the meaning of our civil revolution, what will be its declared aims, on either side? You must, you see, have peace aims as well as war aims, and the truth is that no one has any positive aims for Ulster. Nobody wants us; Great Britain is bored and frightened by the return of the Irish problem, and the Free State wouldn't, indeed, couldn't take on Ulster, not for all the bombs secreted in Belfast."

"You're thinking it'll really be civil war again, then, James?"

"I shouldn't be at all surprised, Caroline."

"Praise the Lord and pass the ammunition," Mab said, breaking the sudden, alert tension.

"But my dear James," Colum argued, "do, at least, define your terms of reference. What, in this book of yours, does civil war mean?"

"Do you want a quantitative evaluation, in terms of the numbers of dead? Do fifty dead mean only civil disobedience, while a hundred corpses mean civil war? I'm afraid such an analysis is beyond me. But, Colum, the martyred dead are not the only measure – nor are the repressive edicts; not even martial law in the province would necessarily mean a state of civil war. But the people. The people are already at war in their hearts."

"Arrant, melodramatic nonsense, James, if you'll forgive me."

"No, there's enough hate about, Colum. God knows, I wish I had a scale, something like a decibel, to measure the degree of hate. It's so high in this province now, it almost exceeds the power of human – what? With what sense does one measure hate?"

"By the pricking of my thumbs."

"Yes, Mab, thank you for that. May I use it?"

"It's only because we did *Macbeth* last term that I thought of it," Mab said grudgingly, as though angry with himself for having made such an acceptable interruption.

"By the pricking of my thumbs. God, Colum, can't you feel it? I sense the mood of the people; so ox-heavy with hate, so laden with suspicion, so utterly, blindly distrustful. No, nothing does any good. The fifty years of Ulster have been too long, too meaningless. At the risk of sounding banal, one must repeat: repression is no substitute for government, whoever does the repressing." James pushed his desert plate aside, as though it were the whole of Ulster.

"Nonsense." Colum jerked to his feet. "Have some brandy. Stop your melodrama, James. Quote *Macbeth* in one of your articles and you'll have every Ulsterman sitting, contemplating his thumbs, and wondering what prickles are supposed to mean. God knows, you'll have them sticking pins in their thumbs, in case they've gone dead on them."

Sarah had made a true and conscious effort to pull herself out of her depression; she'd felt the force of Caroline's rebuke and had been pleased with James for his positive assertion of despair over Ulster; maternally, she'd watched her little Mab, her fellow countryman, had loved his efforts to behave himself according to her standards, aware that, here, he had none of his own, but suddenly she felt herself outside again. Bored. On her last night she'd wished, without having thought of it, a warm, nostalgic mood, a cosiness, an

ease. She was ill, wasn't she? And going away; she had her
rights. She changed the subject before James could answer
Colum's charge; using, cashing in upon her frailty, her femininity. "Caroline, d'you think Mab could sleep in one of your
bunk beds tonight? Unless it's a fearful imposition? I find
that he's booked on the same flight as me tomorrow; I could
give him a lift to the plane and I'd be glad of his company.
Unless it's asking too much, of course?"

"Not a bit of it; he can sleep here if he'll wash up. Take his
mind off the politics. Who'll dry?"

"I will," James said. "He can instruct me in the principles
of Welsh Nationalism."

"No, no, James, I wouldn't hear of it. We'll manage fine;
there's no hurry, none in the world. Let's take our coffee in the
other room. Una may clear the table with Mab, while I pour."

James sat with Sarah on the couch and pressed his thigh
against hers. He was fat; she felt his warmth and knew he
wanted her; he was himself again. How could she manage it?
How with grace and tact could she win for them the chance?
She looked up and into Caroline's eyes, said nothing, but
communicated.

Caroline said, "God, you know something? I'm for my
bed. Young Patrick had us up last night; he's cutting teeth,
and I'm not in the best form just now, James; another little
angel sent to try us. A wee Christmas present, this time."

"Why, that's lovely, Caroline. But I'll not keep you up. It's
time I made for home. God knows what's happening in
Belfast the night. My paper'll have my life, if something
breaks and I've nothing to report."

"Would you not walk James to his car, Sarah? I know he
doesn't trust our avenue; and God knows, Colum, it's time
we had it sorted. I've said enough."

"Yes, dear, I know. But I rather favour it; it fulfils the
function of the medieval moat. Only those who really care to
see us will negotiate that avenue."

"I'll say goodnight then, James. Don't keep yourself so distant. Safe home, and mind yourself. You're at a dangerous game, don't be forgetting."

"Good night, Caroline. Thank you for a lovely meal; I'll be in touch, I promise you."

They walked together slowly down the drive, not touching, the house lights on them. They passed through the everlastingly open gates, and then, by the new-cut hayfield, he turned her to the grass, without a word, and loved her there. The night was still, she saw Orion and the Plough; the stars had wheeled, the earth had moved, she was at peace.

"God," he said, "twice. I've done it twice, in how many hours? Can't be more than thirty-six. You'll bloody well come back, you hear me? Och, come back soon, little Sarah, and listen, love, you mustn't mind. If you get chipped, I think I'll love you more. I'm old, I need a little imperfection, if I'm to keep my *amour propre*. Don't be afraid. Look, when they put you under, give you their anaesthetic, think of me; say 'James', and then you'll wake up with me on your mind. Do that; promise?"

"Yes, I promise. And may I come back again? You're sure?"

"I have to go. Oh, Jesus, yes, I have to go. Good-bye. God bless you Sarah; you'll walk me to the car?"

She saw the dark shape of his car under the stable clock, where the white doves lived. He would get in and drive away, back to his life, his wife, his work. Get into bed with her this very night. Oh, hell, was it for her that she'd revived his powers, only that he might now— ? No. That was bad form, she mustn't think of that; it was like thinking of one's parents; one must preserve the decencies.

"Well, sweetheart, this is it." He stood with his hand on the car door, the car keys dangling, ticking to be off. He kissed her lightly, feinted at her chin. "Keep cheerful; we'll all win through, in time." And then he watched her walk

away; tall, elegant, her head with all that rich abundance of
fair hair bowed now; dear Sarah, who'd ever guess the
passion hidden there? Pray God she'd be all right.

It was then the bullets tore apart the night, from the
ambush of the clock tower. He tottered, fell, screamed something. She heard the bullets, heard the scream and ran, high-
heeled, incompetent. Sarah forgot the guns, forgot the threat;
he lay there, in the shadow of his car, all folded over, crumpled, lost, like an abandoned teddy bear. She knelt and turned
his head into her arms. He mumbled words, a groan, a curse
that might have been a prayer. She knew she ought to go, to
look for help, get him a doctor, save his life, but his pathetic
mouthings held her there, they made no sense, she had to
hear him out. His lips were clogged, his breathing harsh and
shallow, his head a ton weight on her arm. She felt him struggle, fight to speak, "Sarah," he mumbled, "My Evelyn. No
scandal." The effort was too much for what was left. His
mouth fell open, his loved eyes stared. He frightened her. She
dropped him then, and his head fell, bounded heavy, like a
waterlogged football, and she ran, abandoned him. Ran to the
house, to Colum's arms.

"He's dead. Shot. He's by his car. Do something, Colum.
I tell you James is shot. One shot, one death; you have it now,
have it with my compliments. Go, please, I left him there."

Colum called out to Mab and ran, and Caroline, dressing-
gowned, rocked Sarah in her arms. "I saw him die, I, said the
fly, I saw him die. James is finished, Caroline. He's over and
done with. He loved me first before they got him. Look," she
said, lifting up her skirts. "You see my hand, this on my
fingers? That's his spunk; it's warm, it's still alive. But,
Caroline, he sent me away. 'My Evelyn,' he said. Did you
ever know her name was Evelyn? He should have known;
you couldn't but be frigid with a name like that. You might
as well be Ethel, mightn't you? 'My Evelyn. No scandal.'
You told me that I had no right. I have no rights, no rites. His

body's hers, the mourning's hers; he's hers forevermore. She has him now."

"God rest his soul. Jesus, Mary, Joseph and all the saints in Heaven preserve him. Holy Mary, Mother of God—"

"No, Caroline, no, don't take yourself away. You know the Mother of God's as meaningless to me and to him as a dead codfish. Stay with me, here on earth. Help me, here."

"Aye, but you'll forgive me if I cross myself. Here, drink this brandy Una's poured out for youse. Now look, you'll have to cope, to testify. There'll be the police: you didn't see who—?"

"No, nothing; I didn't think. He said no scandal; somehow you and Colum will have to cover up. He wanted me away. Christ, Caroline, d'you think they watched us, gave him time? Oh, God, Caroline—"

"All right now, yes, all right. We'd better get you off to bed. Here, take these pills; I wear them in my pocket, with my beads. Yes, swallow these, take all the three, the brandy'll keep them down. Yes, that's the girl, you're best in bed, and out of this. Una'll help you up; she'll sleep with you. If we're to hide you, you must sleep. Go up now, go with Una, that's my girl. We'll cover up, we'll cope. Just go to sleep. Do that for James, do what he asked."

"Come with me, Una, help me up. I left him, did I tell you that? I left him on his own out there. I dropped his poor old head and heard it bounce. How could I, Una, how could I? I just up and left him. His eyes, James-eyes, were open. And his mouth. He has a new gold tooth. Did you notice that new gold tooth? I thought it somewhat vulgar; but, mind, I didn't mention it. I never would have hurt him, not old James. And yet, I bounced his head. Bang, bang. How could I leave him, Una? Alone and in the dark starlight?"

"You had to come for help. What could you do? You fetched the men; you had to, so you did. Don't worry now. Take off your dress; look, here's your nightie; you lie down and I'll take off your paint. Shut up about your teeth, they'll do the night; when we were kids we only had the one toothbrush for the five of us and once Caroline took it on holiday and left us to our dirty teeth. Don't fuss, they'll do; lie down if I'm to take your makeup off. There now, just you relax, Una will mind you, sure she will. There, Sarah, there, you go to sleep, my lamb, my little girl." Sarah felt Una take her hand, felt comfort and security, her thoughts were all through-other, gone away. She held the hand. Too doped, too buffeted to know what she had said, she said, "But where are your children, girl?" And slept.

It was Colum who came back to the house, leaving Mab to stay with the body by the car.

"Yes, it's true, Caroline, he's dead. Where is she?"

"Una's helped her to her bed. I gave her those wee tablets the doctor gave me when I couldn't sleep that time. They'll knock her out. She'll sleep the night, poor bitch."

"We'll have to keep her name out of all this. You know that? We can't have us condoning immorality."

"You knew?"

"Of course I knew. D'you think I'm blind? He came here to dinner, that's all, and then set off alone, and then we heard the shots. And I rushed down with Mab; that's all we know. All right?"

"We heard no shots, Colum, it's too far. You may think again."

"Yes, well, James McNeil went off and then I went out with Mab – is that his name? It's grossly unconvincing, I must say. But I went out with Mab to breathe the air, and we found James beside his car. We know no more than that he's dead. I'll telephone the sergeant at the barracks then, shall I?"

"Yes. But don't forget, you don't know how he died. He seems to be dead, that's all. But, Colum, is there any need to mention Mab? You went to breathe the air, just you. No complications."

"Yes, you may be right. I'll do it then. I was alone, I don't know how he died, I only know he seems to be dead."

He telephoned the barracks, told his story, got Mab away to bed, and left all that remained of James McNeil to the Ulster police and their discretion. Like Caroline, he knew the force, the meaning of one shot, one death.

He told the sergeant all he could about his guests, said they knew nothing, were asleep. They were to leave tomorrow. Should he let them go?

"Och, yes," the sergeant said. He saw no reason why they ought to stay. They weren't involved, sure; weren't they only foreigners?

Colum agreed.

"Yes, let them go." No need to be officious, inconsiderate, sure there wasn't? The lady had to go to hospital? Suspected cancer; who'd have thought? The lady was a lady, so she was; a five-pound cheque it was she'd given for the Police Ball.

CHAPTER 15

Sarah slept through the strident telephone call that woke the others early on the thirteenth of July. A call from the district inspector, the sergeant's boss. He thanked Professor Moore for his prompt action on the previous night. The Professor would doubtless be interested to know that Mr. McNeil had died of a heart condition that had been troubling him for some time. There was no question of his having eaten anything harmful at the Professor's house, none at all. In the circumstances, they wouldn't ask Professor Moore to testify as to his finding of the body. There had been slight haemorrhaging, not unusual, not at all surprising; not that the district inspector knew much about these physical details, but his medical colleagues had assured him that all the symptoms were consistent.There had, in fact, been an earlier prognosis. Professor Moore hadn't known? Well, there it was, an unhappy end to their dinner party, most distressing for them all, most unfortunate. Mrs. Moore, in her present condition, was none the worse for the shock? Splendid, splendid. Mr. McNeil was said to have been a likeable man, a very lively journalist. A pity. But there it was.

"Yes," Colum agreed, "a pity. He tried to be a kind of bridge—"

"Quite, professor, quite. Unless there's anything else, then, we'll not trouble you again. Good day to you." Slowly Colum replaced the telephone receiver; looked out over his garden, at William Butler slobbering at the window and Brendan, with supreme indifference and complete concentration, sorting maggots on the bank outside. Colum put his hand up to his brow, tightened his fingers as though to rein his thoughts, then dragged his hand down, slowly, clenching at his face; the traces of his fingers were a livid white against the sallow skin. His eyes stared, out of focus, as he paced the length of the dining room, and compulsively tied and untied and retied the belt of his dressing gown. He felt the incongruity of his slippered feet, his vulnerability in pyjamas, his unwashed face and night-clogged teeth and hair on end. He heard the others talking in the drawing room, knew they were waiting, worried, but he couldn't face them, fight them, as he was. He ran upstairs and took a shower, cleaned his teeth and brushed his hair, put on a fake efficiency with clothes and shoes and socks.

Sarah slept on while Colum joined the others in the drawing room and while he instructed Mab in the facts of death. A heart condition.

"But you're talking balls; I don't know what you're saying, mun. He was murdered; shot. Good God, I got blood on my hands when I moved him off that wheel. He looked so uncomfortable, so lost; daft, I know, when he was dead and everything, but I couldn't help myself. Look, I got some blood still on my cuff."

"They say he had a haemorrhage."

"Look, Professor, we know the bloke was shot down, don't we?"

"We only have Sarah's word for the shooting."

"What about this blood, then?"

"They explained that, I tell you. A haemorrhage."

"You don't get a haemorrhage with a heart attack. I remember when old Jim Kremlin dropped dead in the pub one night—"

"Christ, Christ, Christ," Una hammered. She stood staring out of the window, thin and gaunt in Sarah's floral dressing gown, her arms wrapped around her as though to keep her in one piece. "Christ, it's true. They do it. They really do it. And we have to stand by. Are we going to stand by, Colum? You may have been conned into accepting this, but don't you dare imagine you can legislate for the rest of us. By God, you won't; I promise you."

"Sorry to be so daft, so simple-minded, for all I know," Mab said, his face unwashed, long red hair on end, in a grimy white vest, blue jeans and dirty bare feet. "But will you, for God's sake, tell me what you're on about? I'm just not with you. Murder is murder, isn't it?"

"Not in Ulster, Mab. Remember the Special Powers Act I told you about yesterday?"

"About arresting, and searching houses without a warrant, and putting blokes in jail on suspicion and keeping them there without trial, and flogging, and not letting prisoners see a lawyer nor their relatives? Of course I do, Una, I remember all that. Who'd forget, isn't it? It's bloody criminal."

"There are some more sections to the Act than I told you about. Under it the police needn't hold an inquest on a dead body if they think that public knowledge of the cause of death might lead to a breakdown of law and order. James McNeil was an honest journalist; he had the guts to write some of the truth. His life had been threatened and the peelers were guarding his home. Now he's been killed and he's a potential martyr. The way things are just now— You wouldn't know."

"Good God! I don't believe it, Una, you're off the beam. If you're right the police could bump off anyone they didn't like and say he'd fallen off a bus?"

"Yes. They're not required to hold an inquest when a prisoner dies in their hands, either."

"*Iesu*! But here's your chance, isn't it? Why don't we just tell the truth and show them up?"

Caroline had been sitting, unkempt and silent, her hair in plastic curlers, in a far corner of the big room, her face flushed and pulled awry. "Mab, love," she said, "we'd have to show up more than them. Tell him about James and Sarah, Colum. I'm away to be sick."

"Yes, well, Mab" — Colum spoke slowly, fumbling for his words — "James and Sarah had been lovers years ago and the last thing that James said to Sarah, as he died, indeed, was that she should go away and create no scandal. He was thinking of his wife; perhaps, too, of his own obituaries. Far more people knew of their old affair than Sarah realised. Ulster is a small community and James was a public figure. They broke it off, but, for reasons we can understand, and indeed feel compassion for — we mustn't judge — Sarah came back and they took up with each other again. Her name will be muddied if we fight this thing. Would you want that? And James' memory besmirched? Remember that the so-called permissive society has not yet penetrated the barricades of Ulster. Think of the filthy innuendos, all the dirt. Caroline and I would be accused of abetting them in their immorality."

"Sarah? With Mr. McNeil? I – I never thought, I didn't dream. But she's as old as my mother. Good God."

"Yes, Mab, as old as your mam. Hard to take, isn't it, boy?"

Sarah was at the open door, a painted mask on her face, the eyelids green, lips vivid, like the coral on her nails. But her eyes were sunk and dark beneath the painted lids and the heavy mask of makeup wasn't thick enough to cover up the twitch that pleated her face, contorted it.

"Did you really have to tell him, Colum? You might have tried to preserve his little innocence. But there, it's over now, it's done, isn't it, darlings?"

"How are you, Sarah? God, I'm sorry. Come, sit here beside me." Colum led her to the sofa, held her hand. "Look, we had to tell Mab because the thing is, Sarah, that the police have telephoned. They say James died of a heart condition; they're going to cover up the shooting."

Sarah's laughter rang out like machine-gun fire, obscene, indecent in the Sunday hush of that gracious room. "A heart

condition, did you say? I'd never have believed them so per-
cipient. Poor old James, dead of a heart condition. Yes, you
could call it that; he did die of his silly heart, of his stupid
generosity to me. I ought never to have come, you know that,
don't you, Colum? I was never really serious; I shot a line,
that's all. What did you say about a cover-up?"

"In the 'present state of discontent' the police obviously
feel that to disclose the circumstances of James' death would
be unwise. There might well be trouble here."

"And you've decided to go along with them? But that
would surely be to deny all that he stood for, all he tried to
do? Are you sure, Colum? Wouldn't his martyrdom be politically expedient to your side?" Her mouth twisted into something like a smile. "Yes, let him have his martyrdom. And
ease my burden just that much."

"Thank God for you, old Sarah." Una spun away from the
window, throwing back her lank hair, her hands spread out,
as though to accept a gift. "Here's our chance, at last. To hell
with Colum and respectability. If you're prepared to do it,
we'll face them out. We'll beat them, Mab. Westminster'll
have to take a bit of notice with two British residents here to
testify to the facts. 'This is a consummation devoutly to be
wished.'" She knelt before Sarah, clutched at Sarah's hands.
"You'll do it, won't you? You'll sacrifice his reputation to the
Cause? You'll tell the truth?"

"Wait, Una, I'm sorry; I'm not sure that I quite understand. James' death a consummation devoutly to be
wished?"

Una's clutch on Sarah's hands relaxed. She sat back, on
her haunches, moved, swung away from her.

"Forgive me, it's all those pills you made me take last
night; I'm slow just now. Yes, me you may sacrifice to any
cause, of course, but you mustn't talk of sacrificing James.
He's dead. He has no say. And I'm sorry to be stupid, honestly, but I'm at sea in all this."

"What Una wants is to insist upon a proper inquest and inquiry into James' death, Sarah. You would have to testify about the shooting, explain why you should have been walking with him to his car, tell them why you came to Ulster and why James came here. I hate to be harsh, Sarah, but you'd have to tell the court just why it took you half an hour to get from this house to James' car." Colum's voice was cold, despite his gentle hand that fondled hers.

"And who the hell's to know what time it was they left this house?" Una demanded.

"We'd have to testify on oath ourselves. Would you perjure yourself, Una?"

"Sure, I'd take the reserved oath. For the Cause," she said, still sitting on the floor at Sarah's feet and staring at her, with the intensity of a cornered cat, ready to spit.

"I, for one, could certainly not bring myself. And you know Caroline." Colum shook his death's head. "It's no good, Una. Give it up."

"What are you all saying? God help me out; I want to do what's right, God knows. Una wants me to confess that James came here to comfort me? But that's no use. I can't. You know I can't, I promised him. Can he be a martyr without me?"

"Of course he can't, you fool, you sentimental lunatic," Una shouted, hammering the floor. "This is an issue that transcends your stupid loyalties. His bloody wife. Is one frigid female to deny us this opportunity, this break?"

"He has children too. He's proud of them. If you can't rule me out, then he'll have to miss his martyrdom. I promised him. His last thought was for his wife. I'd never known her name was Evelyn. It was a bitter pill for me to swallow last night, that last request, but I've taken it. By now it's only a minor discomfort, an aspirin that sticks sourly in the throat, no more. But I did promise him, there in the dark, by his car." Memory curdled her face, but she went on. "No, Una, I'll not testify if it means his reputation; I hadn't thought it out. And anyway, don't base your case on me; I may not be around that long."

Caroline came back into the room, encumbered with two children. She sat down heavily beside Sarah and Colum on the sofa. "Hello, Sarah, love. You made it then? You look all right, you'll do. Colum told you, did he?"

"Yes, thank you, Caroline, I know James died of a heart condition. Died of me."

"Och, no, now, Sarah; they were after him, they'd vowed to get him. Sure, wasn't I after telling him that very afternoon when we stood talking here? Jesus, no, don't blame yourself, blame Ulster."

"All right, I didn't hold the gun. I only brought him here to kiss my wound. While there were plenty of others who would have done as well. If only I could convince myself that he had really mattered in my life. My journey wasn't necessary, you see, I should have stayed at home." Her voice was strangely light and thin, a medieval ballad voice. The accents of despair. She looked cancelled out, reduced and paper thin.

"Sarah," Mab shouted at her, his voice an adolescent croak. "That Special Powers Act is vile; I mean, who'd ever believe? You ought to have the guts to fight it. You told me I ought to be in a proper fight, remember? This is it, mun. This is their chance, indeed to God it is. You got no right—"

Sarah looked up at Mab in all his innocence; at Una, sitting in her embittered hunch on the floor in the thin floral dressing gown. "Yes, yes, of course. You've made your point; it's an old-fashioned problem, that one of personal loyalty against the general principle. I'm with you all the way, you know, in theory. I wish—" She shook and shook her head as though she'd never stop. "But can't you see, we'd never do? Not you and me, Mab. Look at us, *bach*, Una's two British citizens. They'll say that I came over here because

I'm a whore. And you? Will you be a very pretty witness in this case? Colum thinks you are a mere accident, picked up by Una in the village pub. But you'd have to tell the enquiry why you came to Ulster, what you did and where you went. Will you rank as a creditable, worthwhile character? Will you, Mab? A lad on the run because he blew up, or failed to blow up, a sergeant and a telephone kiosk. An adulteress and you, boyo; those are your reliable witnesses. How would you describe yourself for the *Belfast News-Letter*, Mabon Vavasour?" Sarah's oddly high-pitched voice broke. She hid her painted face in her hands, turned to Colum's arms and broke her heart.

Speaking over Sarah's head as he rocked her in his arms, Colum said, "There's that small detail, Una and Mab, that you'll neither of you have given thought to. I hate to bring it up and grant you that it's petty, but Caroline and I gave Sarah house room, we encouraged James to meet her here. How will we look, good Catholics, if you insist this scandal break? We were condoning immorality. I never would have counte- nanced it, Mab, but Sarah may have cancer in her breast. One didn't have the heart."

"No, boy, don't look like that," Caroline burst in. "There in the breast it's not so bad. Sure, don't I know of dozens?"

"So we let the fascists get away with it again? God, Caroline, for once we know, we have the evidence ourselves. Jesus, this is what his death was all about."

"Aye, and what his life was all about, poor beast. But, our Una, McNeil was a family man. He had no business carrying on. Adultery never suited. Martyrs are like the saints; you've got to be awful careful who you choose."

"But who's to know? We could lie in our teeth."

"Una, Sarah's here, you want her evidence; the sergeant saw her; dear God, she gave him money for the ball, no less. And there's plenty knew about them; you know the size of Ulster, and James a public man."

"But Sarah hasn't been here for five years."

"What's five years and the man crossing the water whenever he felt like it? Five years is like five minutes in Ireland and well you know it, my girl."

Sarah lifted her ravaged face from Colum's shoulder. "Did he often cross the water? He never came to Cambridge."

"Whisht now; you're a bit irrelevant for a wee while."

"Yes, I know, Caroline; I always was, you know."

"Och, Sarah, quit. This is important. Act your age." Caroline had never any patience to spare for what she thought was mere whimsy; and Colum, released now from the constraint of Sarah's tears, got up from the sofa. He walked to the fireplace and while his fingertips caressed a porcelain Chelsea shepherdess on the mantelpiece, he said, "We don't know who fired those shots Una. The earlier threats against his life may have prompted his murder for some other and quite different cause. Sarah need not have been the only one. Perhaps some other husband, who can tell?"

"You're going to accept it, then? You'll take it?"

"We all will, Una. You and Mab, Sarah, Caroline and I – 'for the purposes of peace and maintaining order.'"

"But Mab and I have no interest in your peace. Indeed, we positively wish to destroy your order."

"No, Una, I've my childer. I'll take no risk, no more I will. We'll take it and like it. And thank God it wasn't worse. I'll make some breakfast; they've that plane to catch. You may give up, young Una, give it up. And get your clothes on you; we'll need to pack that dressing gown you've got on."

Mrs. Savidge came to do the morning chores and Caroline gave her the official version of the death of James McNeil. That, somehow, set the seal on it.

"Och, madam, no! The dear knows. D'you tell me that? The poor wee soul; in life we are in death, God knows. But it wasn't them crabs, madam; fresh as a newborn babe they was. And sure, wouldn't the rest of youse have been poorly? No, it was nothing he took here, praise God, and yourselves the other sort. And it the Twelfth of July. No, don't let it cost you a thought. God moves in mysterious ways his wonders to perform. Yes, I'll mind the childer with Miss Una, so I will. Go youse with Mrs. Thomas to the airport. She's in poor form, the lady?"

"She was poorly before she came, and now the shock."

"Aye, the soul. Away now; we'll get by."

"Aye, well, God help us all. Mrs. Thomas isn't at herself, you know? She asked me to give you this wee present for all your trouble. She said to thank you and bid you good-bye for her."

"Three pound? Madam, no, it's far too much."

"No, take it; sure it's what she wants. She's grateful to you, but she's in a state. Mr. McNeil was an old friend of hers. She's not at herself, you understand?"

"Aye, this world's the hard place, so it is."

CHAPTER 16

Una stood in the drive, with Patrick in her arms, to watch them go. She looked like a frustrated fury, like a disappointed witch, the long hair in black, tangled wisps about her face and hanging over her slumped shoulders. It was as though she'd retreated into her hair, like a monk into his cowl. For Una, Sarah's departure meant more than yet another symbol of victory for the Special Powers Act; that wasn't why she felt deprived, solitary and abandoned. A certain sanity in Sarah had beckoned to her, had sorely tempted her to snap her sentimentalities, to change gear, to accept the seductions of undistorted, rational and honest thoughts. Not, of course, that Sarah was any examplar of rational behaviour, but she had half opened a door, had pointed a way. Och, well, that was yet another chance she'd missed, nothing new in that; and thank God too, in a way. Patrick, at least, could put his arms around her neck with trust. His flesh was warm and smooth and rounded. He smelled a bit, the baby smell of wet wool and powder and traces of sick. She clutched him, hard, like a little girl with a teddy bear, and he promptly bit her neck.

She was appalled by the look of Sarah, who had hardly spoken since her acceptance of irrelevance that morning, her collapse in Colum's arms. Now Sarah sat beside Caroline in the back seat of the big car. They both sat up, formal and stiff, like mourners at a public funeral; both clutched their handbags in their laps, a rigid pose, like statuary. There had been no question of Sarah's driving the little Mini to the airport. Colum skirted it, abandoned, in the drive. Someone would return it, sometime.

Sarah waved a mechanical good-bye to Una and then to Bridget and Brendan in the drive, Bridget still in Sarah's big, sexy black hat. The others talked around her in the car, constrained and unnatural. They pointed out the sights, the views, to Mab. They passed the "wee loanie," went through the long, thin villages, but Sarah's eyes were closed, she paid no heed.

They came to Belfast. On the morning after. The city still bedecked, still bedecked for triumph; but the bedecking, in the morning light, was more than ever sordid, one week more tatty than when Sarah had seen it first, the streets now like a waking woman who'd gone to bed unwashed, with all her makeup on. The flags, triumphal arches, and the king on terraced gable ends like latter-day mascara, rouge and clogged-up pores, sordid reminders. There were no obvious signs of violence, as yet; not one pathetic, burned-out refugee in sight. The Twelfth had come and gone in sullen, grim passivity. A number of the pubs had broken windows boarded up and, in the Sandy Row, charred bits of bonfires littered the street, the plate glass of a few shop windows shattered in the heat of prejudice. Policemen patrolled in couples, with guns; heavy, stolid, inhuman, in long coats, faces anonymous under the hard hats.

A Sunday morning; the people on the streets all gloved and summer-hatted, decorous, respectable. Their Sunday luncheons organised, the cabbage washed, the frozen peas prim in their waiting packets, rice puddings turned out of the tins. In Belfast Mab forgot his shock and his constraint; terrier alert again, his eyes alight to watch for signs of violence, for all that fighting he'd have wished to see and had to miss. But there was nothing yet. The Twelfth had come and gone, and hardly anything, hardly a flick.

After Belfast, the country villages again, with flags and bunting. Serene, small villages; the Orange Hall secure, safe bastion of the Protestant supremacy; and, quite suddenly, the new and modern road that took them to the airport and the end.

Sarah opened her green-lidded, heavy eyes, gave Mab her ticket and the money for his fare. "You do it, Mab, and join us in the bar."

With Caroline she climbed the modern, international, functional steps that took them to the airport bar. "I've got to have a drink. Get me a double, Caroline, quick. What? Closed? What can you mean?"

"It's Sunday, love, no drink. But we'll just sit here, anyway. I hate to see a bar like this, you know that? With that grille thing over the works and not a barman in sight. It's so awful naked-looking, don't you think? And this smell of old dust and sorrows that you'd never notice with a decent drink before youse. Och, Sarah, I wish you didn't have to go. I see you so lonely in that bloody flat tonight."

"There'll be company tomorrow in the nursing home. Birds of a feather."

"What about your family? Would they not come?"

"I couldn't burden them. I brought about his death. You know that, don't you?"

"Yes, if you want the truth. I'll tell no lie. But I'll pray for you."

"What will you pray for, Caroline? But please pray, anyway. And get those nuns of yours to pray as well."

"God knows, they're at it already. I had no embroidery to take to Mother Superior that day we went to Ardmore and you saw Sally's Lough. It was prayers I went for; aye, those poor bitches have corns on their knees for you, you know that?"

"They don't know what they're on about, do they? Caroline, d'you think they watched us in the grass? Gave him time to finish? Enjoyed us first and laughed? Was I vicariously fucked by murderers?"

"Would you not just try to put it out of your mind? God knows, you're punished enough...."

Mab came up then, with Colum, who had parked his car, and a voice coughed at them and warned them to assemble at Gate Six.

Colum and Caroline, up at the high windows, watched them come out onto the apron. Mab, in his dark-red sweater and his shabby jeans, carried Sarah's little bag. She walked beside him; you would never have known that she was any different from the rest. The sun shone on her lovely, heavy hair, on his red head, and they mounted the steps and went on, into the aeroplane.